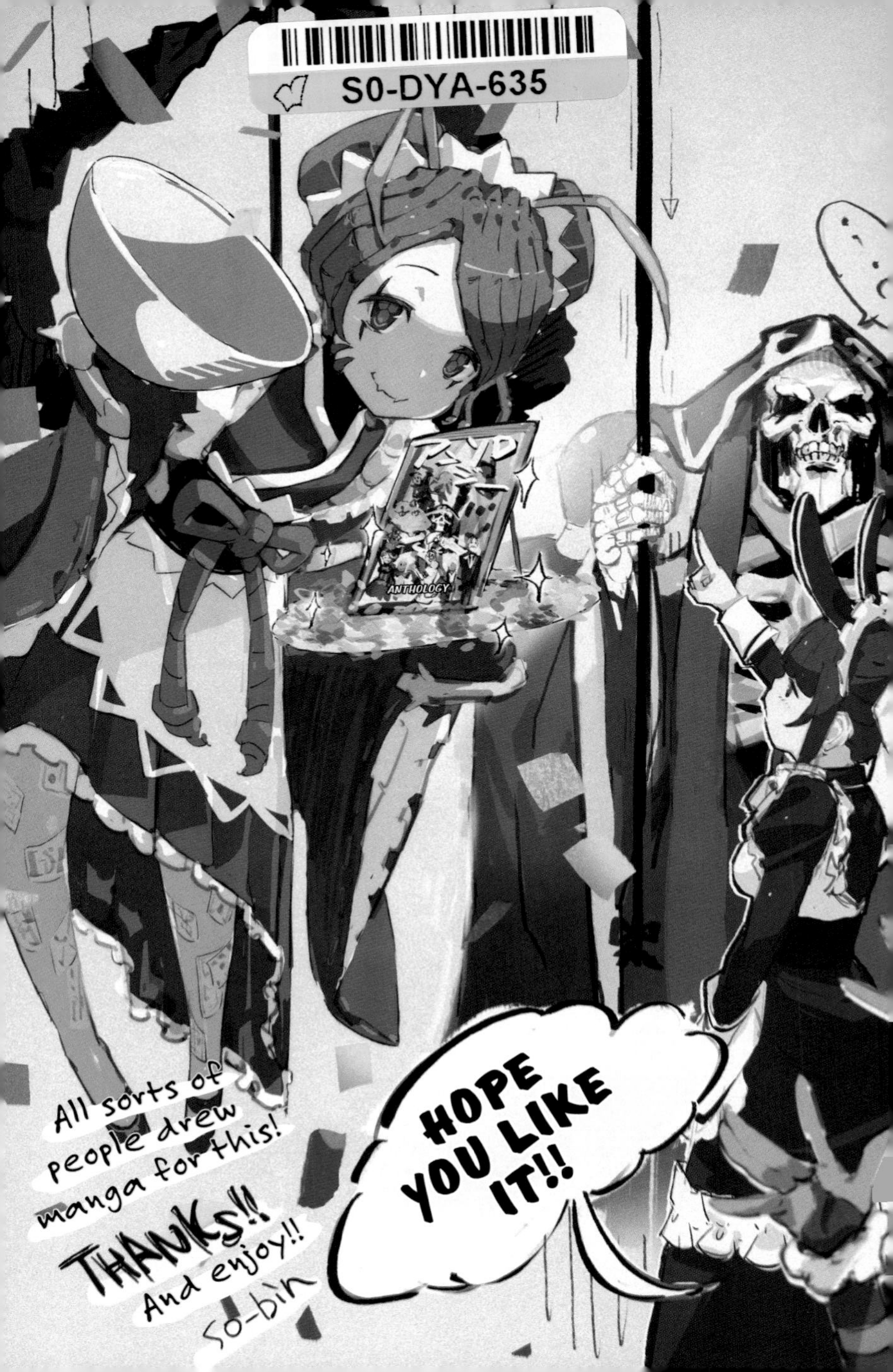
ANTHOLOGY
HOPE YOU LIKE IT!!
All sorts of people drew manga for this!
THANKS!! And enjoy!!
so-bin

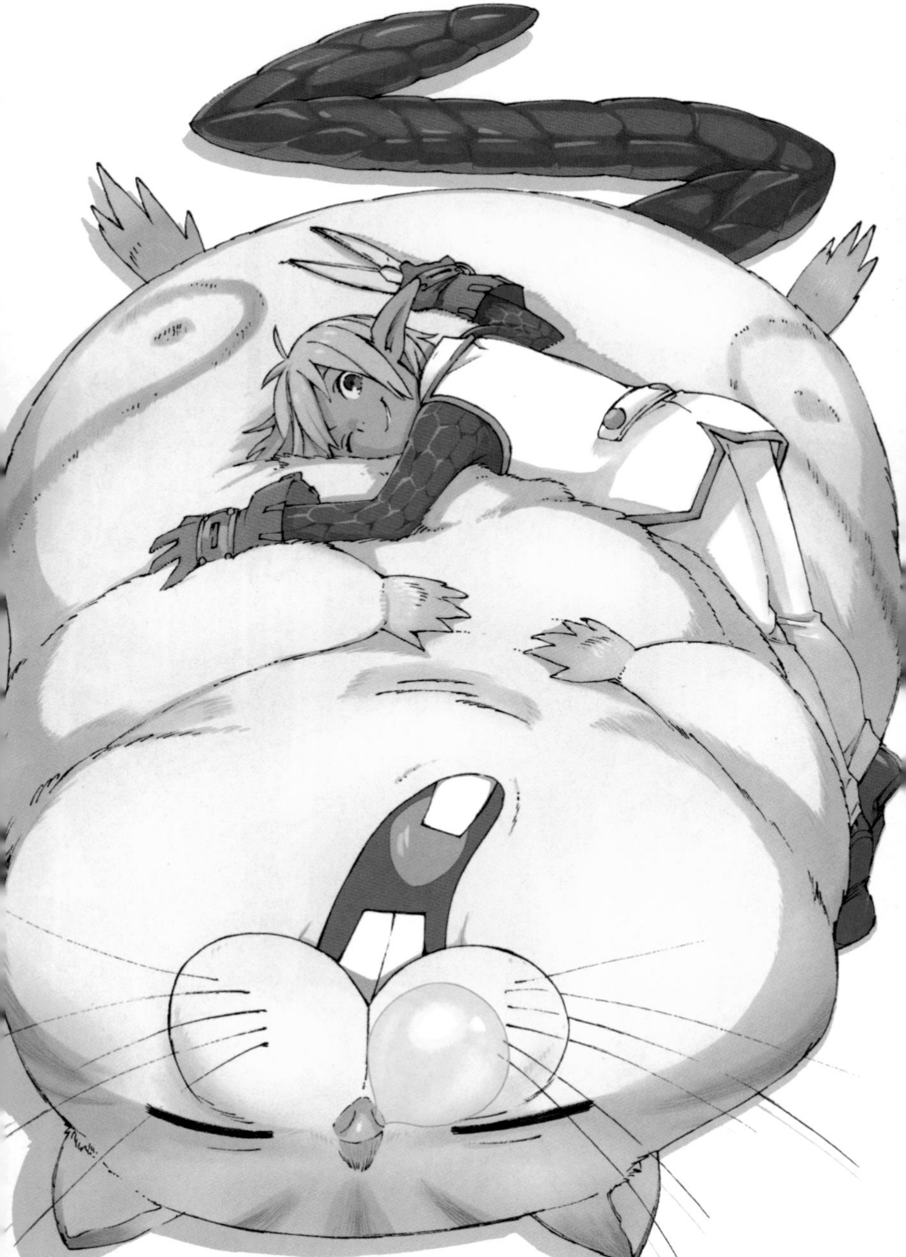

illustration / Hugin Miyama

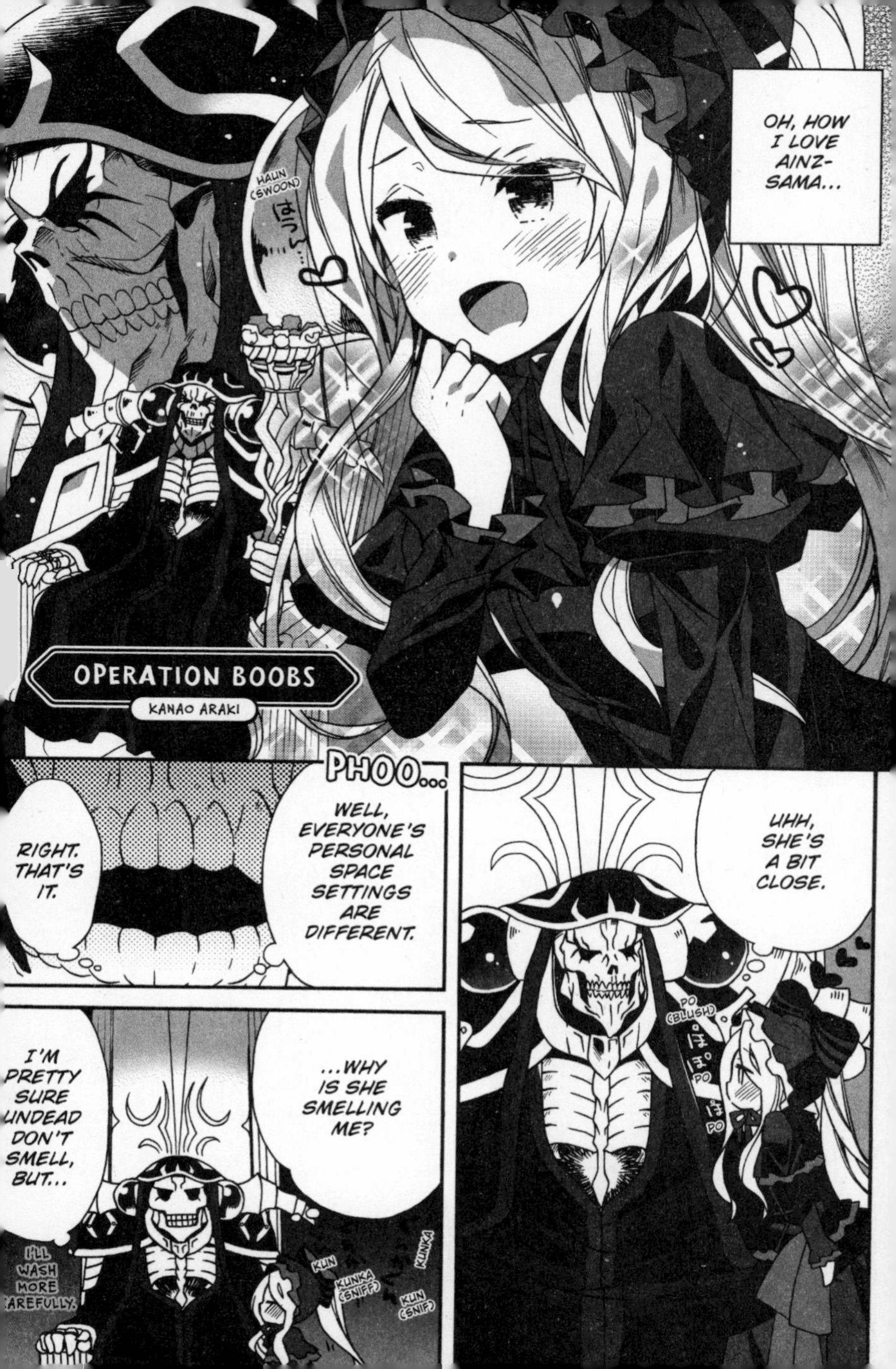
OH, HOW I LOVE AINZ-SAMA...
HAUN (SWOON)
OPERATION BOOBS
KANAO ARAKI
UHH, SHE'S A BIT CLOSE.
PO (BLUSH)
PO
PO
PHOO...
WELL, EVERYONE'S PERSONAL SPACE SETTINGS ARE DIFFERENT.
RIGHT. THAT'S IT.
...WHY IS SHE SMELLING ME?
I'M PRETTY SURE UNDEAD DON'T SMELL, BUT...
KUNKA
KUN
KUNKA (SNIFF)
KUN (SNIFF)
I'LL WASH MORE CAREFULLY.

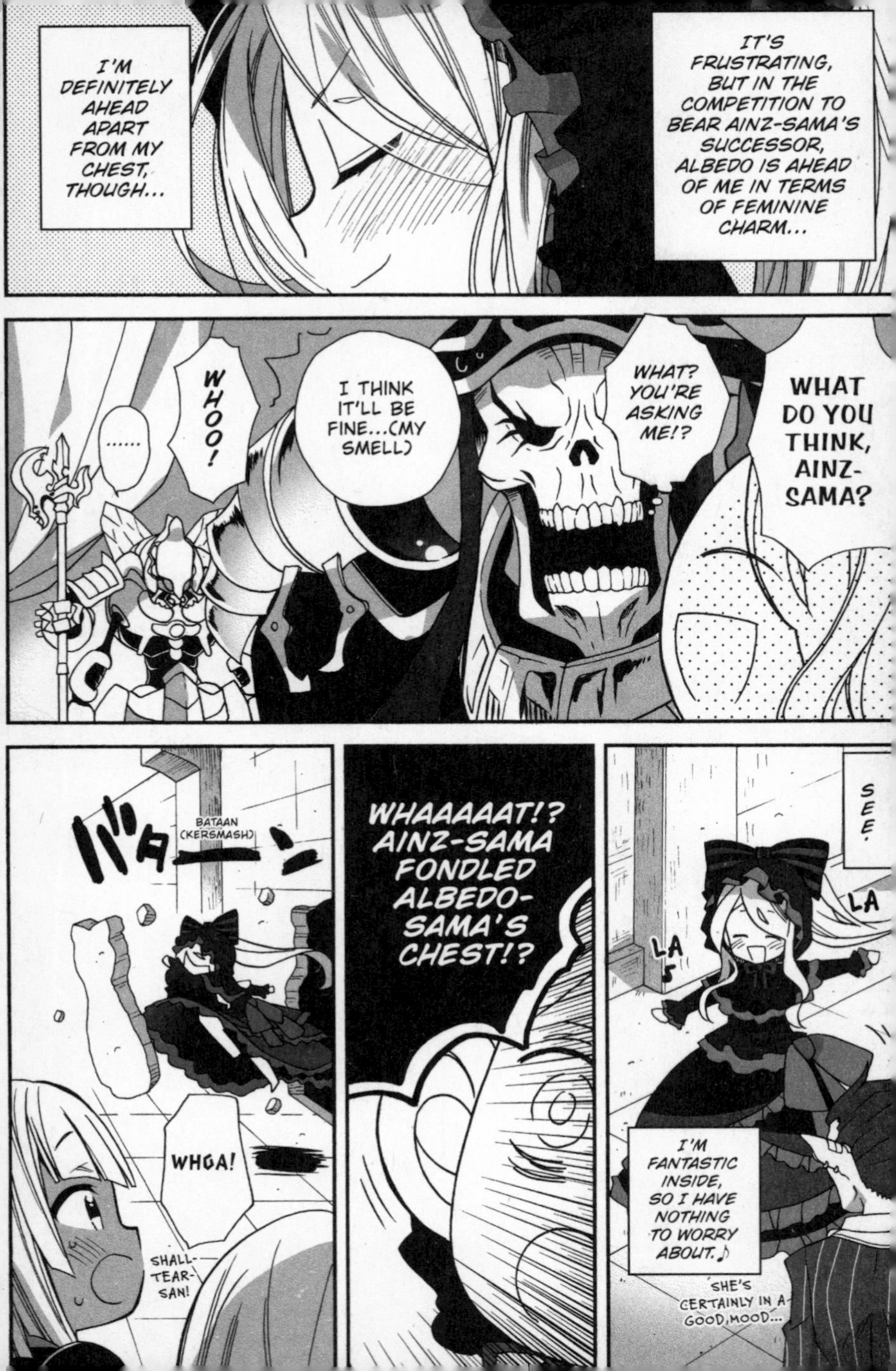
IT'S FRUSTRATING, BUT IN THE COMPETITION TO BEAR AINZ-SAMA'S SUCCESSOR, ALBEDO IS AHEAD OF ME IN TERMS OF FEMININE CHARM...
I'M DEFINITELY AHEAD APART FROM MY CHEST, THOUGH...
WHAT DO YOU THINK, AINZ-SAMA?
WHAT? YOU'RE ASKING ME!?
I THINK IT'LL BE FINE...(MY SMELL)
WHOO!
......
SEE.
LA
LA
I'M FANTASTIC INSIDE, SO I HAVE NOTHING TO WORRY ABOUT.♪
SHE'S CERTAINLY IN A GOOD MOOD...
WHAAAAAT!? AINZ-SAMA FONDLED ALBEDO-SAMA'S CHEST!?
BATAAN (KERSMASH)
WHGA!
SHALL-TEAR-SAN!

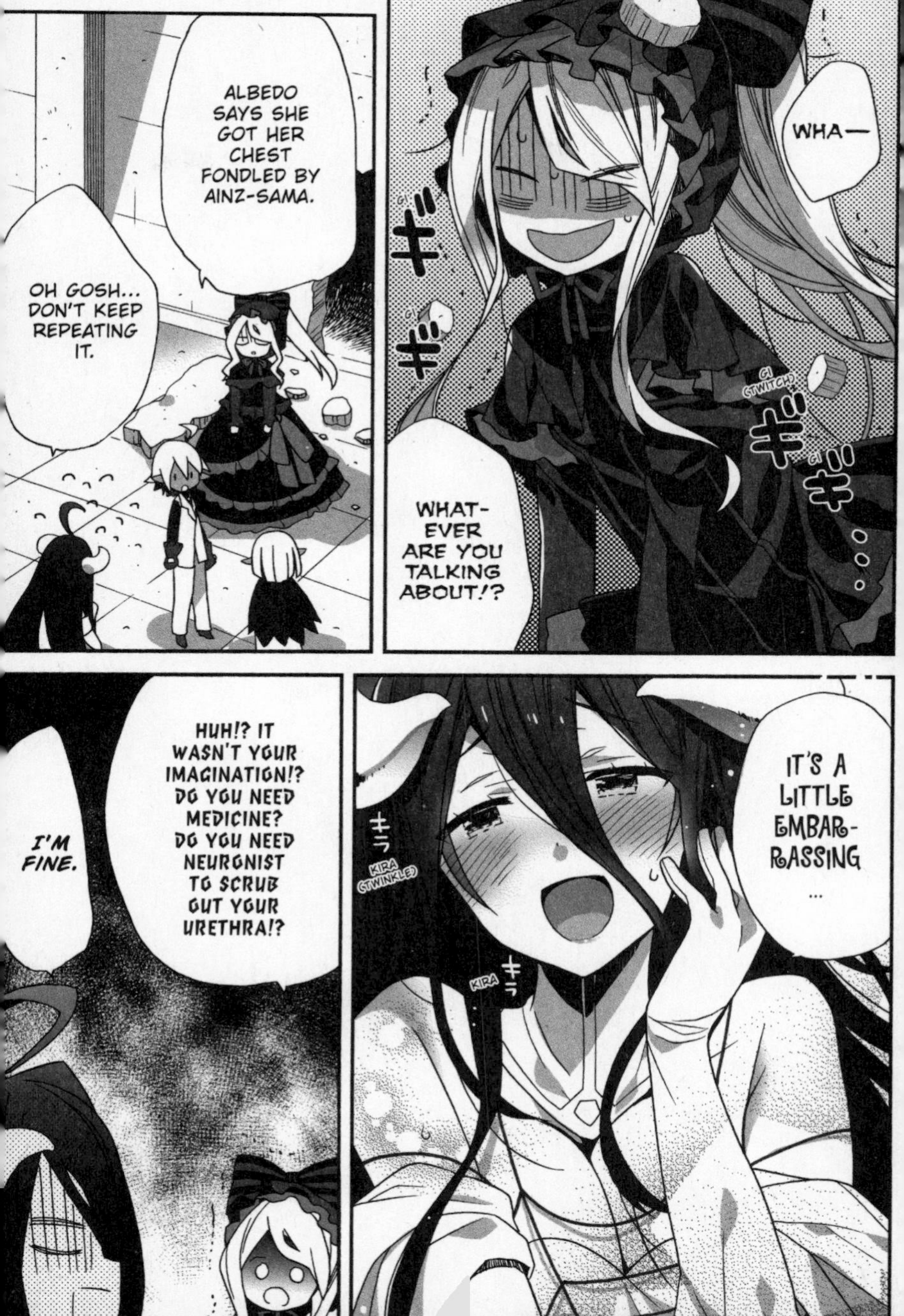
WHA—
GI
GI
GI (TWITCH)
GI
WHAT-EVER ARE YOU TALKING ABOUT!?
ALBEDO SAYS SHE GOT HER CHEST FONDLED BY AINZ-SAMA.
OH GOSH... DON'T KEEP REPEATING IT.
IT'S A LITTLE EMBARRASSING...
KIRA (TWINKLE)
KIRA
HUH!? IT WASN'T YOUR IMAGINATION!? DO YOU NEED MEDICINE? DO YOU NEED NEURONIST TO SCRUB OUT YOUR URETHRA!?
I'M FINE.

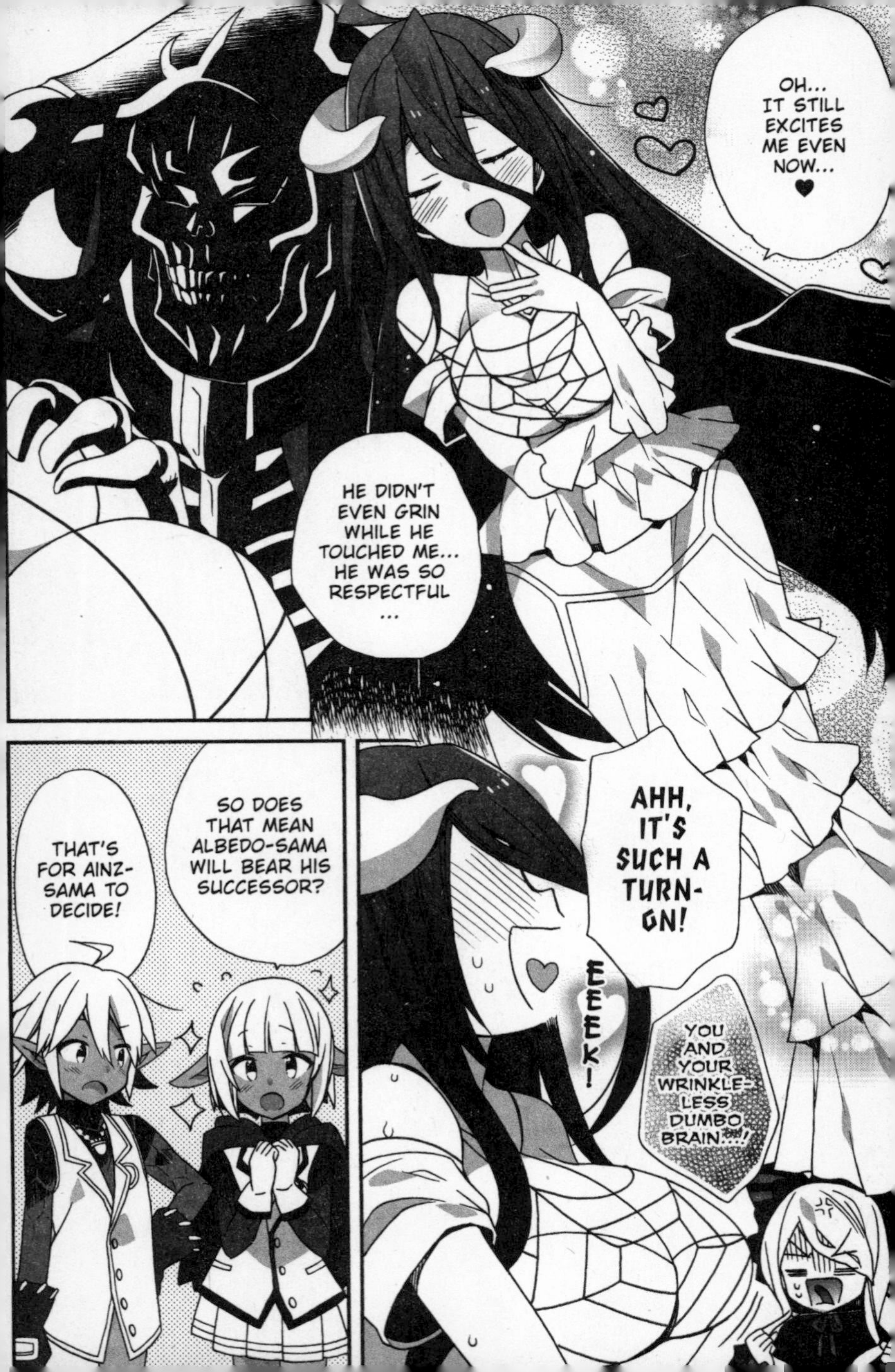
OH... IT STILL EXCITES ME EVEN NOW... ♥
HE DIDN'T EVEN GRIN WHILE HE TOUCHED ME... HE WAS SO RESPECTFUL ...
AHH, IT'S SUCH A TURN-GN!
EEEEK!
YOU AND YOUR WRINKLE-LESS DUMBO BRAIN...!
SO DOES THAT MEAN ALBEDO-SAMA WILL BEAR HIS SUCCESSOR?
THAT'S FOR AINZ-SAMA TO DECIDE!

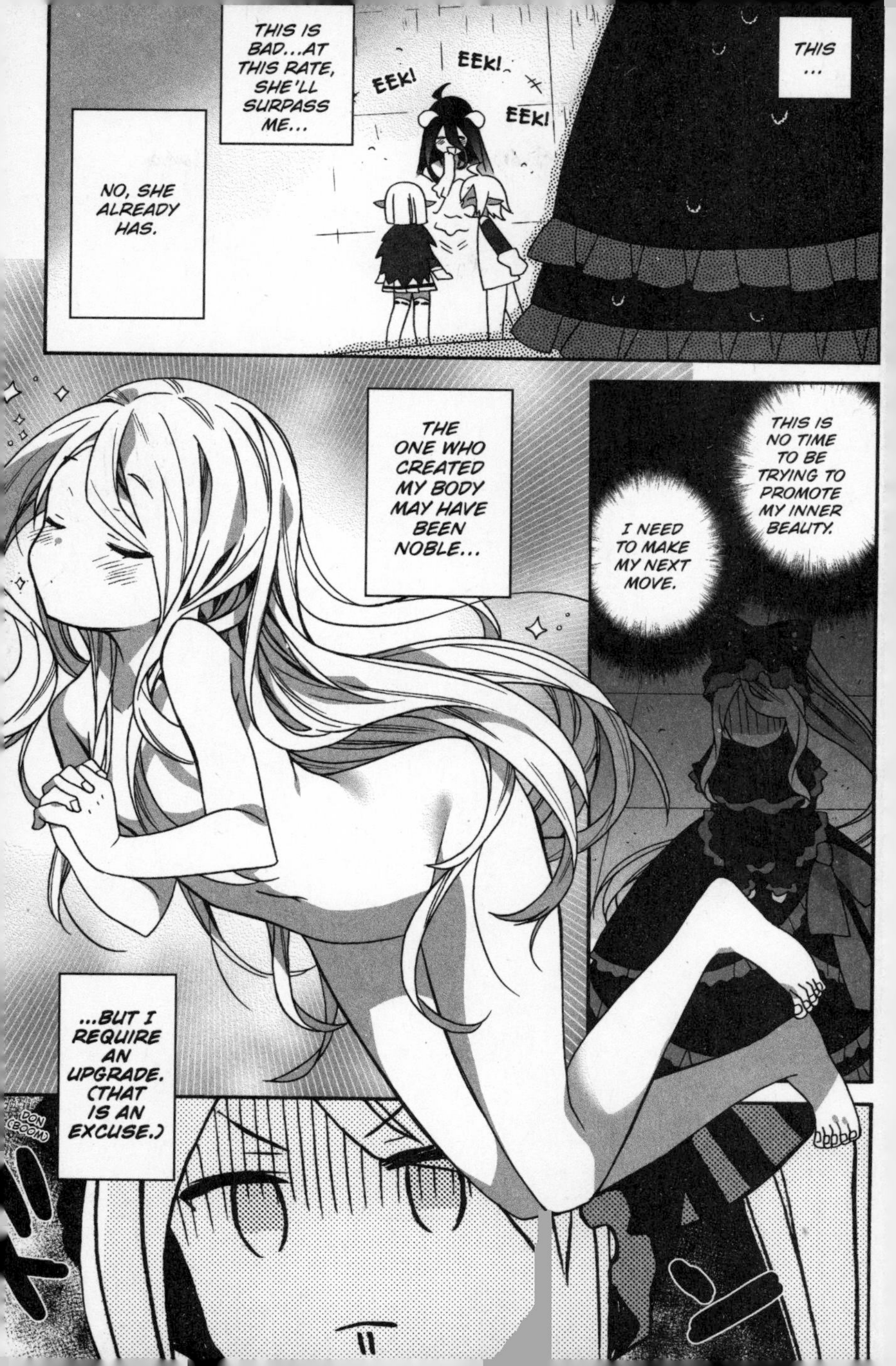
THIS...
EEK!
EEK!
EEK!
THIS IS BAD...AT THIS RATE, SHE'LL SURPASS ME...
NO, SHE ALREADY HAS.
THIS IS NO TIME TO BE TRYING TO PROMOTE MY INNER BEAUTY.
I NEED TO MAKE MY NEXT MOVE.
THE ONE WHO CREATED MY BODY MAY HAVE BEEN NOBLE...
...BUT I REQUIRE AN UPGRADE. (THAT IS AN EXCUSE.)
DON (BOOM)

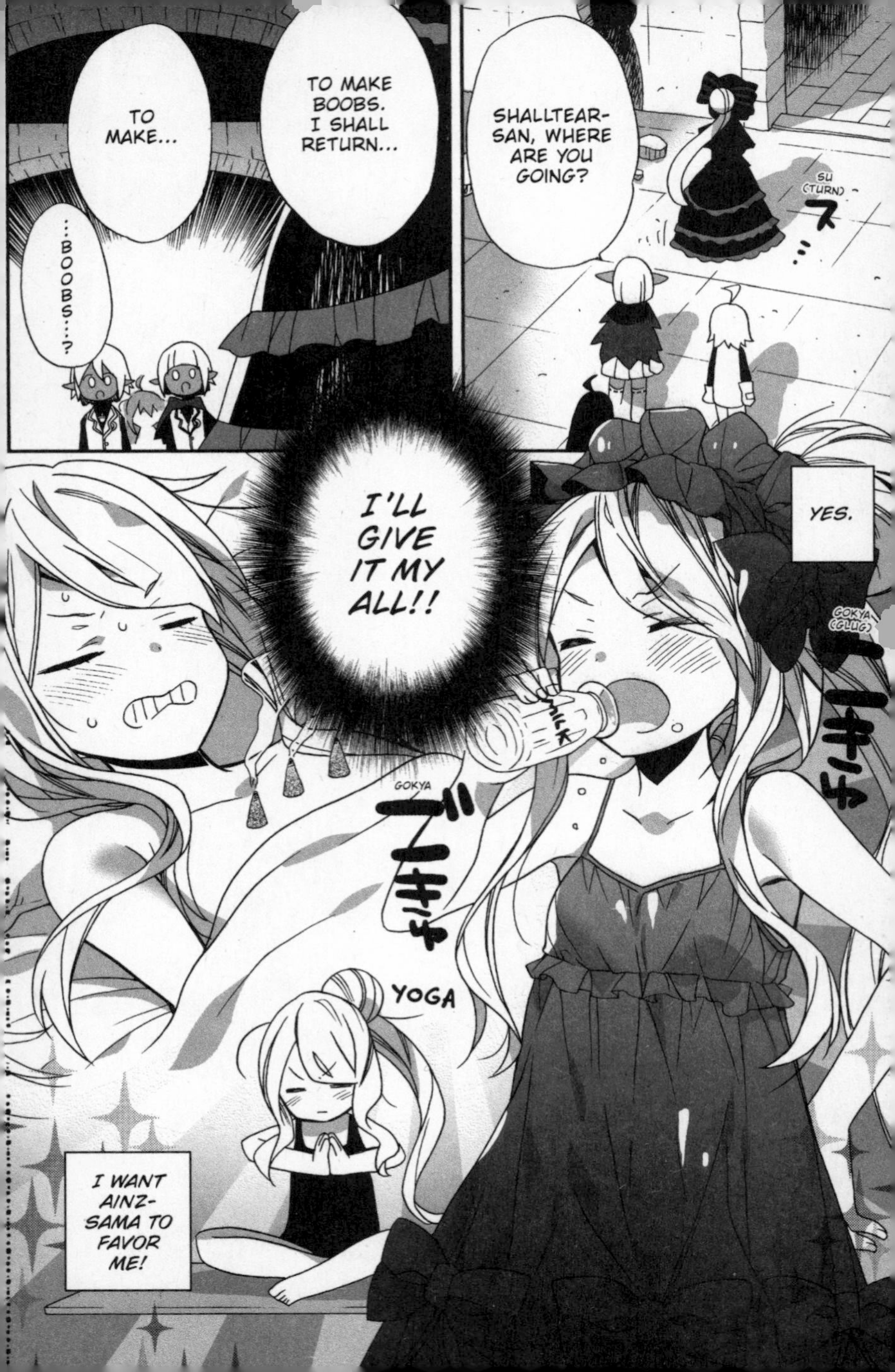
SHALLTEAR-SAN, WHERE ARE YOU GOING?
SU (TURN)
ス
TO MAKE BOOBS. I SHALL RETURN...
TO MAKE...
...BOOBS...?
YES.
GOKYA (GLUG)
I'LL GIVE IT MY ALL!!
MILK
GOKYA
YOGA
I WANT AINZ-SAMA TO FAVOR ME!

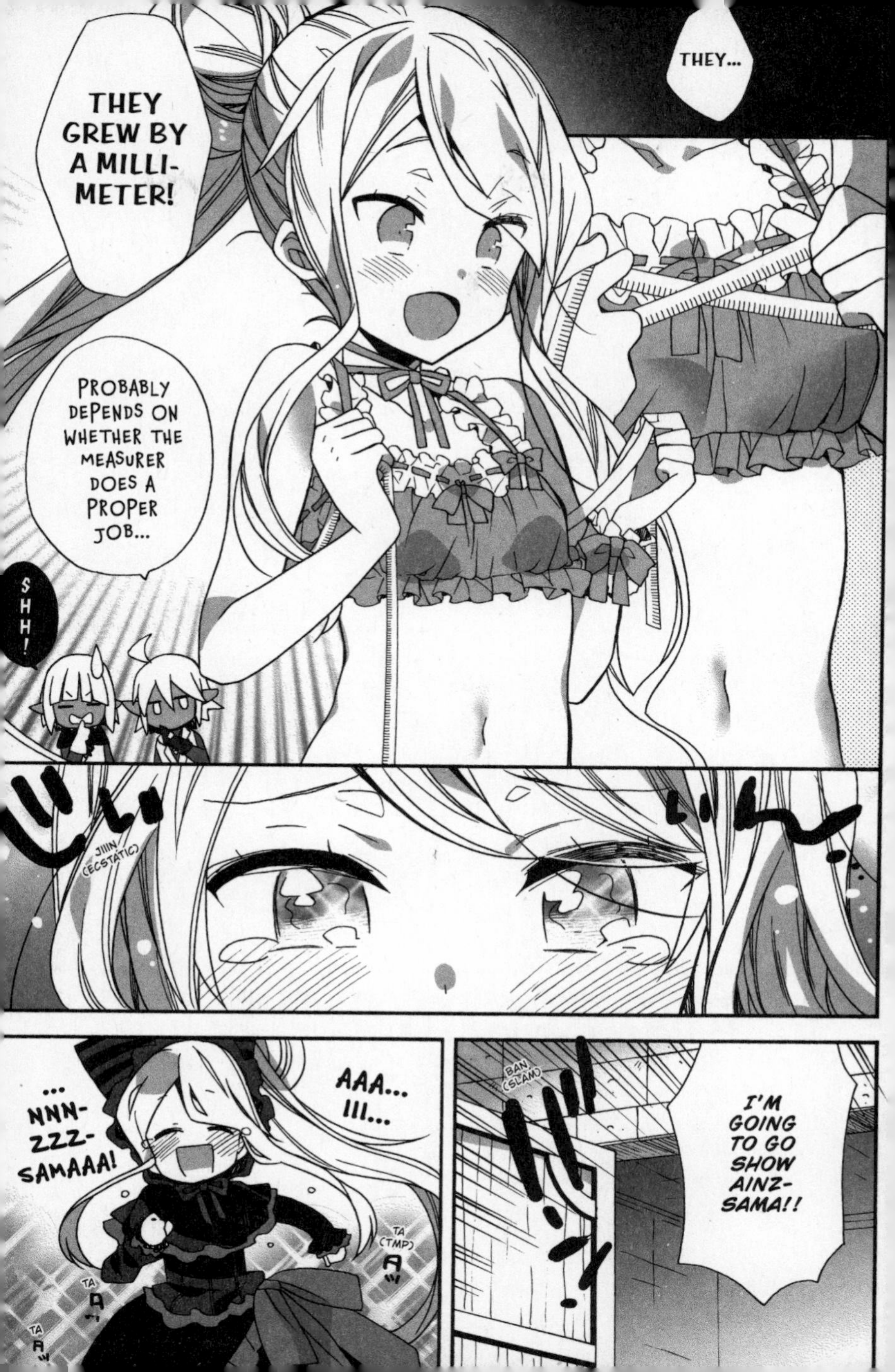
THEY...
THEY GREW BY A MILLI-METER!
PROBABLY DEPENDS ON WHETHER THE MEASURER DOES A PROPER JOB...
SHH!
JIIIN (ECSTATIC)
I'M GOING TO GO SHOW AINZ-SAMA!!
BAN (SLAM)
AAA... III...
... NNN-ZZZ-SAMAAA!
TA (TMP)
TA
TA

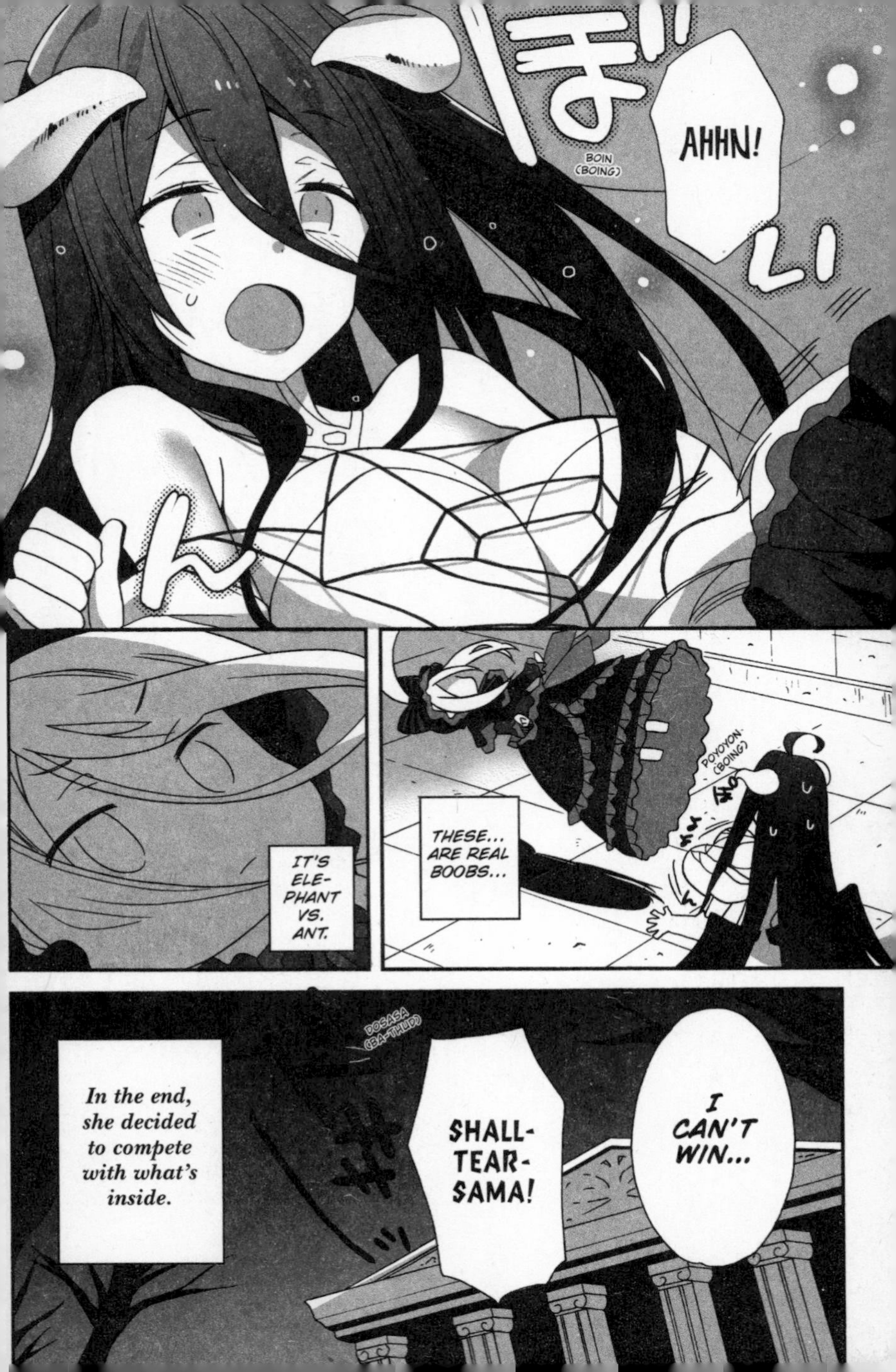

AHHN!
BOIN (BOING)
POYOYON (BOING)
THESE... ARE REAL BOOBS...
IT'S ELE-PHANT VS. ANT.
I CAN'T WIN...
SHALL-TEAR-SAMA!
DOSASA (BA-THUD)
In the end, she decided to compete with what's inside.

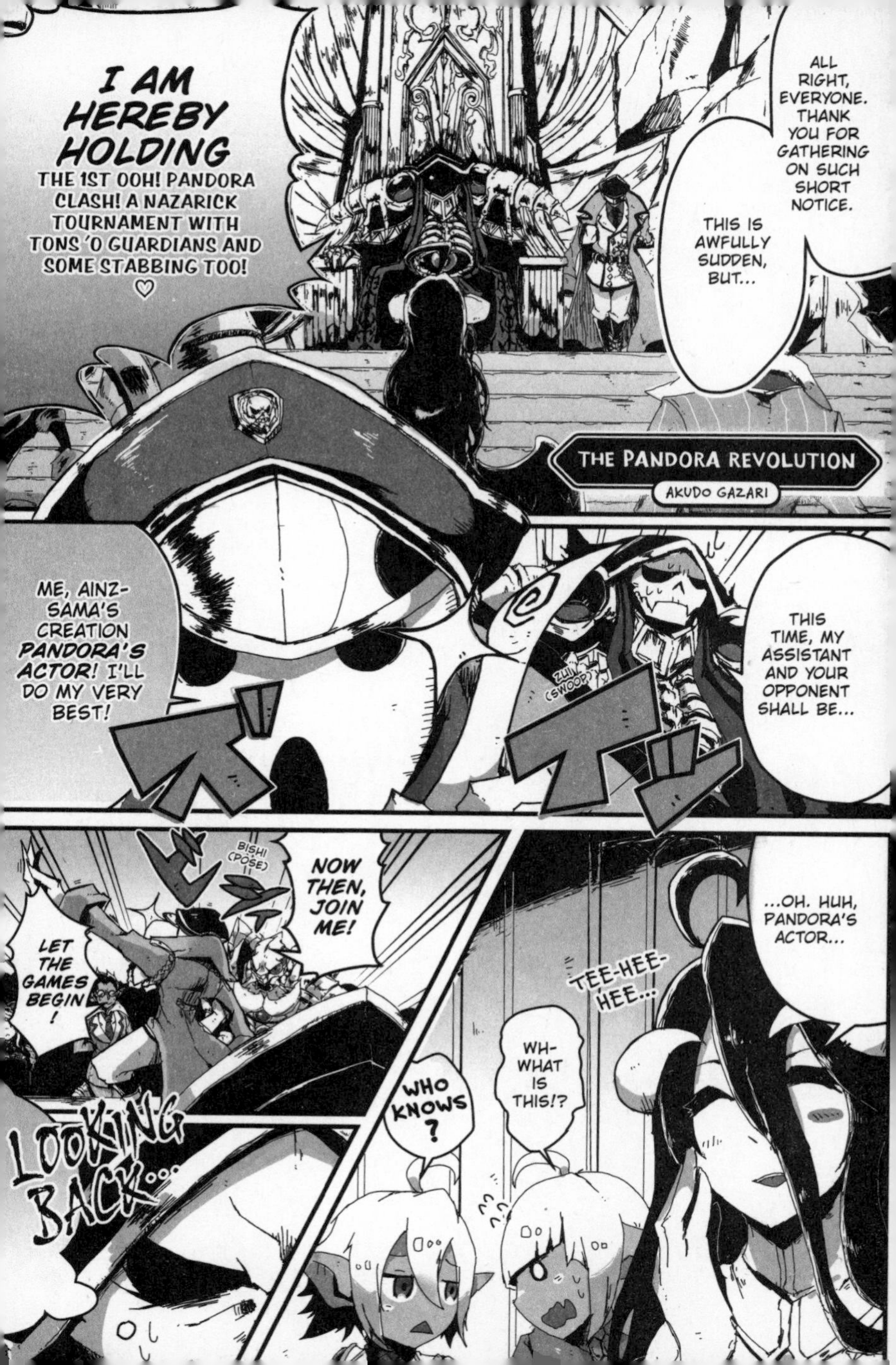
ALL RIGHT, EVERYONE. THANK YOU FOR GATHERING ON SUCH SHORT NOTICE.
THIS IS AWFULLY SUDDEN, BUT...
I AM HEREBY HOLDING THE 1ST OOH! PANDORA CLASH! A NAZARICK TOURNAMENT WITH TONS 'O GUARDIANS AND SOME STABBING TOO! ♡
THE PANDORA REVOLUTION
AKUDO GAZARI
THIS TIME, MY ASSISTANT AND YOUR OPPONENT SHALL BE...
ZUI (SWOOP)
ME, AINZ-SAMA'S CREATION PANDORA'S ACTOR! I'LL DO MY VERY BEST!
...OH. HUH, PANDORA'S ACTOR...
TEE-HEE-HEE...
WH-WHAT IS THIS!?
WHO KNOWS?
NOW THEN, JOIN ME!
BISHI (POSE)
LET THE GAMES BEGIN!
LOOKING BACK...

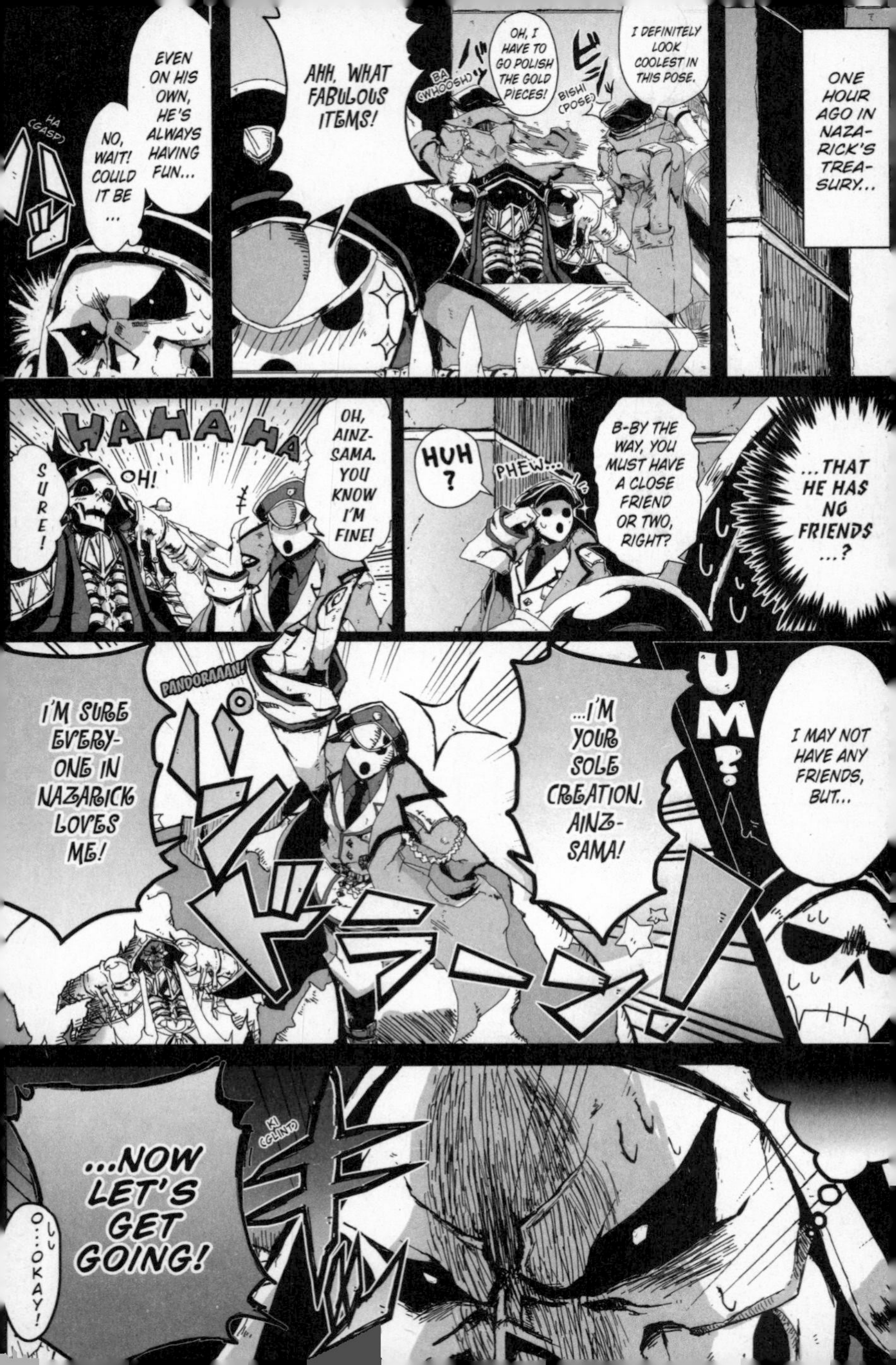

ONE HOUR AGO IN NAZARICK'S TREASURY...
I DEFINITELY LOOK COOLEST IN THIS POSE.
BISHI (POSE)
OH, I HAVE TO GO POLISH THE GOLD PIECES!
BA (WHOOSH)
AHH, WHAT FABULOUS ITEMS!
EVEN ON HIS OWN, HE'S ALWAYS HAVING FUN...
NO, WAIT! COULD IT BE ...
HA (GASP)
...THAT HE HAS NO FRIENDS ...?
B-BY THE WAY, YOU MUST HAVE A CLOSE FRIEND OR TWO, RIGHT?
PHEW...
HUH?
OH, AINZ-SAMA. YOU KNOW I'M FINE!
HAHAHAHA
OH!
SURE!
UM?
I MAY NOT HAVE ANY FRIENDS, BUT...
...I'M YOUR SOLE CREATION, AINZ-SAMA!
PANDORAAAN!
I'M SURE EVERYONE IN NAZARICK LOVES ME!
KI (GLINT)
...NOW LET'S GET GOING!
O...OKAY!

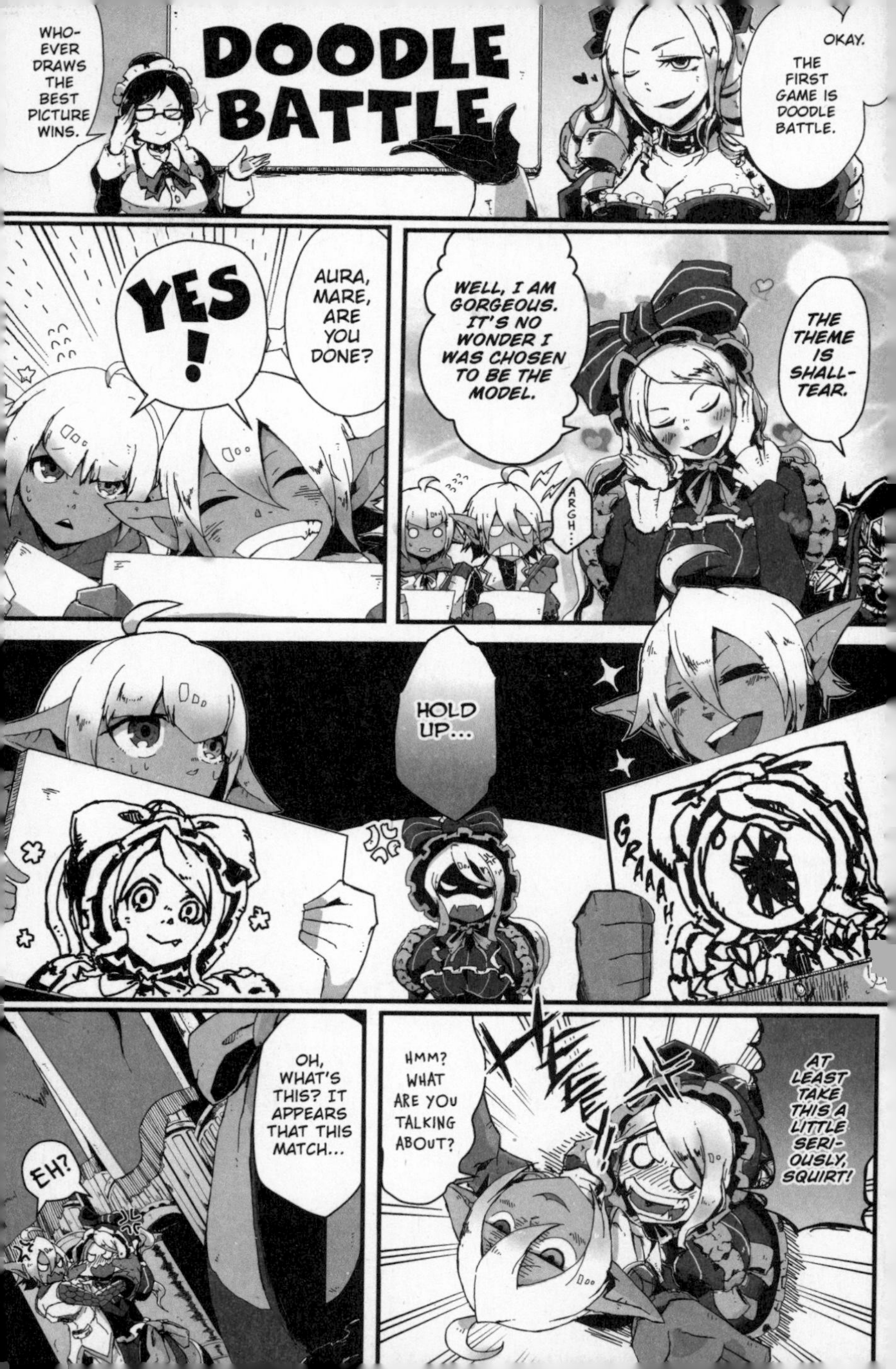
OKAY. THE FIRST GAME IS DOODLE BATTLE.
DOODLE BATTLE
WHO-EVER DRAWS THE BEST PICTURE WINS.
THE THEME IS SHALL-TEAR.
WELL, I AM GORGEOUS. IT'S NO WONDER I WAS CHOSEN TO BE THE MODEL.
ARGH...
AURA, MARE, ARE YOU DONE?
YES!
HOLD UP...
GRAAAAH!
AT LEAST TAKE THIS A LITTLE SERI-OUSLY, SQUIRT!
HMM? WHAT ARE YOU TALKING ABOUT?
OH, WHAT'S THIS? IT APPEARS THAT THIS MATCH...
EH?

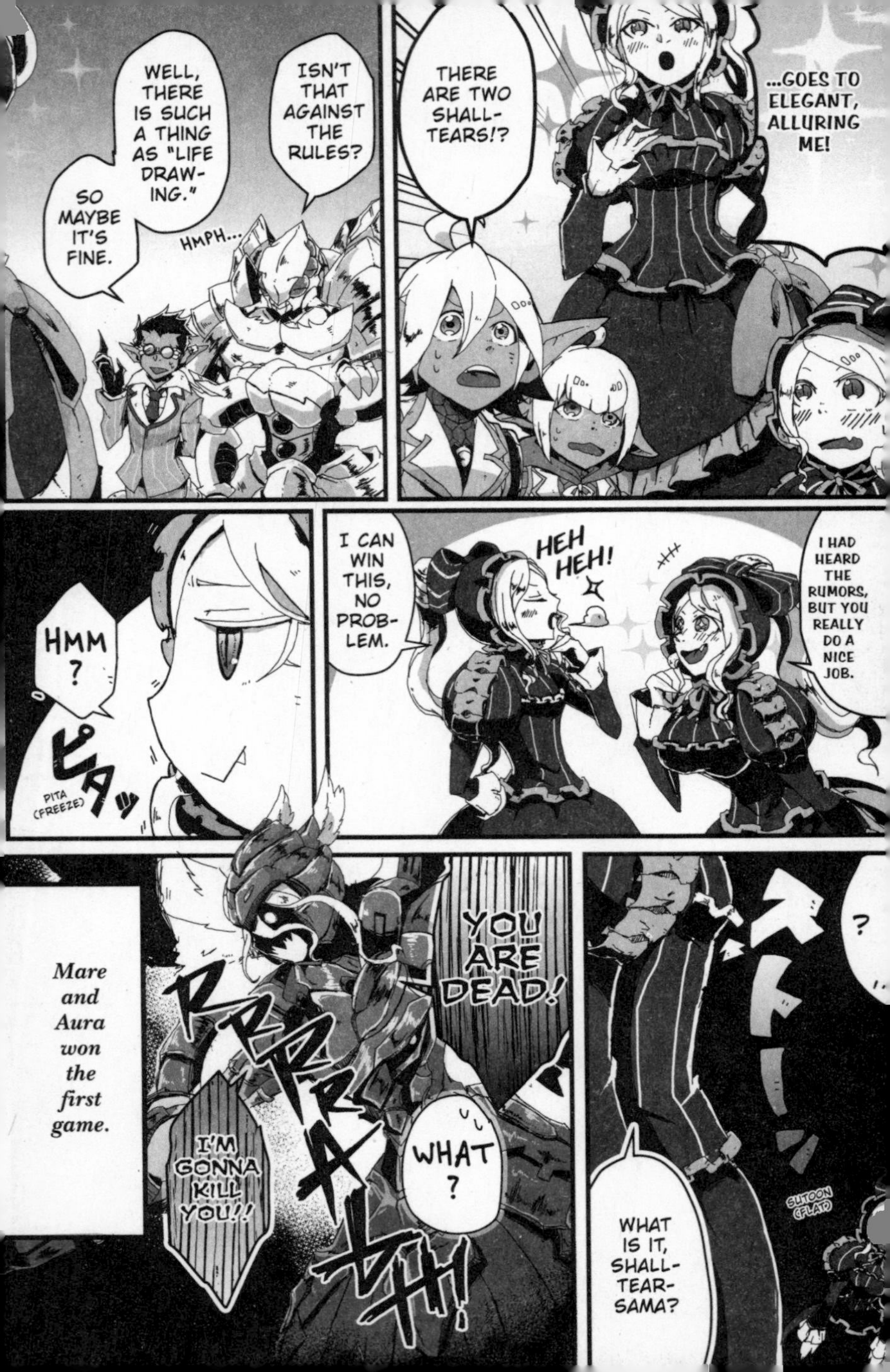
...GOES TO ELEGANT, ALLURING ME!
THERE ARE TWO SHALL-TEARS!?
ISN'T THAT AGAINST THE RULES?
HMPH...
WELL, THERE IS SUCH A THING AS "LIFE DRAWING."
SO MAYBE IT'S FINE.
I HAD HEARD THE RUMORS, BUT YOU REALLY DO A NICE JOB.
HEH HEH!
I CAN WIN THIS, NO PROBLEM.
HMM?
ピタッ
PITA (FREEZE)
?
SUTOON (FLAT)
WHAT IS IT, SHALL-TEAR-SAMA?
YOU ARE DEAD!
WHAT?
RRRRAAHH!
I'M GONNA KILL YOU!!
Mare and Aura won the first game.

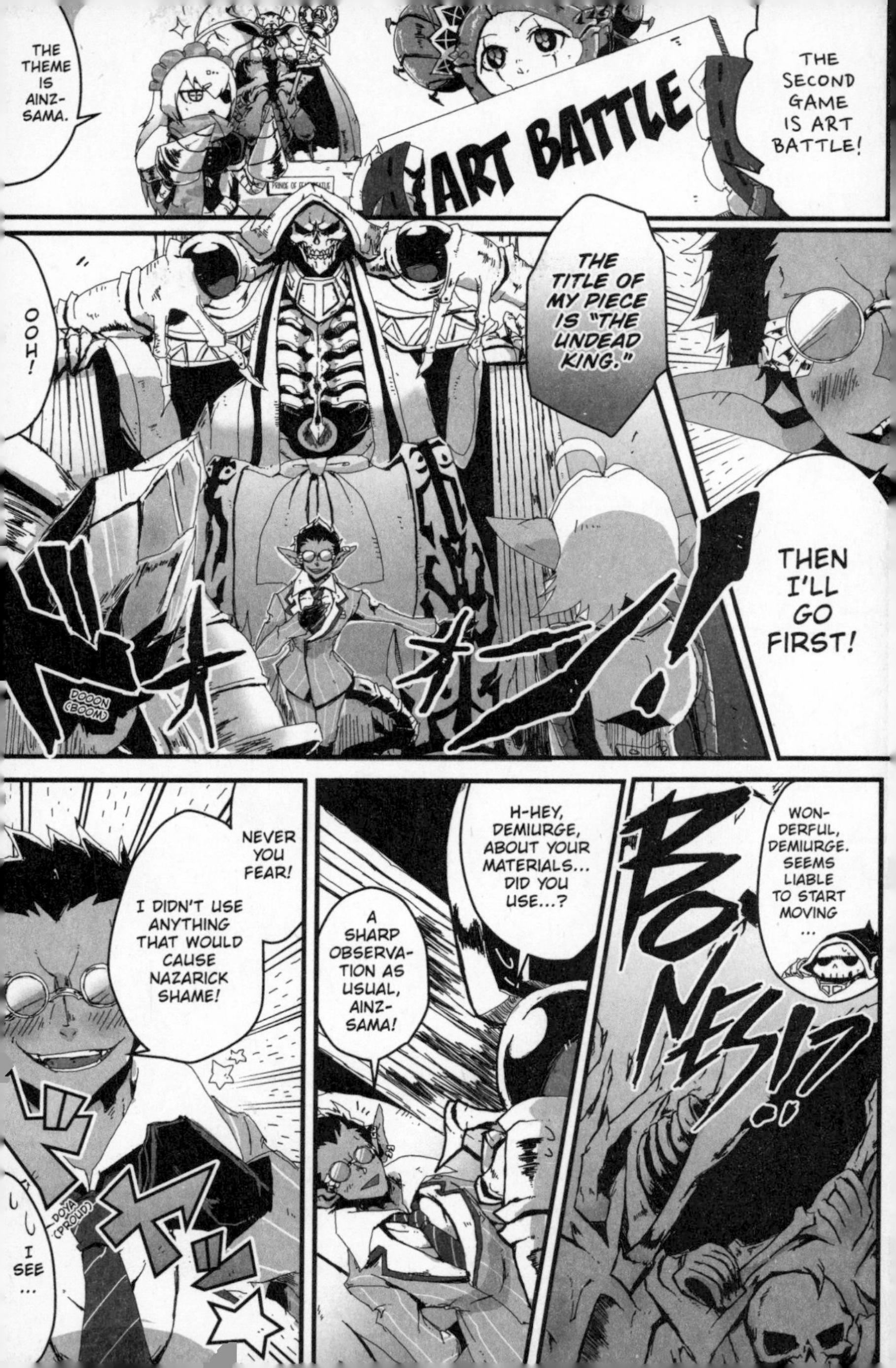

THE SECOND GAME IS ART BATTLE!
ART BATTLE
THE THEME IS AINZ-SAMA.
THEN I'LL GO FIRST!
THE TITLE OF MY PIECE IS "THE UNDEAD KING."
OOH!
DOOON (BOOM)
WON-DERFUL, DEMIURGE. SEEMS LIABLE TO START MOVING ...
BONES!?
H-HEY, DEMIURGE, ABOUT YOUR MATERIALS... DID YOU USE...?
A SHARP OBSERVA-TION AS USUAL, AINZ-SAMA!
NEVER YOU FEAR!
I DIDN'T USE ANYTHING THAT WOULD CAUSE NAZARICK SHAME!
DOYA (PROUD)
I SEE ...

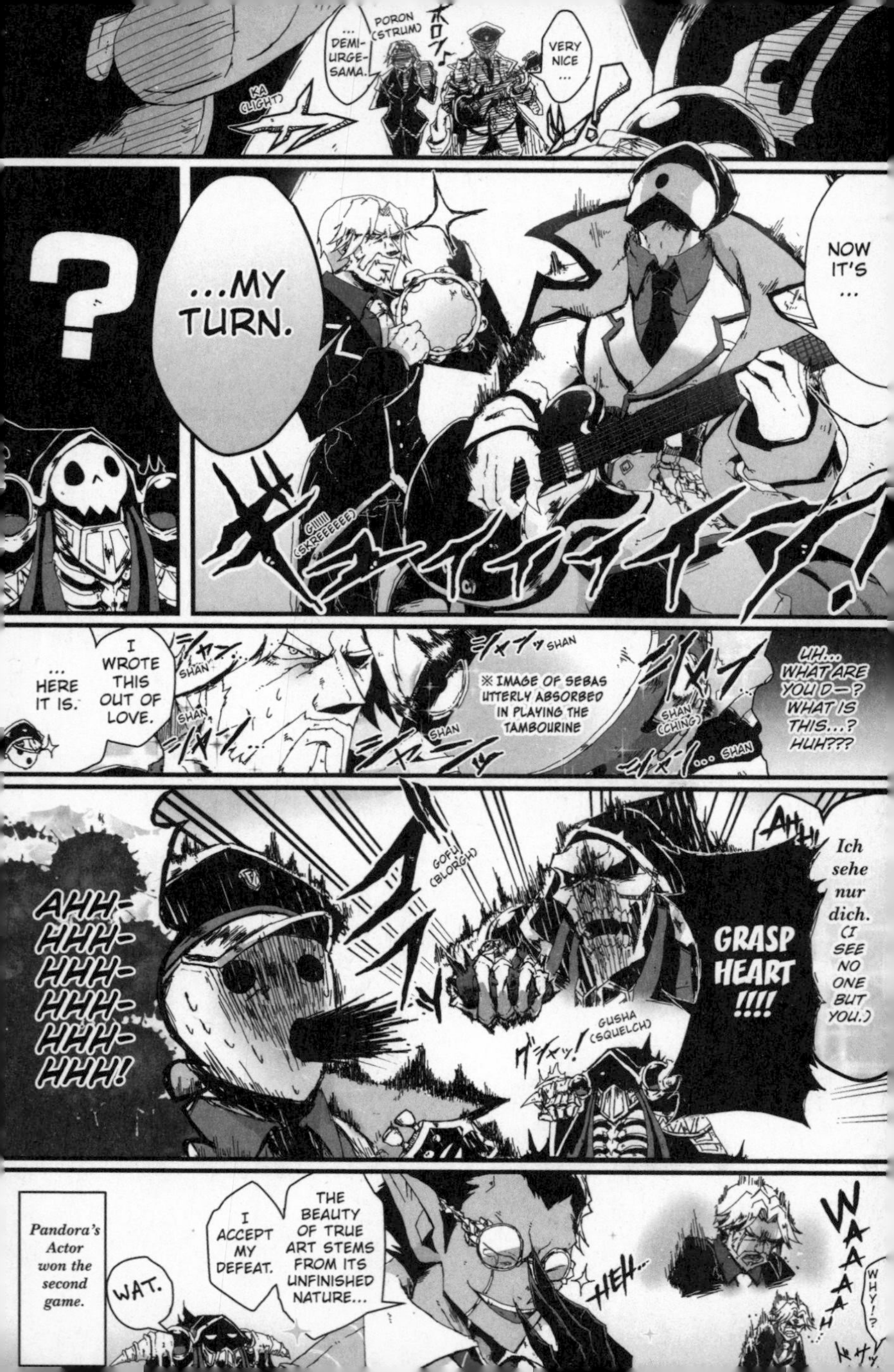

VERY NICE ...
PORON (STRUM)
... DEMIURGE-SAMA.
KA (LIGHT)
NOW IT'S ...
...MY TURN.
GIIIIII (SKREEEEEEE)
?
UH... WHAT ARE YOU D—? WHAT IS THIS...? HUH???
SHAN
SHAN (CHING)
SHAN
SHAN
※IMAGE OF SEBAS UTTERLY ABSORBED IN PLAYING THE TAMBOURINE
SHAN
SHAN
I WROTE THIS OUT OF LOVE.
... HERE IT IS.
Ich sehe nur dich. (I SEE NO ONE BUT YOU.)
AHH!
GRASP HEART!!!!
GOFU (BLORGH)
GUSHA (SQUELCH)
AHH-HHH-HHH-HHH-HHH-HHH!
WAAAAAH
WHY!?
HEH...
THE BEAUTY OF TRUE ART STEMS FROM ITS UNFINISHED NATURE...
I ACCEPT MY DEFEAT.
WAT.
Pandora's Actor won the second game.

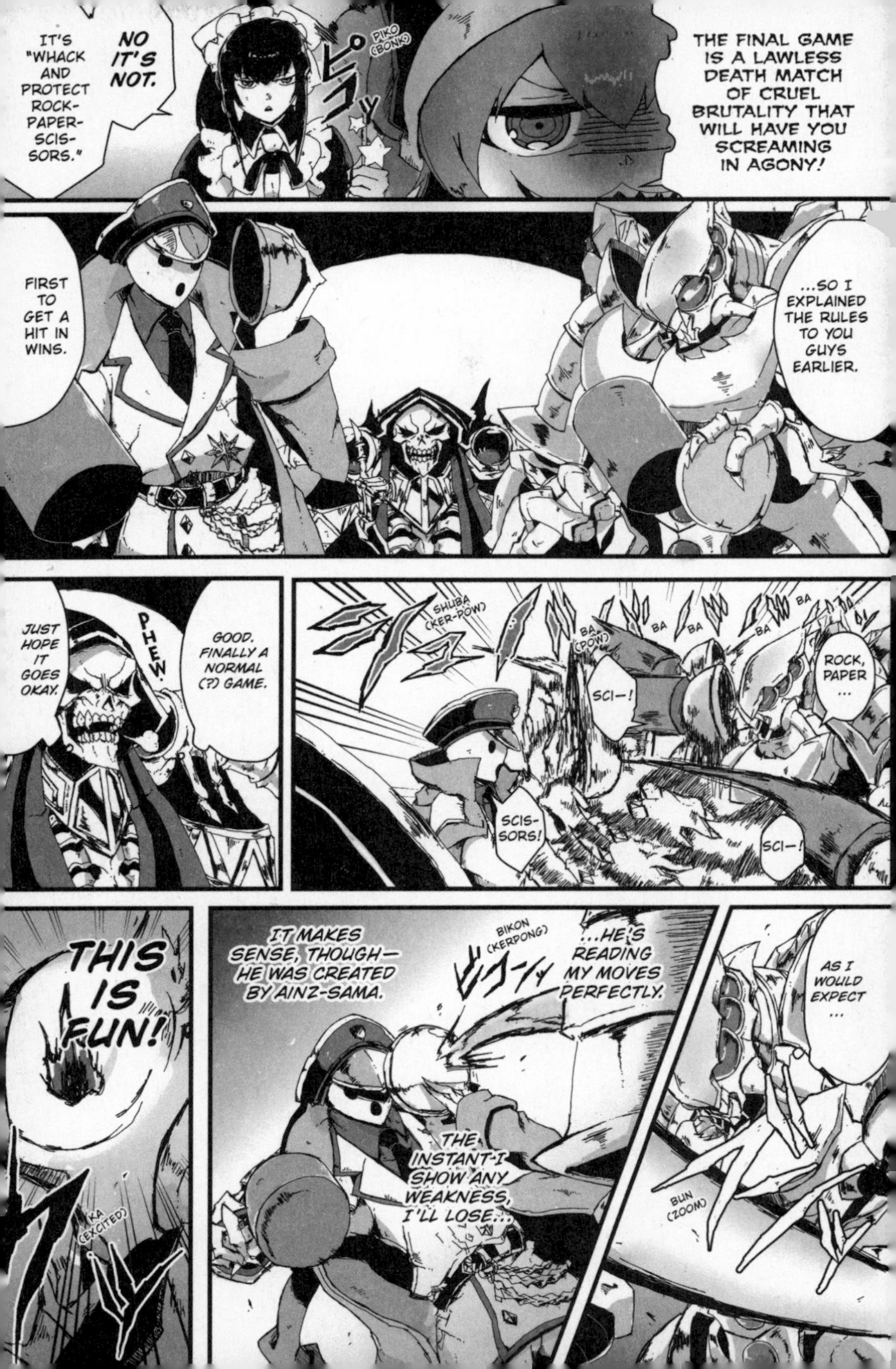
THE FINAL GAME IS A LAWLESS DEATH MATCH OF CRUEL BRUTALITY THAT WILL HAVE YOU SCREAMING IN AGONY!
PIKO (BONK)
NO IT'S NOT.
IT'S "WHACK AND PROTECT ROCK-PAPER-SCISSORS."
...SO I EXPLAINED THE RULES TO YOU GUYS EARLIER.
FIRST TO GET A HIT IN WINS.
BA BA BA BA
ROCK, PAPER ...
BA (POW)
SCI—!
SHUBA (KER-POW)
SCISSORS!
SCI—!
GOOD. FINALLY A NORMAL (?) GAME.
PHEW!
JUST HOPE IT GOES OKAY.
AS I WOULD EXPECT ...
BUN (ZOOM)
...HE'S READING MY MOVES PERFECTLY.
BIKON (KERPONG)
IT MAKES SENSE, THOUGH—HE WAS CREATED BY AINZ-SAMA.
THE INSTANT I SHOW ANY WEAKNESS, I'LL LOSE...
THIS IS FUN!
KA (EXCITED)

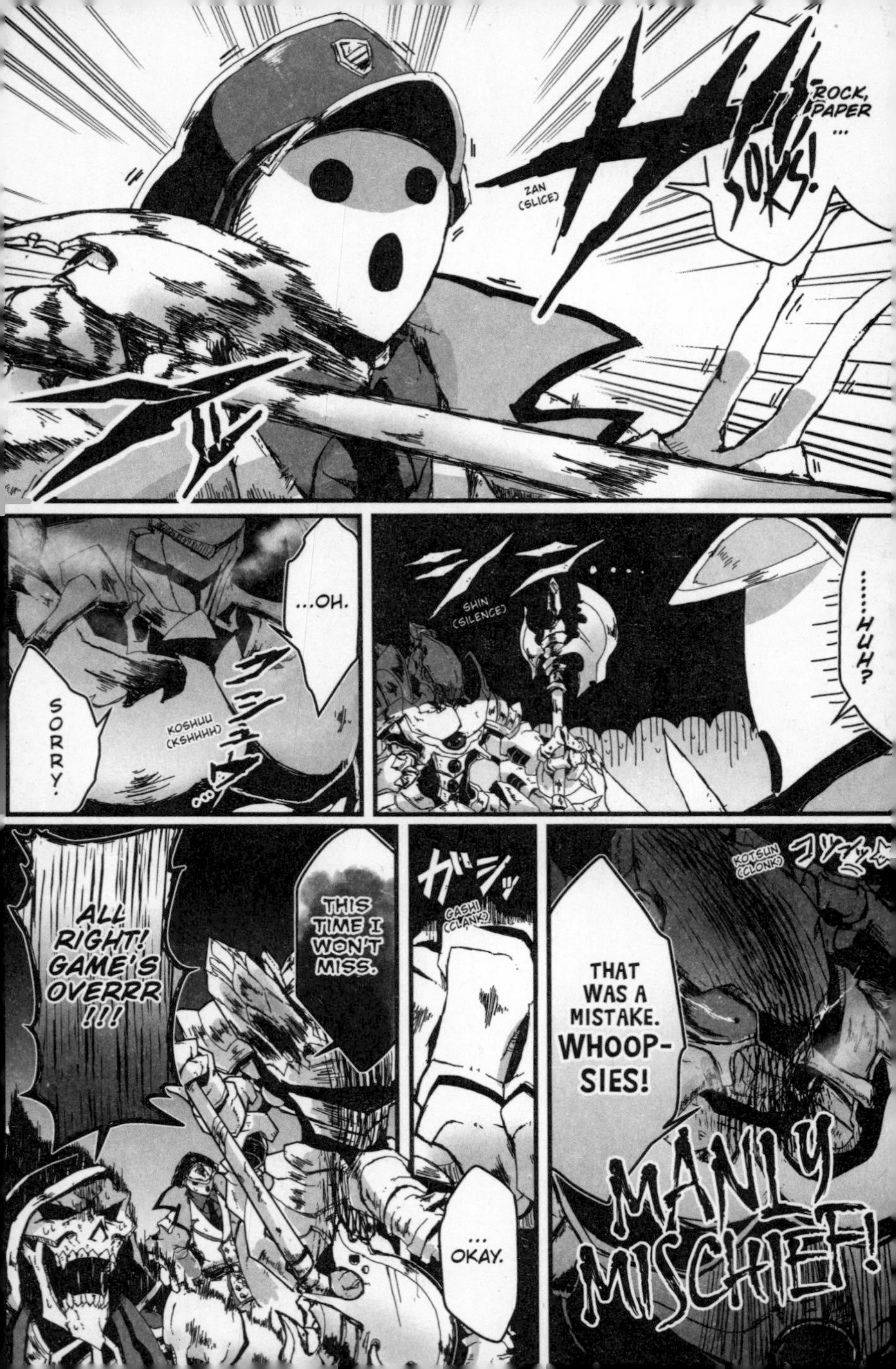

ROCK, PAPER ...
SOKS!
ZAN (SLICE)
......HUH?
SHIN (SILENCE)
...
...OH.
KOSHUU (KSHHHH)
SORRY.
KOTSUN (CLONK)
THAT WAS A MISTAKE. WHOOPSIES!
MANLY MISCHIEF!
GASHI (CLANK)
...OKAY.
THIS TIME I WON'T MISS.
ALL RIGHT! GAME'S OVERRR!!!

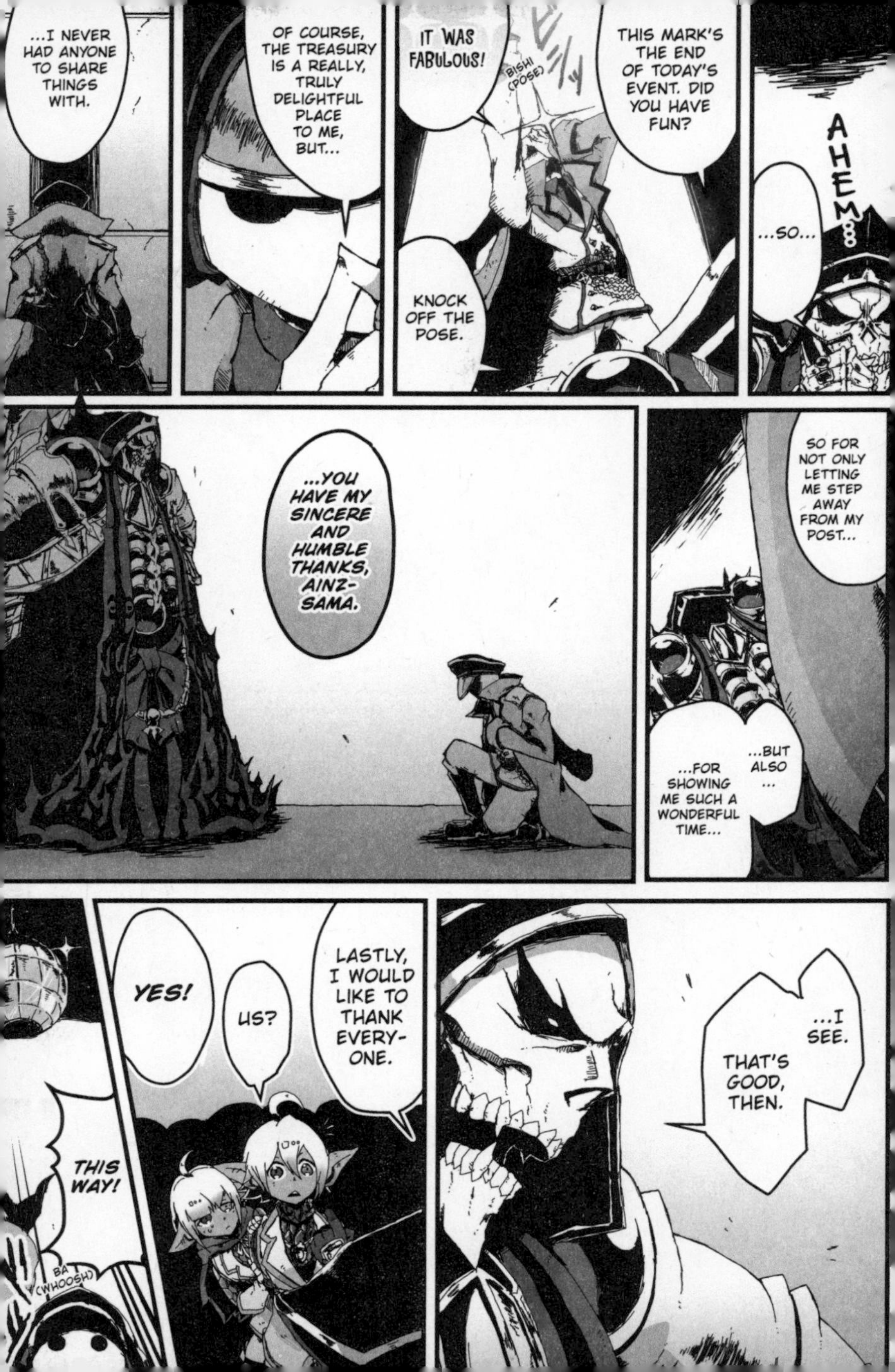
AHEM...
...SO...
THIS MARK'S THE END OF TODAY'S EVENT. DID YOU HAVE FUN?
BISHI (POSE)
IT WAS FABULOUS!
KNOCK OFF THE POSE.
OF COURSE, THE TREASURY IS A REALLY, TRULY DELIGHTFUL PLACE TO ME, BUT...
...I NEVER HAD ANYONE TO SHARE THINGS WITH.
SO FOR NOT ONLY LETTING ME STEP AWAY FROM MY POST...
...BUT ALSO...
...FOR SHOWING ME SUCH A WONDERFUL TIME...
...YOU HAVE MY SINCERE AND HUMBLE THANKS, AINZ-SAMA.
...I SEE.
THAT'S GOOD, THEN.
LASTLY, I WOULD LIKE TO THANK EVERYONE.
US?
YES!
THIS WAY!
BA (WHOOSH)

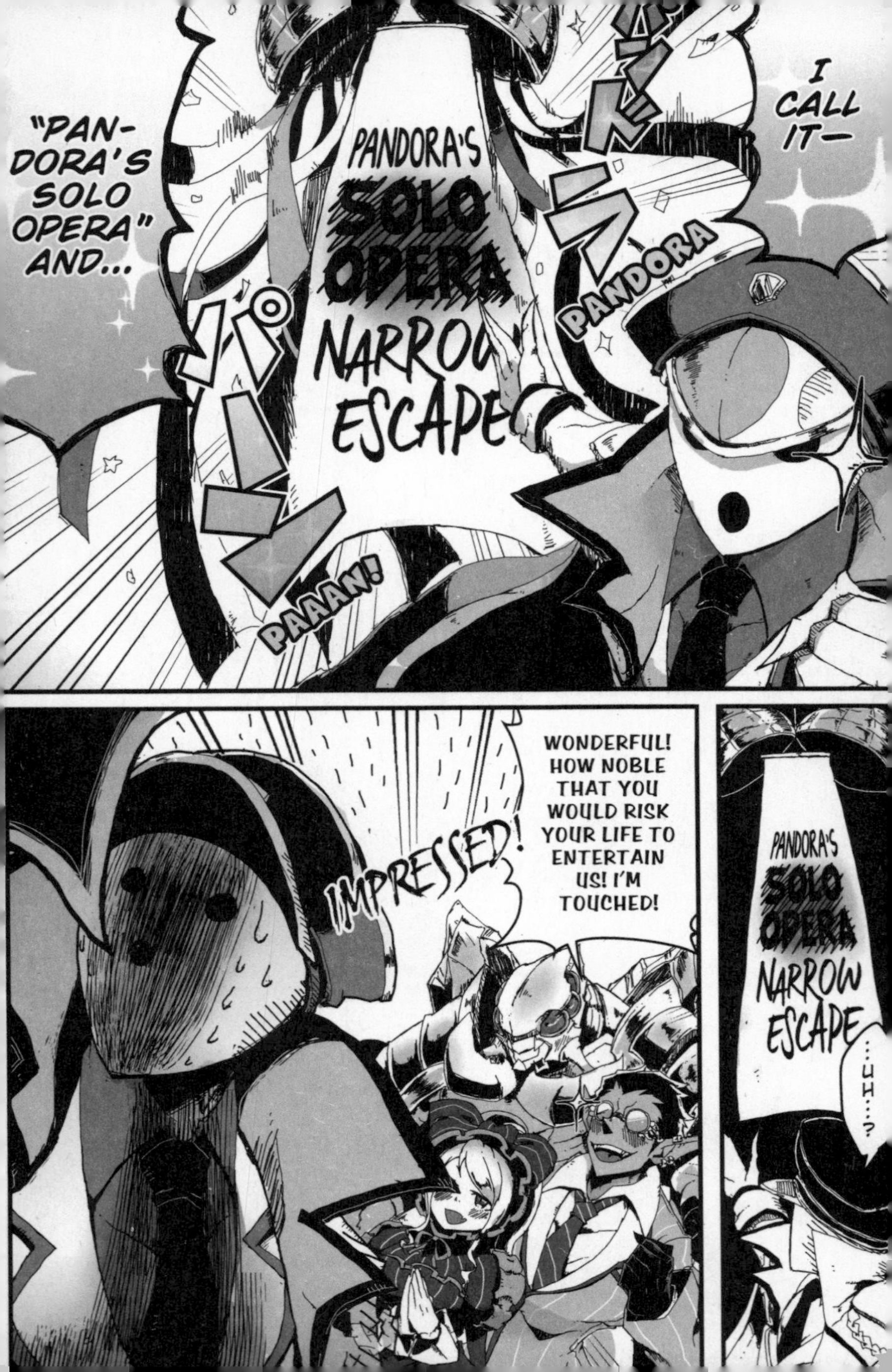
I CALL IT—
PANDORA
PANDORA'S SOLO OPERA NARROW ESCAPE
"PAN-DORA'S SOLO OPERA" AND...
PAAAN!
PANDORA'S SOLO OPERA NARROW ESCAPE
...UH...?
WONDERFUL! HOW NOBLE THAT YOU WOULD RISK YOUR LIFE TO ENTERTAIN US! I'M TOUCHED!
IMPRESSED!

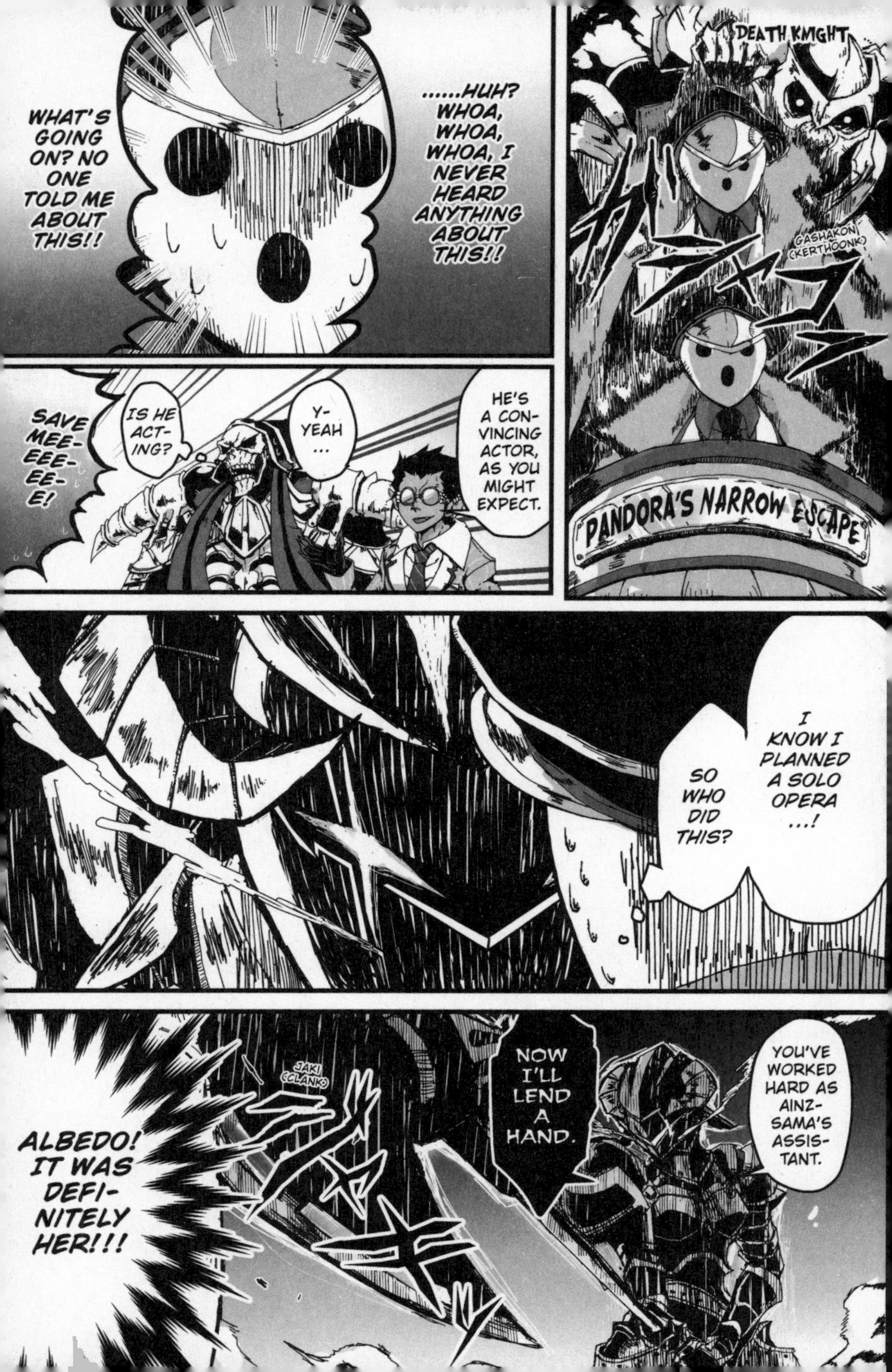
DEATH KNIGHT
GASHAKON (KERTHOONK)
PANDORA'S NARROW ESCAPE
......HUH? WHOA, WHOA, WHOA, I NEVER HEARD ANYTHING ABOUT THIS!!
WHAT'S GOING ON? NO ONE TOLD ME ABOUT THIS!!
HE'S A CON-VINCING ACTOR, AS YOU MIGHT EXPECT.
Y-YEAH ...
IS HE ACT-ING?
SAVE MEE-EEE-EE-E!
I KNOW I PLANNED A SOLO OPERA ...!
SO WHO DID THIS?
YOU'VE WORKED HARD AS AINZ-SAMA'S ASSIS-TANT.
NOW I'LL LEND A HAND.
JAKI (CLANK)
ALBEDO! IT WAS DEFI-NITELY HER!!!

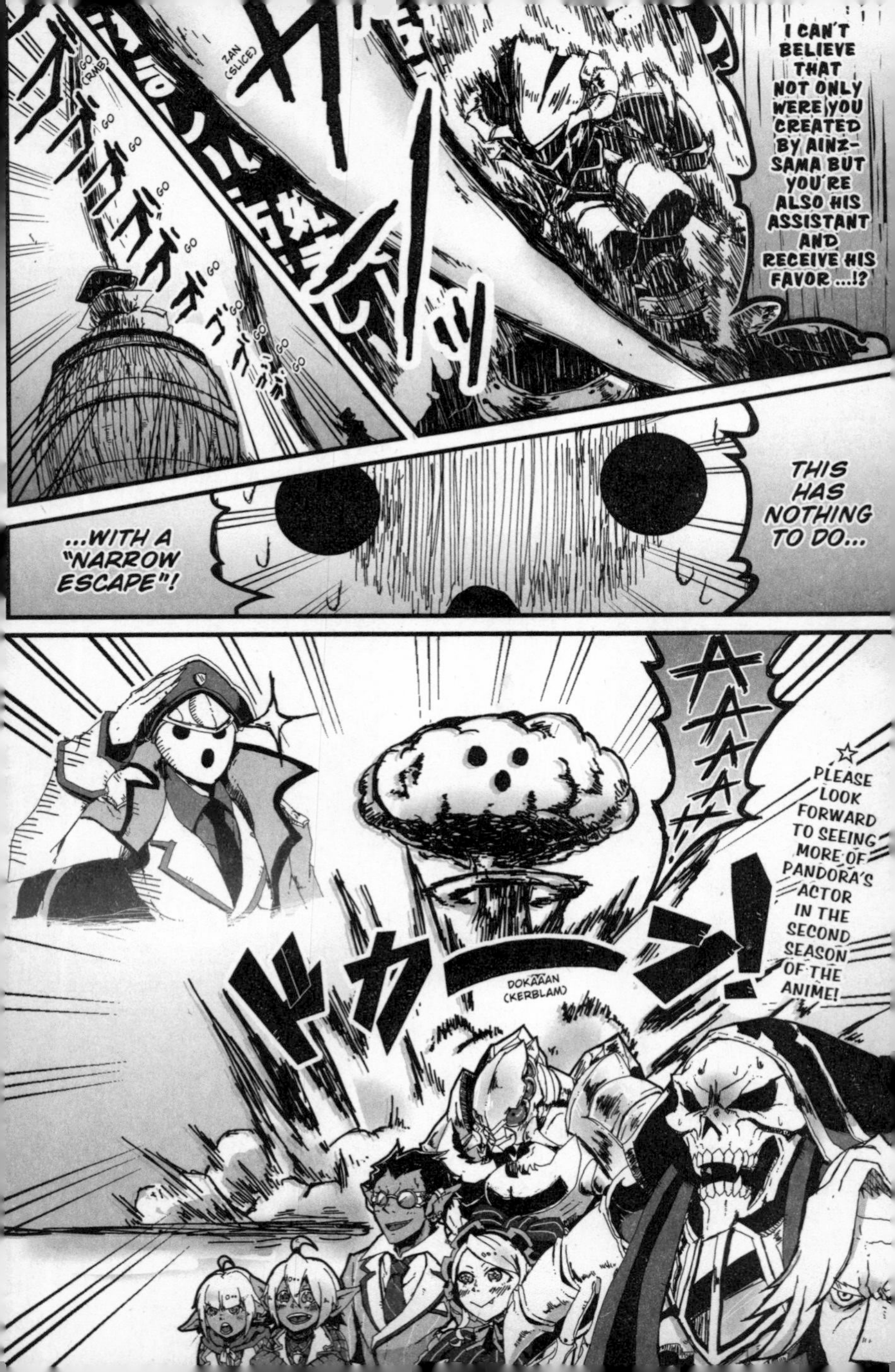
I CAN'T BELIEVE THAT NOT ONLY WERE YOU CREATED BY AINZ-SAMA BUT YOU'RE ALSO HIS ASSISTANT AND RECEIVE HIS FAVOR ...!?
ZAN (SLICE)
GO (RMB)
GO GO GO GO GO GO GO GO
THIS HAS NOTHING TO DO...
...WITH A "NARROW ESCAPE"!
☆ PLEASE LOOK FORWARD TO SEEING MORE OF PANDORA'S ACTOR IN THE SECOND SEASON OF THE ANIME!
DOKAAAN (KERBLAM)

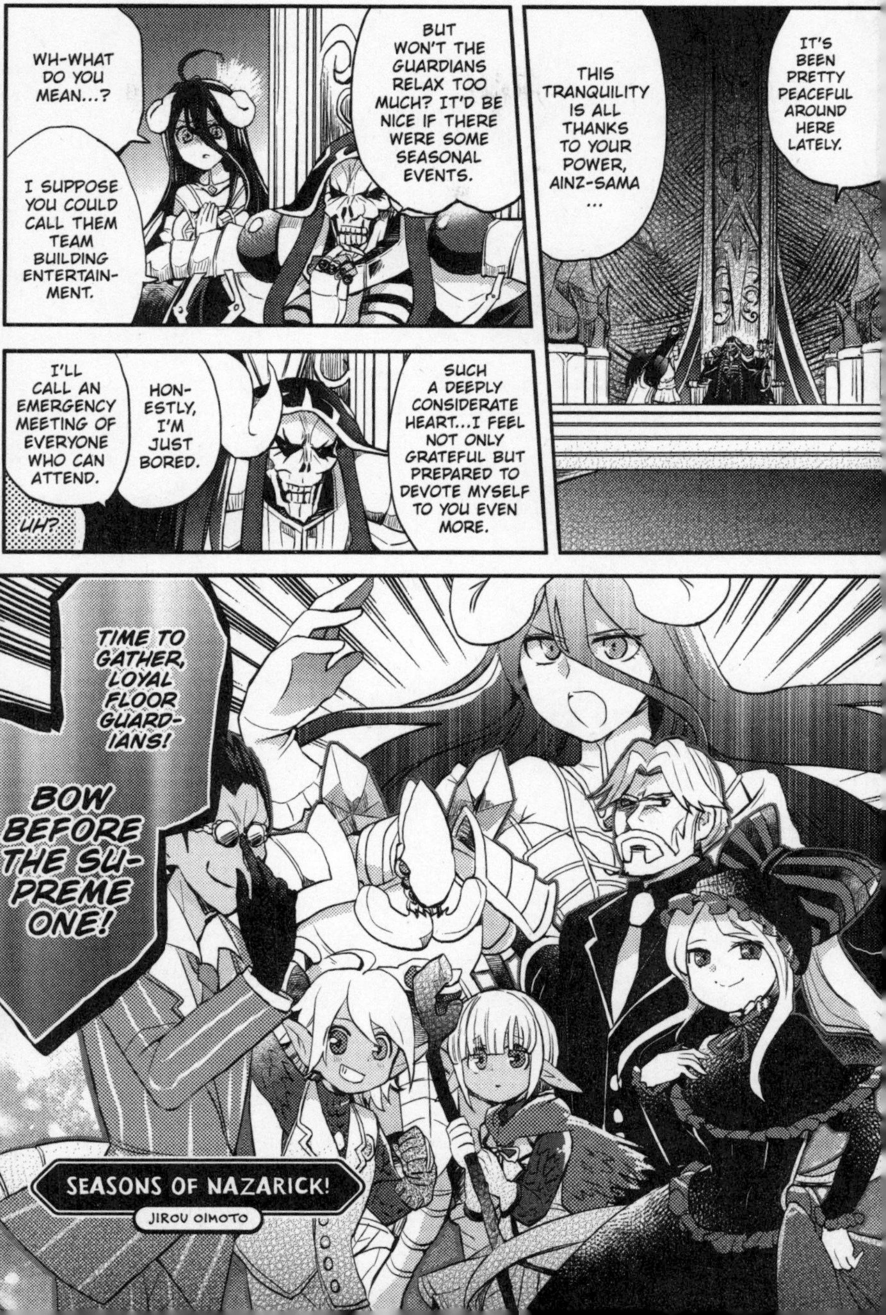
IT'S BEEN PRETTY PEACEFUL AROUND HERE LATELY.
THIS TRANQUILITY IS ALL THANKS TO YOUR POWER, AINZ-SAMA...
BUT WON'T THE GUARDIANS RELAX TOO MUCH? IT'D BE NICE IF THERE WERE SOME SEASONAL EVENTS.
WH-WHAT DO YOU MEAN...?
I SUPPOSE YOU COULD CALL THEM TEAM BUILDING ENTERTAINMENT.
SUCH A DEEPLY CONSIDERATE HEART...I FEEL NOT ONLY GRATEFUL BUT PREPARED TO DEVOTE MYSELF TO YOU EVEN MORE.
HON-ESTLY, I'M JUST BORED.
I'LL CALL AN EMERGENCY MEETING OF EVERYONE WHO CAN ATTEND.
UH?
TIME TO GATHER, LOYAL FLOOR GUARD-IANS!
BOW BEFORE THE SU-PREME ONE!
SEASONS OF NAZARICK!
JIROU OIMOTO

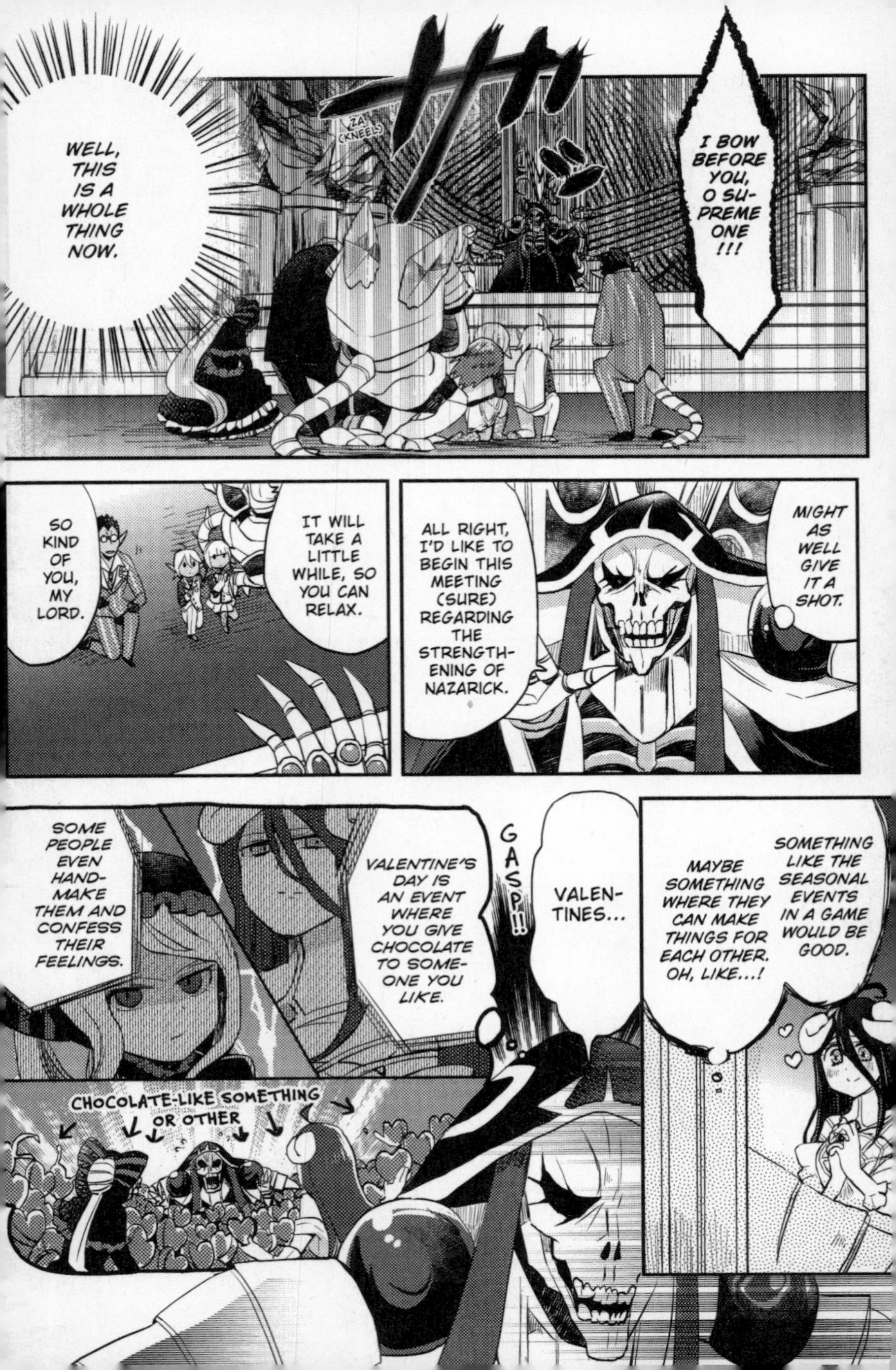
I BOW BEFORE YOU, O SUPREME ONE!!!
ZA (KNEELS)
WELL, THIS IS A WHOLE THING NOW.
MIGHT AS WELL GIVE IT A SHOT.
ALL RIGHT, I'D LIKE TO BEGIN THIS MEETING (SURE) REGARDING THE STRENGTHENING OF NAZARICK.
IT WILL TAKE A LITTLE WHILE, SO YOU CAN RELAX.
SO KIND OF YOU, MY LORD.
SOMETHING LIKE THE SEASONAL EVENTS IN A GAME WOULD BE GOOD.
MAYBE SOMETHING WHERE THEY CAN MAKE THINGS FOR EACH OTHER. OH, LIKE...!
VALENTINES...
GASP!!
VALENTINE'S DAY IS AN EVENT WHERE YOU GIVE CHOCOLATE TO SOMEONE YOU LIKE.
SOME PEOPLE EVEN HANDMAKE THEM AND CONFESS THEIR FEELINGS.
CHOCOLATE-LIKE SOMETHING OR OTHER

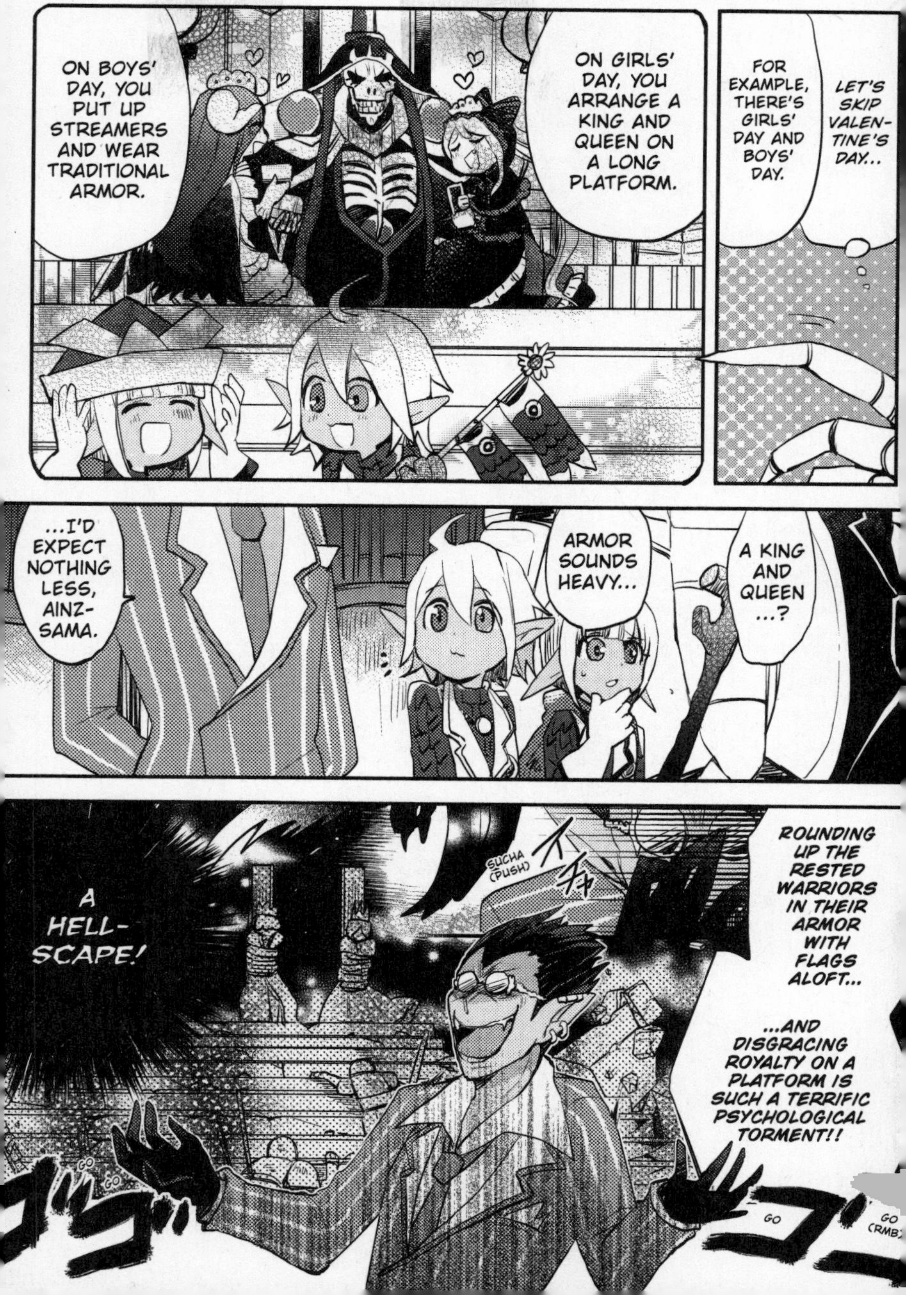
LET'S SKIP VALEN-TINE'S DAY...
FOR EXAMPLE, THERE'S GIRLS' DAY AND BOYS' DAY.
ON GIRLS' DAY, YOU ARRANGE A KING AND QUEEN ON A LONG PLATFORM.
ON BOYS' DAY, YOU PUT UP STREAMERS AND WEAR TRADITIONAL ARMOR.
A KING AND QUEEN ...?
ARMOR SOUNDS HEAVY...
...I'D EXPECT NOTHING LESS, AINZ-SAMA.
ROUNDING UP THE RESTED WARRIORS IN THEIR ARMOR WITH FLAGS ALOFT...
...AND DISGRACING ROYALTY ON A PLATFORM IS SUCH A TERRIFIC PSYCHOLOGICAL TORMENT!!
SUCHA (PUSH)
A HELL-SCAPE!
GO GO (RMB)
GO GO

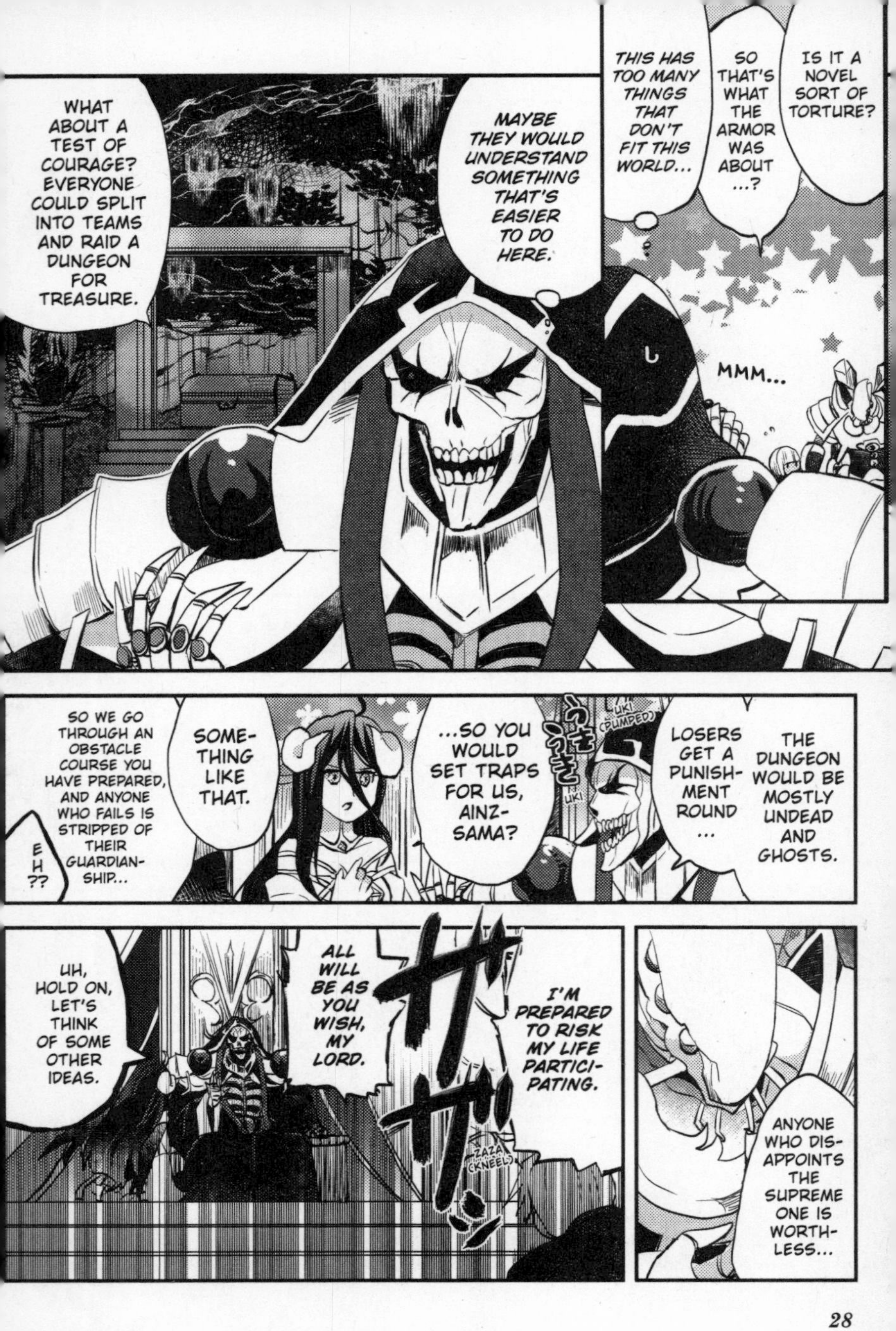
IS IT A NOVEL SORT OF TORTURE?
SO THAT'S WHAT THE ARMOR WAS ABOUT ...?
THIS HAS TOO MANY THINGS THAT DON'T FIT THIS WORLD...
MMM...
MAYBE THEY WOULD UNDERSTAND SOMETHING THAT'S EASIER TO DO HERE.
WHAT ABOUT A TEST OF COURAGE? EVERYONE COULD SPLIT INTO TEAMS AND RAID A DUNGEON FOR TREASURE.
THE DUNGEON WOULD BE MOSTLY UNDEAD AND GHOSTS.
LOSERS GET A PUNISHMENT ROUND ...
うき うき
UKI (PUMPED) UKI
...SO YOU WOULD SET TRAPS FOR US, AINZ-SAMA?
SOMETHING LIKE THAT.
SO WE GO THROUGH AN OBSTACLE COURSE YOU HAVE PREPARED, AND ANYONE WHO FAILS IS STRIPPED OF THEIR GUARDIANSHIP...
EH??
ANYONE WHO DISAPPOINTS THE SUPREME ONE IS WORTHLESS...
I'M PREPARED TO RISK MY LIFE PARTICIPATING.
ALL WILL BE AS YOU WISH, MY LORD.
ZAZA (KNEEL)
UH, HOLD ON, LET'S THINK OF SOME OTHER IDEAS.

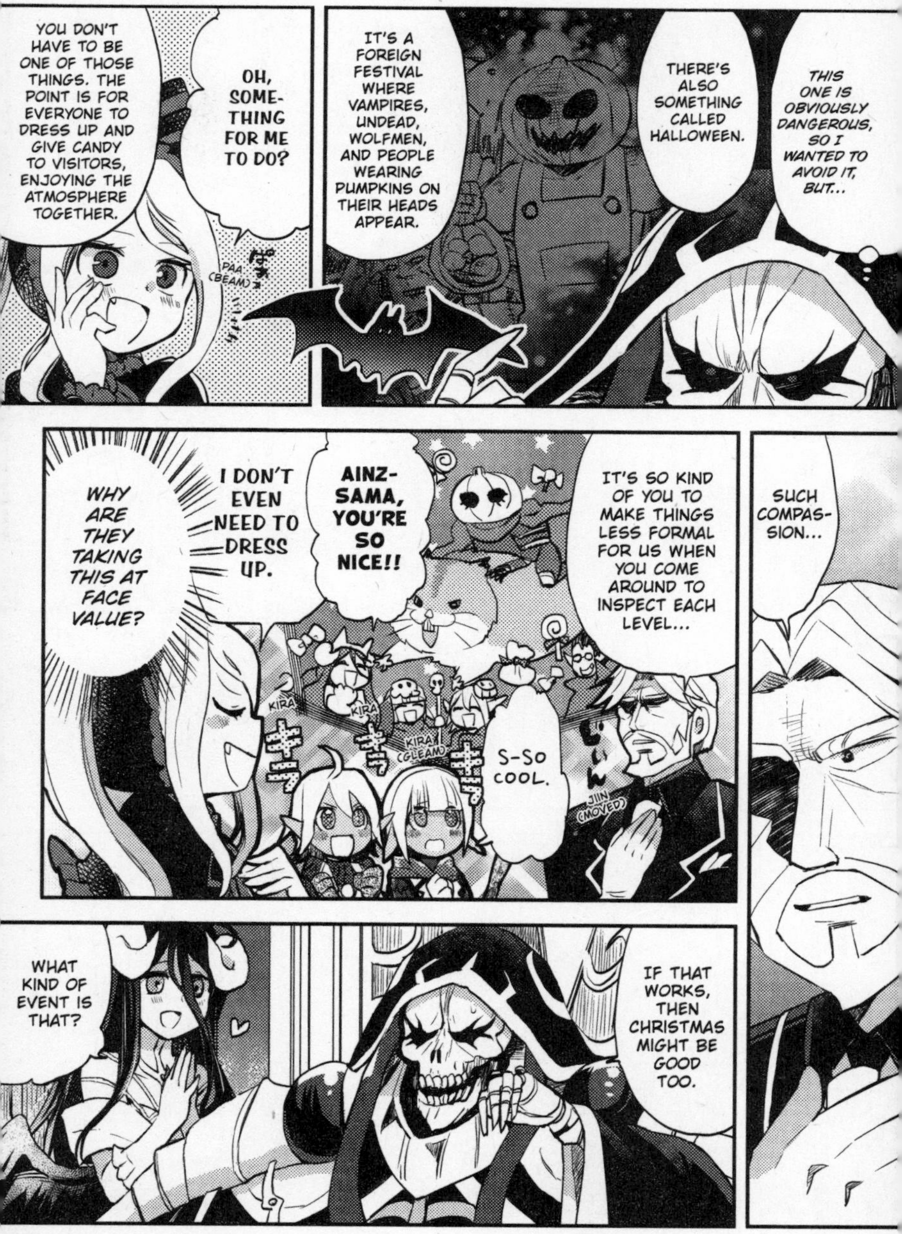
THIS ONE IS OBVIOUSLY DANGEROUS, SO I WANTED TO AVOID IT, BUT...
THERE'S ALSO SOMETHING CALLED HALLOWEEN.
IT'S A FOREIGN FESTIVAL WHERE VAMPIRES, UNDEAD, WOLFMEN, AND PEOPLE WEARING PUMPKINS ON THEIR HEADS APPEAR.
OH, SOMETHING FOR ME TO DO?
YOU DON'T HAVE TO BE ONE OF THOSE THINGS. THE POINT IS FOR EVERYONE TO DRESS UP AND GIVE CANDY TO VISITORS, ENJOYING THE ATMOSPHERE TOGETHER.
PAA (BEAM)
SUCH COMPASSION...
IT'S SO KIND OF YOU TO MAKE THINGS LESS FORMAL FOR US WHEN YOU COME AROUND TO INSPECT EACH LEVEL...
AINZ-SAMA, YOU'RE SO NICE!!
I DON'T EVEN NEED TO DRESS UP.
WHY ARE THEY TAKING THIS AT FACE VALUE?
JIIN (MOVED)
S-SO COOL.
KIRA
KIRA
KIRA (GLEAM)
IF THAT WORKS, THEN CHRISTMAS MIGHT BE GOOD TOO.
WHAT KIND OF EVENT IS THAT?

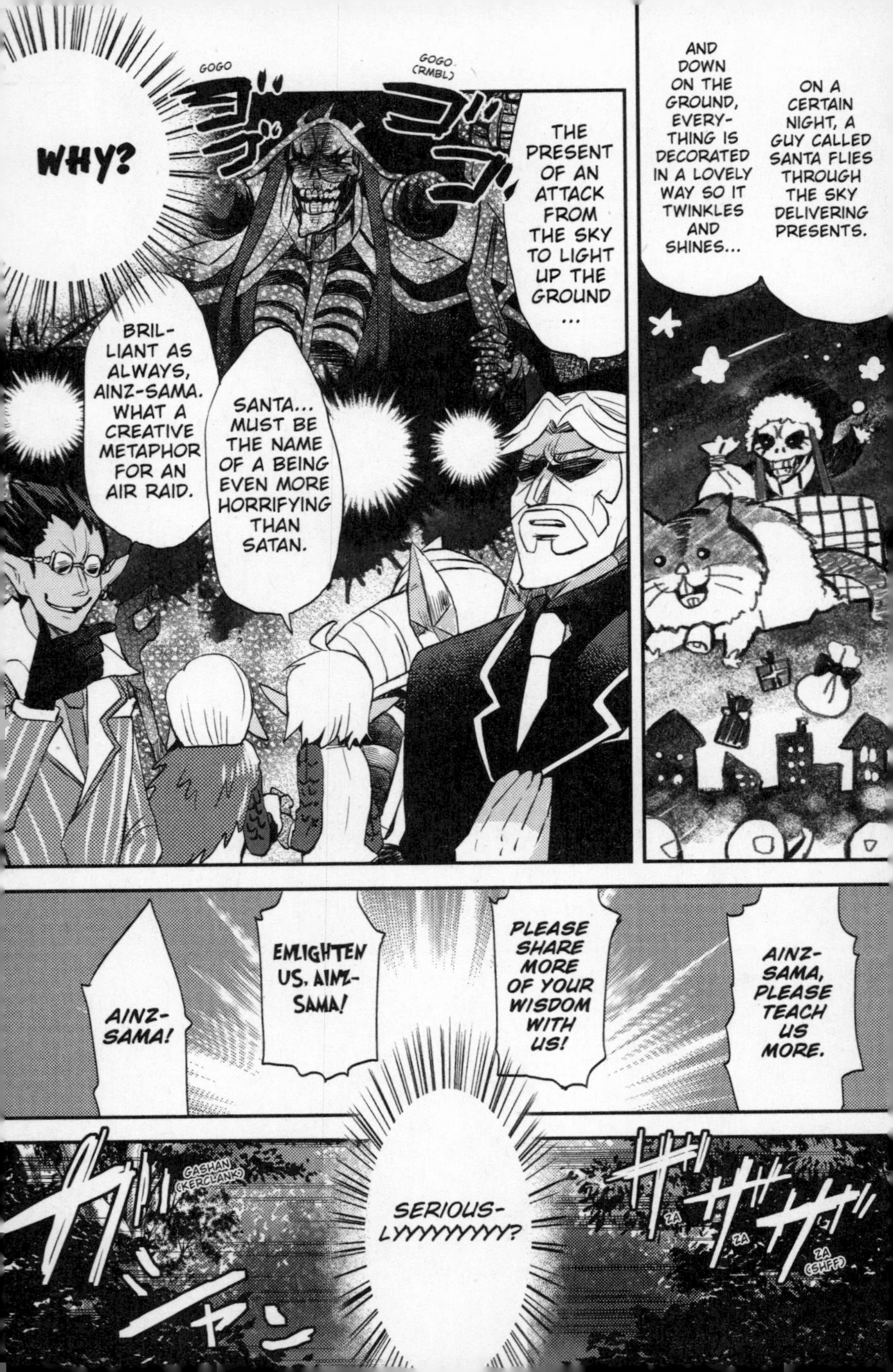
ON A CERTAIN NIGHT, A GUY CALLED SANTA FLIES THROUGH THE SKY DELIVERING PRESENTS.
AND DOWN ON THE GROUND, EVERY-THING IS DECORATED IN A LOVELY WAY SO IT TWINKLES AND SHINES...
THE PRESENT OF AN ATTACK FROM THE SKY TO LIGHT UP THE GROUND ...
GOGO (RMBL)
GOGO
WHY?
SANTA... MUST BE THE NAME OF A BEING EVEN MORE HORRIFYING THAN SATAN.
BRIL-LIANT AS ALWAYS, AINZ-SAMA. WHAT A CREATIVE METAPHOR FOR AN AIR RAID.
AINZ-SAMA, PLEASE TEACH US MORE.
PLEASE SHARE MORE OF YOUR WISDOM WITH US!
ENLIGHTEN US, AINZ-SAMA!
AINZ-SAMA!
ZA
ZA
ZA (SHFF)
SERIOUS-LYYYYYYYYY?
GASHAN (KERCLANK)

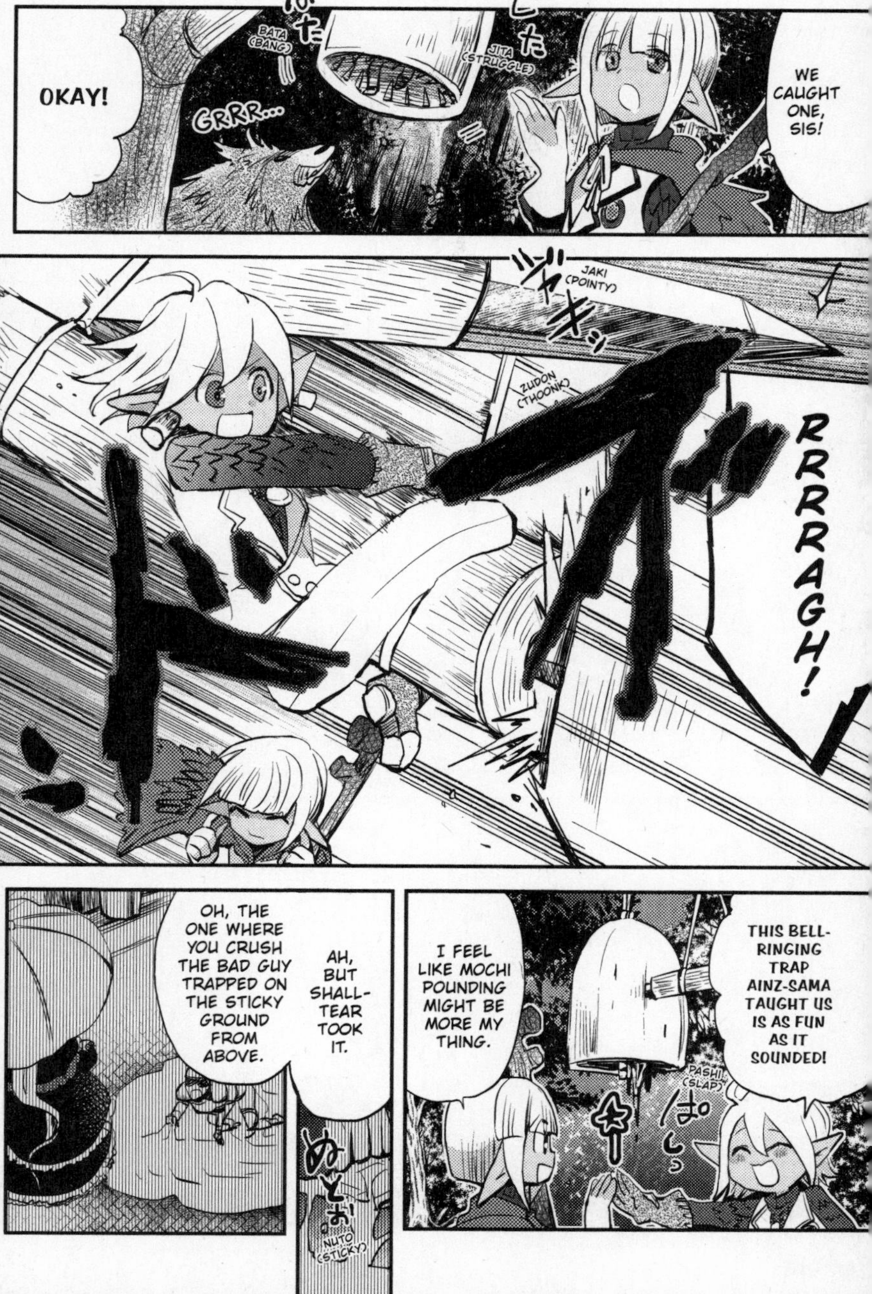
WE CAUGHT ONE, SIS!
じた
JITA (STRUGGLE)
ばた
BATA (BANG)
GRRR...
OKAY!
ジャキッ
JAKI (POINTY)
ZUDON (THOONK)
RRRRAGH!
THIS BELL-RINGING TRAP AINZ-SAMA TAUGHT US IS AS FUN AS IT SOUNDED!
ぱしっ
PASHI (SLAP)
I FEEL LIKE MOCHI POUNDING MIGHT BE MORE MY THING.
AH, BUT SHALLTEAR TOOK IT.
OH, THE ONE WHERE YOU CRUSH THE BAD GUY TRAPPED ON THE STICKY GROUND FROM ABOVE.
ぬとぉ!
NUTO (STICKY)

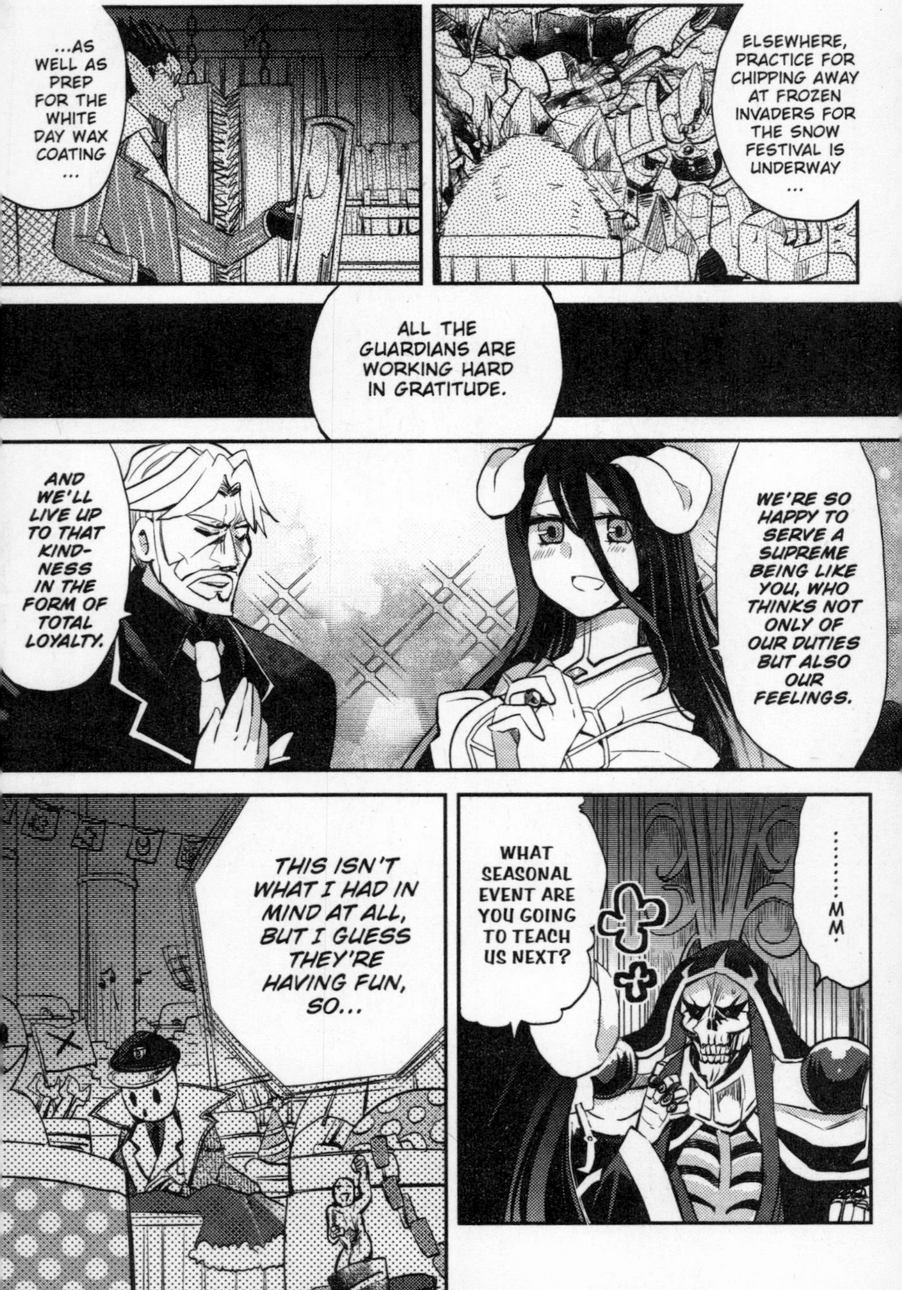
ELSEWHERE, PRACTICE FOR CHIPPING AWAY AT FROZEN INVADERS FOR THE SNOW FESTIVAL IS UNDERWAY ...
...AS WELL AS PREP FOR THE WHITE DAY WAX COATING ...
ALL THE GUARDIANS ARE WORKING HARD IN GRATITUDE.
WE'RE SO HAPPY TO SERVE A SUPREME BEING LIKE YOU, WHO THINKS NOT ONLY OF OUR DUTIES BUT ALSO OUR FEELINGS.
AND WE'LL LIVE UP TO THAT KINDNESS IN THE FORM OF TOTAL LOYALTY.
WHAT SEASONAL EVENT ARE YOU GOING TO TEACH US NEXT?
......MM.
THIS ISN'T WHAT I HAD IN MIND AT ALL, BUT I GUESS THEY'RE HAVING FUN, SO...

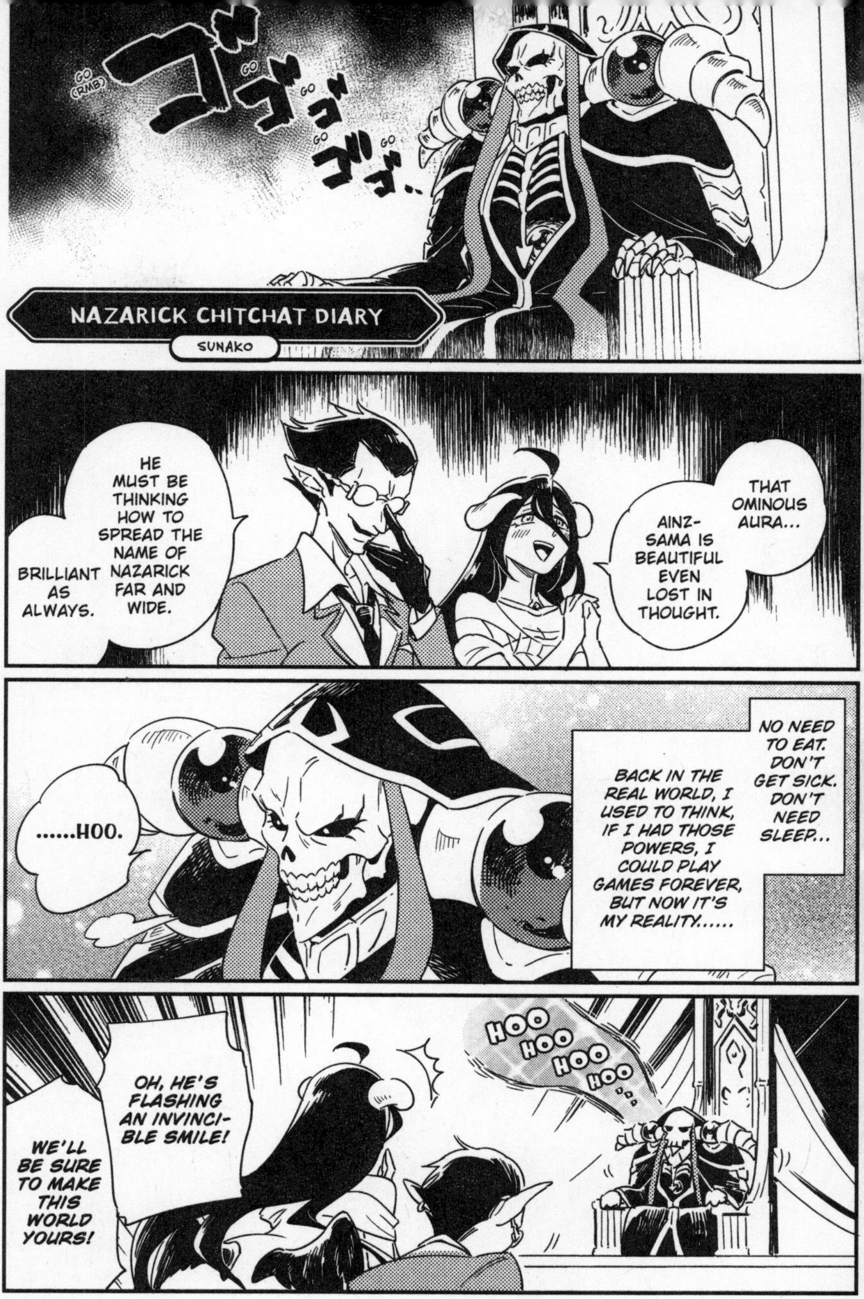
ゴゴゴゴゴ…
GO (RMB) GO GO GO GO
NAZARICK CHITCHAT DIARY
SUNAKO
THAT OMINOUS AURA...
AINZ-SAMA IS BEAUTIFUL EVEN LOST IN THOUGHT.
HE MUST BE THINKING HOW TO SPREAD THE NAME OF NAZARICK FAR AND WIDE.
BRILLIANT AS ALWAYS.
NO NEED TO EAT. DON'T GET SICK. DON'T NEED SLEEP...
BACK IN THE REAL WORLD, I USED TO THINK, IF I HAD THOSE POWERS, I COULD PLAY GAMES FOREVER, BUT NOW IT'S MY REALITY......
......HOO.
HOO HOO HOO HOO...
OH, HE'S FLASHING AN INVINCIBLE SMILE!
WE'LL BE SURE TO MAKE THIS WORLD YOURS!

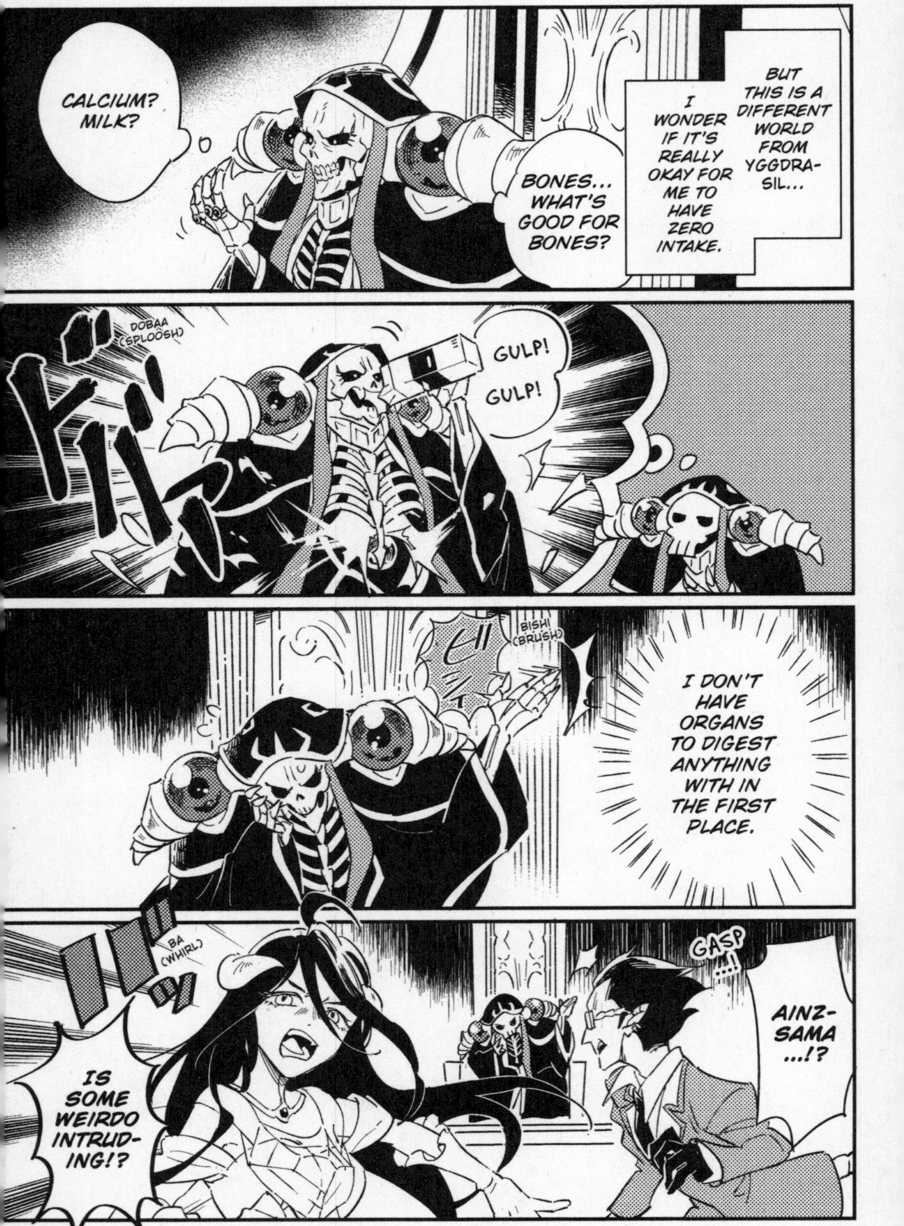
BUT THIS IS A DIFFERENT WORLD FROM YGGDRA-SIL...
I WONDER IF IT'S REALLY OKAY FOR ME TO HAVE ZERO INTAKE.
BONES... WHAT'S GOOD FOR BONES?
CALCIUM? MILK?
GULP! GULP!
DOBAA (SPLOOSH)
I DON'T HAVE ORGANS TO DIGEST ANYTHING WITH IN THE FIRST PLACE.
BISHI (BRUSH)
AINZ-SAMA ...!?
GASP ...!
BA (WHIRL)
IS SOME WEIRDO INTRUD-ING!?

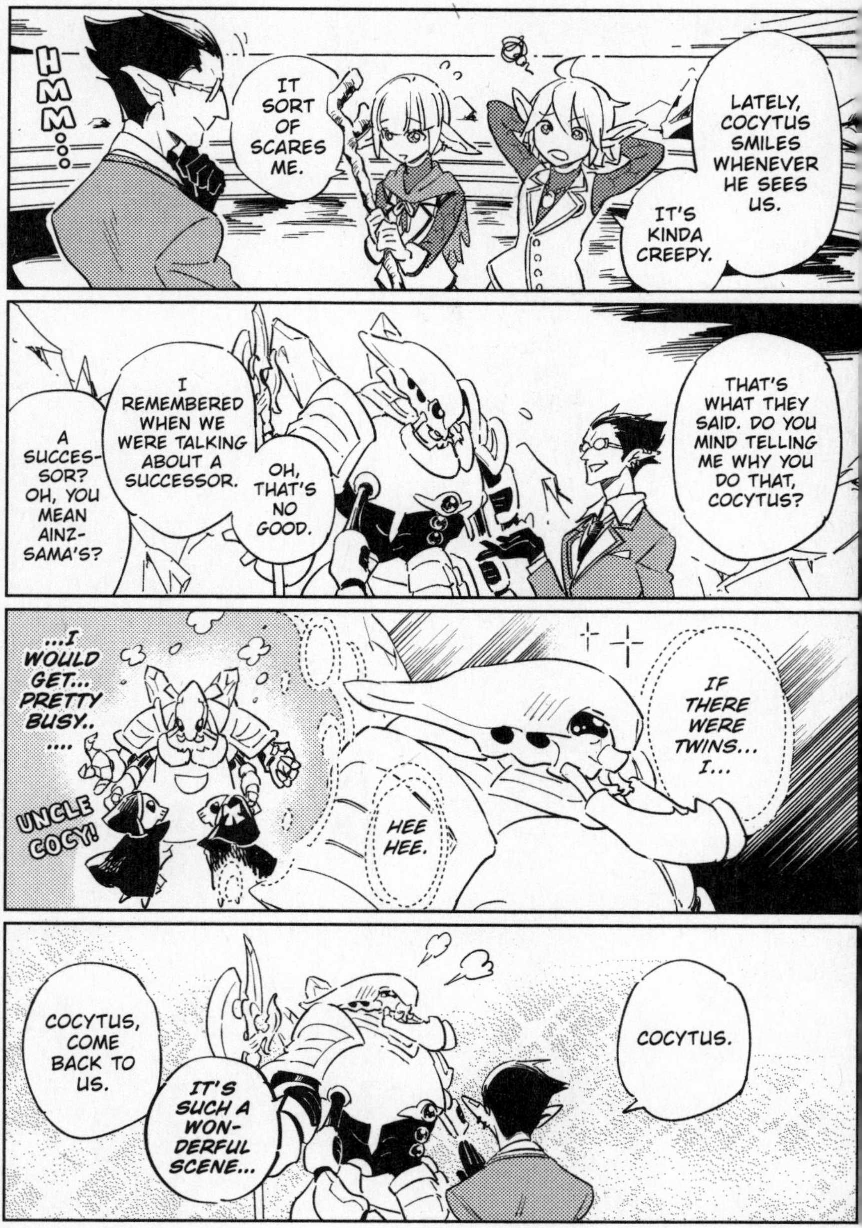
LATELY, COCYTUS SMILES WHENEVER HE SEES US.
IT'S KINDA CREEPY.
IT SORT OF SCARES ME.
HMM...
THAT'S WHAT THEY SAID. DO YOU MIND TELLING ME WHY YOU DO THAT, COCYTUS?
OH, THAT'S NO GOOD.
I REMEMBERED WHEN WE WERE TALKING ABOUT A SUCCESSOR.
A SUCCES-SOR? OH, YOU MEAN AINZ-SAMA'S?
IF THERE WERE TWINS... I...
HEE HEE.
...I WOULD GET... PRETTY BUSY.. ....
UNCLE COCY!
COCYTUS.
IT'S SUCH A WONDERFUL SCENE...
COCYTUS, COME BACK TO US.

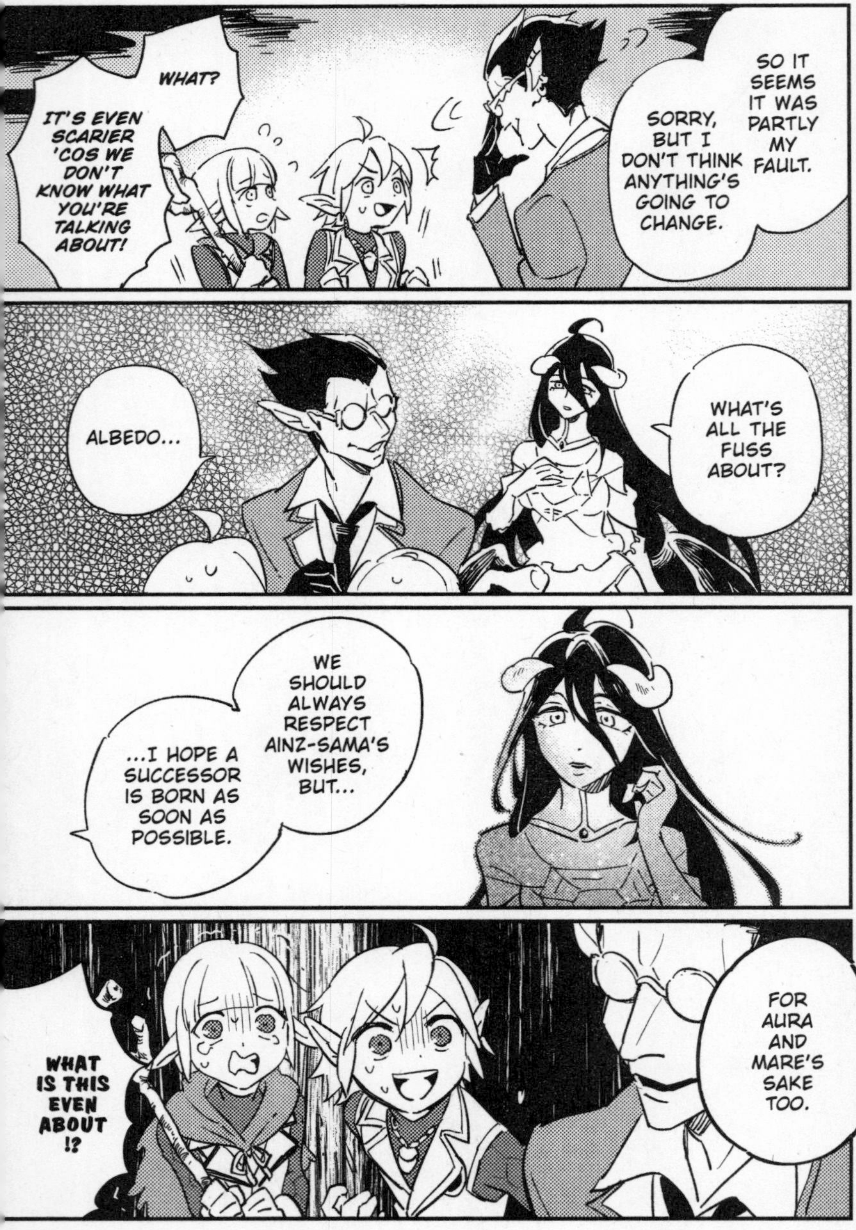
SO IT SEEMS IT WAS PARTLY MY FAULT.
SORRY, BUT I DON'T THINK ANYTHING'S GOING TO CHANGE.
WHAT?
IT'S EVEN SCARIER 'COS WE DON'T KNOW WHAT YOU'RE TALKING ABOUT!
WHAT'S ALL THE FUSS ABOUT?
ALBEDO...
WE SHOULD ALWAYS RESPECT AINZ-SAMA'S WISHES, BUT...
...I HOPE A SUCCESSOR IS BORN AS SOON AS POSSIBLE.
FOR AURA AND MARE'S SAKE TOO.
WHAT IS THIS EVEN ABOUT!?

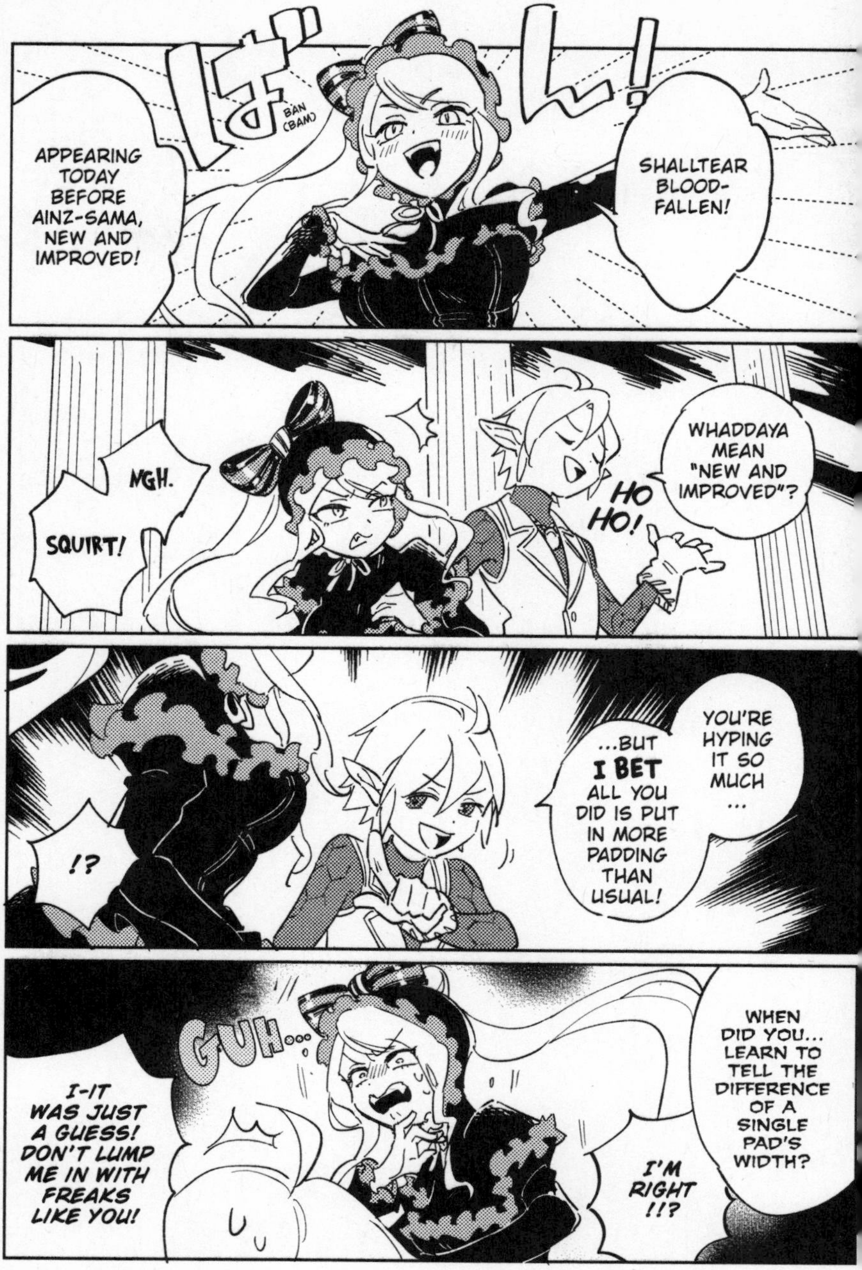
ばん!
BAN (BAM)
SHALLTEAR BLOOD-FALLEN!
APPEARING TODAY BEFORE AINZ-SAMA, NEW AND IMPROVED!
WHADDAYA MEAN "NEW AND IMPROVED"?
HO HO!
NGH.
SQUIRT!
YOU'RE HYPING IT SO MUCH...
...BUT I BET ALL YOU DID IS PUT IN MORE PADDING THAN USUAL!
!?
WHEN DID YOU... LEARN TO TELL THE DIFFERENCE OF A SINGLE PAD'S WIDTH?
I'M RIGHT!!?
GUH...
I-IT WAS JUST A GUESS! DON'T LUMP ME IN WITH FREAKS LIKE YOU!

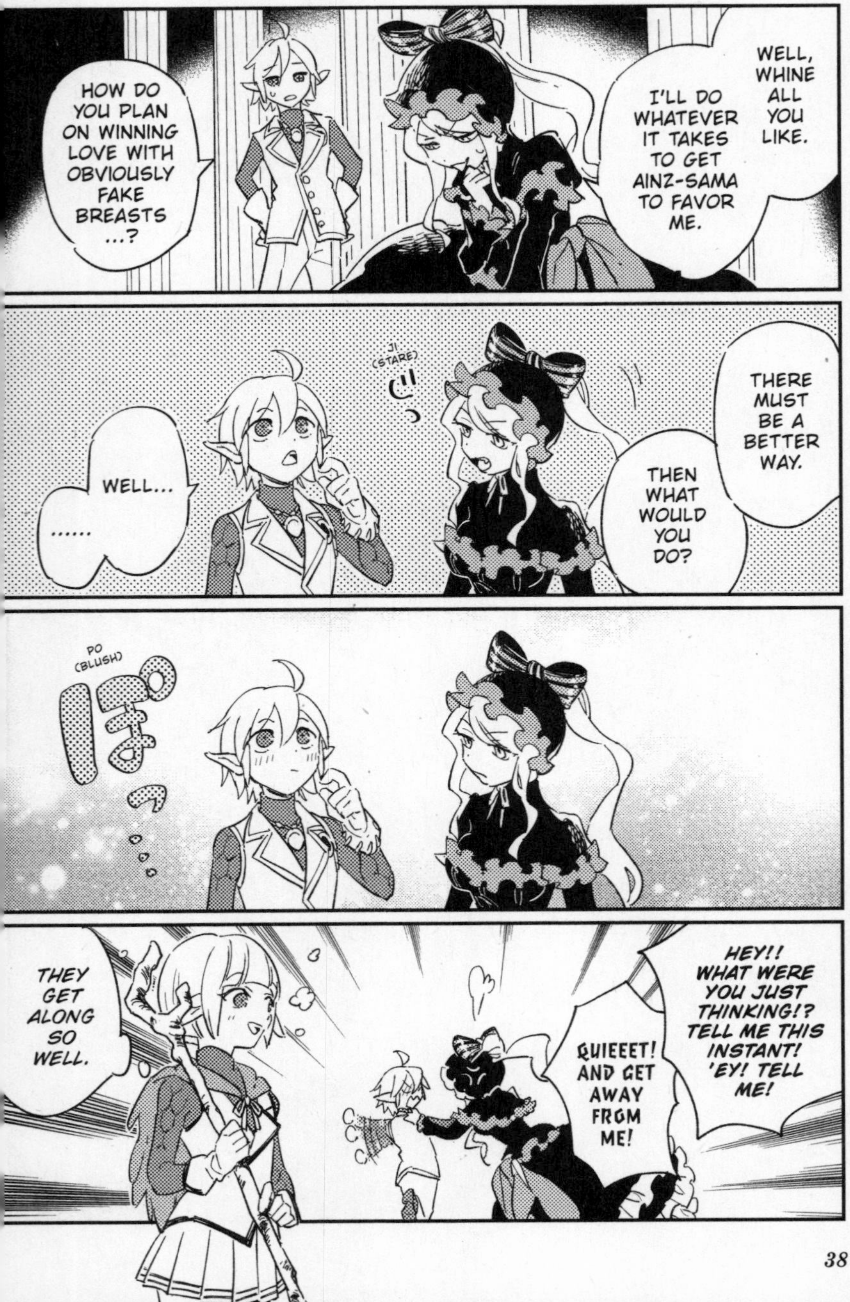
WELL, WHINE ALL YOU LIKE.
I'LL DO WHATEVER IT TAKES TO GET AINZ-SAMA TO FAVOR ME.
HOW DO YOU PLAN ON WINNING LOVE WITH OBVIOUSLY FAKE BREASTS ...?
THERE MUST BE A BETTER WAY.
THEN WHAT WOULD YOU DO?
JI (STARE)
WELL... ......
PO (BLUSH)
HEY!! WHAT WERE YOU JUST THINKING!? TELL ME THIS INSTANT! 'EY! TELL ME!
QUIEEET! AND GET AWAY FROM ME!
THEY GET ALONG SO WELL.

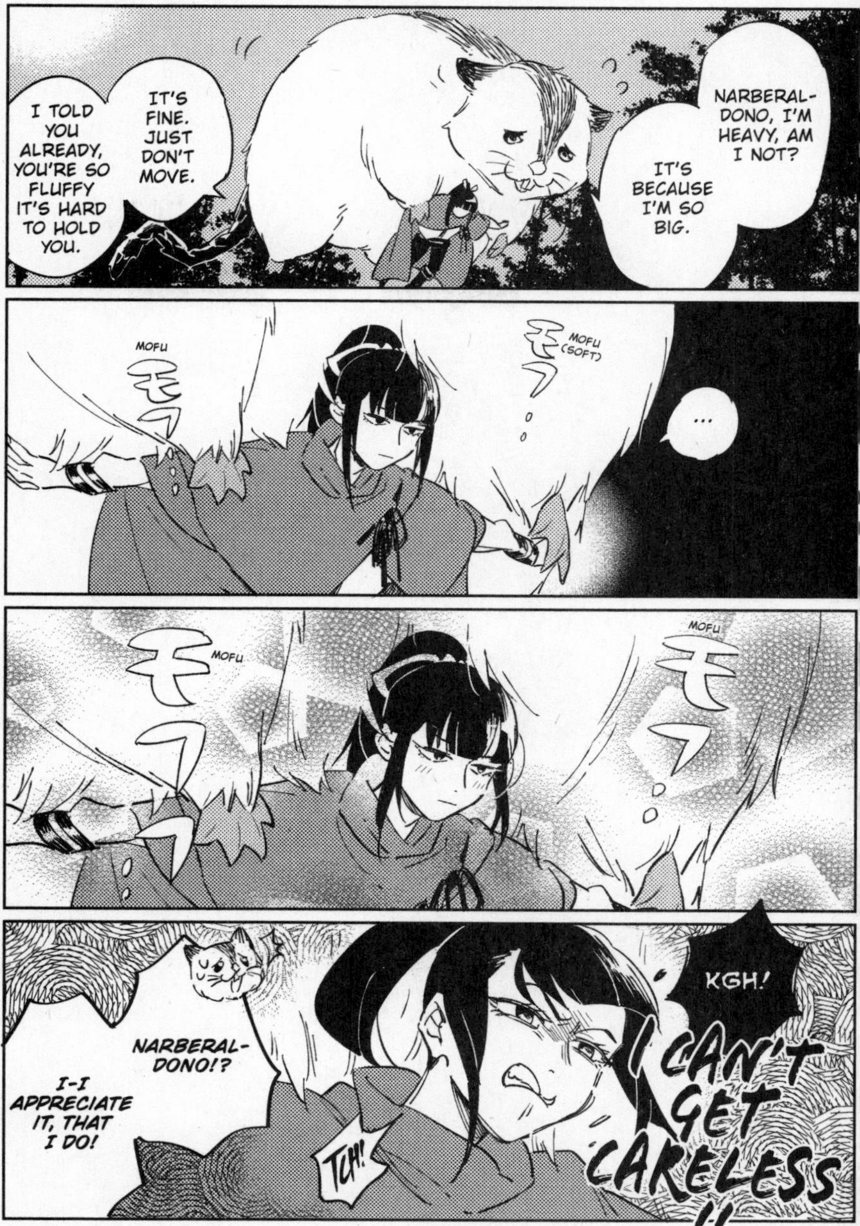
NARBERAL-DONO, I'M HEAVY, AM I NOT?
IT'S BECAUSE I'M SO BIG.
IT'S FINE. JUST DON'T MOVE.
I TOLD YOU ALREADY, YOU'RE SO FLUFFY IT'S HARD TO HOLD YOU.
...
MOFU (SOFT)
MOFU
MOFU
MOFU
KGH!
I CAN'T GET CARELESS!!
TCH!
NARBERAL-DONO!?
I-I APPRECIATE IT, THAT I DO!

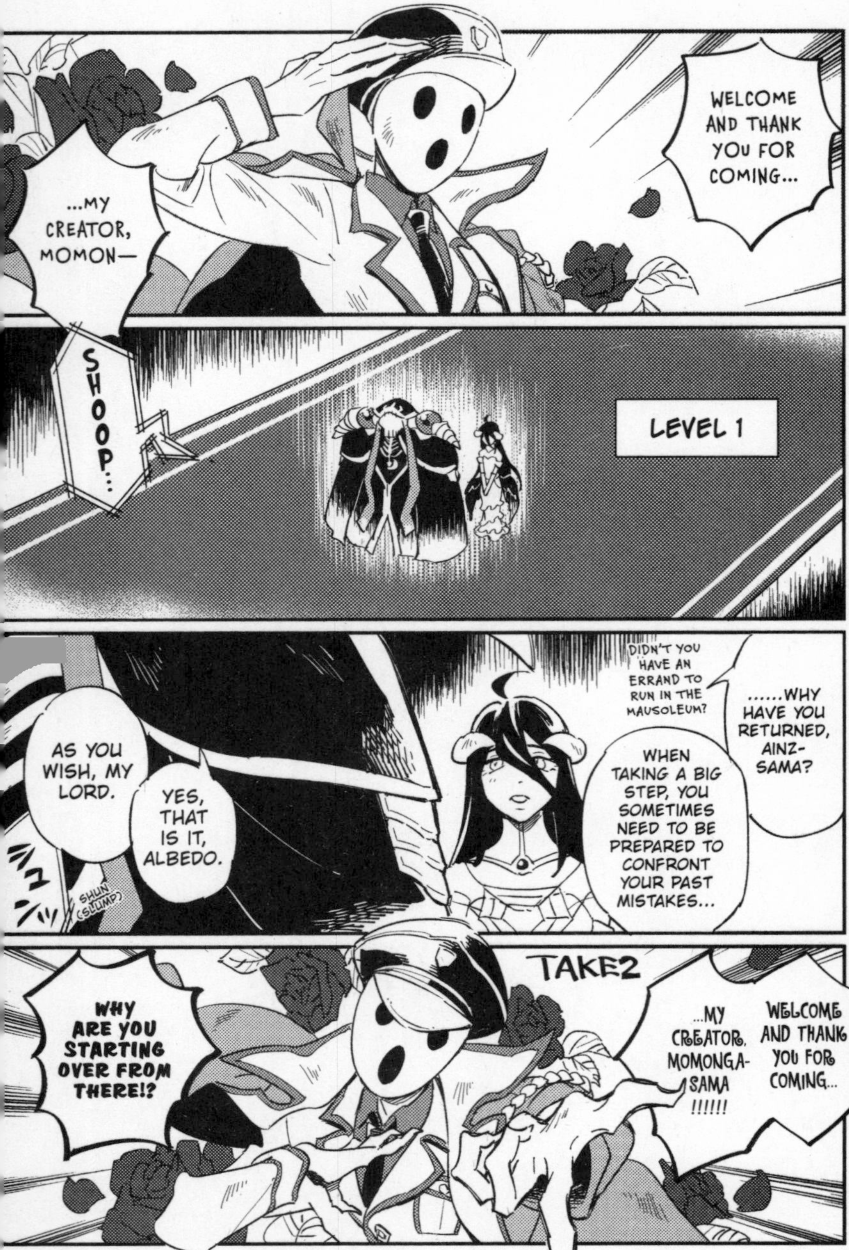
WELCOME AND THANK YOU FOR COMING...
...MY CREATOR, MOMON—
LEVEL 1
SHOOP...
......WHY HAVE YOU RETURNED, AINZ-SAMA?
DIDN'T YOU HAVE AN ERRAND TO RUN IN THE MAUSOLEUM?
WHEN TAKING A BIG STEP, YOU SOMETIMES NEED TO BE PREPARED TO CONFRONT YOUR PAST MISTAKES...
YES, THAT IS IT, ALBEDO.
AS YOU WISH, MY LORD.
SHUN (SLUMP)
TAKE2
WELCOME AND THANK YOU FOR COMING...
...MY CREATOR, MOMONGA-SAMA !!!!!!
WHY ARE YOU STARTING OVER FROM THERE!?

THE SUPREME MAGICAL BEAST NAMER

KOU1

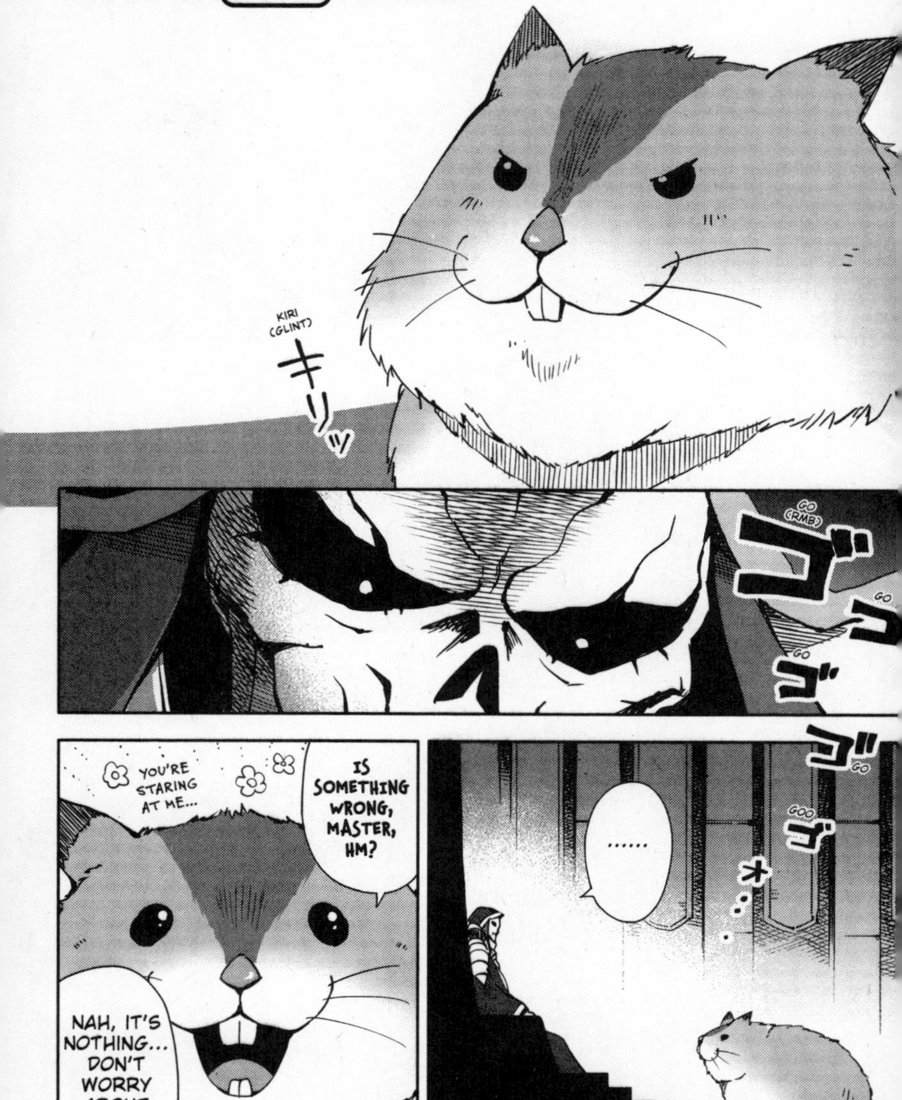

KIRI (GLINT)
キリッ
GO (RMB)
GO
GO
GO
GOO
ゴゴゴゴォ・・・
......
IS SOMETHING WRONG, MASTER, HM?
YOU'RE STARING AT ME...
NAH, IT'S NOTHING... DON'T WORRY ABOUT IT.

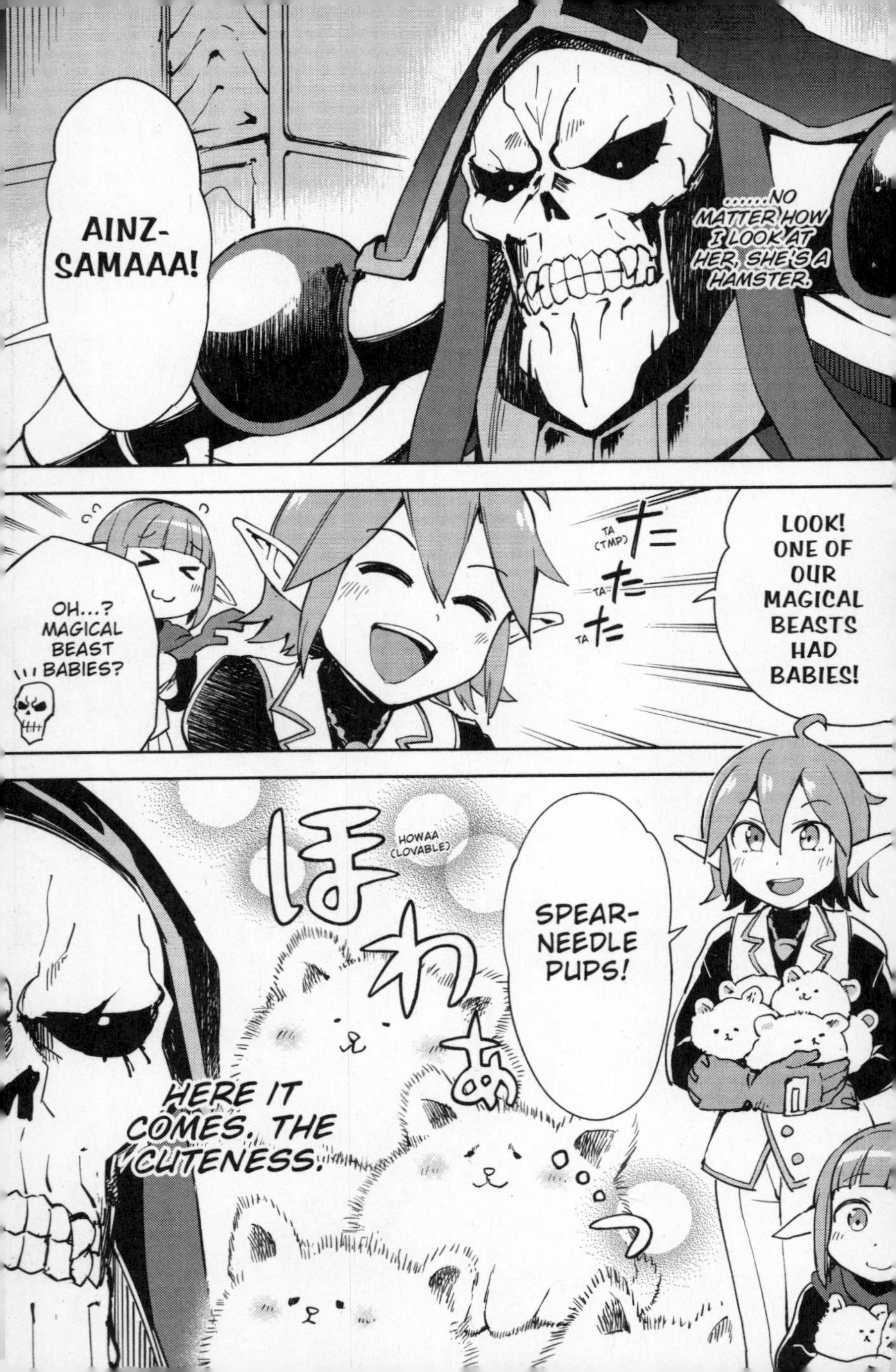

......NO MATTER HOW I LOOK AT HER, SHE'S A HAMSTER.
AINZ-SAMAAA!
LOOK! ONE OF OUR MAGICAL BEASTS HAD BABIES!
TA (TMP) た
TA た
TA た
OH...? MAGICAL BEAST BABIES?
SPEAR-NEEDLE PUPS!
HOWAA (LOVABLE) ほわぁ
HERE IT COMES. THE CUTENESS.

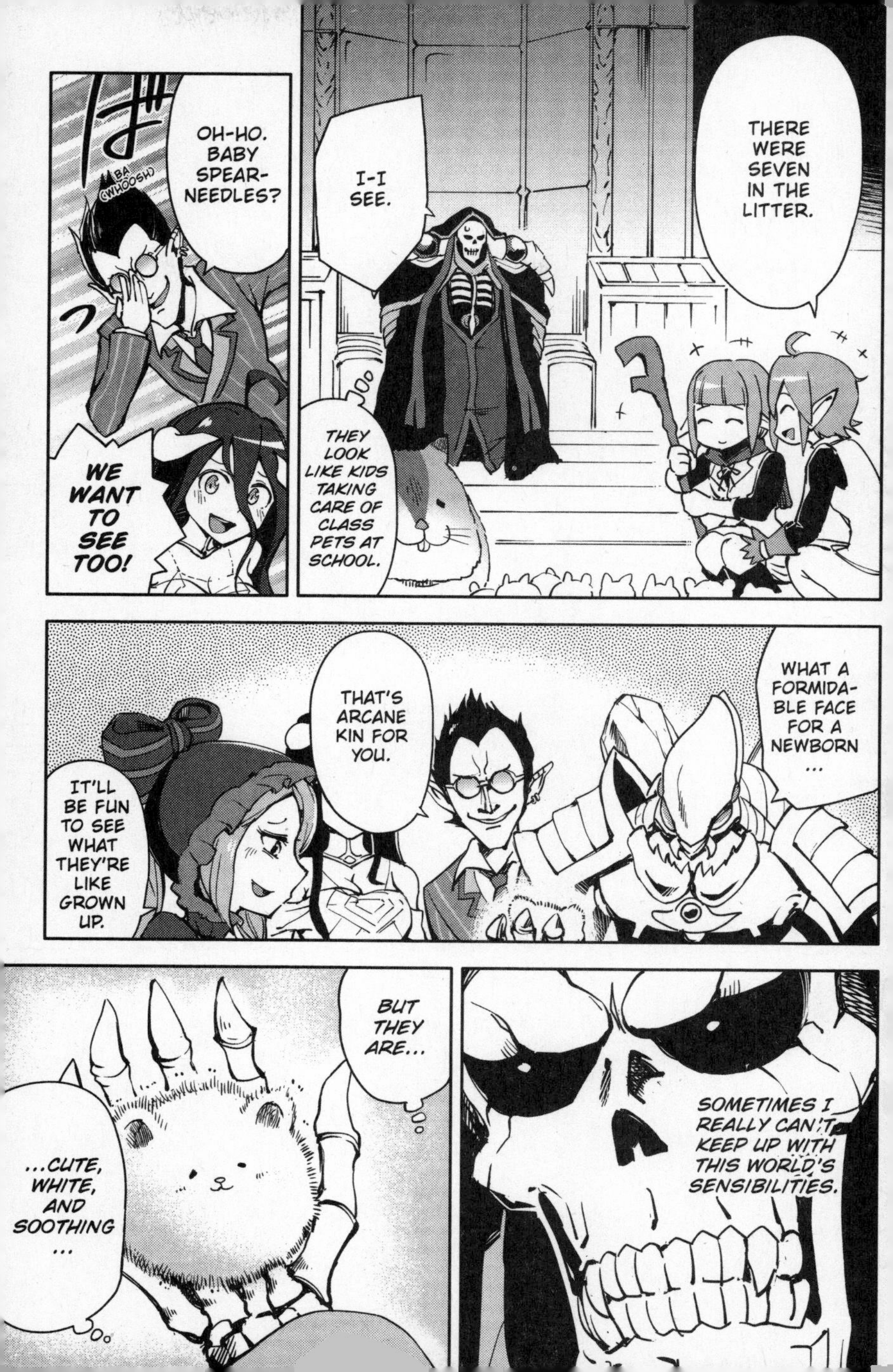
THERE WERE SEVEN IN THE LITTER.
I-I SEE.
THEY LOOK LIKE KIDS TAKING CARE OF CLASS PETS AT SCHOOL.
OH-HO. BABY SPEAR-NEEDLES?
BA (WHOOSH)
WE WANT TO SEE TOO!
WHAT A FORMIDABLE FACE FOR A NEWBORN...
THAT'S ARCANE KIN FOR YOU.
IT'LL BE FUN TO SEE WHAT THEY'RE LIKE GROWN UP.
SOMETIMES I REALLY CAN'T KEEP UP WITH THIS WORLD'S SENSIBILITIES.
BUT THEY ARE...
...CUTE, WHITE, AND SOOTHING...

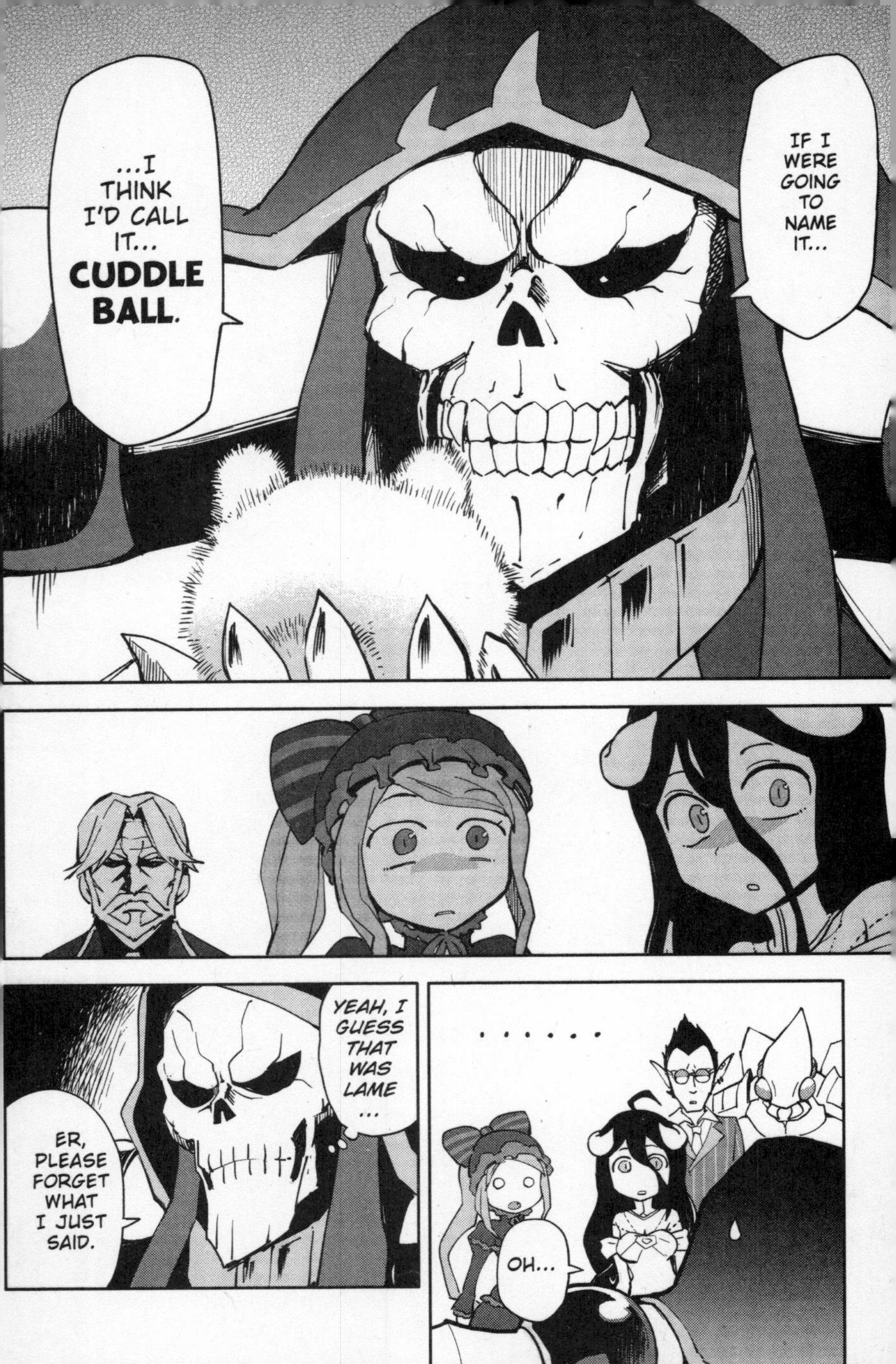
IF I WERE GOING TO NAME IT...
...I THINK I'D CALL IT... **CUDDLE BALL**.
......
OH...
YEAH, I GUESS THAT WAS LAME ...
ER, PLEASE FORGET WHAT I JUST SAID.

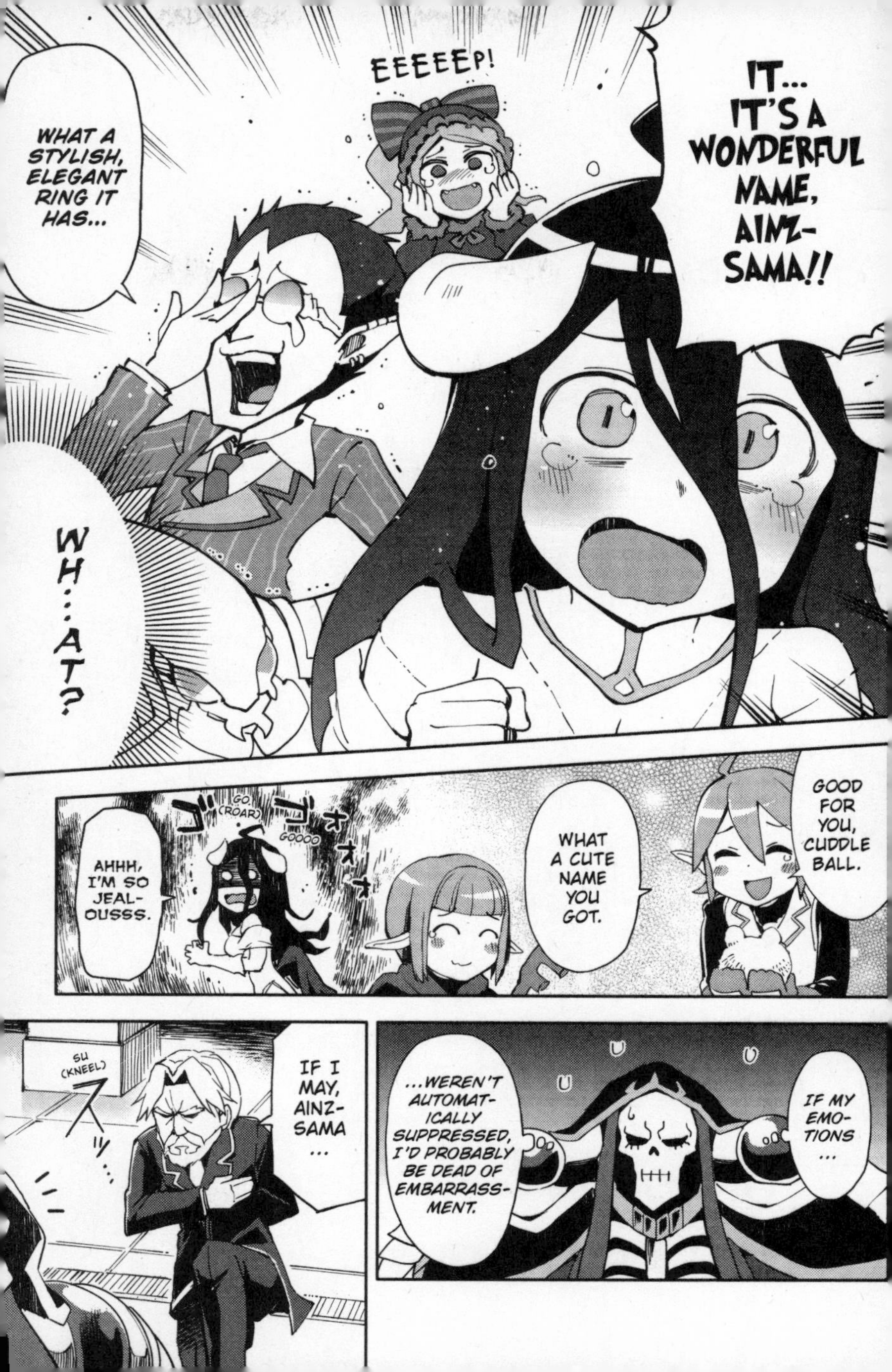
IT... IT'S A WONDERFUL NAME, AINZ-SAMA!!
EEEEEP!
WHAT A STYLISH, ELEGANT RING IT HAS...
WH...AT?
GOOD FOR YOU, CUDDLE BALL.
WHAT A CUTE NAME YOU GOT.
GO (ROAR) GOOOO
AHHH, I'M SO JEAL-OUSSS.
IF MY EMO-TIONS...
...WEREN'T AUTOMAT-ICALLY SUPPRESSED, I'D PROBABLY BE DEAD OF EMBARRASS-MENT.
IF I MAY, AINZ-SAMA...
SU (KNEEL)

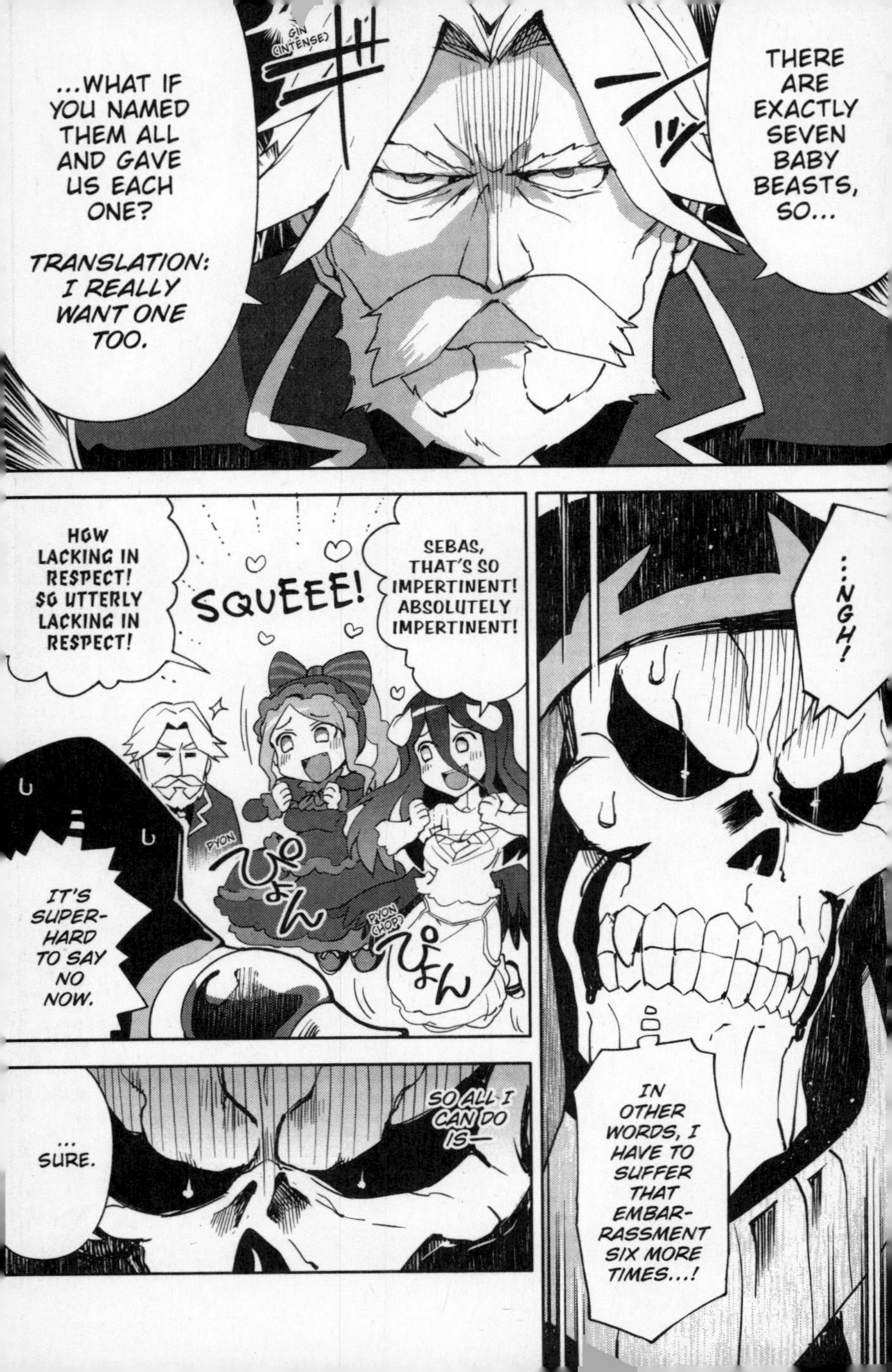
THERE ARE EXACTLY SEVEN BABY BEASTS, SO...
GIN (INTENSE)
...WHAT IF YOU NAMED THEM ALL AND GAVE US EACH ONE?
TRANSLATION: I REALLY WANT ONE TOO.
...NGH!
IN OTHER WORDS, I HAVE TO SUFFER THAT EMBARRASSMENT SIX MORE TIMES...!
SEBAS, THAT'S SO IMPERTINENT! ABSOLUTELY IMPERTINENT!
SQUEEE!
HOW LACKING IN RESPECT! SO UTTERLY LACKING IN RESPECT!
PYON
ぴょん
PYON (HOP)
ぴょん
IT'S SUPER-HARD TO SAY NO NOW.
SO ALL I CAN DO IS—
... SURE.

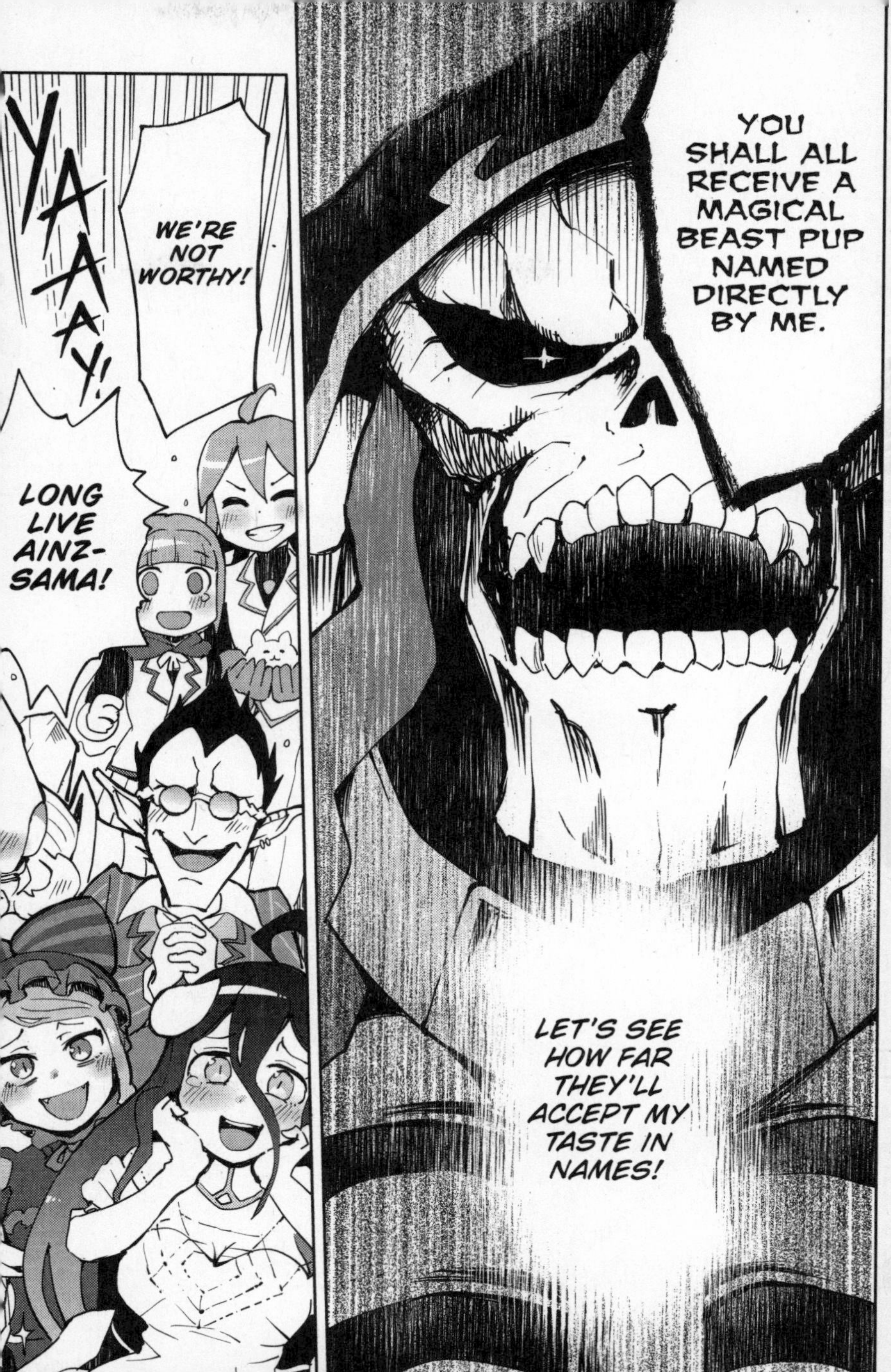
YOU SHALL ALL RECEIVE A MAGICAL BEAST PUP NAMED DIRECTLY BY ME.
LET'S SEE HOW FAR THEY'LL ACCEPT MY TASTE IN NAMES!
WE'RE NOT WORTHY!
YAAAY!
LONG LIVE AINZ-SAMA!

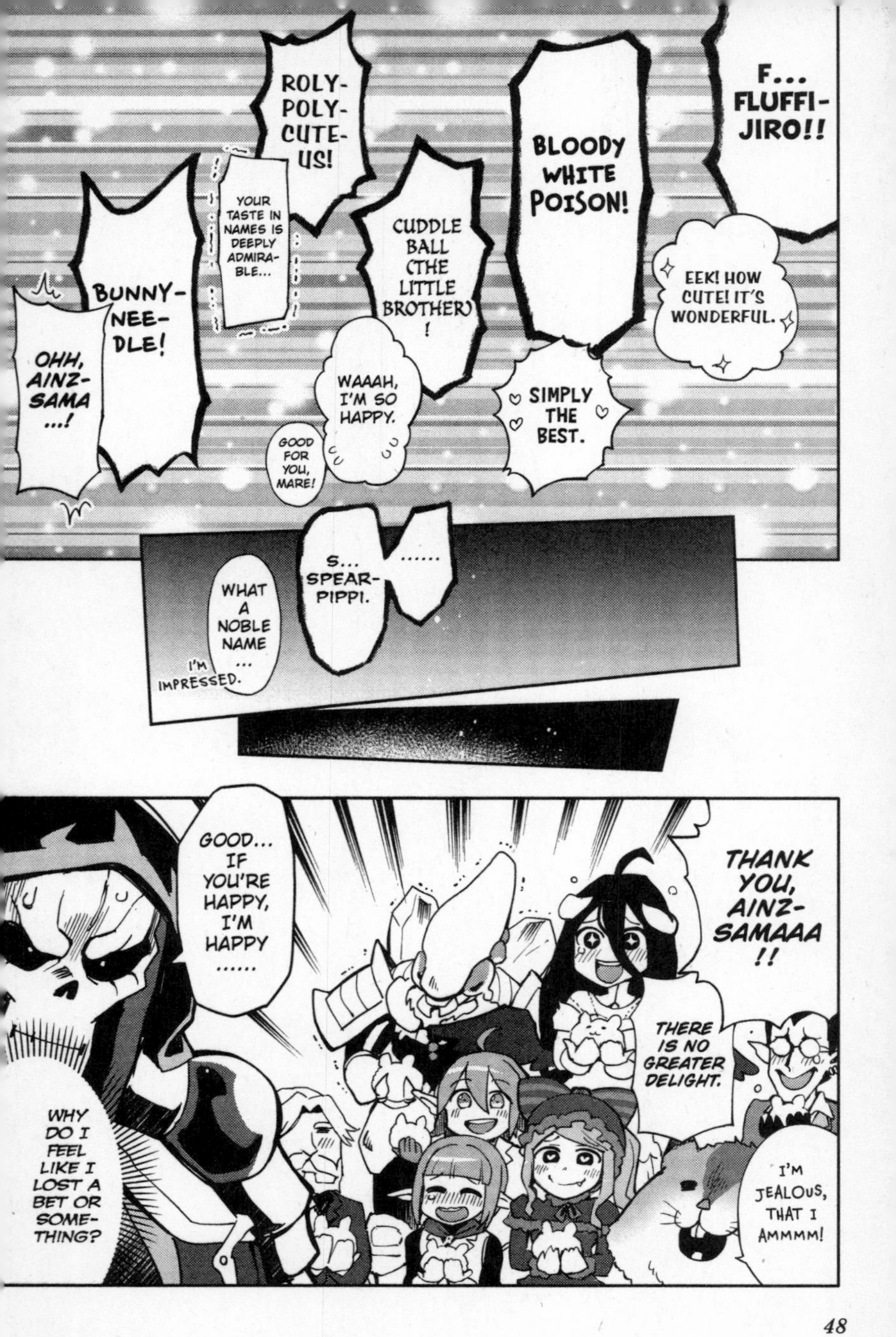

F... FLUFFI-JIRO!!
EEK! HOW CUTE! IT'S WONDERFUL.
BLOODY WHITE POISON!
SIMPLY THE BEST.
ROLY-POLY-CUTE-US!
CUDDLE BALL (THE LITTLE BROTHER)!
WAAAH, I'M SO HAPPY.
GOOD FOR YOU, MARE!
YOUR TASTE IN NAMES IS DEEPLY ADMIRABLE...
BUNNY-NEEDLE!
OHH, AINZ-SAMA...!
......
S... SPEAR-PIPPI.
WHAT A NOBLE NAME...
I'M IMPRESSED.
THANK YOU, AINZ-SAMAAA!!
I'M JEALOUS, THAT I AMMMM!
THERE IS NO GREATER DELIGHT.
GOOD... IF YOU'RE HAPPY, I'M HAPPY......
WHY DO I FEEL LIKE I LOST A BET OR SOMETHING?

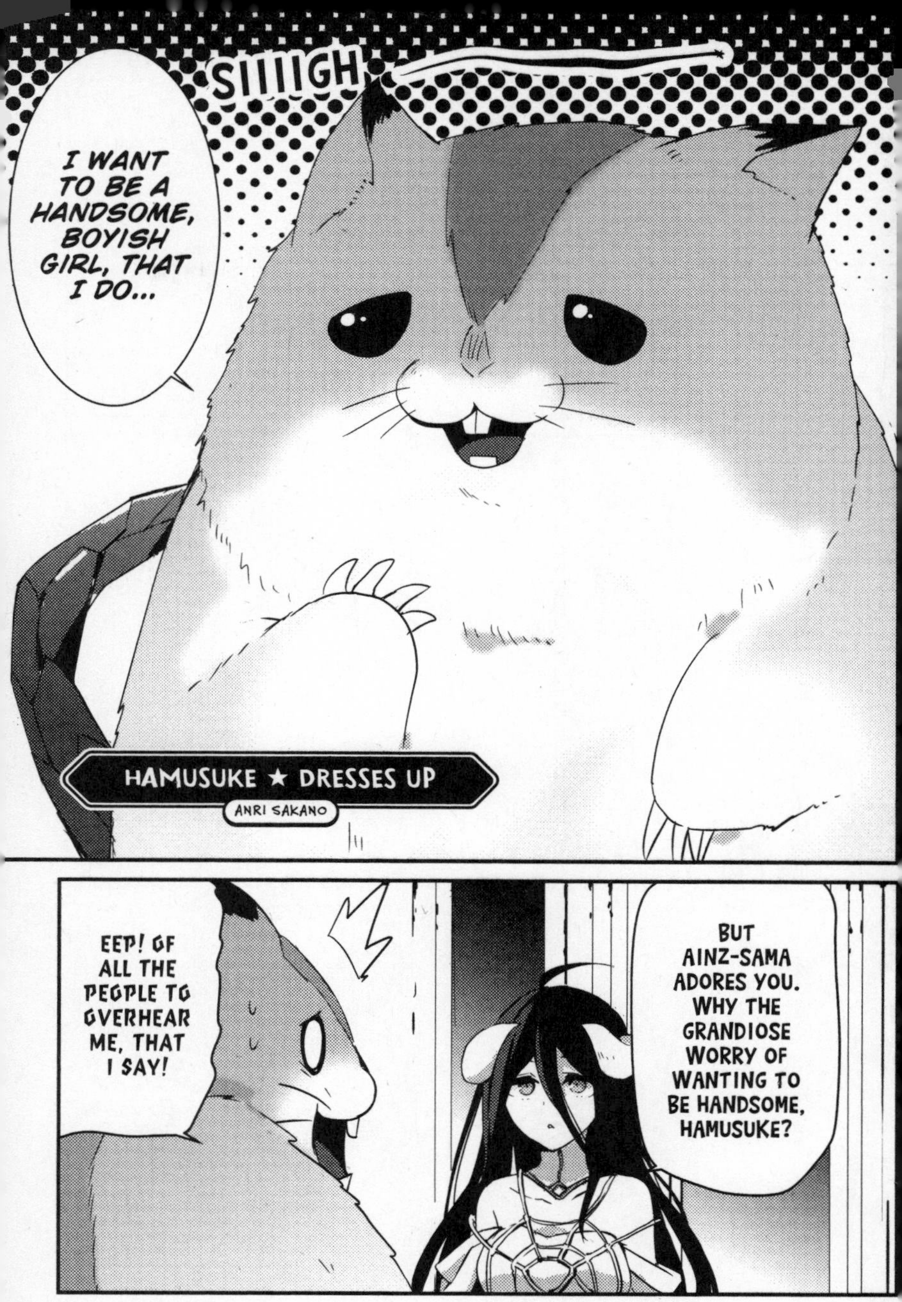
SIIIIGH
I WANT TO BE A HANDSOME, BOYISH GIRL, THAT I DO...
HAMUSUKE ★ DRESSES UP
ANRI SAKANO
BUT AINZ-SAMA ADORES YOU. WHY THE GRANDIOSE WORRY OF WANTING TO BE HANDSOME, HAMUSUKE?
EEP! OF ALL THE PEOPLE TO OVERHEAR ME, THAT I SAY!

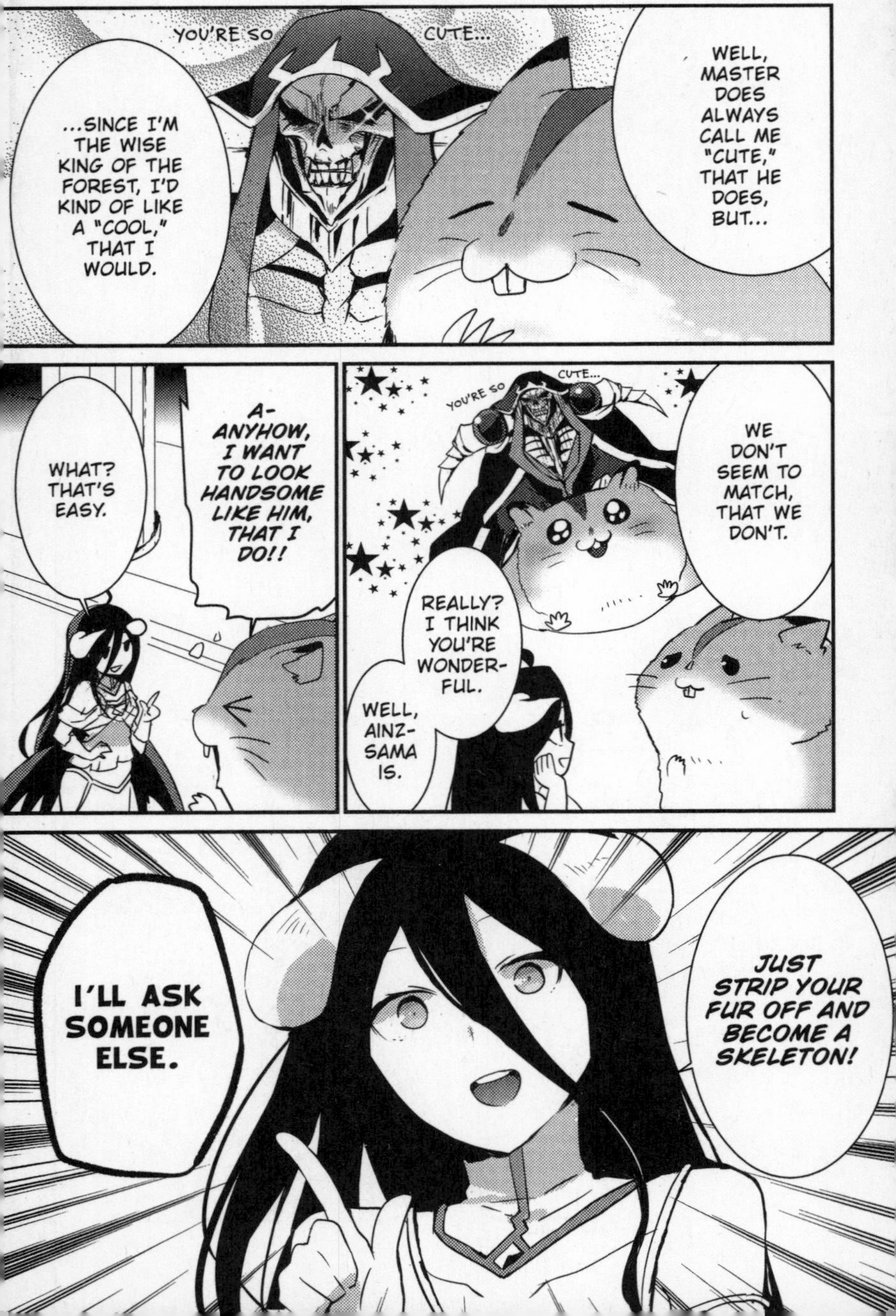
WELL, MASTER DOES ALWAYS CALL ME "CUTE," THAT HE DOES, BUT...
YOU'RE SO CUTE...
...SINCE I'M THE WISE KING OF THE FOREST, I'D KIND OF LIKE A "COOL," THAT I WOULD.
WE DON'T SEEM TO MATCH, THAT WE DON'T.
YOU'RE SO CUTE...
REALLY? I THINK YOU'RE WONDER-FUL.
WELL, AINZ-SAMA IS.
A- ANYHOW, I WANT TO LOOK HANDSOME LIKE HIM, THAT I DO!!
WHAT? THAT'S EASY.
JUST STRIP YOUR FUR OFF AND BECOME A SKELETON!
I'LL ASK SOMEONE ELSE.

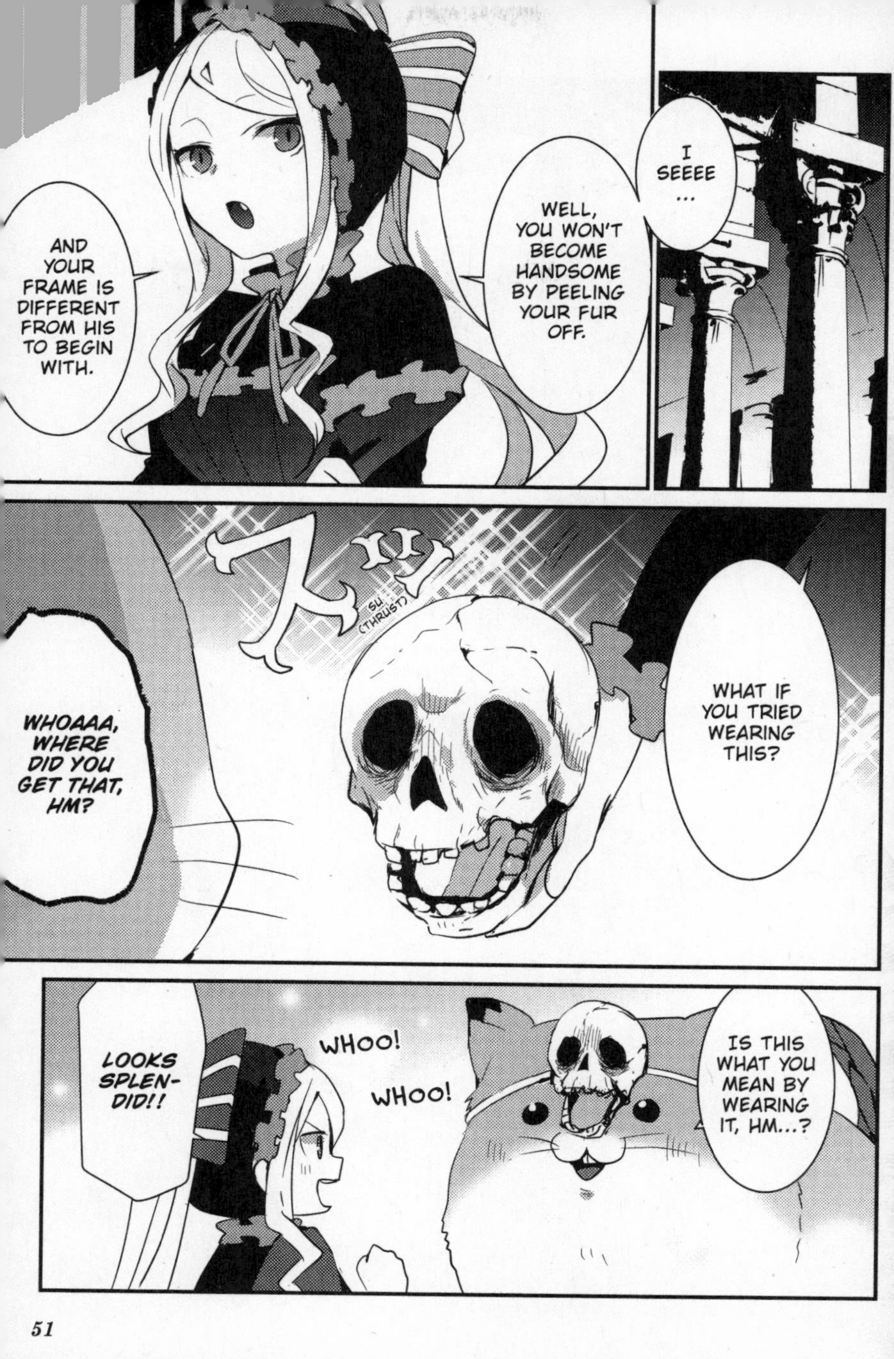
I SEEEE...
WELL, YOU WON'T BECOME HANDSOME BY PEELING YOUR FUR OFF.
AND YOUR FRAME IS DIFFERENT FROM HIS TO BEGIN WITH.
スッ
SU (THRUST)
WHAT IF YOU TRIED WEARING THIS?
WHOAAA, WHERE DID YOU GET THAT, HM?
IS THIS WHAT YOU MEAN BY WEARING IT, HM...?
WHOO!
WHOO!
LOOKS SPLEN-DID!!

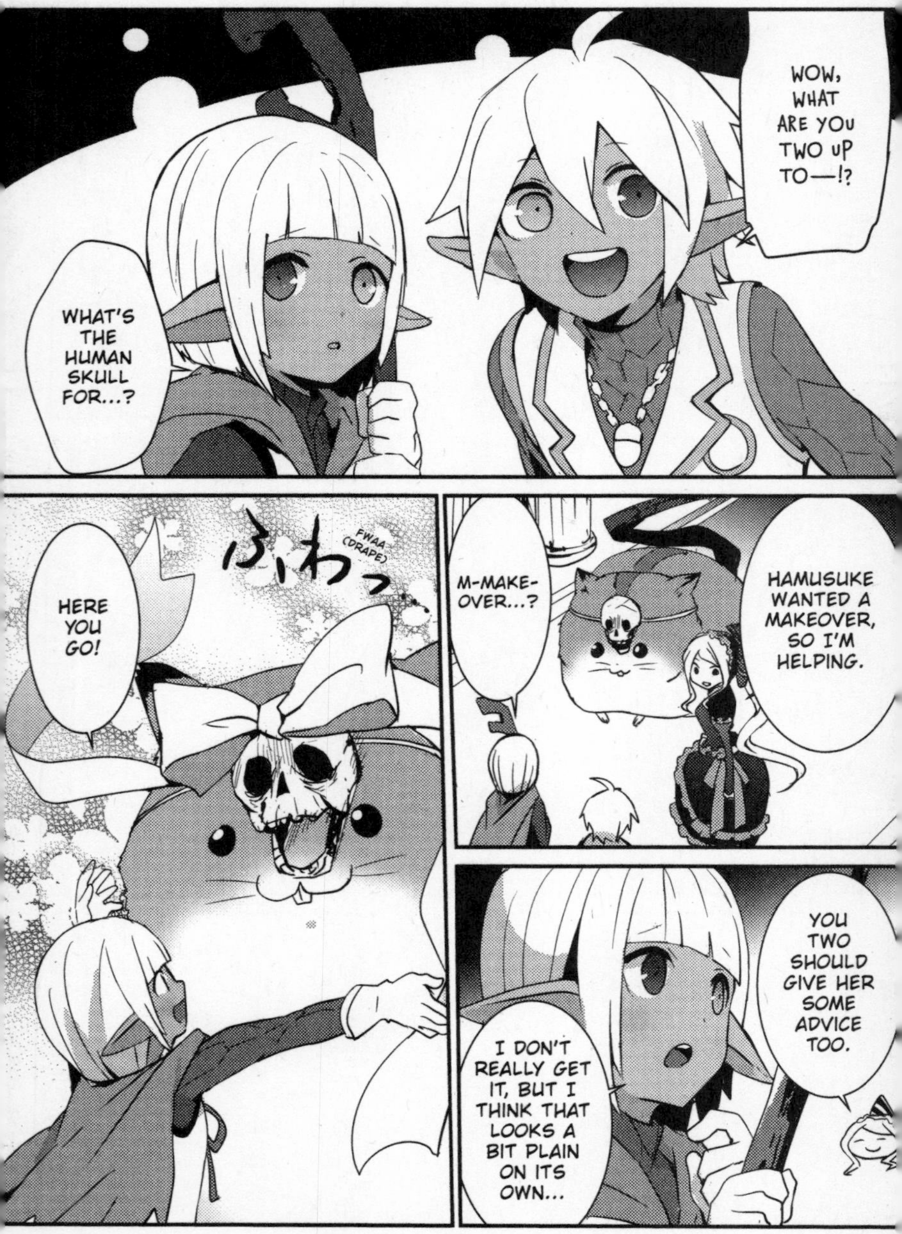
WOW, WHAT ARE YOU TWO UP TO—!?
WHAT'S THE HUMAN SKULL FOR...?
HAMUSUKE WANTED A MAKEOVER, SO I'M HELPING.
M-MAKE-OVER...?
YOU TWO SHOULD GIVE HER SOME ADVICE TOO.
I DON'T REALLY GET IT, BUT I THINK THAT LOOKS A BIT PLAIN ON ITS OWN...
ふわっ
FWAA (DRAPE)
HERE YOU GO!

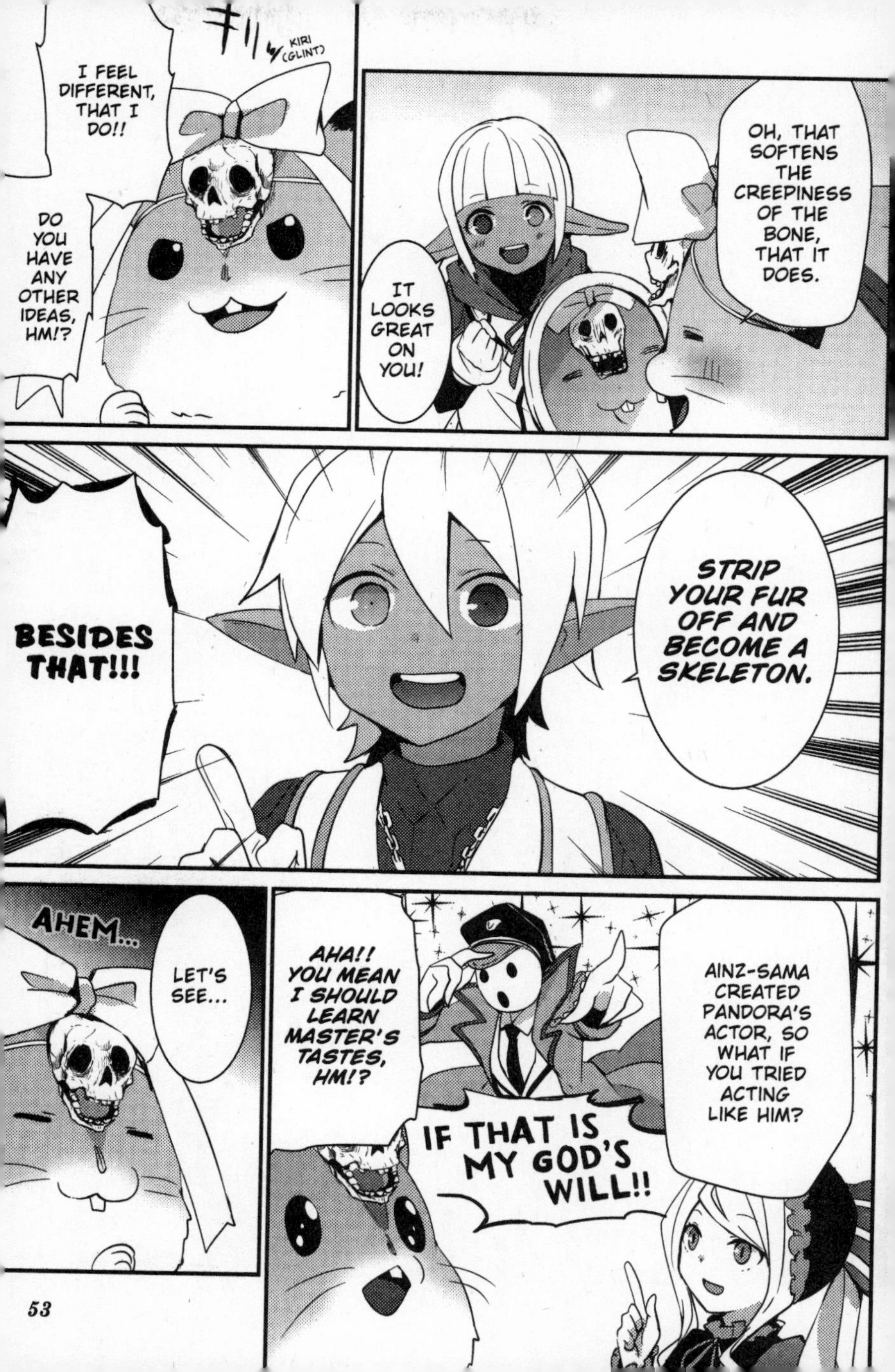
OH, THAT SOFTENS THE CREEPINESS OF THE BONE, THAT IT DOES.
IT LOOKS GREAT ON YOU!
KIRI (GLINT)
I FEEL DIFFERENT, THAT I DO!!
DO YOU HAVE ANY OTHER IDEAS, HM!?
STRIP YOUR FUR OFF AND BECOME A SKELETON.
BESIDES THAT!!!
AINZ-SAMA CREATED PANDORA'S ACTOR, SO WHAT IF YOU TRIED ACTING LIKE HIM?
AHA!! YOU MEAN I SHOULD LEARN MASTER'S TASTES, HM!?
IF THAT IS MY GOD'S WILL!!
AHEM...
LET'S SEE...

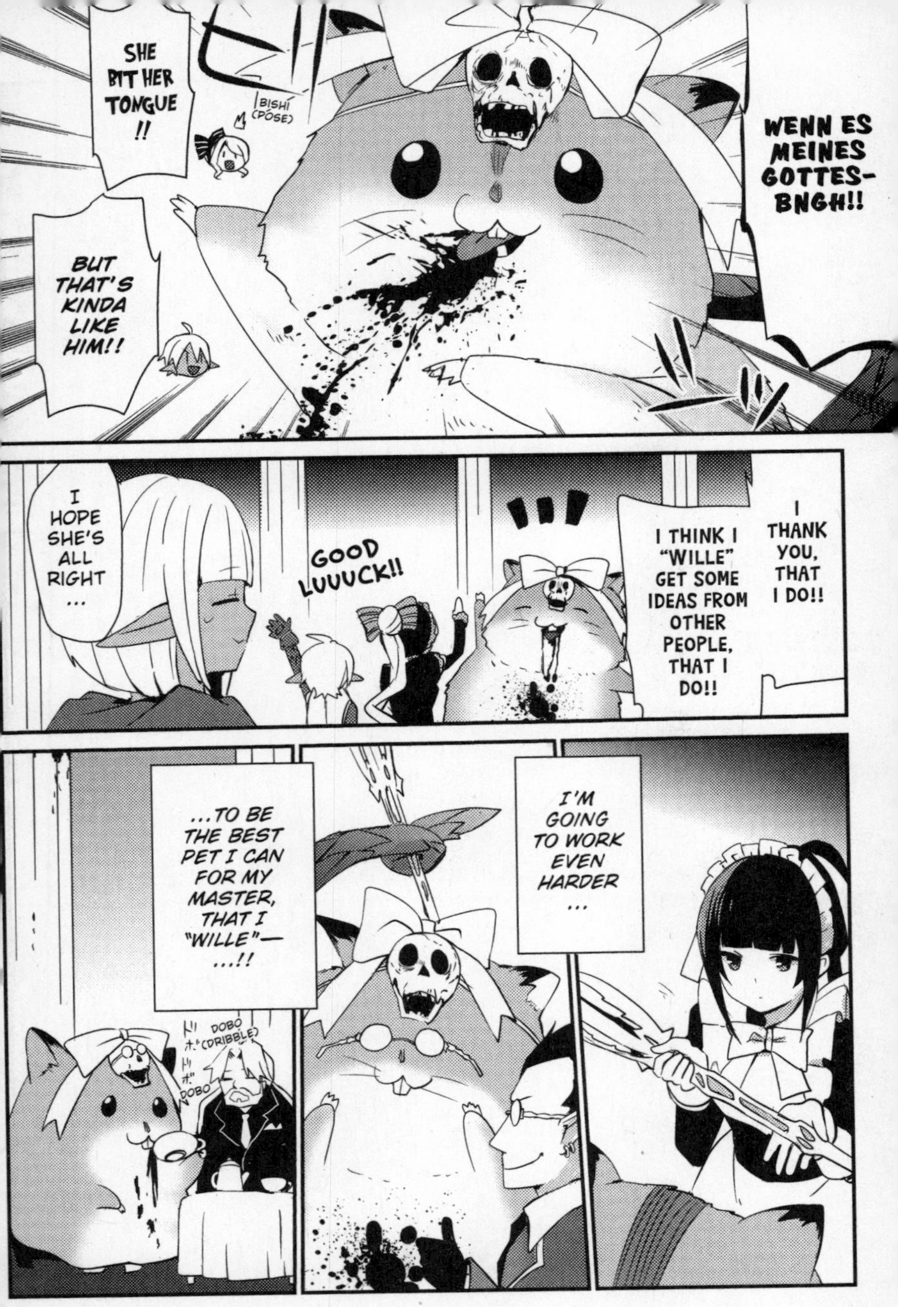
WENN ES MEINES GOTTES-BNGH!!
SHE BIT HER TONGUE!!
BISHI (POSE)
BUT THAT'S KINDA LIKE HIM!!
I THANK YOU, THAT I DO!!
I THINK I "WILLE" GET SOME IDEAS FROM OTHER PEOPLE, THAT I DO!!
GOOD LUUUCK!!
I HOPE SHE'S ALL RIGHT...
I'M GOING TO WORK EVEN HARDER...
...TO BE THE BEST PET I CAN FOR MY MASTER, THAT I "WILLE"—...!!
DOBO (DRIBBLE)
DOBO

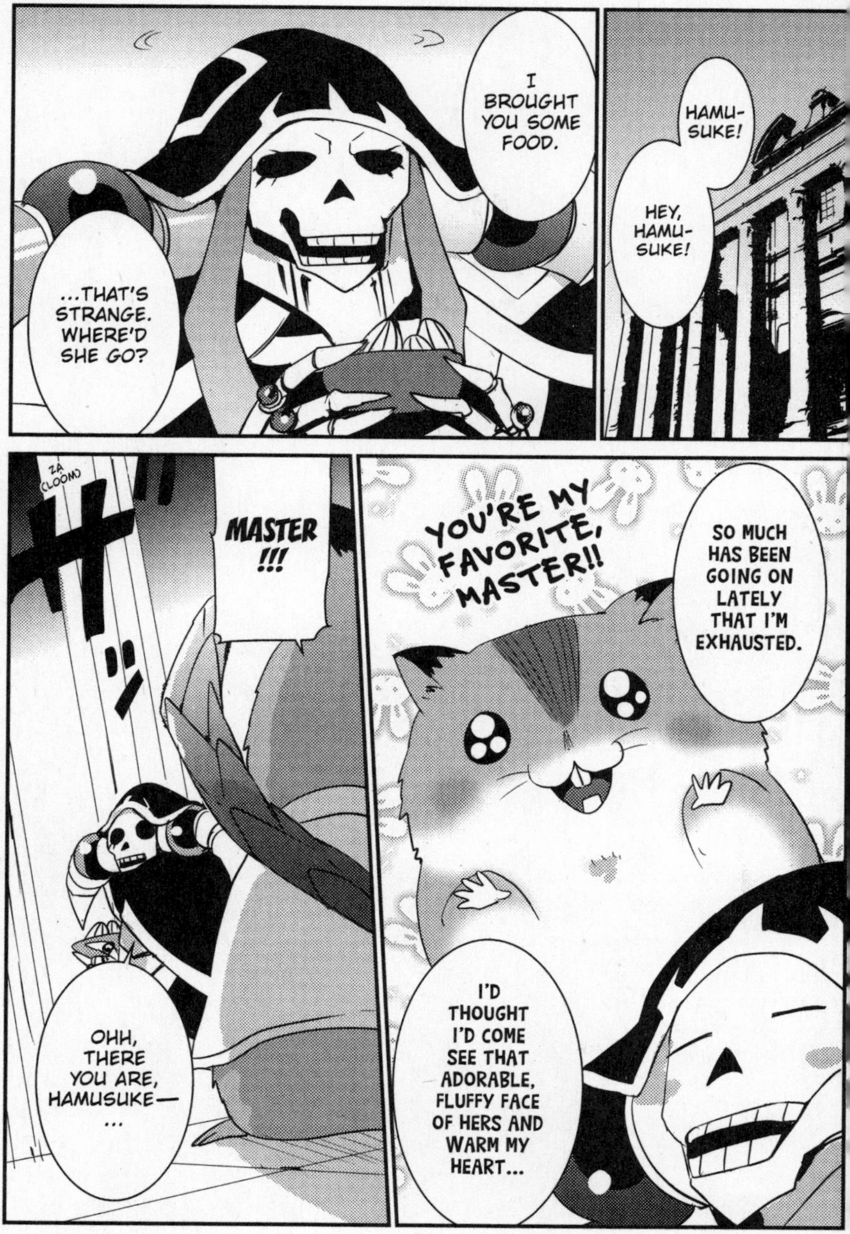
HAMU-SUKE!
HEY, HAMU-SUKE!
I BROUGHT YOU SOME FOOD.
...THAT'S STRANGE. WHERE'D SHE GO?
SO MUCH HAS BEEN GOING ON LATELY THAT I'M EXHAUSTED.
YOU'RE MY FAVORITE, MASTER!!
I'D THOUGHT I'D COME SEE THAT ADORABLE, FLUFFY FACE OF HERS AND WARM MY HEART...
ZA (CLOOM)
MASTER !!!
OHH, THERE YOU ARE, HAMUSUKE— ...

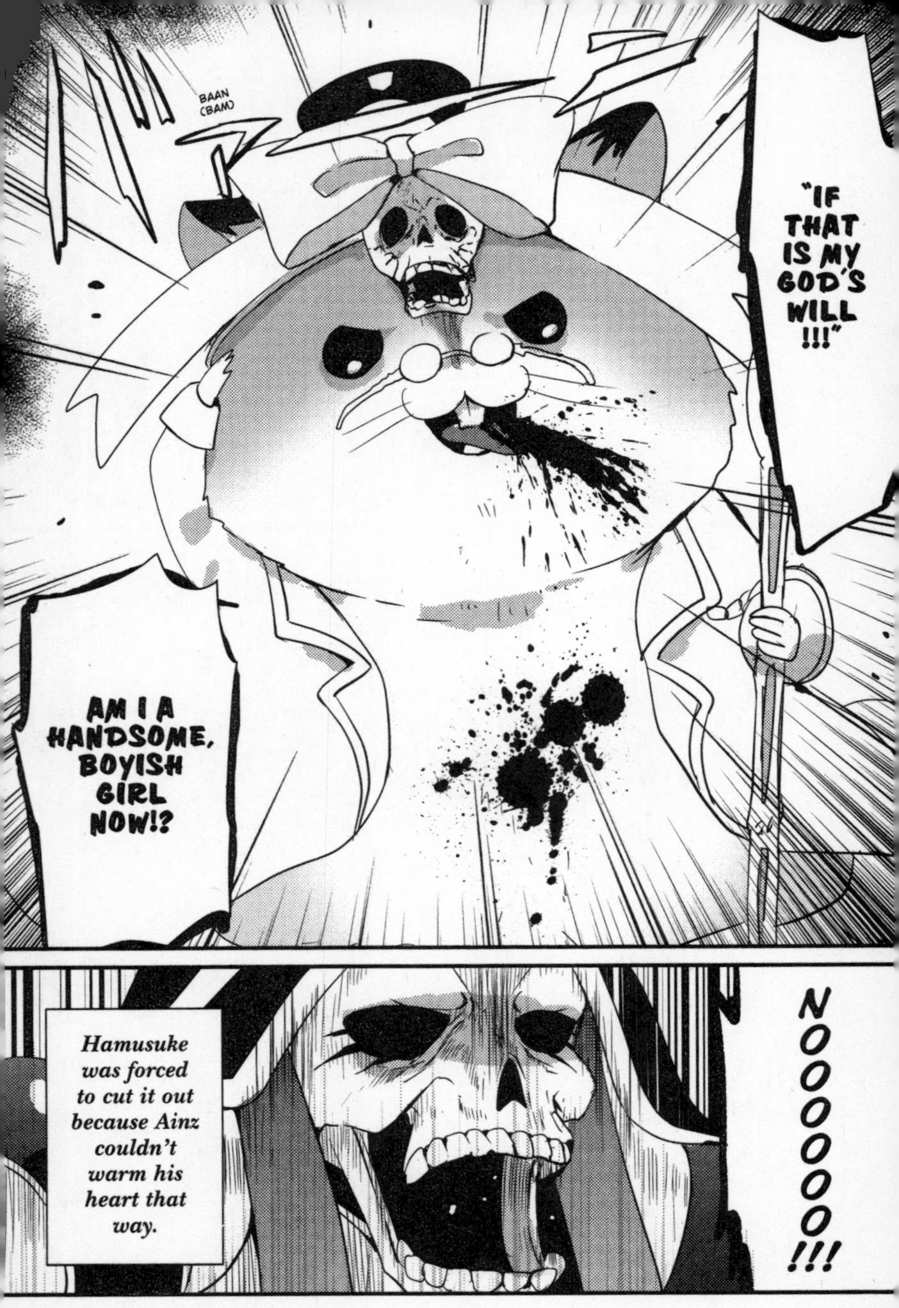
"IF THAT IS MY GOD'S WILL !!!"
BAAN (BAM)
AM I A HANDSOME, BOYISH GIRL NOW!?
NOOOOOOOO !!!
Hamusuke was forced to cut it out because Ainz couldn't warm his heart that way.

OVERLORD
À LA CARTE

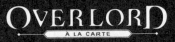

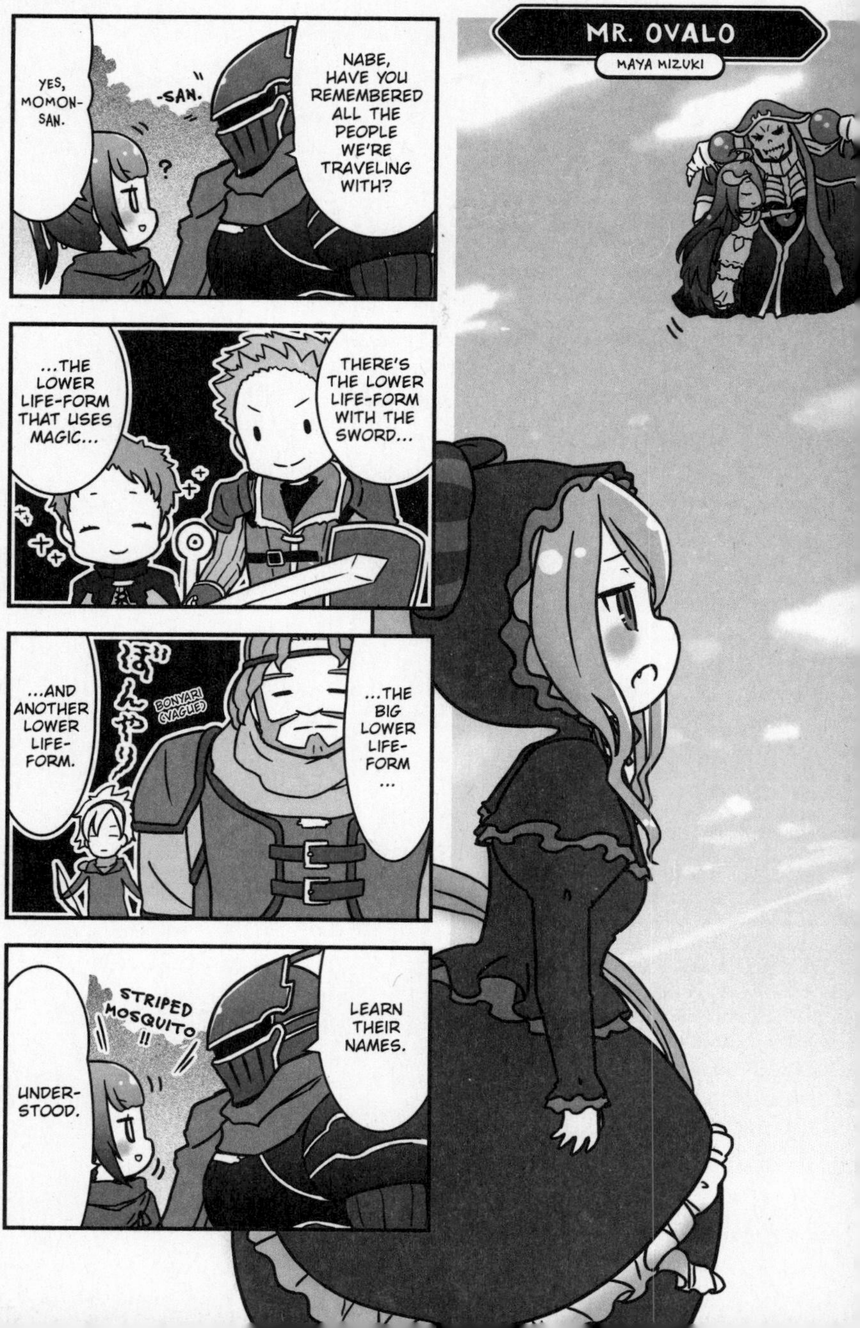
MR. OVALO
MAYA MIZUKI
NABE, HAVE YOU REMEMBERED ALL THE PEOPLE WE'RE TRAVELING WITH?
"-SAN."
YES, MOMON-SAN.
THERE'S THE LOWER LIFE-FORM WITH THE SWORD...
...THE LOWER LIFE-FORM THAT USES MAGIC...
...THE BIG LOWER LIFE-FORM ...
ぼんやり
BONYARI (VAGUE)
...AND ANOTHER LOWER LIFE-FORM.
LEARN THEIR NAMES.
STRIPED MOSQUITO !!
UNDER-STOOD.

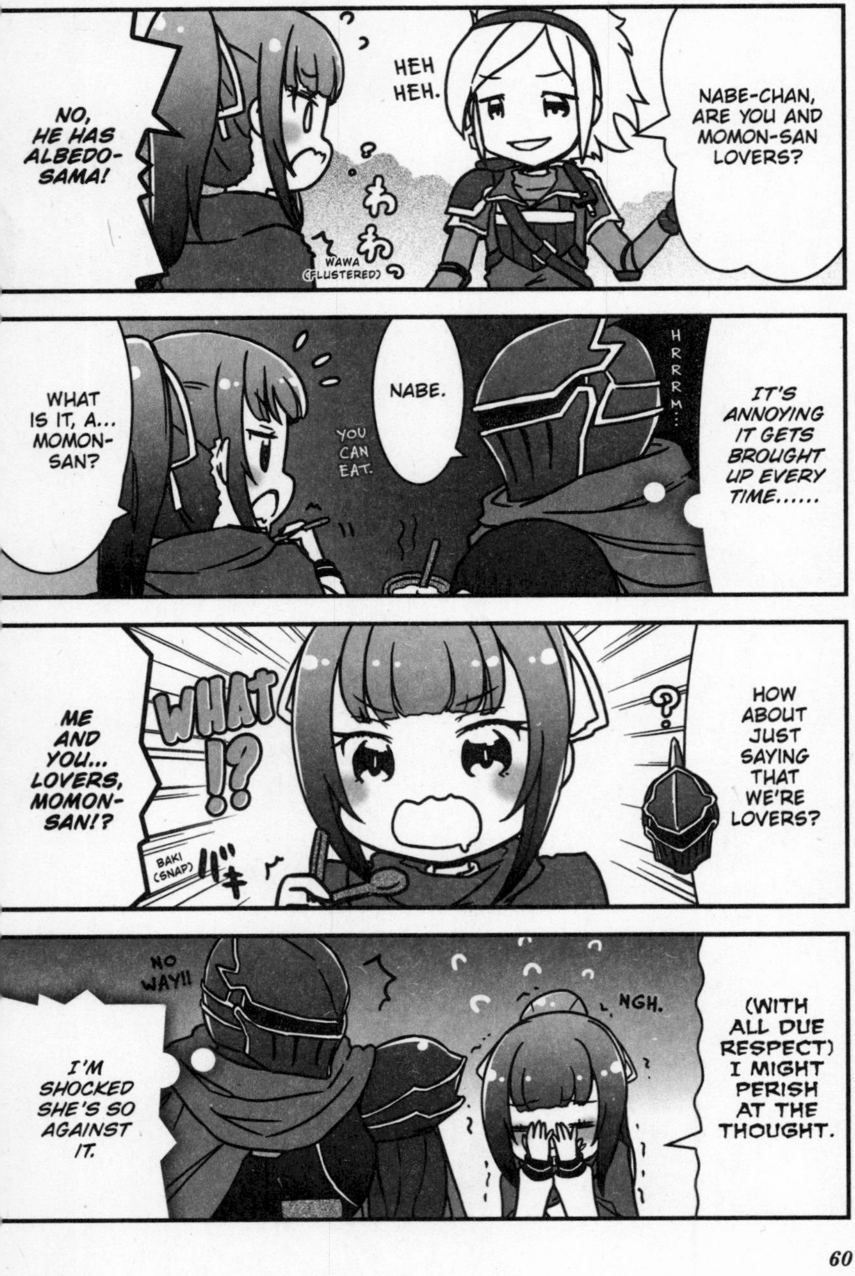
NABE-CHAN, ARE YOU AND MOMON-SAN LOVERS?
HEH HEH.
WAWA (FLUSTERED)
NO, HE HAS ALBEDO-SAMA!
IT'S ANNOYING IT GETS BROUGHT UP EVERY TIME......
HRRRM...
NABE.
YOU CAN EAT.
WHAT IS IT, A... MOMON-SAN?
HOW ABOUT JUST SAYING THAT WE'RE LOVERS?
WHAT!?
BAKI (SNAP)
ME AND YOU... LOVERS, MOMON-SAN!?
(WITH ALL DUE RESPECT) I MIGHT PERISH AT THE THOUGHT.
NGH.
NO WAY!!
I'M SHOCKED SHE'S SO AGAINST IT.

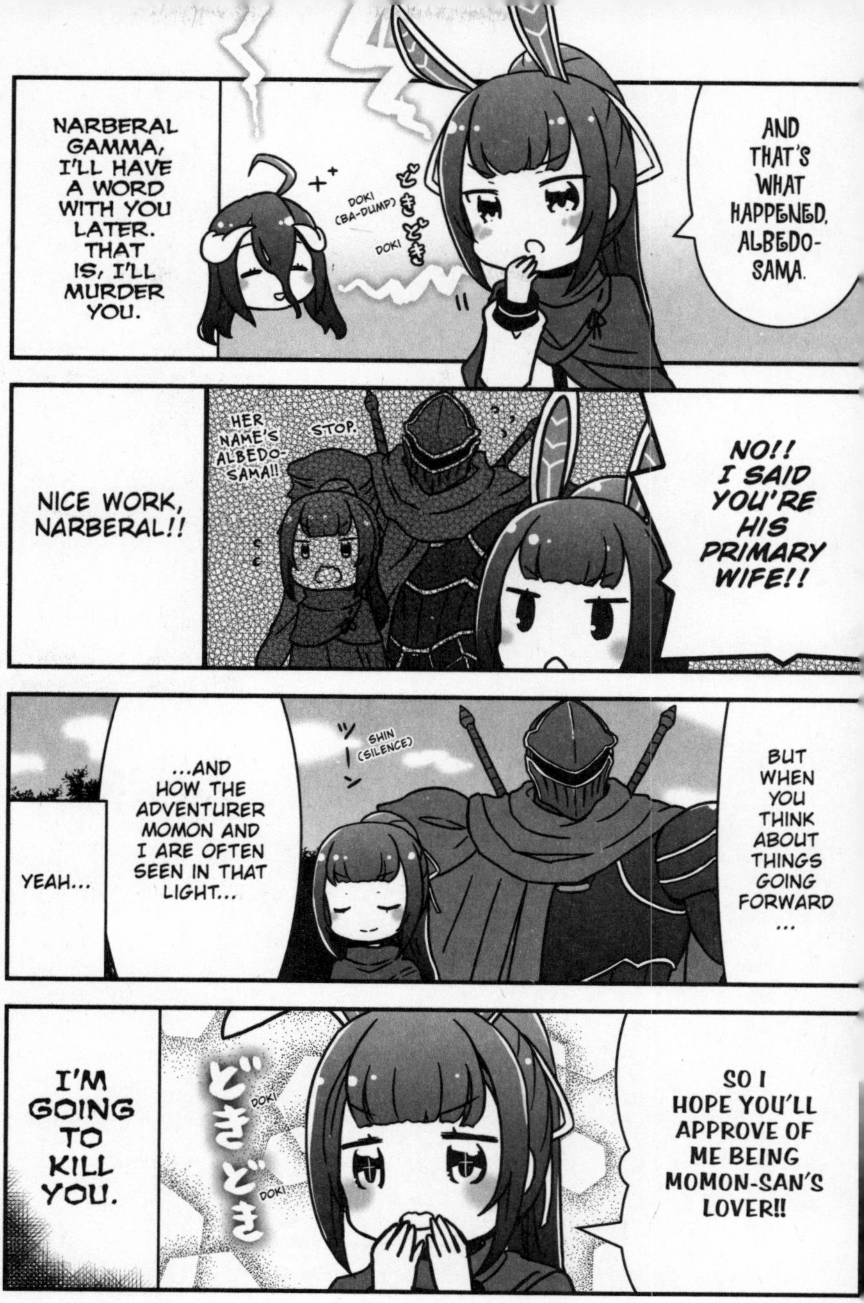
AND THAT'S WHAT HAPPENED, ALBEDO-SAMA.
どきどき
DOKI (BA-DUMP) DOKI
NARBERAL GAMMA, I'LL HAVE A WORD WITH YOU LATER. THAT IS, I'LL MURDER YOU.
NO!! I SAID YOU'RE HIS PRIMARY WIFE!!
STOP.
HER NAME'S ALBEDO-SAMA!!
NICE WORK, NARBERAL!!
BUT WHEN YOU THINK ABOUT THINGS GOING FORWARD...
ツーン
SHIN (SILENCE)
...AND HOW THE ADVENTURER MOMON AND I ARE OFTEN SEEN IN THAT LIGHT...
YEAH...
SO I HOPE YOU'LL APPROVE OF ME BEING MOMON-SAN'S LOVER!!
どきどき
DOKI DOKI
I'M GOING TO KILL YOU.

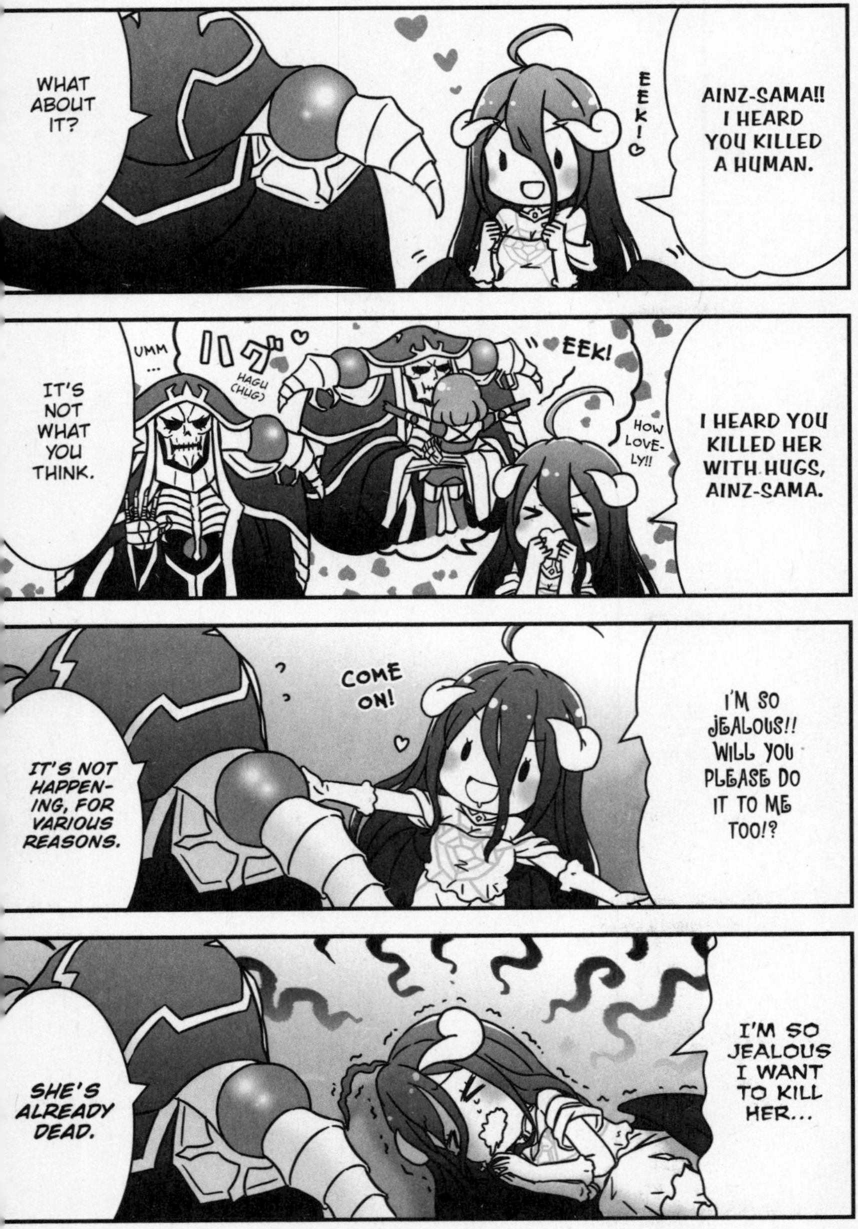
AINZ-SAMA!! I HEARD YOU KILLED A HUMAN.
EEK!
WHAT ABOUT IT?
I HEARD YOU KILLED HER WITH HUGS, AINZ-SAMA.
EEK!
HOW LOVELY!!
ハグ
HAGU (HUG)
UMM ...
IT'S NOT WHAT YOU THINK.
I'M SO JEALOUS!! WILL YOU PLEASE DO IT TO ME TOO!?
COME ON!
IT'S NOT HAPPENING, FOR VARIOUS REASONS.
I'M SO JEALOUS I WANT TO KILL HER...
SHE'S ALREADY DEAD.

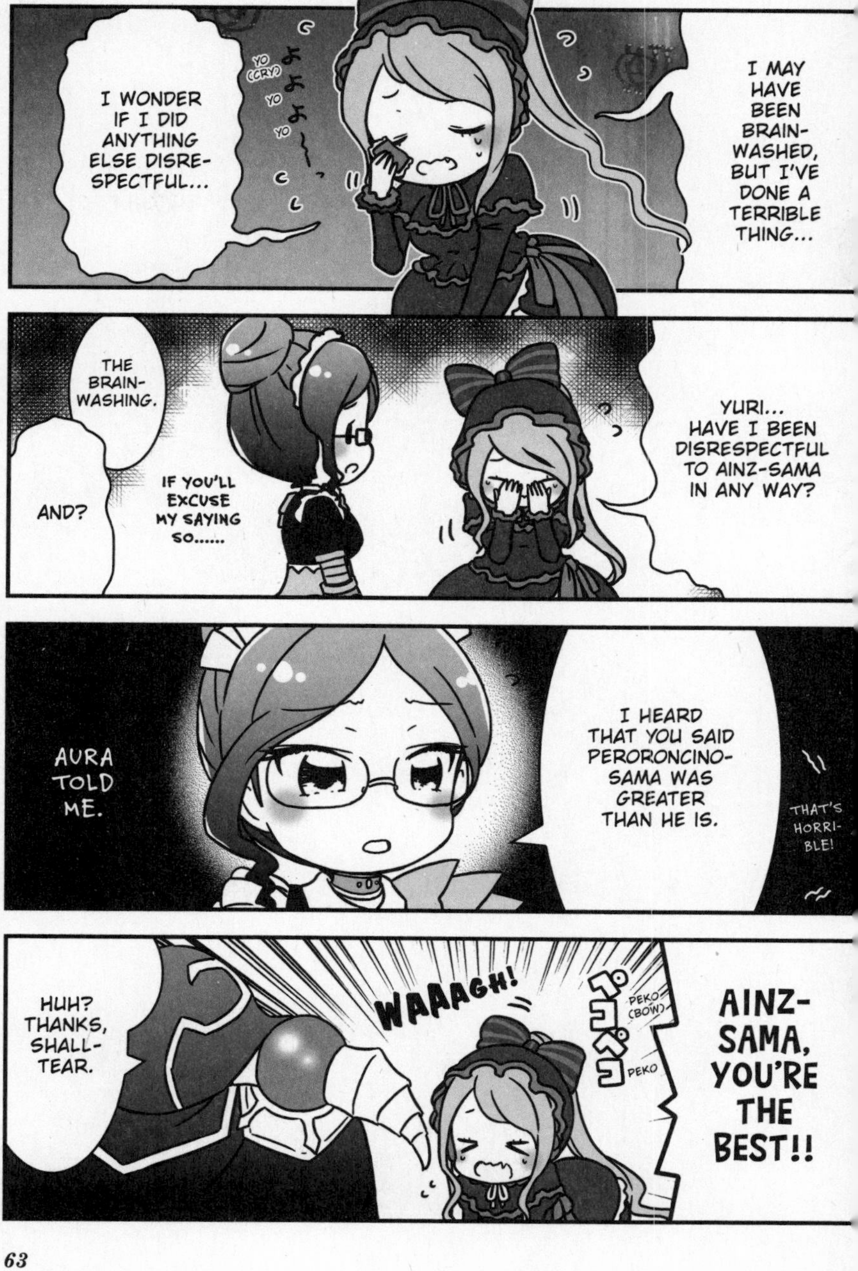
I MAY HAVE BEEN BRAIN-WASHED, BUT I'VE DONE A TERRIBLE THING...
よよよ~
YO (CRY) YO YO
I WONDER IF I DID ANYTHING ELSE DISRE-SPECTFUL...
YURI... HAVE I BEEN DISRESPECTFUL TO AINZ-SAMA IN ANY WAY?
IF YOU'LL EXCUSE MY SAYING SO......
THE BRAIN-WASHING.
AND?
THAT'S HORRI-BLE!
I HEARD THAT YOU SAID PERORONCINO-SAMA WAS GREATER THAN HE IS.
AURA TOLD ME.
AINZ-SAMA, YOU'RE THE BEST!!
PEKO (BOW) PEKO
WAAAGH!
HUH? THANKS, SHALL-TEAR.

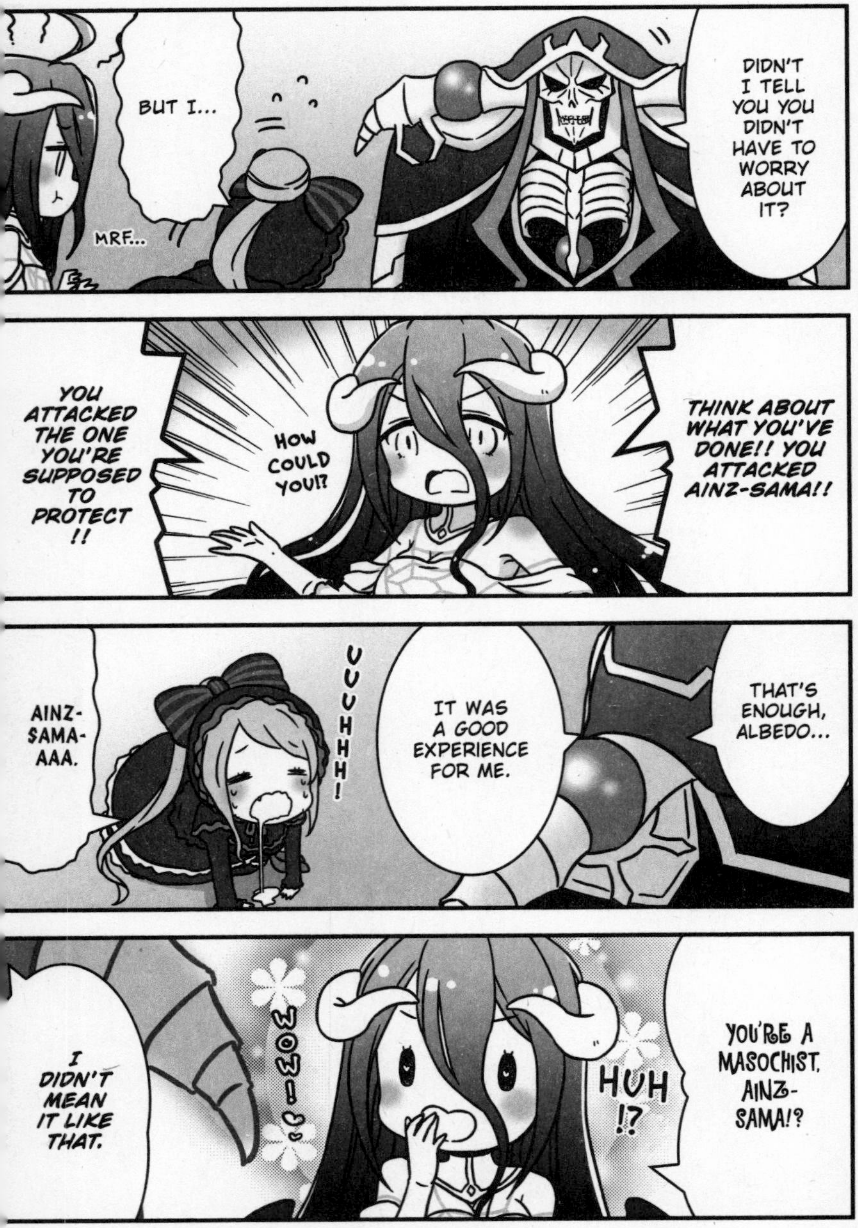
DIDN'T I TELL YOU YOU DIDN'T HAVE TO WORRY ABOUT IT?
BUT I...
MRF...
THINK ABOUT WHAT YOU'VE DONE!! YOU ATTACKED AINZ-SAMA!!
HOW COULD YOU!?
YOU ATTACKED THE ONE YOU'RE SUPPOSED TO PROTECT!!
THAT'S ENOUGH, ALBEDO...
IT WAS A GOOD EXPERIENCE FOR ME.
UUUHHH!
AINZ-SAMA-AAA.
YOU'RE A MASOCHIST, AINZ-SAMA!?
HUH!?
WOW!
I DIDN'T MEAN IT LIKE THAT.

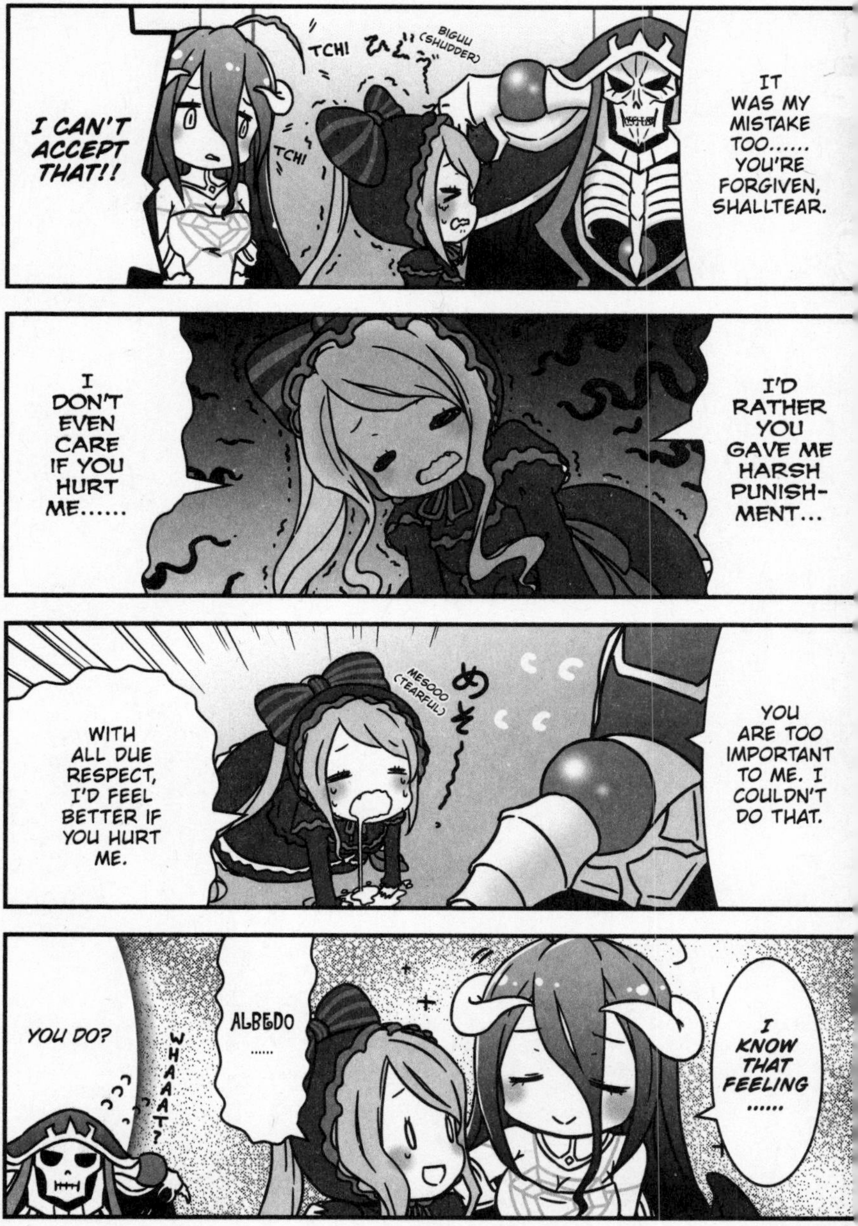
IT WAS MY MISTAKE TOO...... YOU'RE FORGIVEN, SHALLTEAR.
BIGUU (SHUDDER)
TCHI!
TCHI!
I CAN'T ACCEPT THAT!!
I'D RATHER YOU GAVE ME HARSH PUNISHMENT...
I DON'T EVEN CARE IF YOU HURT ME......
YOU ARE TOO IMPORTANT TO ME. I COULDN'T DO THAT.
MESOOO (TEARFUL)
WITH ALL DUE RESPECT, I'D FEEL BETTER IF YOU HURT ME.
I KNOW THAT FEELING......
ALBEDO ......
WHAAAAT?
YOU DO?

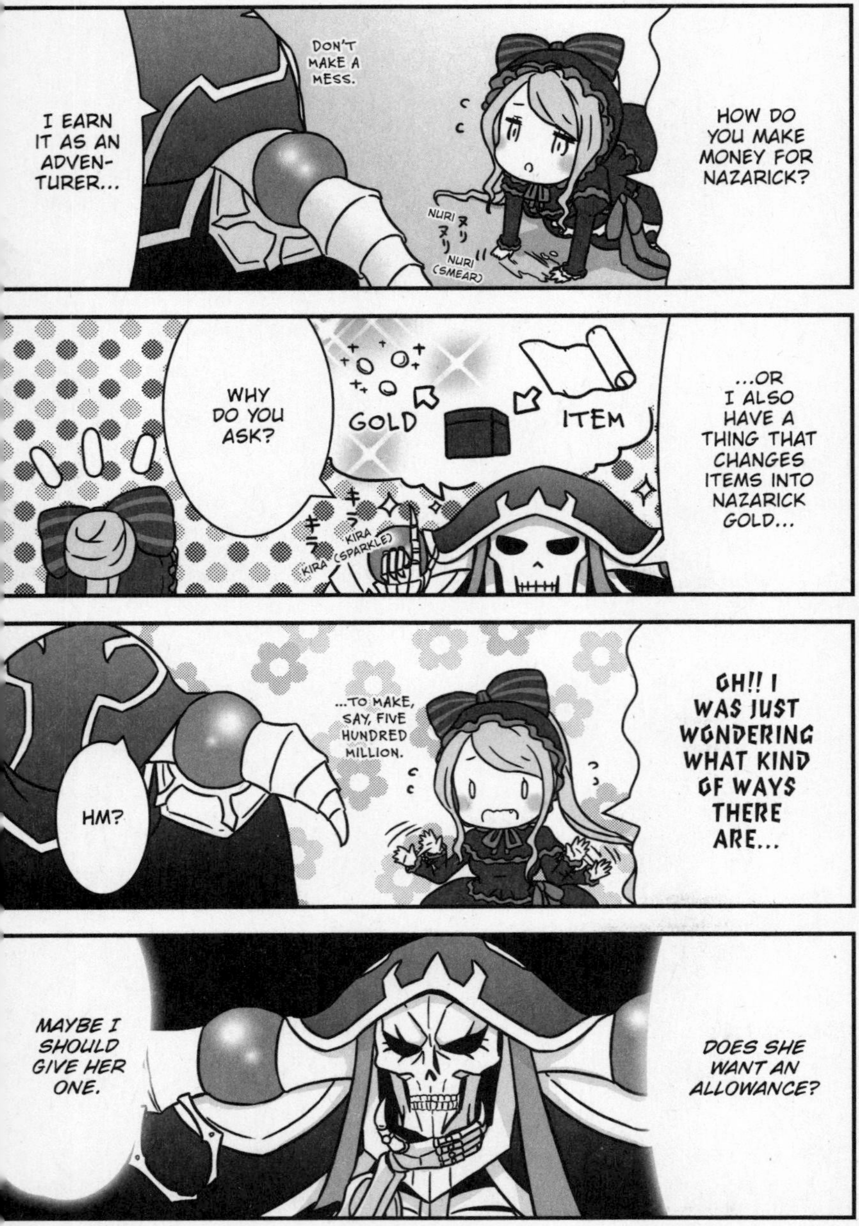
HOW DO YOU MAKE MONEY FOR NAZARICK?
DON'T MAKE A MESS.
I EARN IT AS AN ADVEN-TURER...
NURI ヌリ NURI ヌリ (SMEAR)
...OR I ALSO HAVE A THING THAT CHANGES ITEMS INTO NAZARICK GOLD...
ITEM
GOLD
KIRA キラ KIRA キラ (SPARKLE)
WHY DO YOU ASK?
GH!! I WAS JUST WONDERING WHAT KIND OF WAYS THERE ARE...
...TO MAKE, SAY, FIVE HUNDRED MILLION.
HM?
DOES SHE WANT AN ALLOWANCE?
MAYBE I SHOULD GIVE HER ONE.

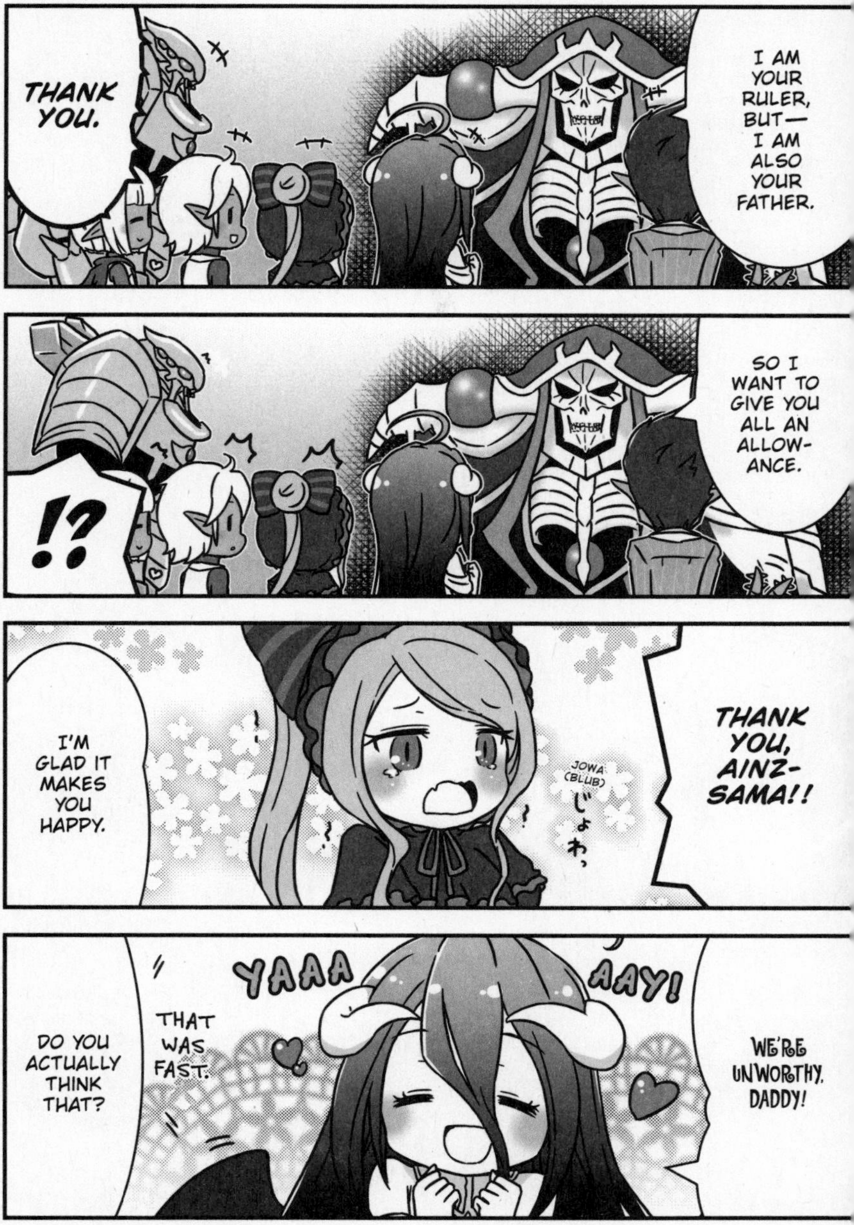
I AM YOUR RULER, BUT— I AM ALSO YOUR FATHER.
THANK YOU.
SO I WANT TO GIVE YOU ALL AN ALLOW-ANCE.
!?
THANK YOU, AINZ-SAMA!!
JOWA (BLUB) じょわっ
I'M GLAD IT MAKES YOU HAPPY.
WE'RE UNWORTHY, DADDY!
YAAA AAY!
THAT WAS FAST.
DO YOU ACTUALLY THINK THAT?

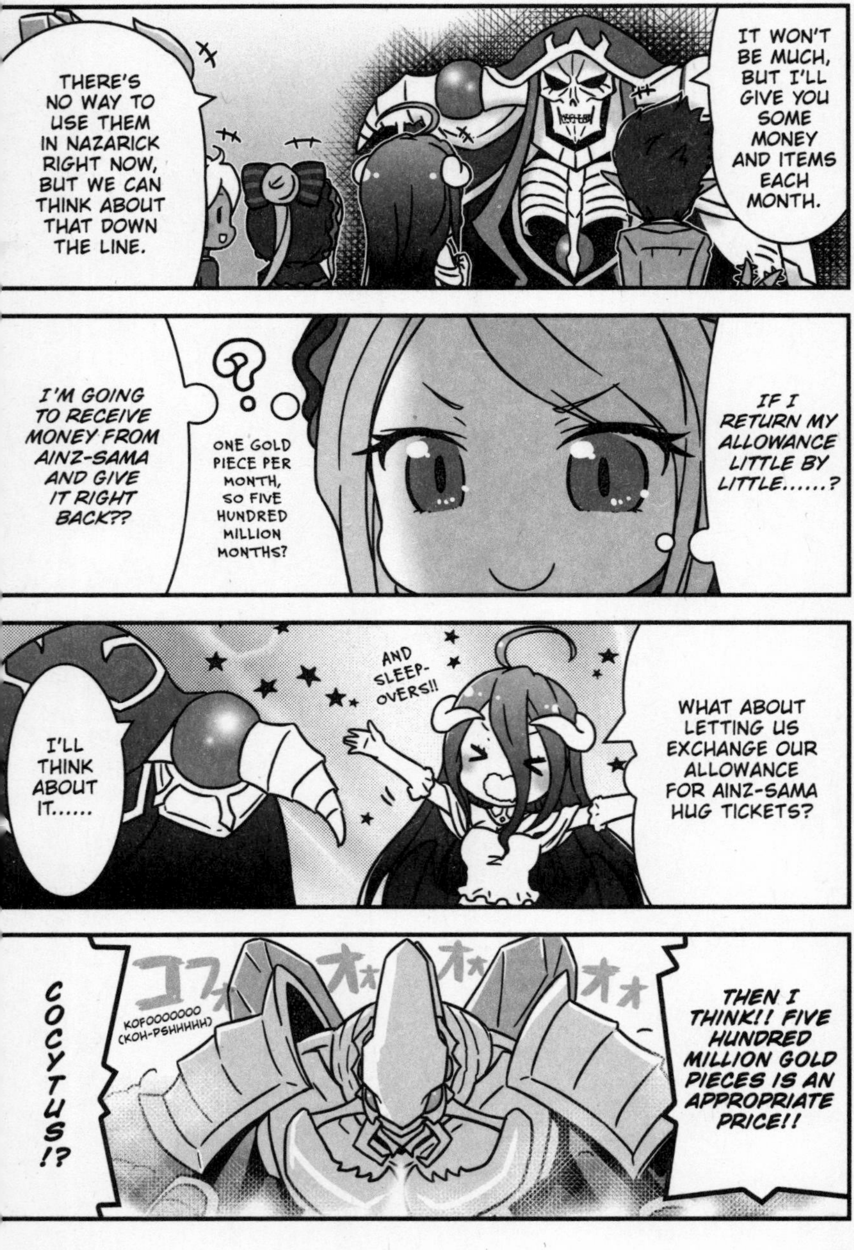
IT WON'T BE MUCH, BUT I'LL GIVE YOU SOME MONEY AND ITEMS EACH MONTH.
THERE'S NO WAY TO USE THEM IN NAZARICK RIGHT NOW, BUT WE CAN THINK ABOUT THAT DOWN THE LINE.
IF I RETURN MY ALLOWANCE LITTLE BY LITTLE......?
ONE GOLD PIECE PER MONTH, SO FIVE HUNDRED MILLION MONTHS?
I'M GOING TO RECEIVE MONEY FROM AINZ-SAMA AND GIVE IT RIGHT BACK??
WHAT ABOUT LETTING US EXCHANGE OUR ALLOWANCE FOR AINZ-SAMA HUG TICKETS?
AND SLEEP-OVERS!!
I'LL THINK ABOUT IT......
THEN I THINK!! FIVE HUNDRED MILLION GOLD PIECES IS AN APPROPRIATE PRICE!!
コフォオオオオ
KOFOOOOOOO (KOH-PSHHHHH)
COCYTUS!?

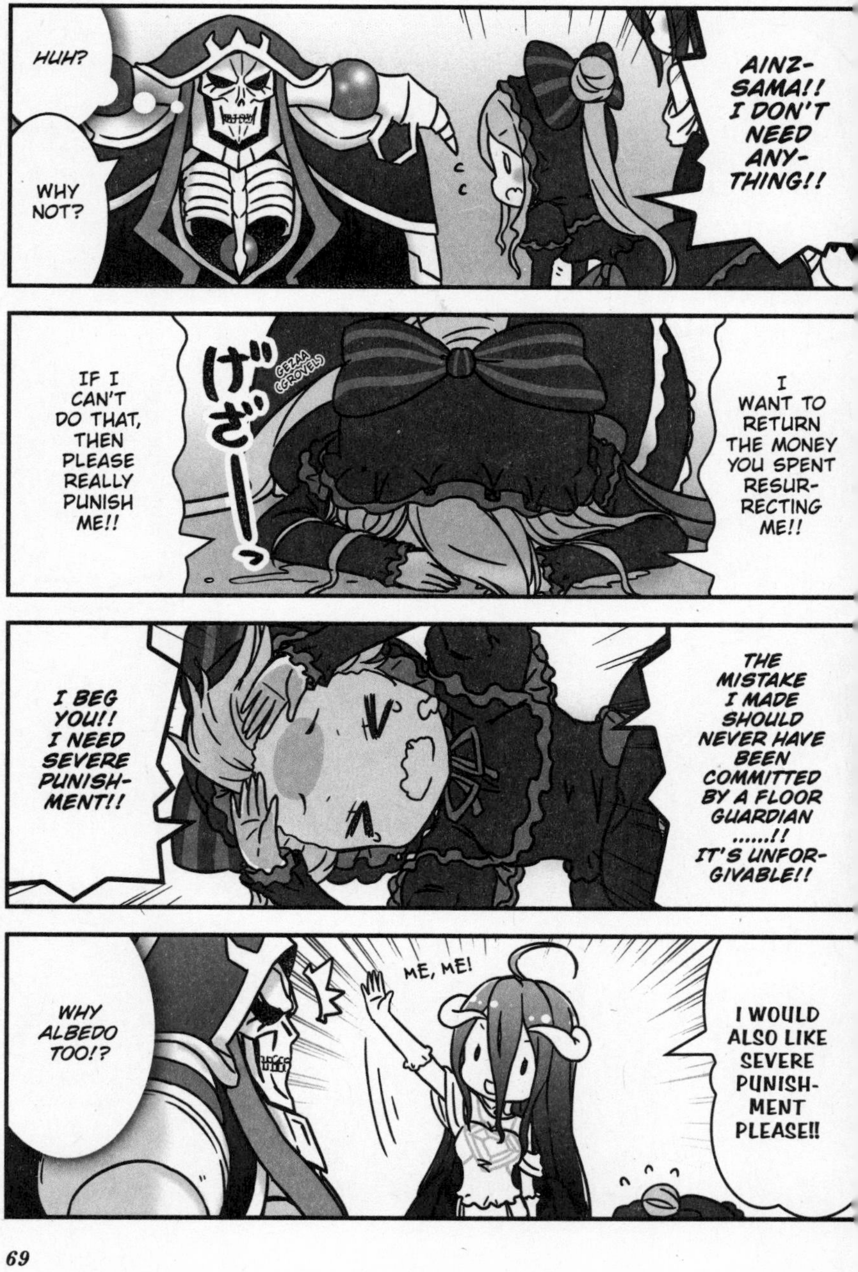
AINZ-SAMA!! I DON'T NEED ANYTHING!!
HUH?
WHY NOT?
I WANT TO RETURN THE MONEY YOU SPENT RESURRECTING ME!!
げざーっ
GEZAA (GROVEL)
IF I CAN'T DO THAT, THEN PLEASE REALLY PUNISH ME!!
THE MISTAKE I MADE SHOULD NEVER HAVE BEEN COMMITTED BY A FLOOR GUARDIAN ......!! IT'S UNFORGIVABLE!!
I BEG YOU!! I NEED SEVERE PUNISHMENT!!
I WOULD ALSO LIKE SEVERE PUNISHMENT PLEASE!!
ME, ME!
WHY ALBEDO TOO!?

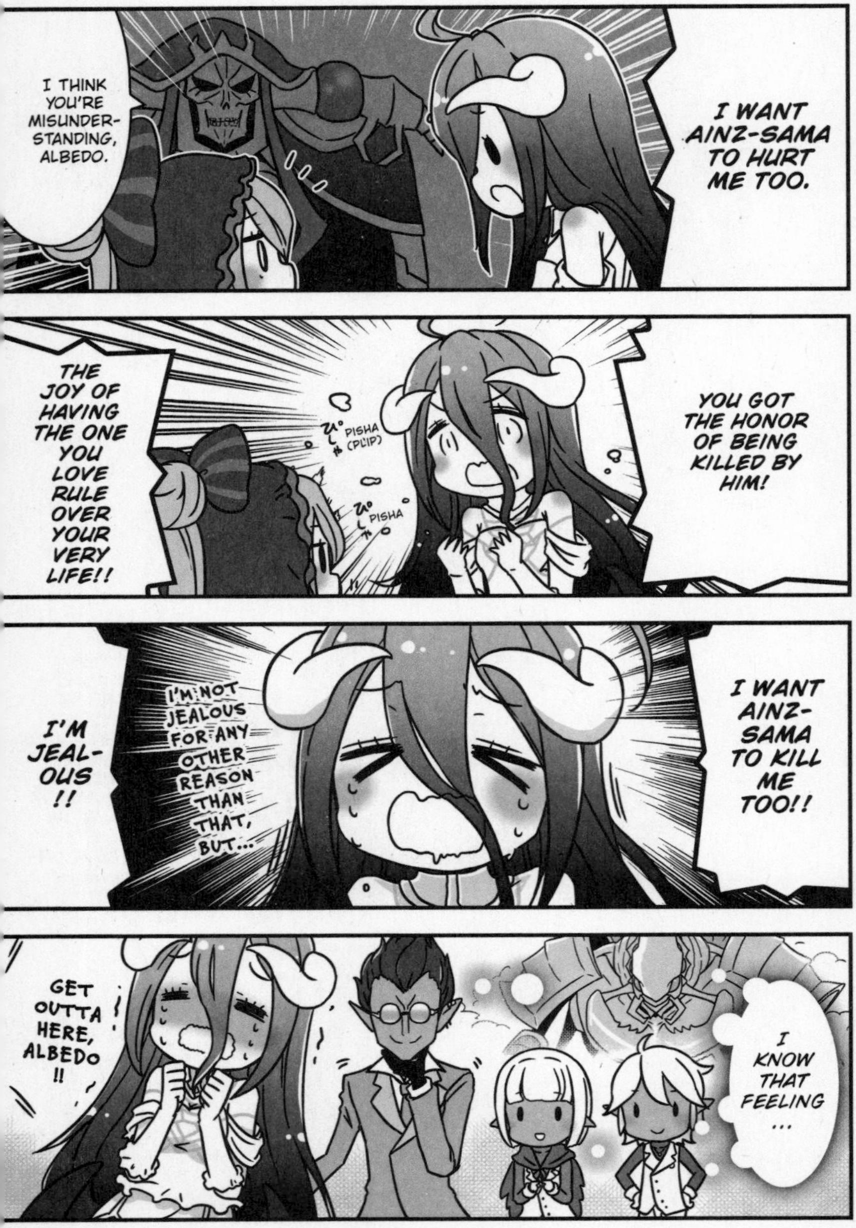
I WANT AINZ-SAMA TO HURT ME TOO.
I THINK YOU'RE MISUNDER-STANDING, ALBEDO.
YOU GOT THE HONOR OF BEING KILLED BY HIM!
ぴしゃ PISHA (PLIP)
ぴしゃ PISHA
THE JOY OF HAVING THE ONE YOU LOVE RULE OVER YOUR VERY LIFE!!
I WANT AINZ-SAMA TO KILL ME TOO!!
I'M NOT JEALOUS FOR ANY OTHER REASON THAN THAT, BUT...
I'M JEAL-OUS!!
I KNOW THAT FEELING...
GET OUTTA HERE, ALBEDO!!

OVERLORD

À LA CARTE

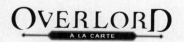

OVERLORD

À LA CARTE

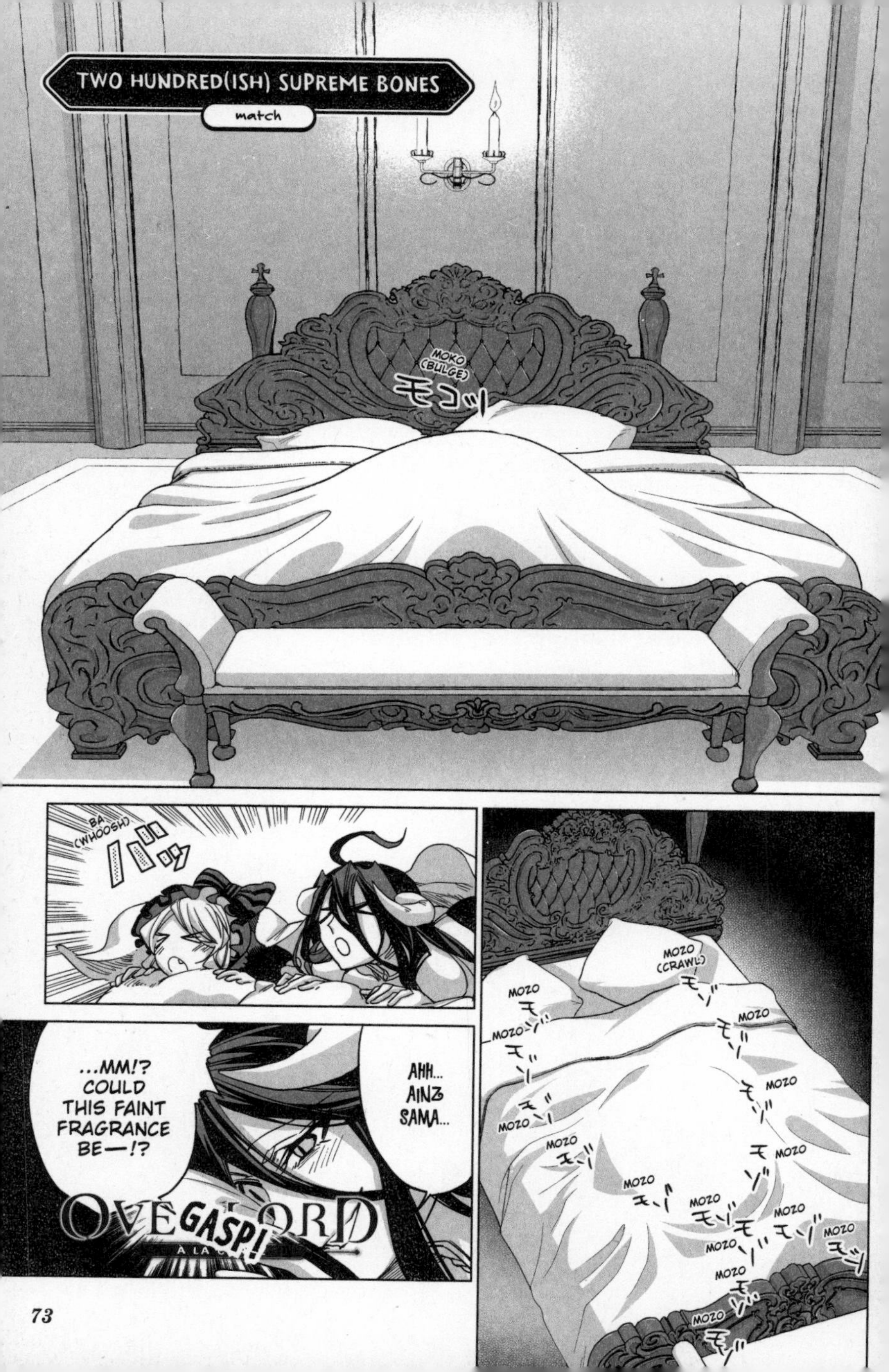
TWO HUNDRED(ISH) SUPREME BONES
match
MOKO (BULGE)
モコッ
MOZO (CRAWL)
モゾ
MOZO
MOZO
MOZO
MOZO
MOZO
MOZO
MOZO
MOZO
MOZO
MOZO
MOZO
MOZO
MOZO
MOZO
BA (WHOOSH)
バッ
...MM!? COULD THIS FAINT FRAGRANCE BE—!?
AHH... AINZ SAMA...
GASP!

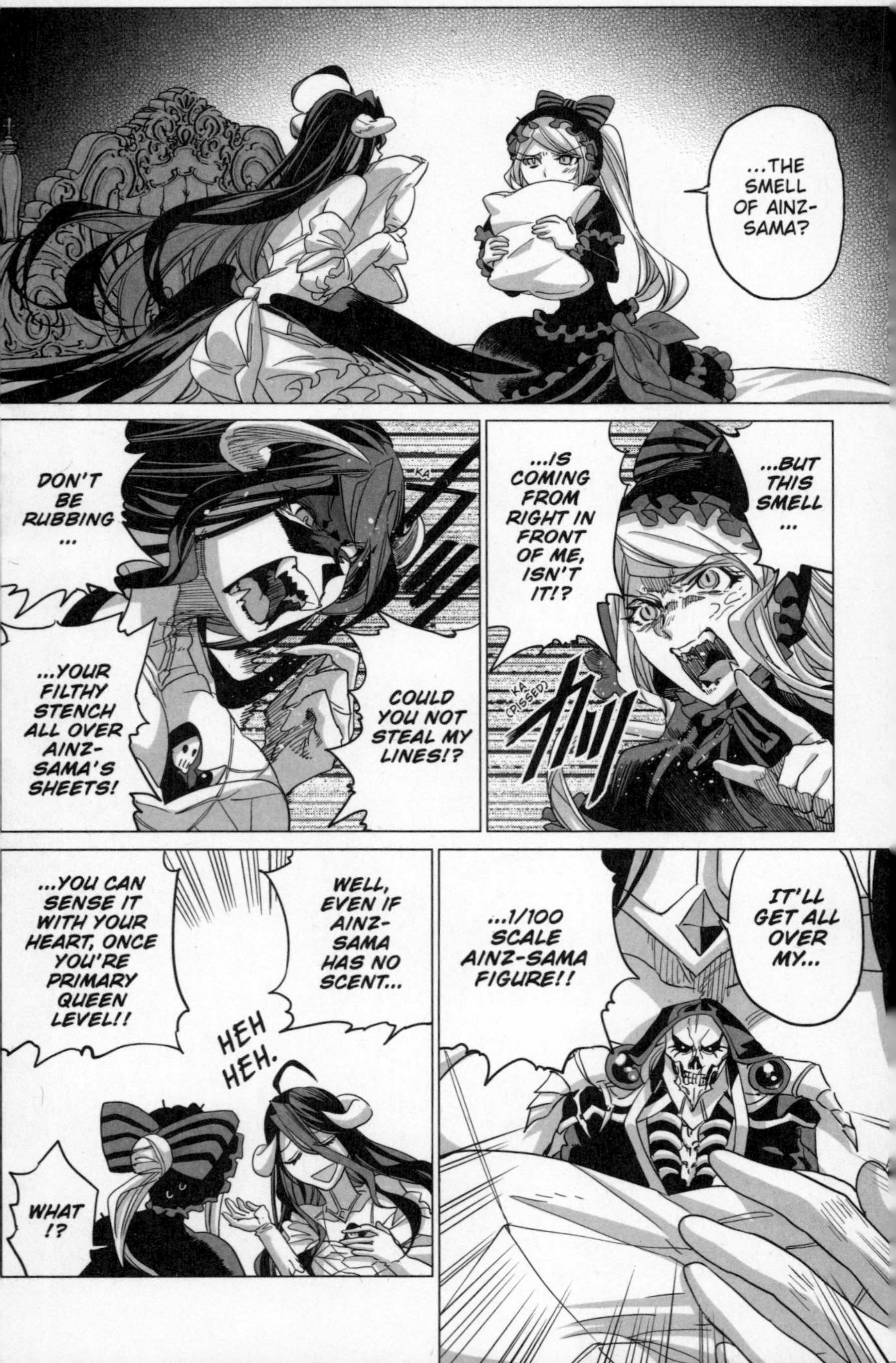

...THE SMELL OF AINZ-SAMA?
...BUT THIS SMELL ...
...IS COMING FROM RIGHT IN FRONT OF ME, ISN'T IT!?
KA (PISSED)
カッ
KA
DON'T BE RUBBING ...
...YOUR FILTHY STENCH ALL OVER AINZ-SAMA'S SHEETS!
COULD YOU NOT STEAL MY LINES!?
IT'LL GET ALL OVER MY...
...1/100 SCALE AINZ-SAMA FIGURE!!
WELL, EVEN IF AINZ-SAMA HAS NO SCENT...
...YOU CAN SENSE IT WITH YOUR HEART, ONCE YOU'RE PRIMARY QUEEN LEVEL!!
HEH HEH.
WHAT!?

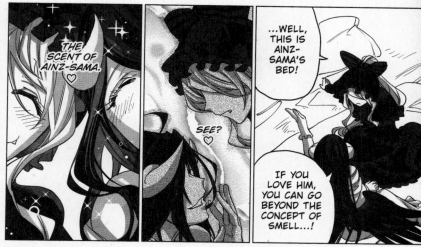

...WELL, THIS IS AINZ-SAMA'S BED!
IF YOU LOVE HIM, YOU CAN GO BEYOND THE CONCEPT OF SMELL...!
SEE? ♡
THE SCENT OF AINZ-SAMA. ♡
BUT WOW, THIS FIGURE IS QUITE IMPRESSIVE.
OF COURSE IT IS.
IT'S AINZ-SAMA AT 1/100 SCALE.
THE BONES ARE SO WELL MOLDED...
YEAH, AINZ-SAMA'S...
...PUBIC BONE IS THE BEST!
...COLLAR-BONE IS THE GREAT-EST!
HYUUU (WHOOOSH)

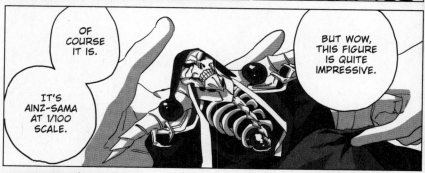

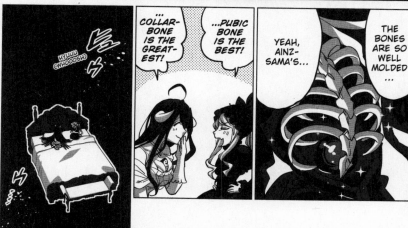

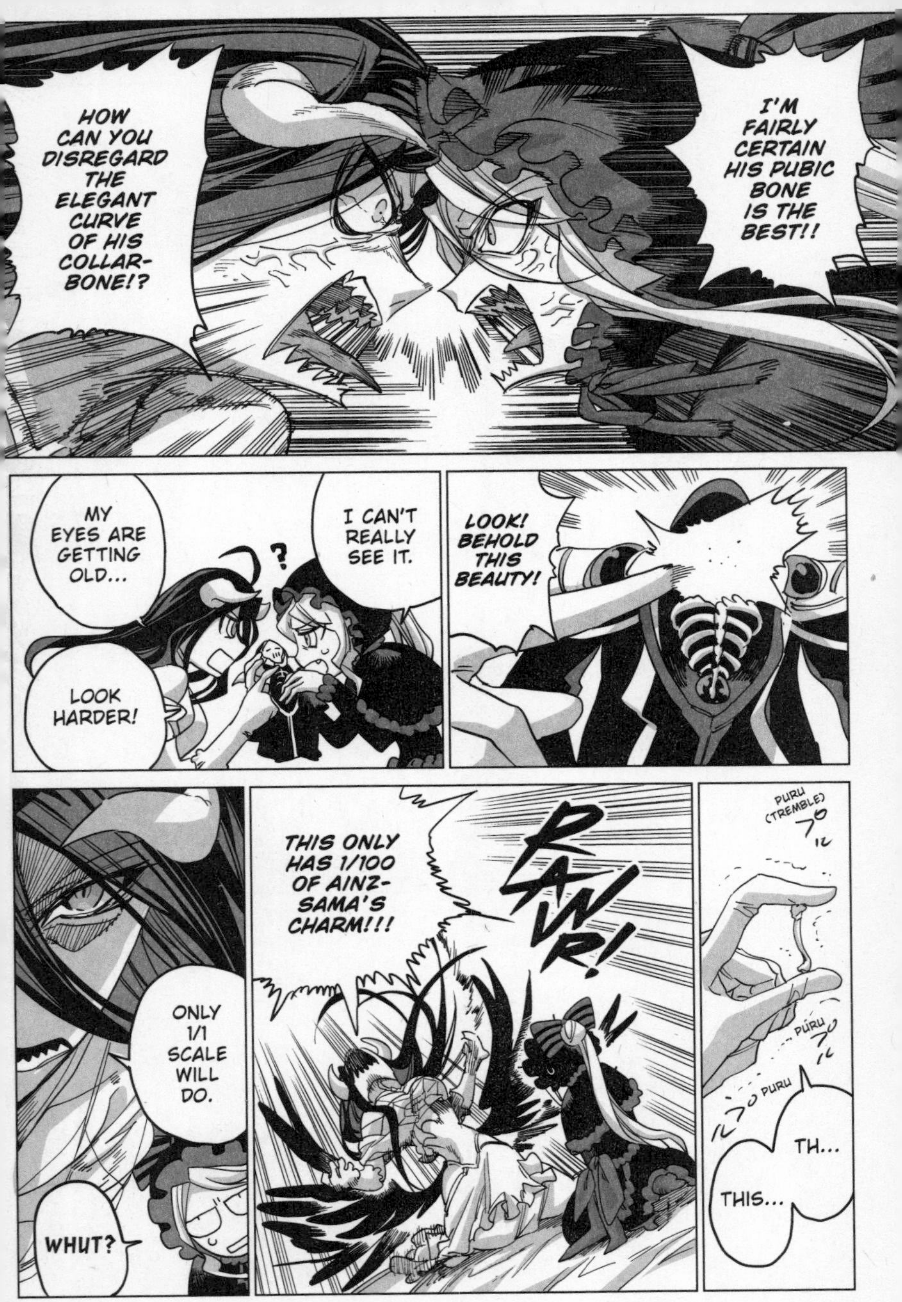
I'M FAIRLY CERTAIN HIS PUBIC BONE IS THE BEST!!
HOW CAN YOU DISREGARD THE ELEGANT CURVE OF HIS COLLAR-BONE!?
LOOK! BEHOLD THIS BEAUTY!
I CAN'T REALLY SEE IT.
MY EYES ARE GETTING OLD...
?
LOOK HARDER!
PURU (TREMBLE)
PURU
PURU
TH...
THIS...
THIS ONLY HAS 1/100 OF AINZ-SAMA'S CHARM!!!
RAWR!
ONLY 1/1 SCALE WILL DO.
WHUT?

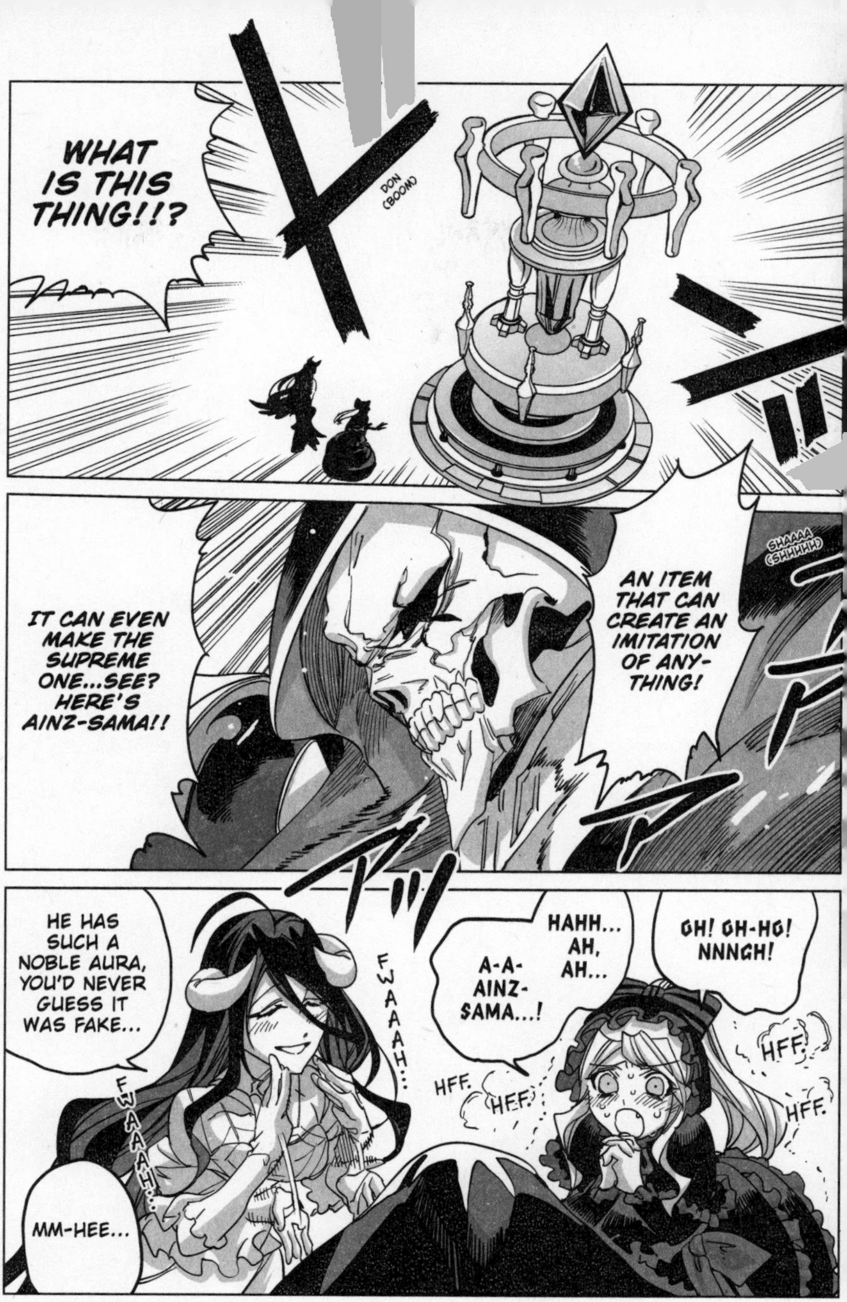
WHAT IS THIS THING!!?
DON (BOOM)
AN ITEM THAT CAN CREATE AN IMITATION OF ANY-THING!
SHAAAA (SHHHHH)
IT CAN EVEN MAKE THE SUPREME ONE...SEE? HERE'S AINZ-SAMA!!
OH! OH-HO! NNNGH!
HFF.
HFF.
HAHH... AH, AH...
A-A-AINZ-SAMA...!
HFF.
HFF.
HE HAS SUCH A NOBLE AURA, YOU'D NEVER GUESS IT WAS FAKE...
FWAAAAH...
FWAAAAH...
MM-HEE...

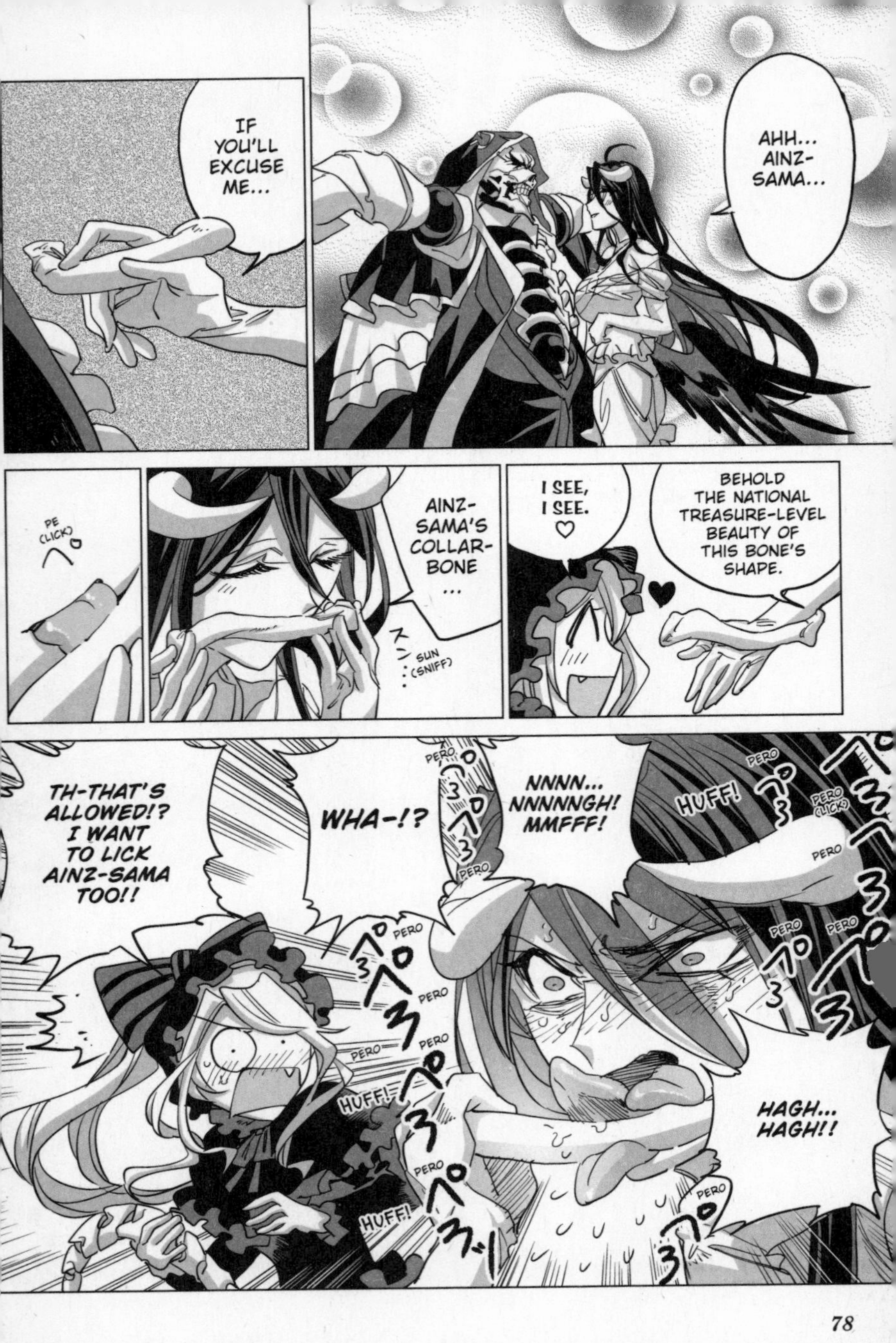
AHH... AINZ-SAMA...
IF YOU'LL EXCUSE ME...
BEHOLD THE NATIONAL TREASURE-LEVEL BEAUTY OF THIS BONE'S SHAPE.
I SEE, I SEE. ♡
AINZ-SAMA'S COLLAR-BONE ...
SUN (SNIFF)
PE (LICK)
HAGH... HAGH!!
PERO (LICK)
HUFF!
PERO
NNNN... NNNNNGH! MMFFF!
PERO
WHA-!?
HUFF!
HUFF!
TH-THAT'S ALLOWED!? I WANT TO LICK AINZ-SAMA TOO!!

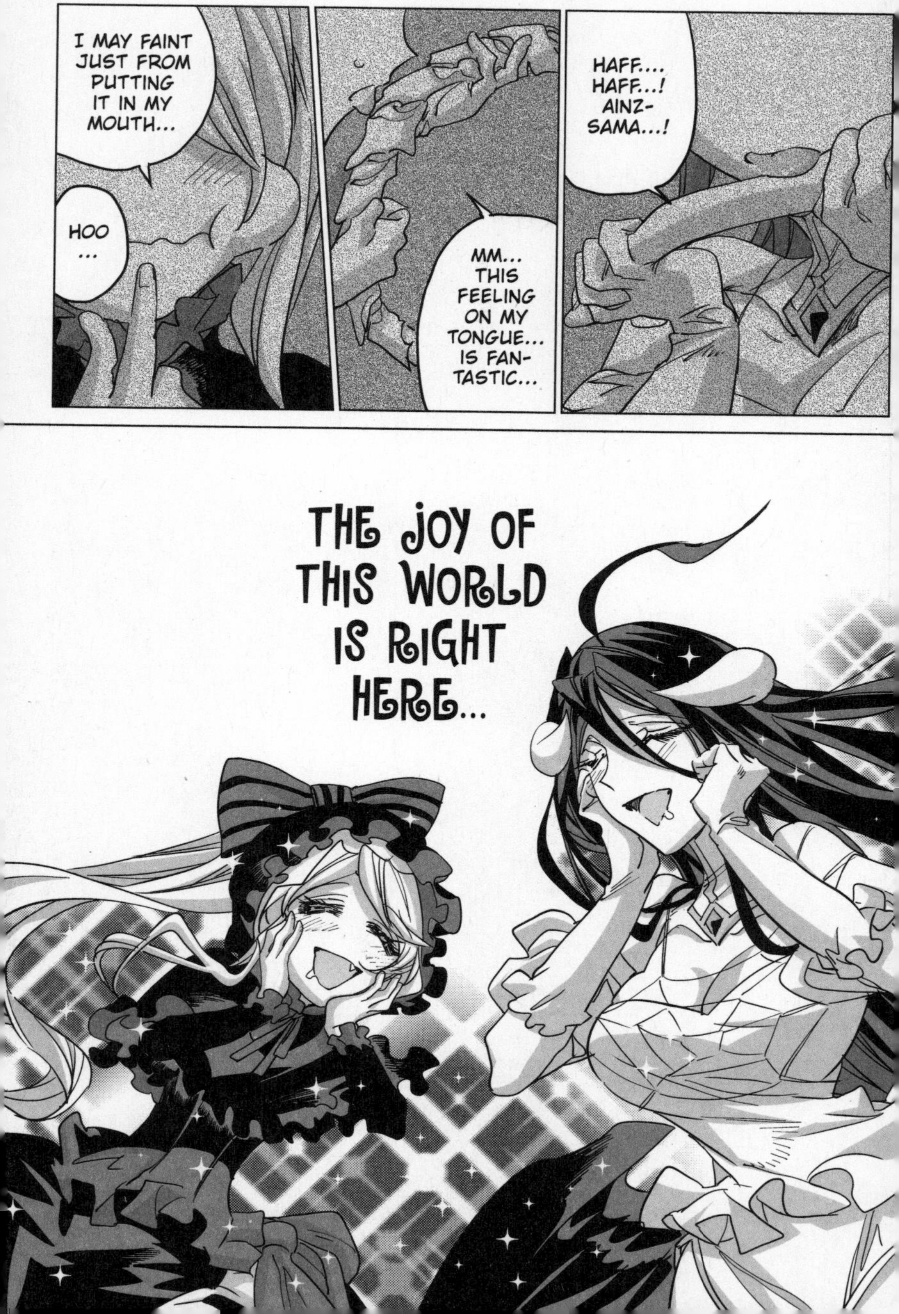
HAFF.... HAFF...! AINZ-SAMA...!
MM... THIS FEELING ON MY TONGUE... IS FANTASTIC...
I MAY FAINT JUST FROM PUTTING IT IN MY MOUTH...
HOO ...
THE JOY OF THIS WORLD IS RIGHT HERE...

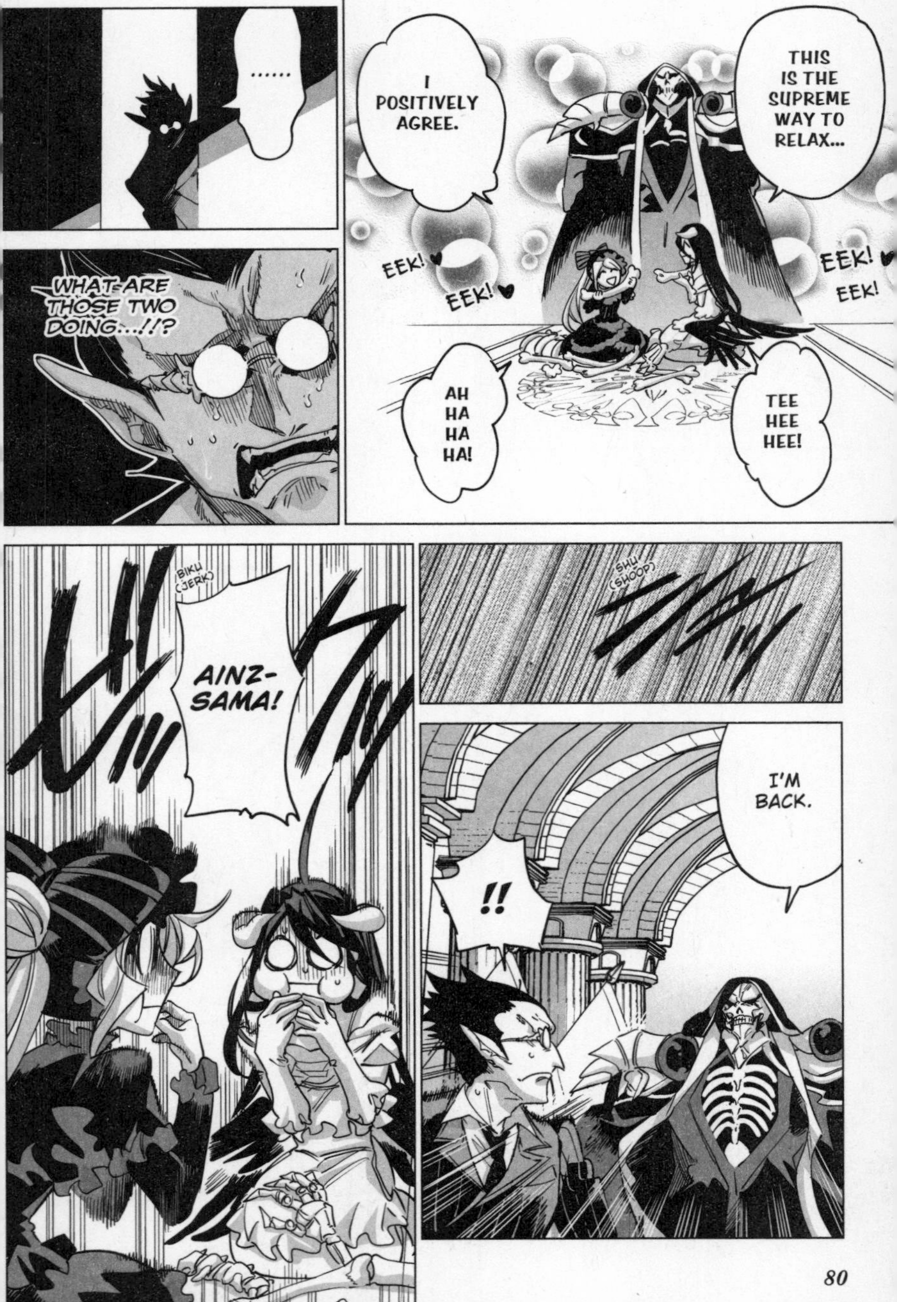
THIS IS THE SUPREME WAY TO RELAX...
I POSITIVELY AGREE.
EEK!
EEK!
EEK!
EEK!
TEE HEE HEE!
AH HA HA HA!
......
WHAT ARE THOSE TWO DOING...!!?
SHU (SHOOP)
I'M BACK.
!!
BIKU (JERK)
AINZ-SAMA!

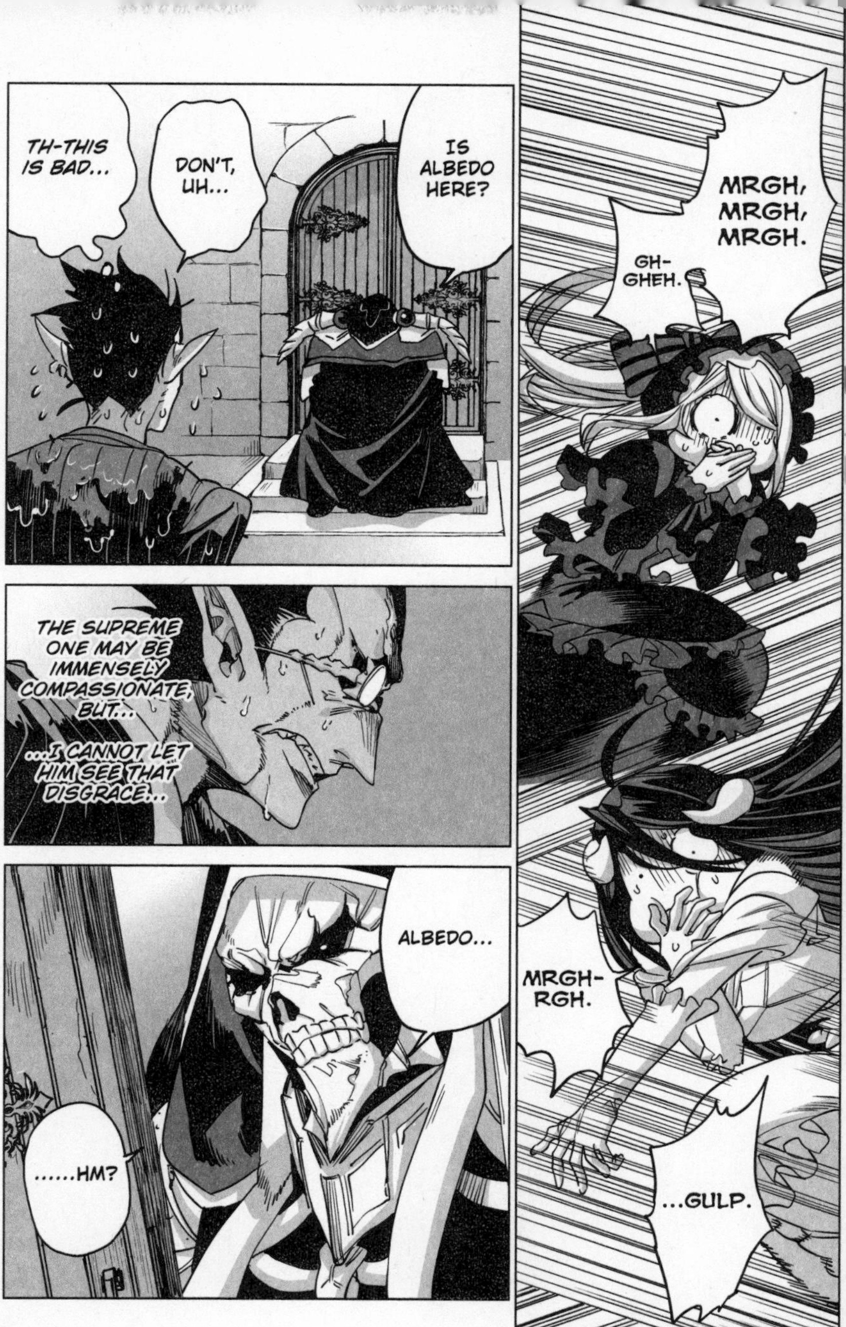
MRGH, MRGH, MRGH.
GH-GHEH.
MRGH-RGH.
...GULP.
IS ALBEDO HERE?
DON'T, UH...
TH-THIS IS BAD...
THE SUPREME ONE MAY BE IMMENSELY COMPASSIONATE, BUT...
...I CANNOT LET HIM SEE THAT DISGRACE...
ALBEDO...
......HM?

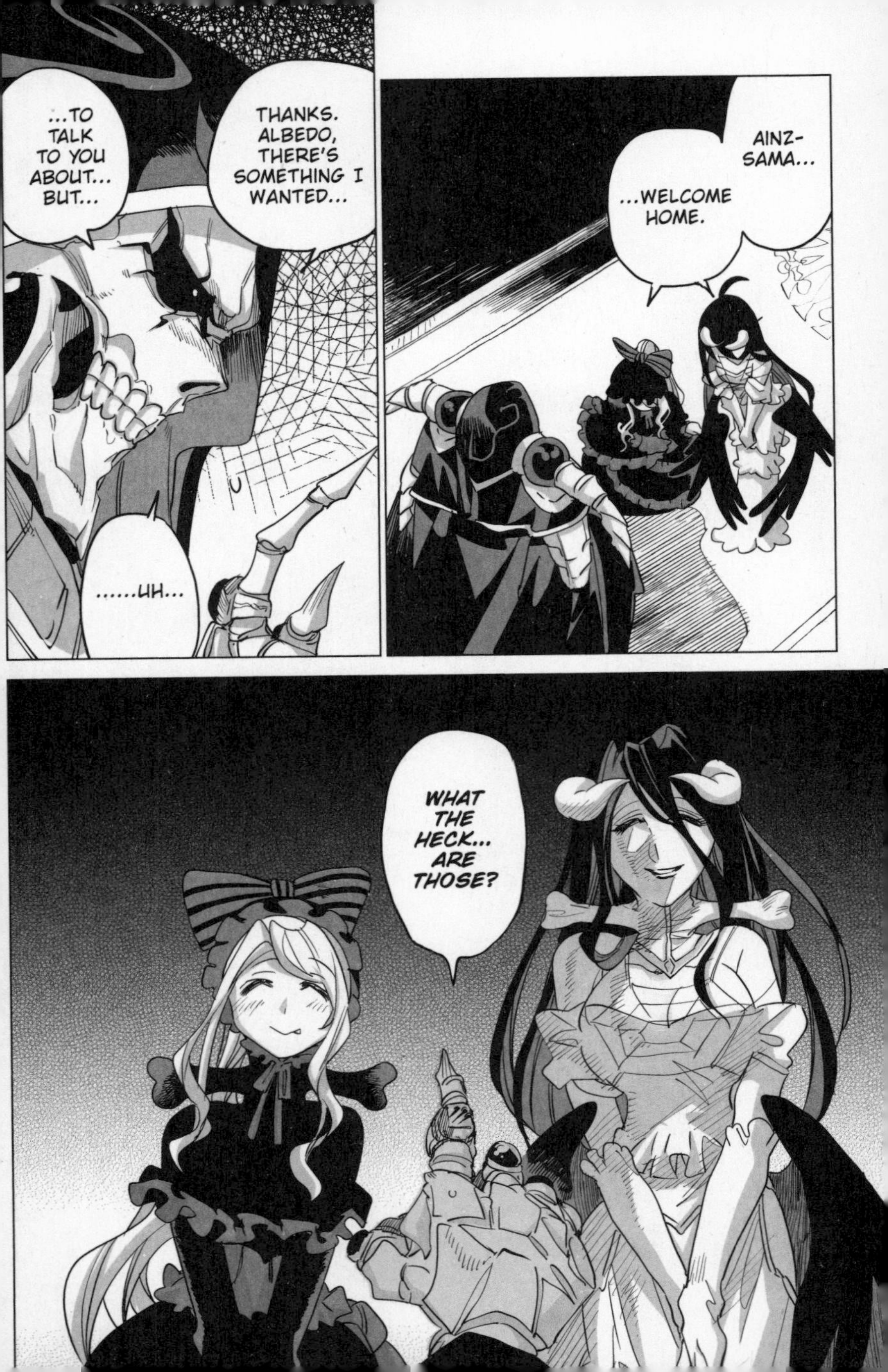
AINZ-SAMA...
...WELCOME HOME.
THANKS. ALBEDO, THERE'S SOMETHING I WANTED...
...TO TALK TO YOU ABOUT... BUT...
......UH...
WHAT THE HECK... ARE THOSE?

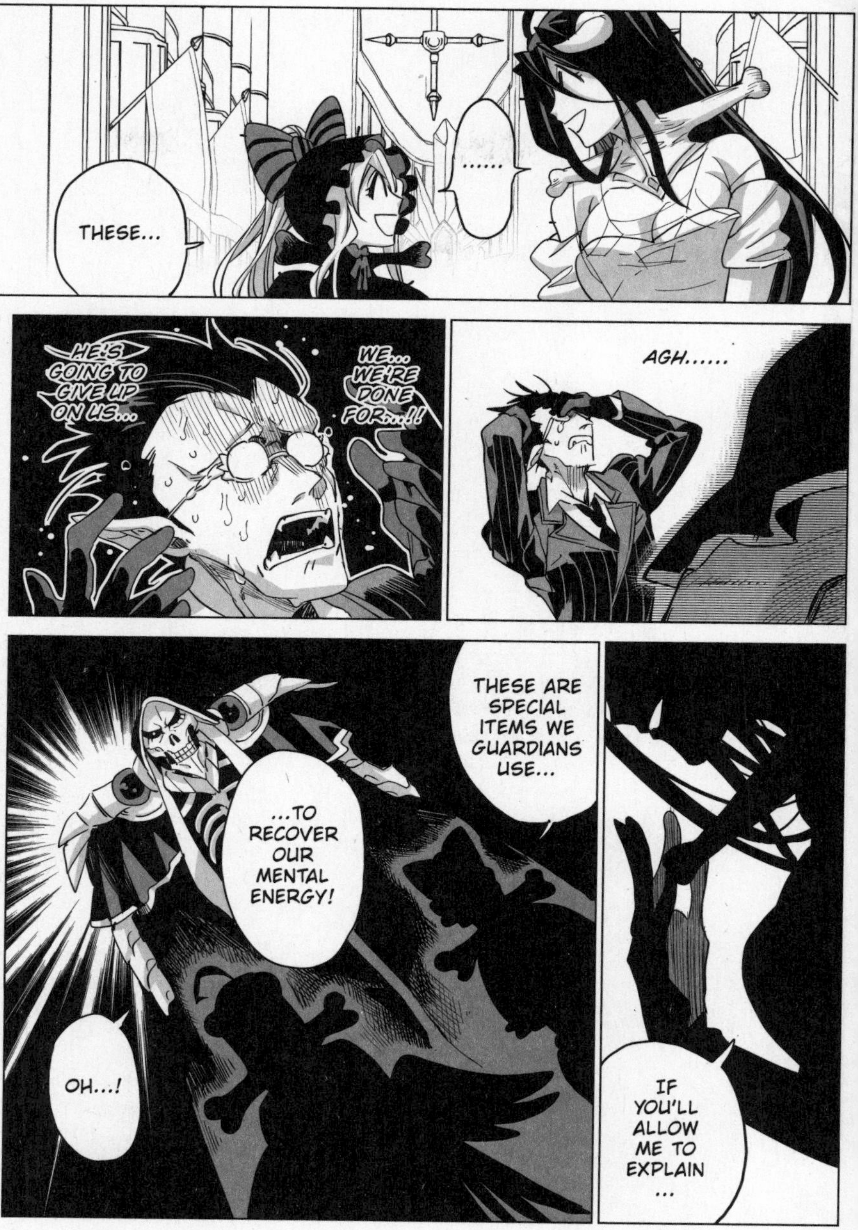
......
THESE...
AGH......
WE... WE'RE DONE FOR...!!
HE'S GOING TO GIVE UP ON US...
IF YOU'LL ALLOW ME TO EXPLAIN ...
THESE ARE SPECIAL ITEMS WE GUARDIANS USE...
...TO RECOVER OUR MENTAL ENERGY!
OH...!

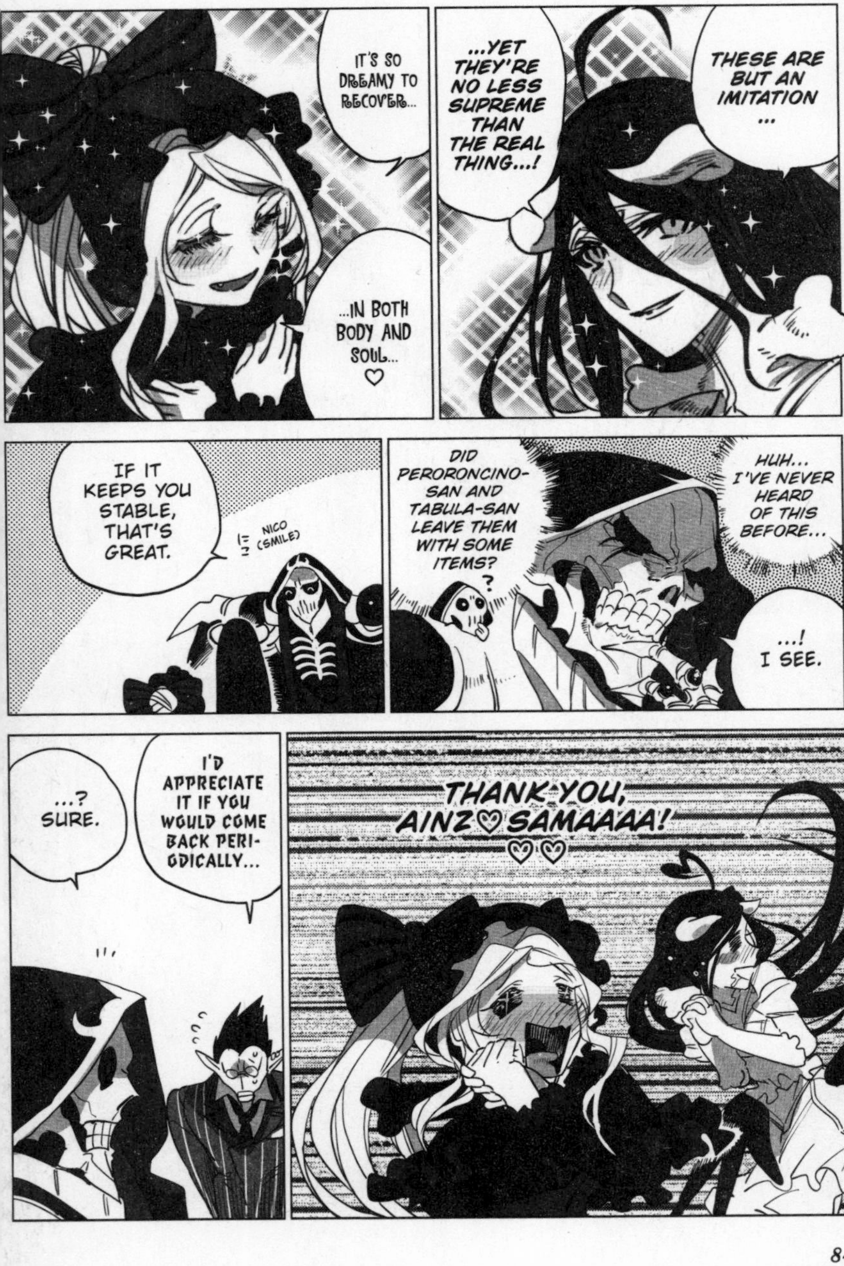
THESE ARE BUT AN IMITATION ...
...YET THEY'RE NO LESS SUPREME THAN THE REAL THING...!
IT'S SO DREAMY TO RECOVER...
...IN BOTH BODY AND SOUL... ♡
HUH... I'VE NEVER HEARD OF THIS BEFORE...
DID PERORONCINO-SAN AND TABULA-SAN LEAVE THEM WITH SOME ITEMS?
?
...! I SEE.
IF IT KEEPS YOU STABLE, THAT'S GREAT.
NICO (SMILE)
THANK YOU, AINZ♡SAMAAAAA!
♡♡
I'D APPRECIATE IT IF YOU WOULD COME BACK PERI-ODICALLY...
...? SURE.

A SPECIAL MEETING REGARDING AGES SIX AND UP

U SETA

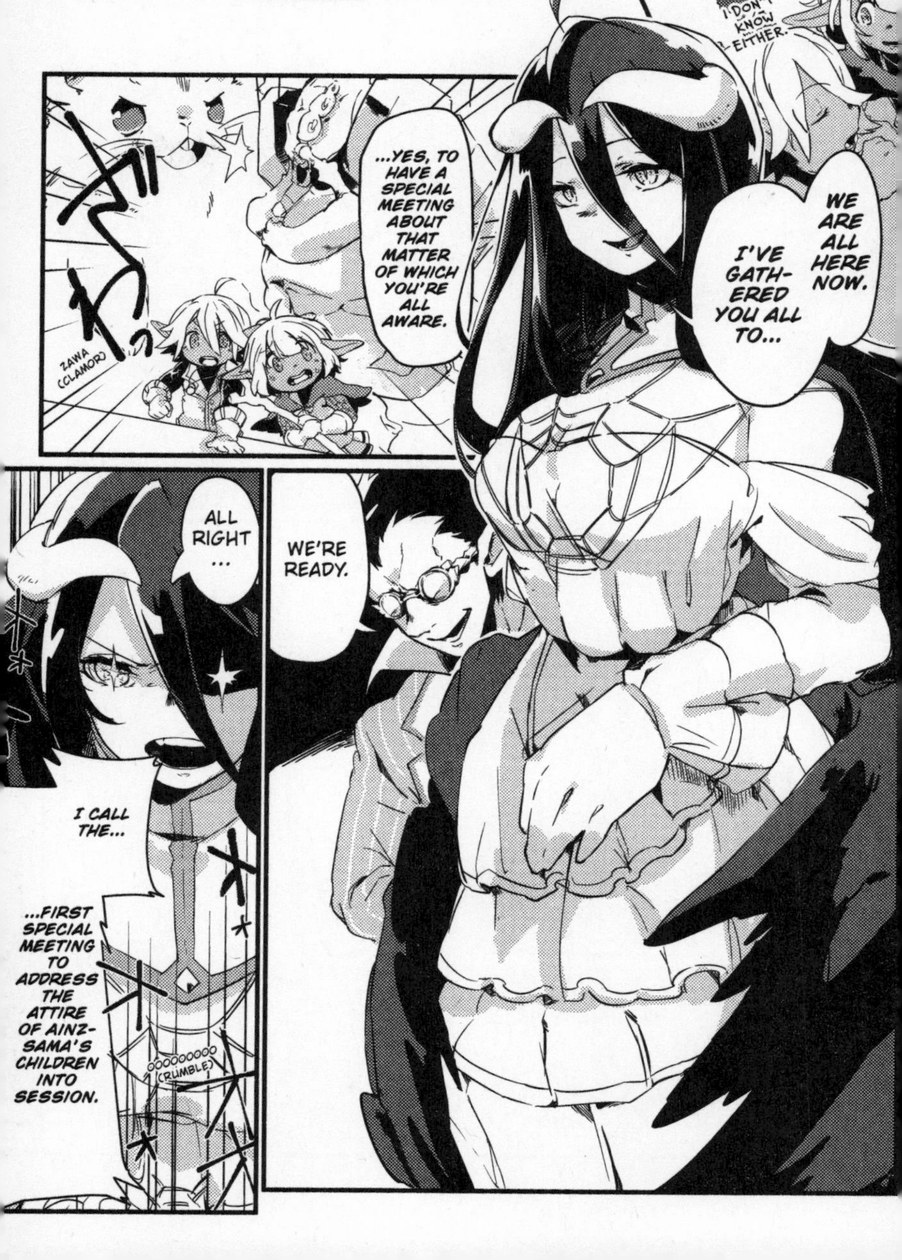
WHAT DO YOU DO IN A SPECIAL MEETING?
I DON'T KNOW EITHER.
WE ARE ALL HERE NOW.
I'VE GATHERED YOU ALL TO...
...YES, TO HAVE A SPECIAL MEETING ABOUT THAT MATTER OF WHICH YOU'RE ALL AWARE.
ZAWA (CLAMOR)
WE'RE READY.
ALL RIGHT...
I CALL THE...
...FIRST SPECIAL MEETING TO ADDRESS THE ATTIRE OF AINZ-SAMA'S CHILDREN INTO SESSION.
OOOOOOOOO (RUMBLE)

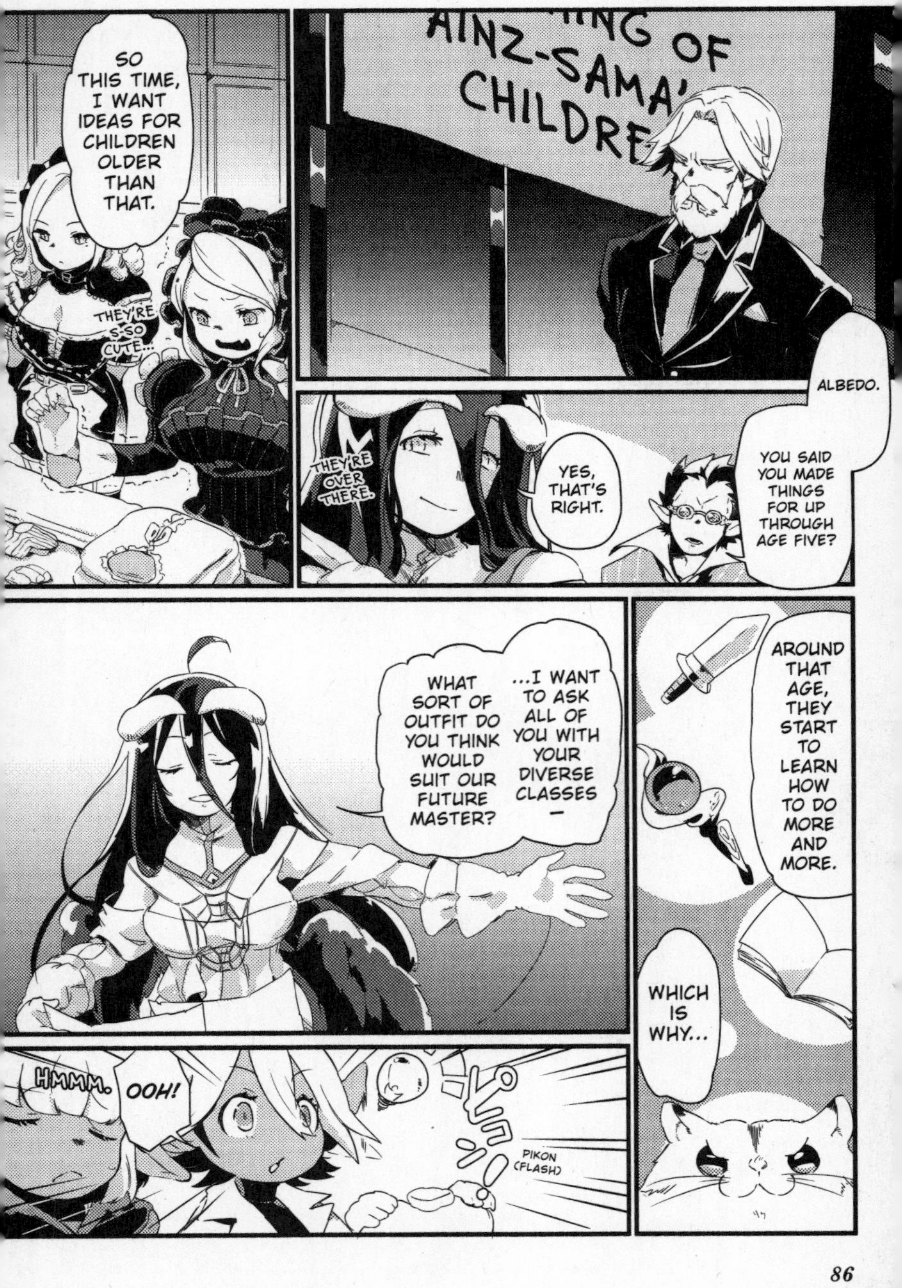
ING OF
AINZ-SAMA'
CHILDRE
ALBEDO.
YOU SAID YOU MADE THINGS FOR UP THROUGH AGE FIVE?
YES, THAT'S RIGHT.
THEY'RE OVER THERE.
SO THIS TIME, I WANT IDEAS FOR CHILDREN OLDER THAN THAT.
THEY'RE S-SO CUTE...
AROUND THAT AGE, THEY START TO LEARN HOW TO DO MORE AND MORE.
WHICH IS WHY...
...I WANT TO ASK ALL OF YOU WITH YOUR DIVERSE CLASSES—
WHAT SORT OF OUTFIT DO YOU THINK WOULD SUIT OUR FUTURE MASTER?
PIKON (FLASH)
OOH!
HMMM.

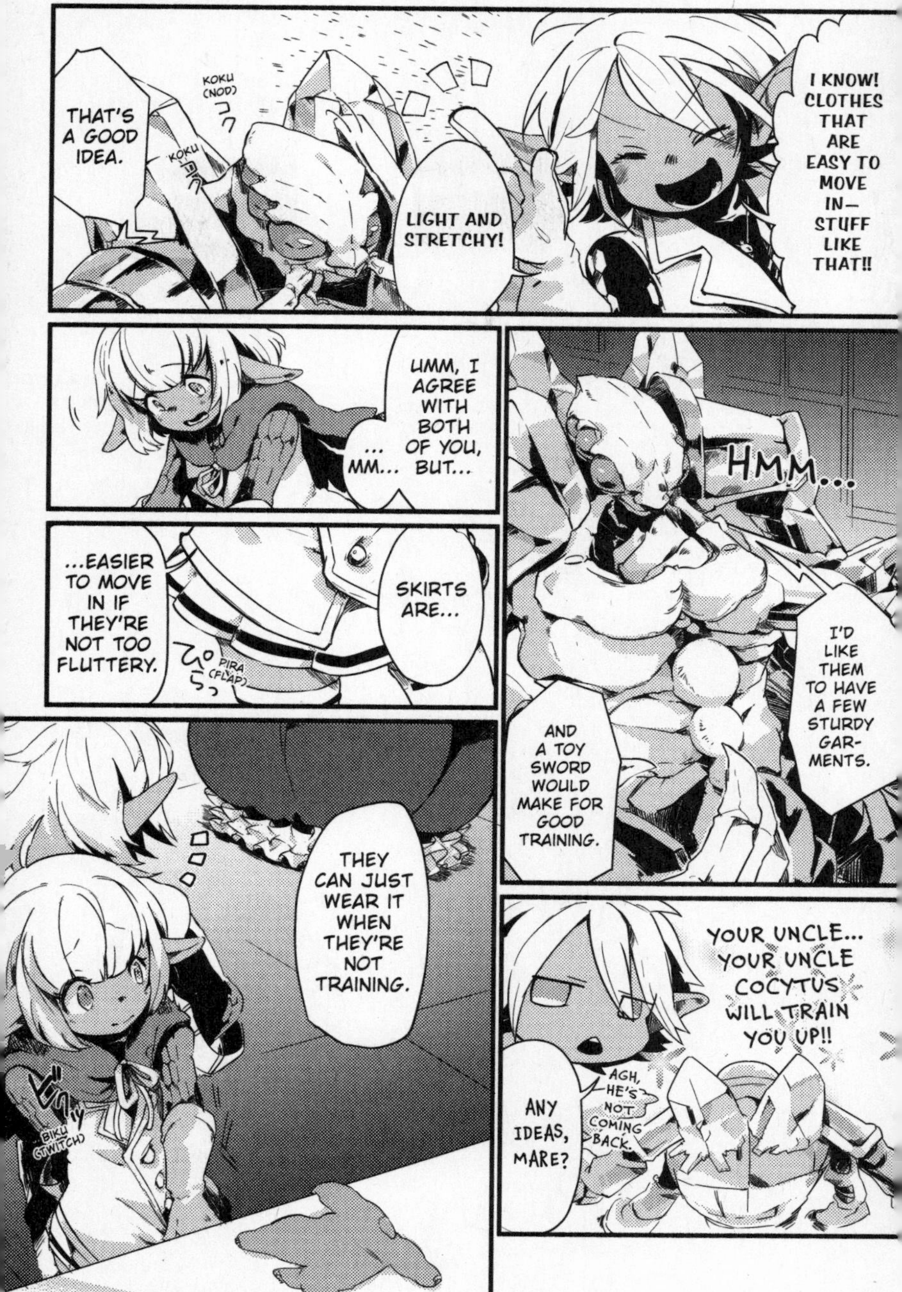
I KNOW! CLOTHES THAT ARE EASY TO MOVE IN— STUFF LIKE THAT!!
LIGHT AND STRETCHY!
KOKU (NOD)
KOKU
THAT'S A GOOD IDEA.
HMM...
I'D LIKE THEM TO HAVE A FEW STURDY GAR-MENTS.
AND A TOY SWORD WOULD MAKE FOR GOOD TRAINING.
UMM, I AGREE WITH BOTH OF YOU, BUT...
...MM...
SKIRTS ARE...
...EASIER TO MOVE IN IF THEY'RE NOT TOO FLUTTERY.
PIRA (FLAP)
THEY CAN JUST WEAR IT WHEN THEY'RE NOT TRAINING.
BIKU (TWITCH)
YOUR UNCLE... YOUR UNCLE COCYTUS WILL TRAIN YOU UP!!
AGH, HE'S NOT COMING BACK.
ANY IDEAS, MARE?

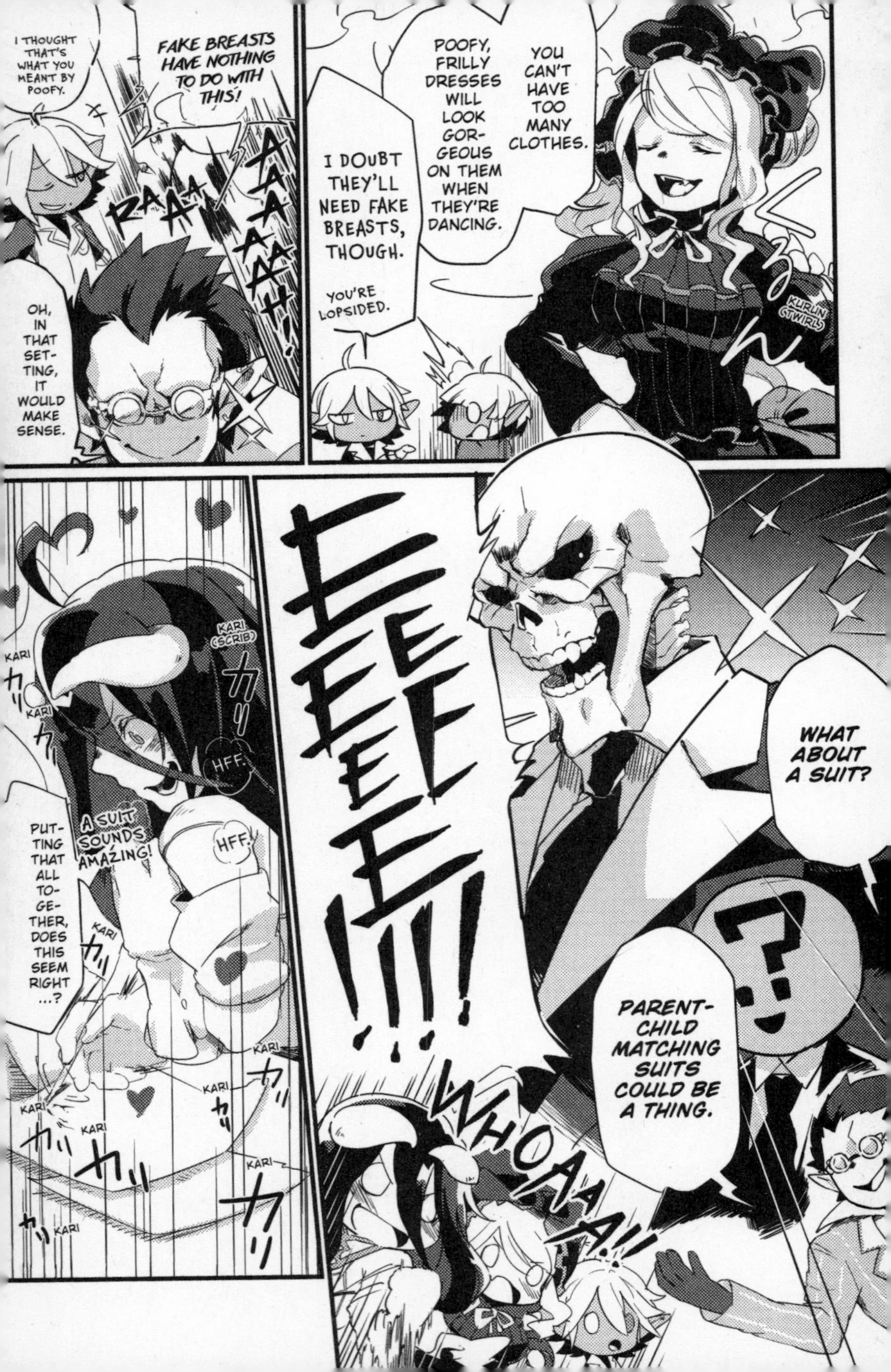
YOU CAN'T HAVE TOO MANY CLOTHES.
POOFY, FRILLY DRESSES WILL LOOK GORGEOUS ON THEM WHEN THEY'RE DANCING.
KURUN (TWIRL)
I DOUBT THEY'LL NEED FAKE BREASTS, THOUGH.
YOU'RE LOPSIDED.
FAKE BREASTS HAVE NOTHING TO DO WITH THIS!
I THOUGHT THAT'S WHAT YOU MEANT BY POOFY.
RAAA AAAAAAH!!
OH, IN THAT SETTING, IT WOULD MAKE SENSE.
WHAT ABOUT A SUIT?
EEEEEE!!!!
?
PARENT-CHILD MATCHING SUITS COULD BE A THING.
WHOAAA!!
KARI (SCRIB)
KARI
KARI
HFF.
HFF.
A SUIT SOUNDS AMAZING!
PUTTING THAT ALL TOGETHER, DOES THIS SEEM RIGHT...?
KARI
KARI
KARI
KARI
KARI
KARI
KARI

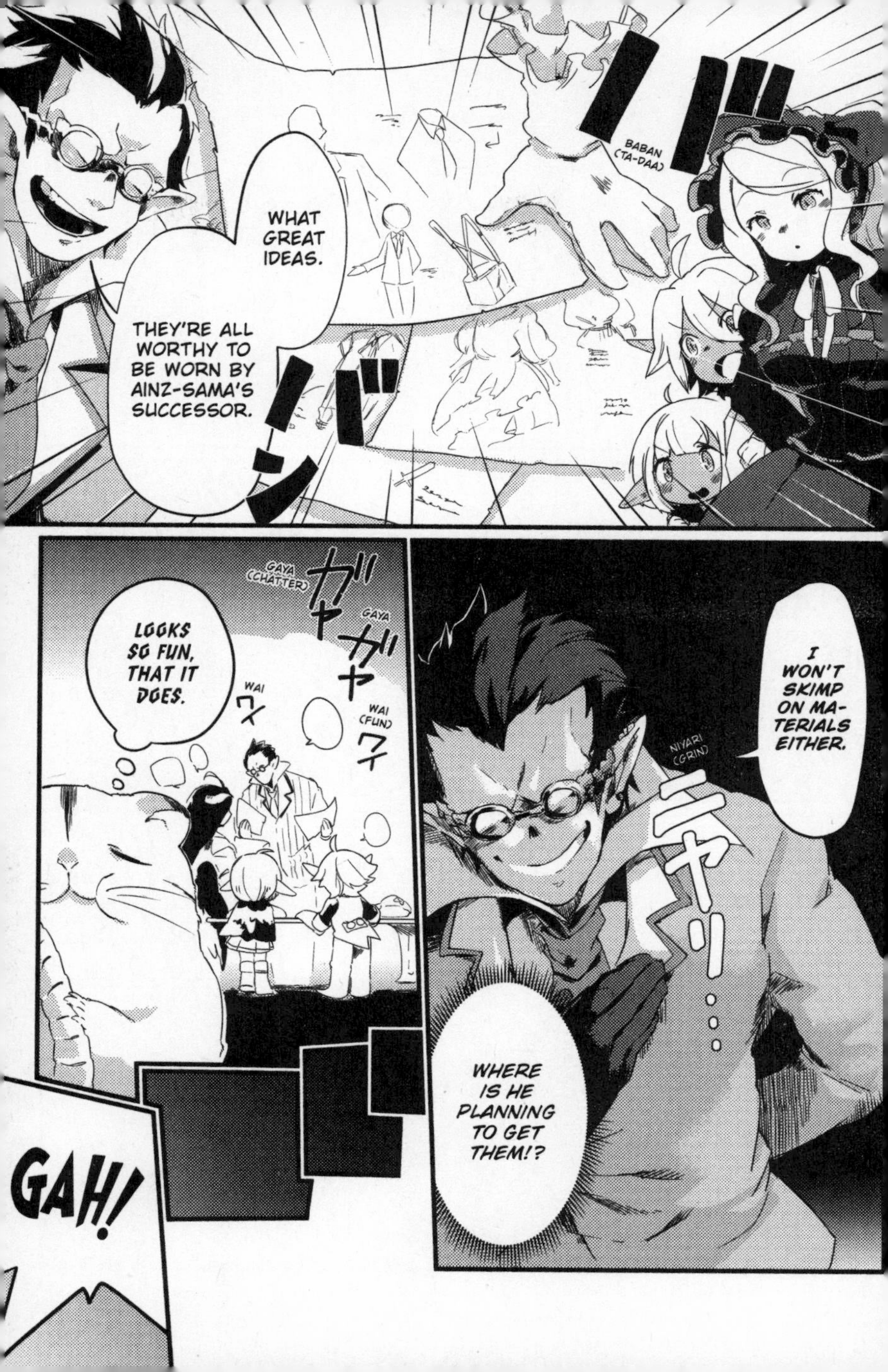
BABAN (TA-DAA)
WHAT GREAT IDEAS.
THEY'RE ALL WORTHY TO BE WORN BY AINZ-SAMA'S SUCCESSOR.
I WON'T SKIMP ON MATERIALS EITHER.
NIYARI (GRIN)
ニヤリ…
WHERE IS HE PLANNING TO GET THEM!?
GAYA (CHATTER)
ガヤ
GAYA
ガヤ
LOOKS SO FUN, THAT IT DOES.
WAI
ワイ
WAI (FUN)
ワイ
GAH!

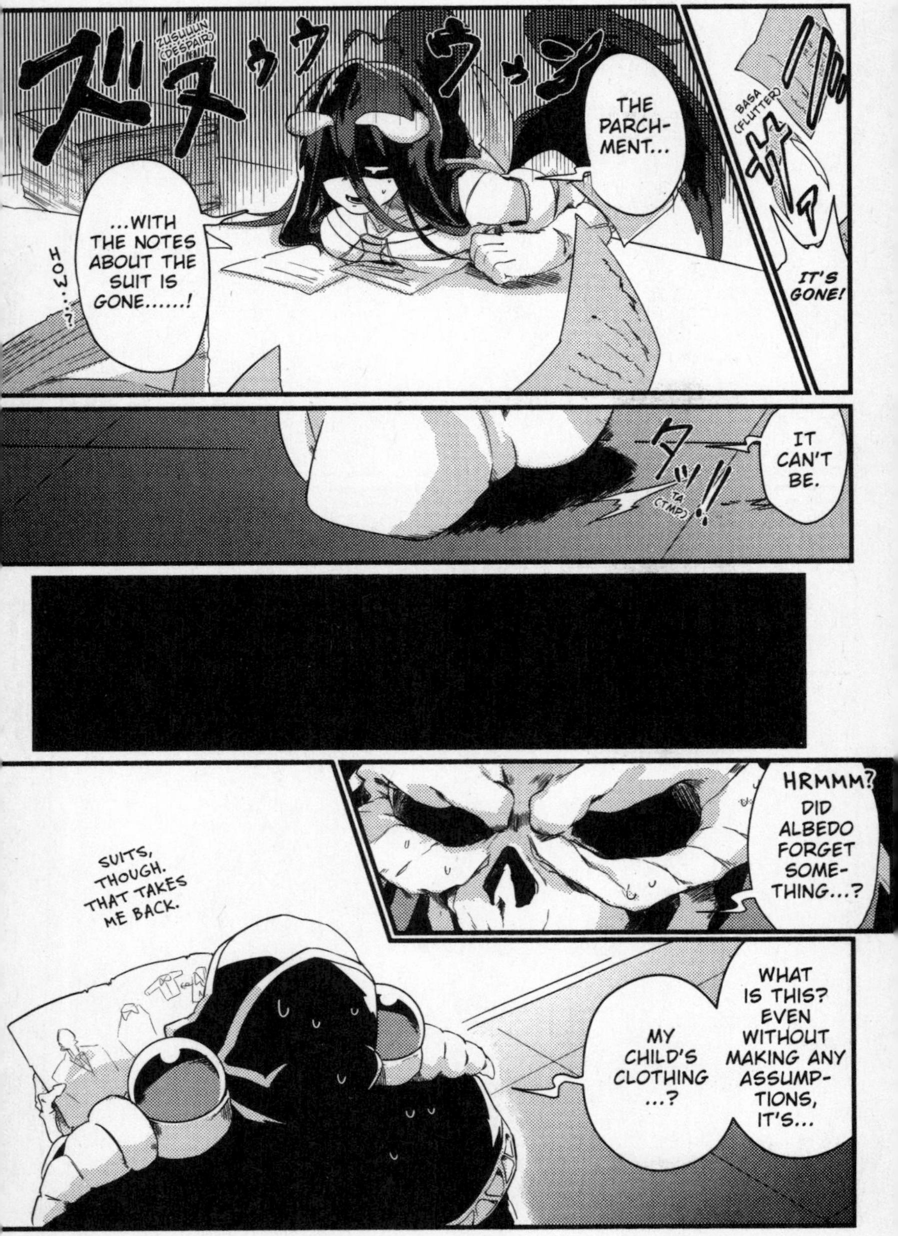
BASA (FLUTTER)
IT'S GONE!
ZUSUUUN (DESPAIR)
THE PARCHMENT...
...WITH THE NOTES ABOUT THE SUIT IS GONE......!
HOW...?
IT CAN'T BE.
TA (TMP)
HRMMM? DID ALBEDO FORGET SOMETHING...?
SUITS, THOUGH. THAT TAKES ME BACK.
WHAT IS THIS? EVEN WITHOUT MAKING ANY ASSUMPTIONS, IT'S...
MY CHILD'S CLOTHING ...?

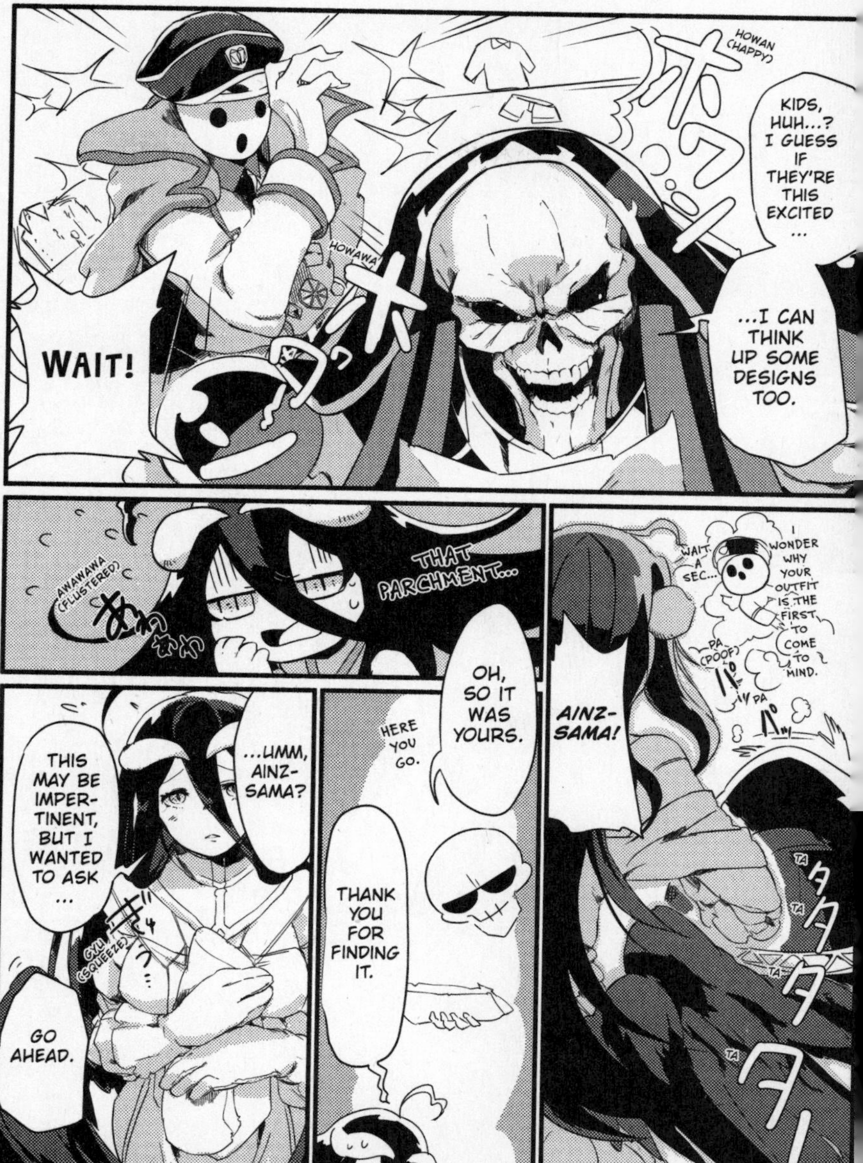
HOWAN (HAPPY)
KIDS, HUH...? I GUESS IF THEY'RE THIS EXCITED ...
...I CAN THINK UP SOME DESIGNS TOO.
HOWAWA
WAIT!
I WONDER WHY YOUR OUTFIT IS THE FIRST TO COME TO MIND.
WAIT. A SEC...
PA (POOF)
PA
AINZ-SAMA!
TA
TA
TA
TA
THAT PARCHMENT...
AWAWAWA (FLUSTERED)
OH, SO IT WAS YOURS.
HERE YOU GO.
THANK YOU FOR FINDING IT.
...UMM, AINZ-SAMA?
THIS MAY BE IMPERTINENT, BUT I WANTED TO ASK ...
GYU (SQUEEZE)
GO AHEAD.

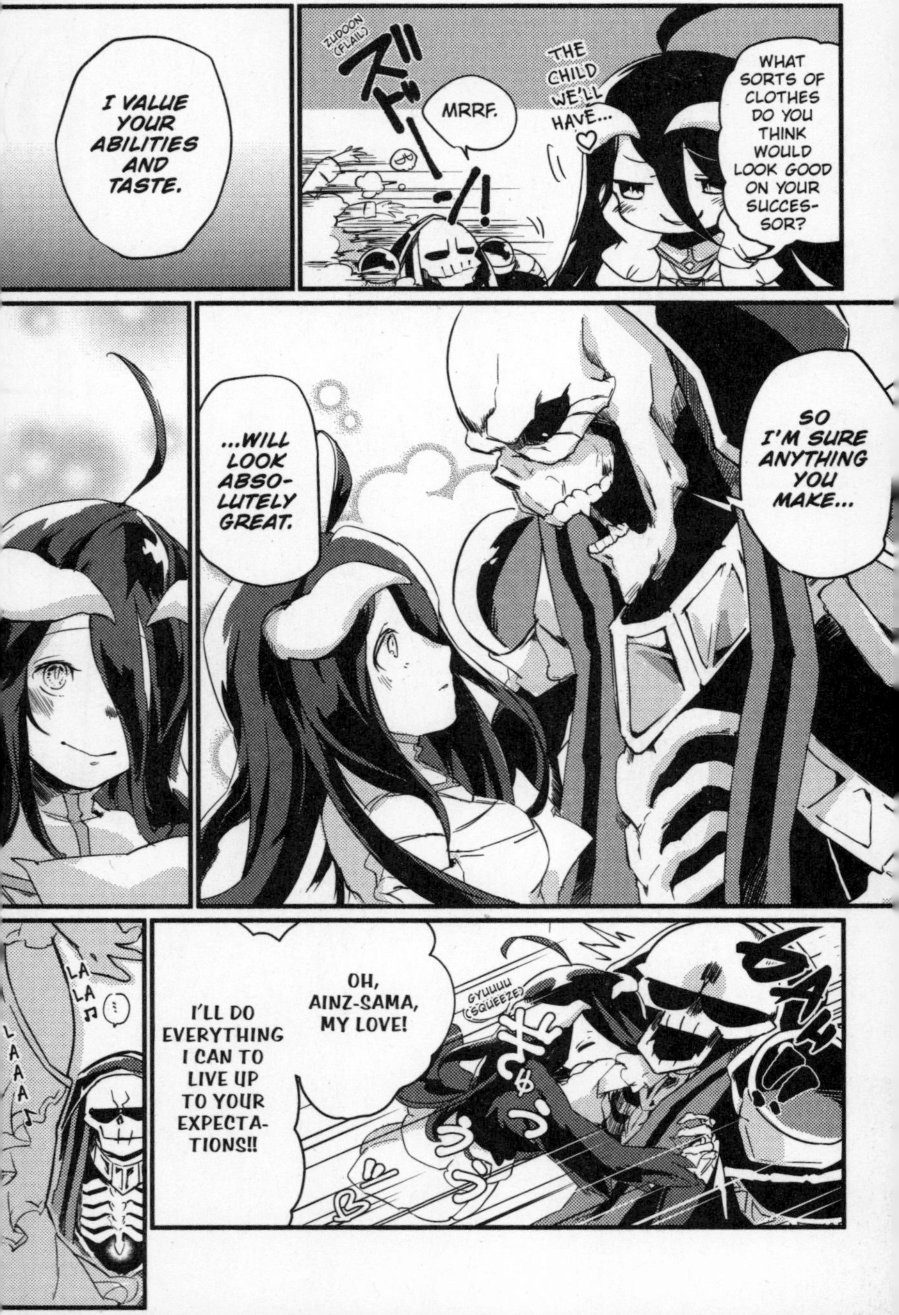
WHAT SORTS OF CLOTHES DO YOU THINK WOULD LOOK GOOD ON YOUR SUCCES-SOR?
THE CHILD WE'LL HAVE... ♡
MRRF.
ZUDOON (FLAIL)
I VALUE YOUR ABILITIES AND TASTE.
SO I'M SURE ANYTHING YOU MAKE...
...WILL LOOK ABSO-LUTELY GREAT.
OH, AINZ-SAMA, MY LOVE!
GYUUUU (SQUEEZE)
I'LL DO EVERYTHING I CAN TO LIVE UP TO YOUR EXPECTA-TIONS!!
LA LA ♫
LAAAA ♪

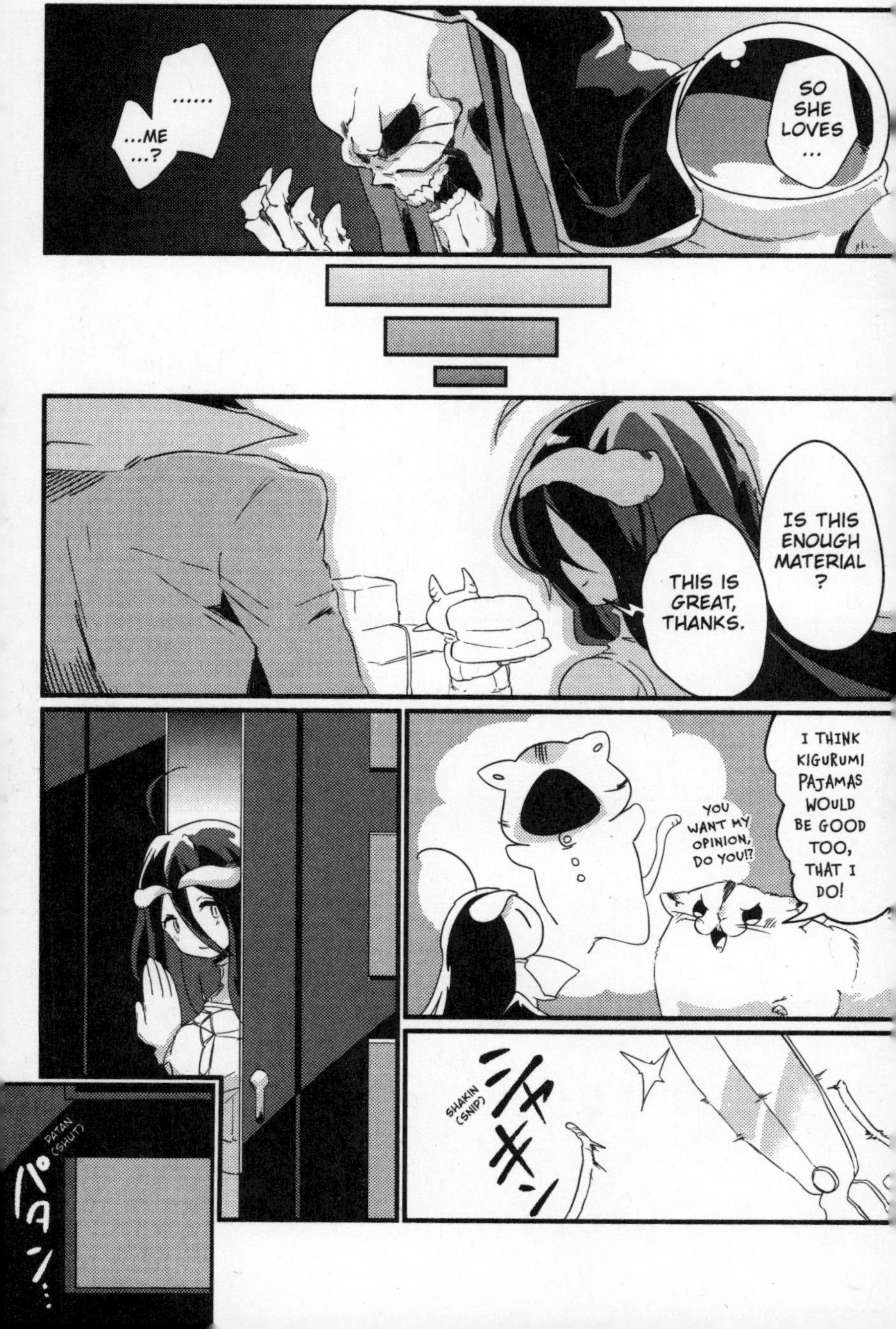
SO SHE LOVES ...
....ME ...?
IS THIS ENOUGH MATERIAL ?
THIS IS GREAT, THANKS.
I THINK KIGURUMI PAJAMAS WOULD BE GOOD TOO, THAT I DO!
YOU WANT MY OPINION, DO YOU!?
シャキン
SHAKIN (SNIP)
パタン…
PATAN (SHUT)

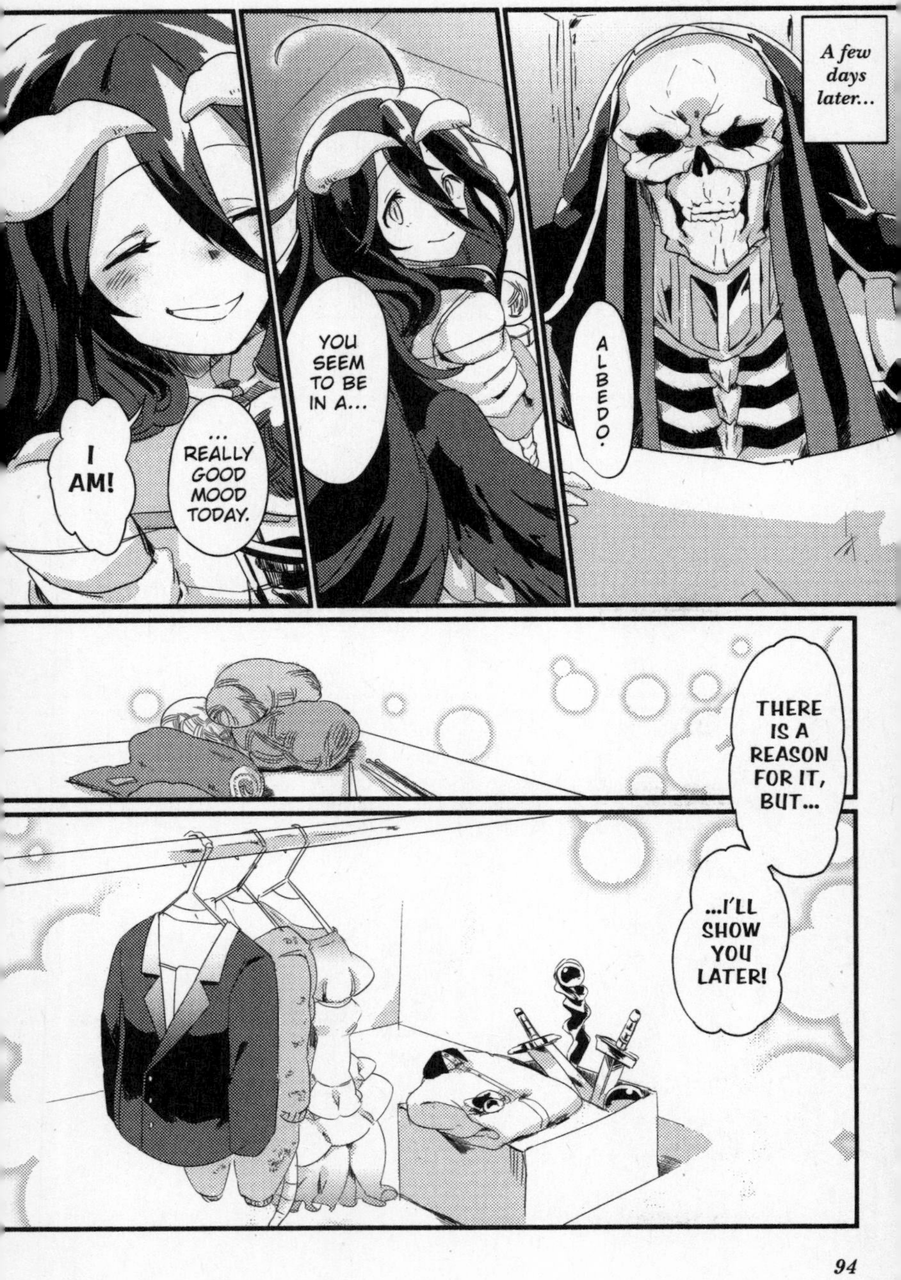
A few days later...
ALBEDO.
YOU SEEM TO BE IN A...
...REALLY GOOD MOOD TODAY.
I AM!
THERE IS A REASON FOR IT, BUT...
...I'LL SHOW YOU LATER!

OVERLORD

À LA CARTE

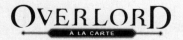

OVERLORD
À LA CARTE

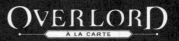

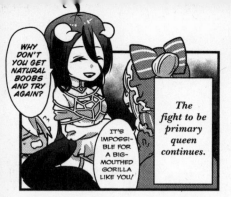

MASTER'S FIRST TIME

KUKO OKANO

The fight to be primary queen continues.
IT'S IMPOSSIBLE FOR A BIG-MOUTHED GORILLA LIKE YOU!
WHY DON'T YOU GET NATURAL BOOBS AND TRY AGAIN?
AH♡, AINZ-SA...
HAVE YOU THOUGHT ABOUT A SUCCESSOR, AINZ-SAMA?
HUH? UH, ER... WELL, DOWN THE LINE, I'M SURE...
A SUCCESSOR...?
THAT IS SOMETHING TO LOOK FORWARD TO.
BUT I DON'T KNOW HOW TO MAKE ONE...
AND I'M A BLANK DOWN THERE...

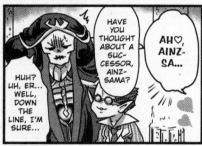

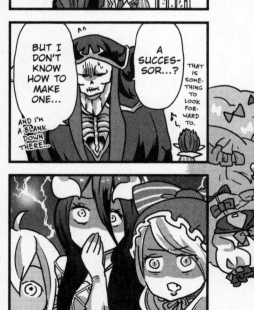

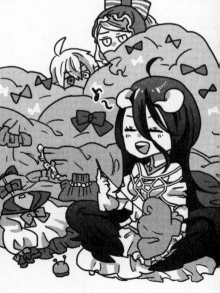

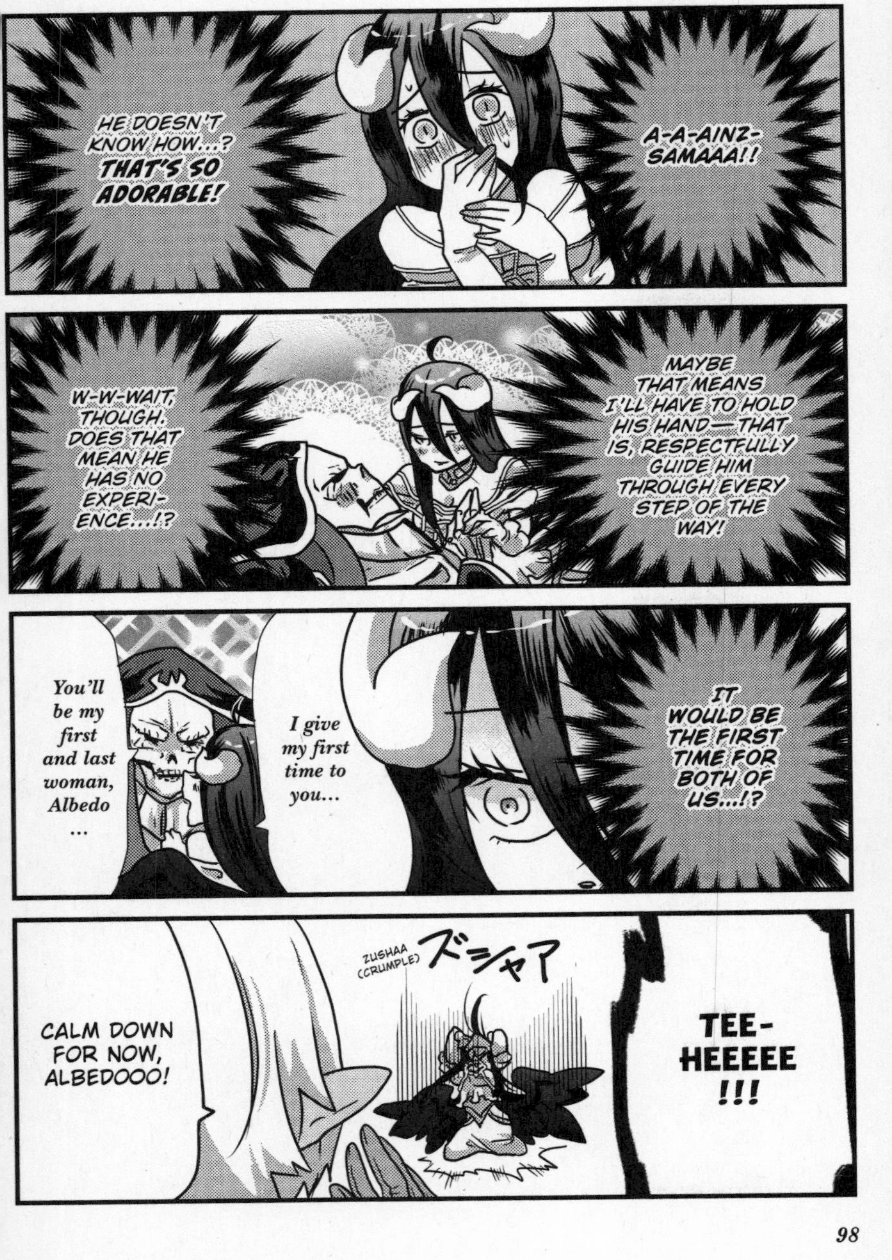
A-A-AINZ-SAMAAA!!
HE DOESN'T KNOW HOW...? **THAT'S SO ADORABLE!**
MAYBE THAT MEANS I'LL HAVE TO HOLD HIS HAND—THAT IS, RESPECTFULLY GUIDE HIM THROUGH EVERY STEP OF THE WAY!
W-W-WAIT, THOUGH. DOES THAT MEAN HE HAS NO EXPERIENCE...!?
IT WOULD BE THE FIRST TIME FOR BOTH OF US...!?
I give my first time to you...
You'll be my first and last woman, Albedo...
TEE-HEEEEE!!!
ズシャア
ZUSHAA (CRUMPLE)
CALM DOWN FOR NOW, ALBEDOOO!

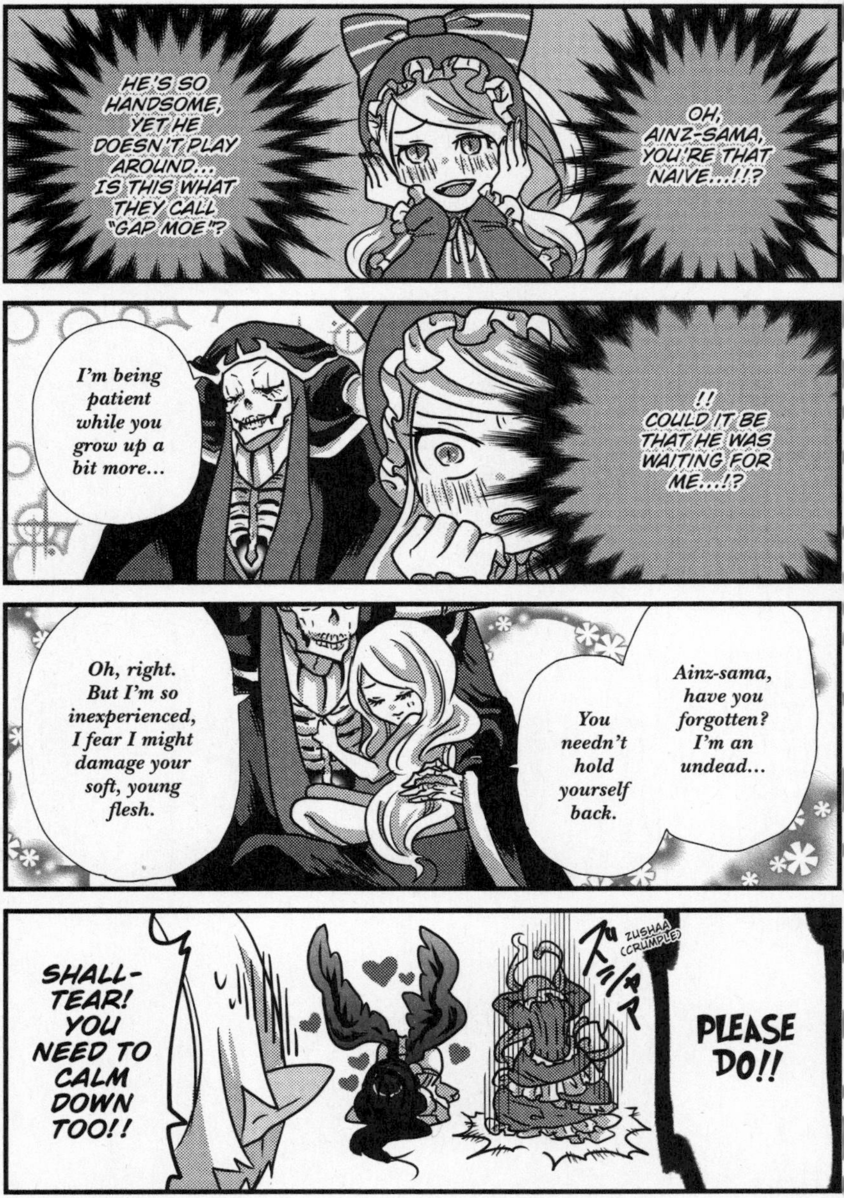
OH, AINZ-SAMA, YOU'RE THAT NAIVE...!!?
HE'S SO HANDSOME, YET HE DOESN'T PLAY AROUND... IS THIS WHAT THEY CALL "GAP MOE"?
!! COULD IT BE THAT HE WAS WAITING FOR ME...!?
I'm being patient while you grow up a bit more...
Ainz-sama, have you forgotten? I'm an undead...
You needn't hold yourself back.
Oh, right. But I'm so inexperienced, I fear I might damage your soft, young flesh.
PLEASE DO!!
ZUSHAA (CRUMPLED)
SHALL-TEAR! YOU NEED TO CALM DOWN TOO!!

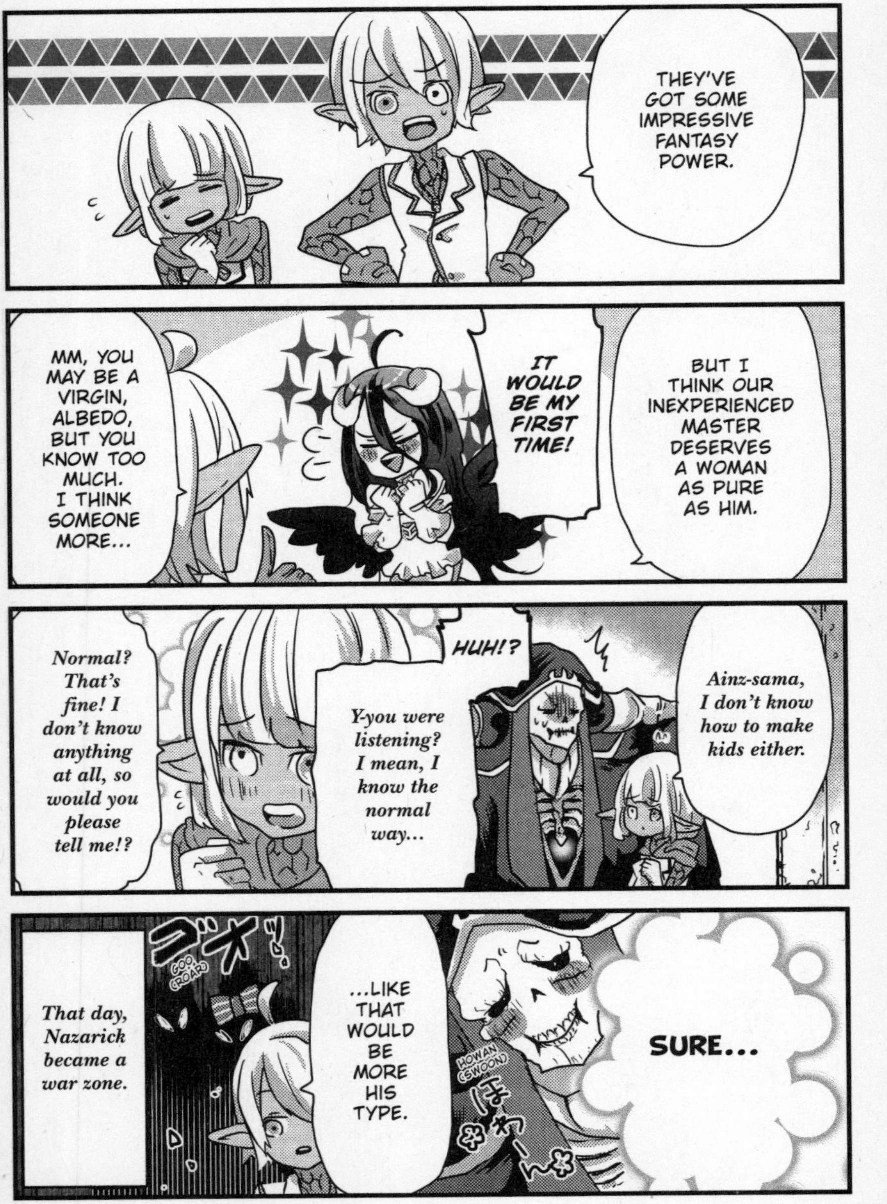

THEY'VE GOT SOME IMPRESSIVE FANTASY POWER.
BUT I THINK OUR INEXPERIENCED MASTER DESERVES A WOMAN AS PURE AS HIM.
IT WOULD BE MY FIRST TIME!
MM, YOU MAY BE A VIRGIN, ALBEDO, BUT YOU KNOW TOO MUCH. I THINK SOMEONE MORE...
Ainz-sama, I don't know how to make kids either.
HUH!?
Y-you were listening? I mean, I know the normal way...
Normal? That's fine! I don't know anything at all, so would you please tell me!?
SURE...
HOWAN (SWOON)
...LIKE THAT WOULD BE MORE HIS TYPE.
GOO (ROAR)
That day, Nazarick became a war zone.

ME AND MASTER'S BABY

KUKO OKANO

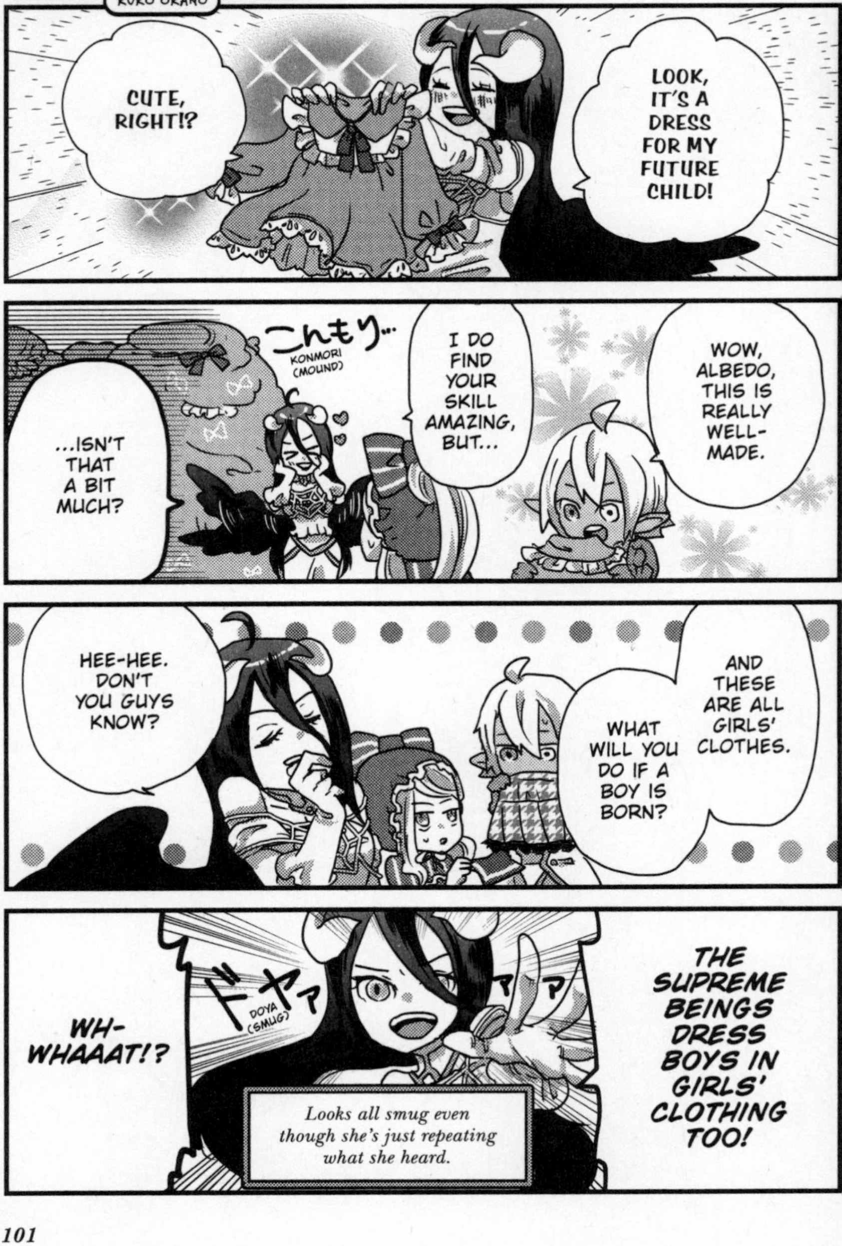
LOOK, IT'S A DRESS FOR MY FUTURE CHILD!
CUTE, RIGHT!?
WOW, ALBEDO, THIS IS REALLY WELL-MADE.
I DO FIND YOUR SKILL AMAZING, BUT...
こんもり…
KONMORI (MOUND)
...ISN'T THAT A BIT MUCH?
AND THESE ARE ALL GIRLS' CLOTHES.
WHAT WILL YOU DO IF A BOY IS BORN?
HEE-HEE. DON'T YOU GUYS KNOW?
THE SUPREME BEINGS DRESS BOYS IN GIRLS' CLOTHING TOO!
ドヤァ
DOYA (SMUG)
WH-WHAAAT!?
Looks all smug even though she's just repeating what she heard.

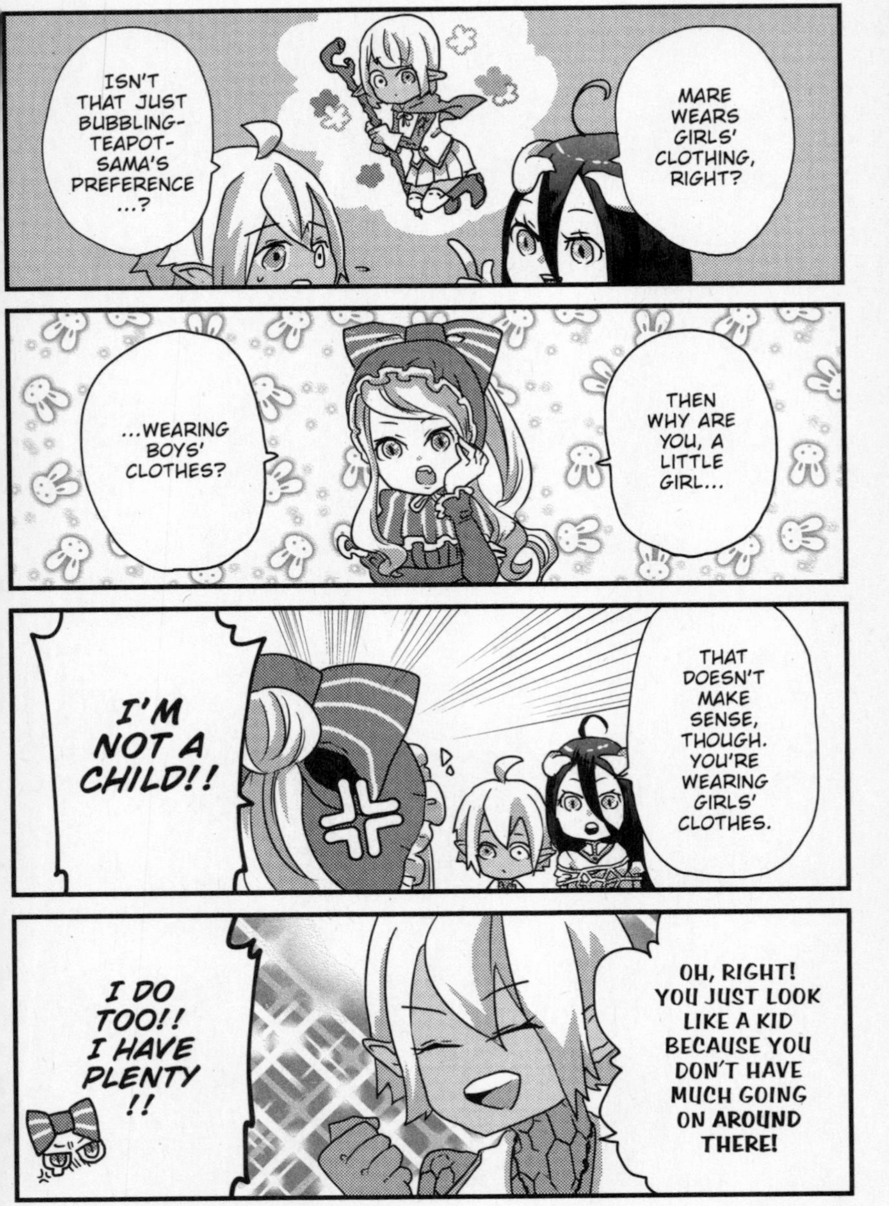
MARE WEARS GIRLS' CLOTHING, RIGHT?
ISN'T THAT JUST BUBBLING-TEAPOT-SAMA'S PREFERENCE ...?
THEN WHY ARE YOU, A LITTLE GIRL...
...WEARING BOYS' CLOTHES?
THAT DOESN'T MAKE SENSE, THOUGH. YOU'RE WEARING GIRLS' CLOTHES.
I'M NOT A CHILD!!
OH, RIGHT! YOU JUST LOOK LIKE A KID BECAUSE YOU DON'T HAVE MUCH GOING ON AROUND THERE!
I DO TOO!! I HAVE PLENTY !!

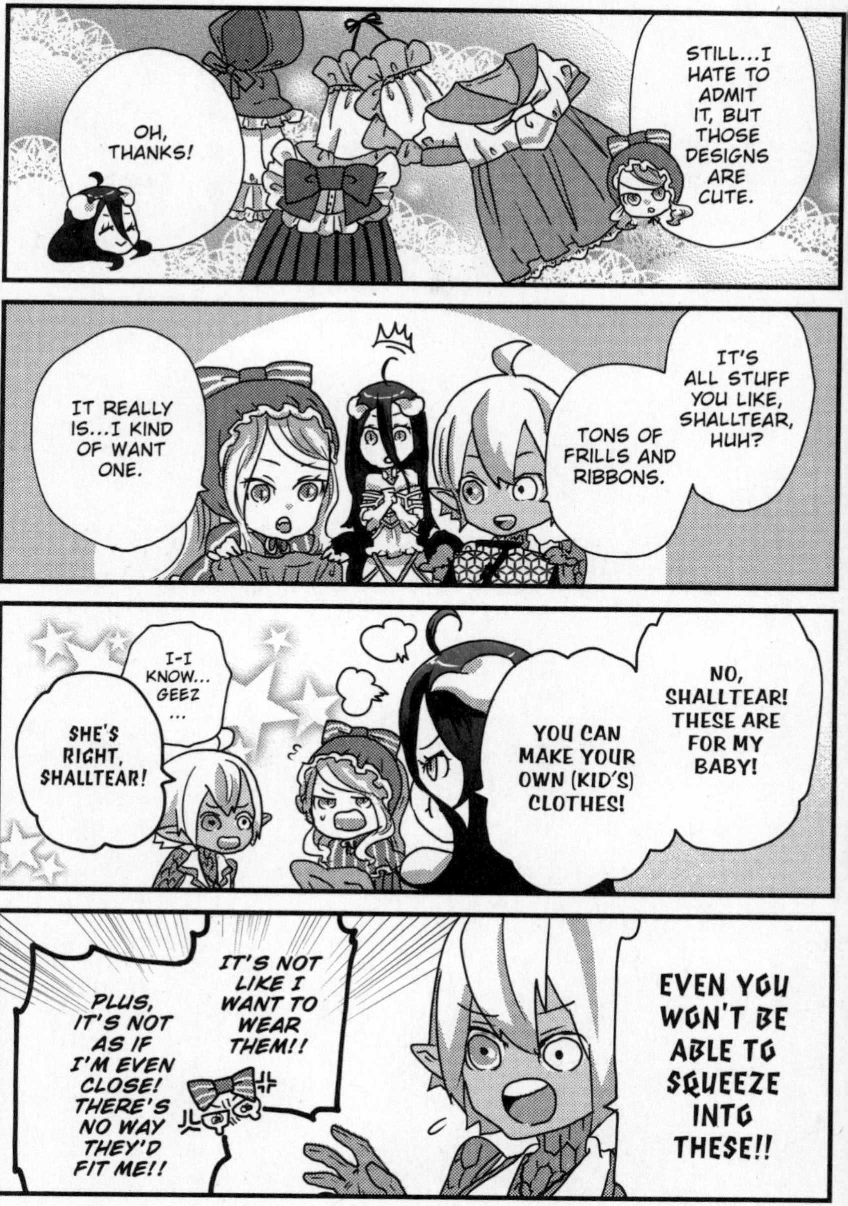
STILL...I HATE TO ADMIT IT, BUT THOSE DESIGNS ARE CUTE.
OH, THANKS!
IT'S ALL STUFF YOU LIKE, SHALLTEAR, HUH?
TONS OF FRILLS AND RIBBONS.
IT REALLY IS...I KIND OF WANT ONE.
NO, SHALLTEAR! THESE ARE FOR MY BABY!
YOU CAN MAKE YOUR OWN (KID'S) CLOTHES!
I-I KNOW... GEEZ...
SHE'S RIGHT, SHALLTEAR!
EVEN YOU WON'T BE ABLE TO SQUEEZE INTO THESE!!
IT'S NOT LIKE I WANT TO WEAR THEM!!
PLUS, IT'S NOT AS IF I'M EVEN CLOSE! THERE'S NO WAY THEY'D FIT ME!!

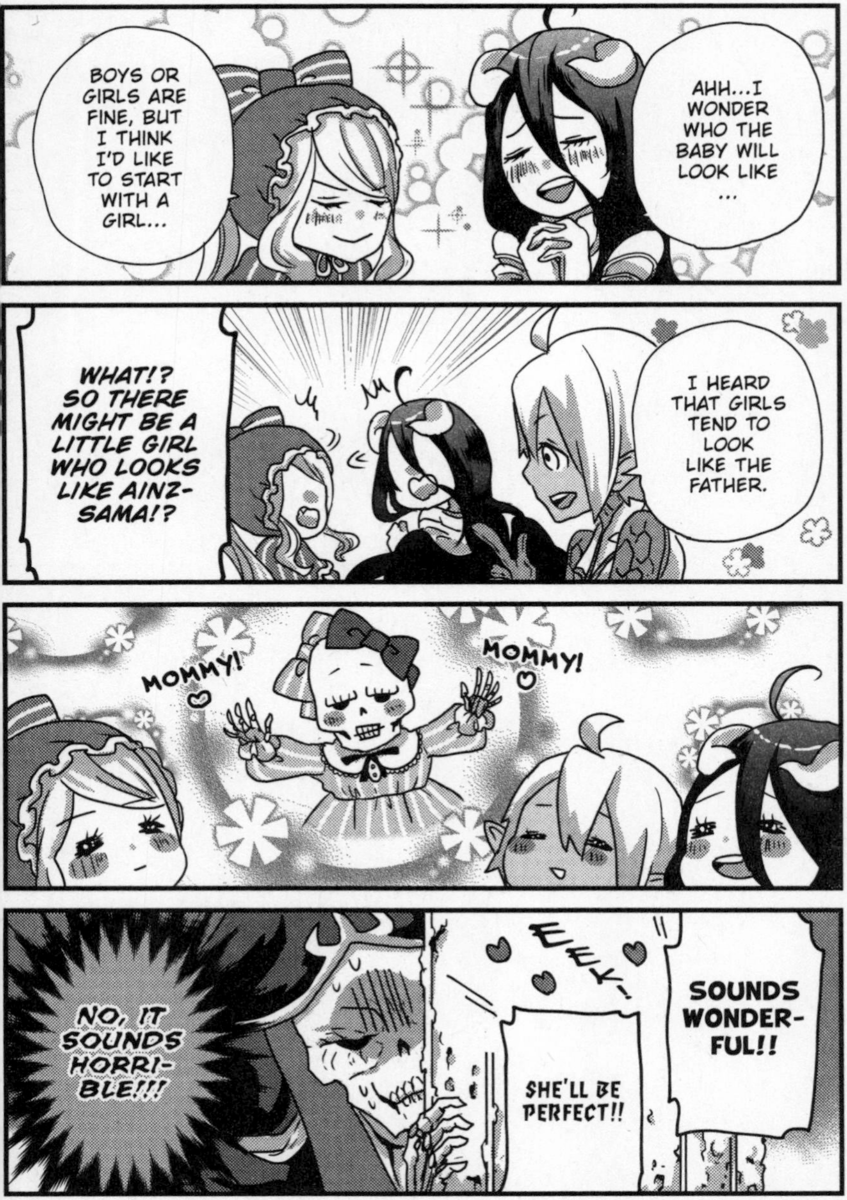
AHH...I WONDER WHO THE BABY WILL LOOK LIKE ...
BOYS OR GIRLS ARE FINE, BUT I THINK I'D LIKE TO START WITH A GIRL...
I HEARD THAT GIRLS TEND TO LOOK LIKE THE FATHER.
WHAT!? SO THERE MIGHT BE A LITTLE GIRL WHO LOOKS LIKE AINZ-SAMA!?
MOMMY!
MOMMY!
SOUNDS WONDERFUL!!
EEEK!
SHE'LL BE PERFECT!!
NO, IT SOUNDS HORRIBLE!!!

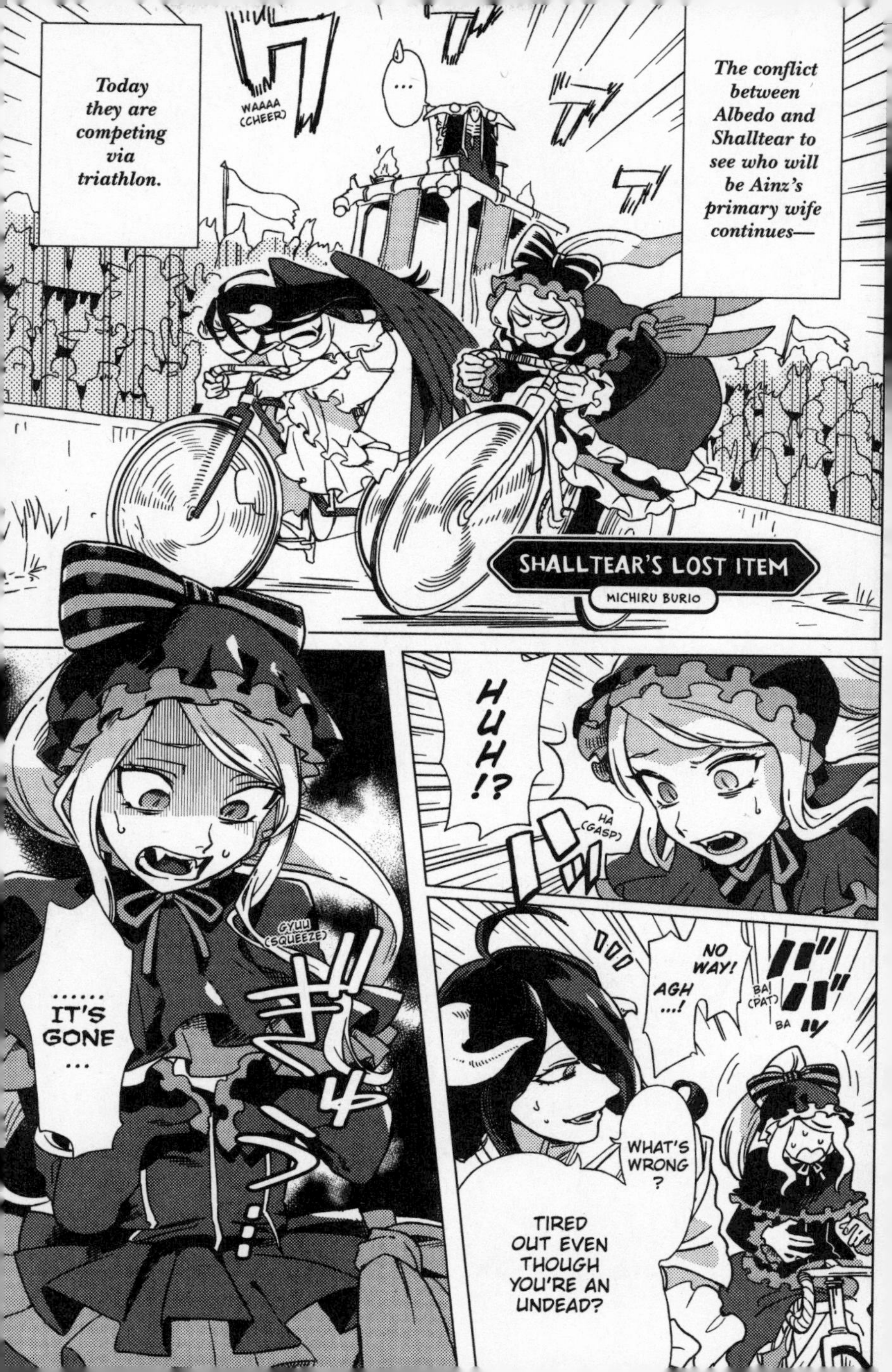
The conflict between Albedo and Shalltear to see who will be Ainz's primary wife continues—
...
WAAAA (CHEER)
Today they are competing via triathlon.
SHALLTEAR'S LOST ITEM
MICHIRU BURIO
HUH!?
HA (GASP)
NO WAY!
AGH ...!
BA (PAT)
BA
WHAT'S WRONG?
TIRED OUT EVEN THOUGH YOU'RE AN UNDEAD?
GYUU (SQUEEZE)
...... IT'S GONE ...

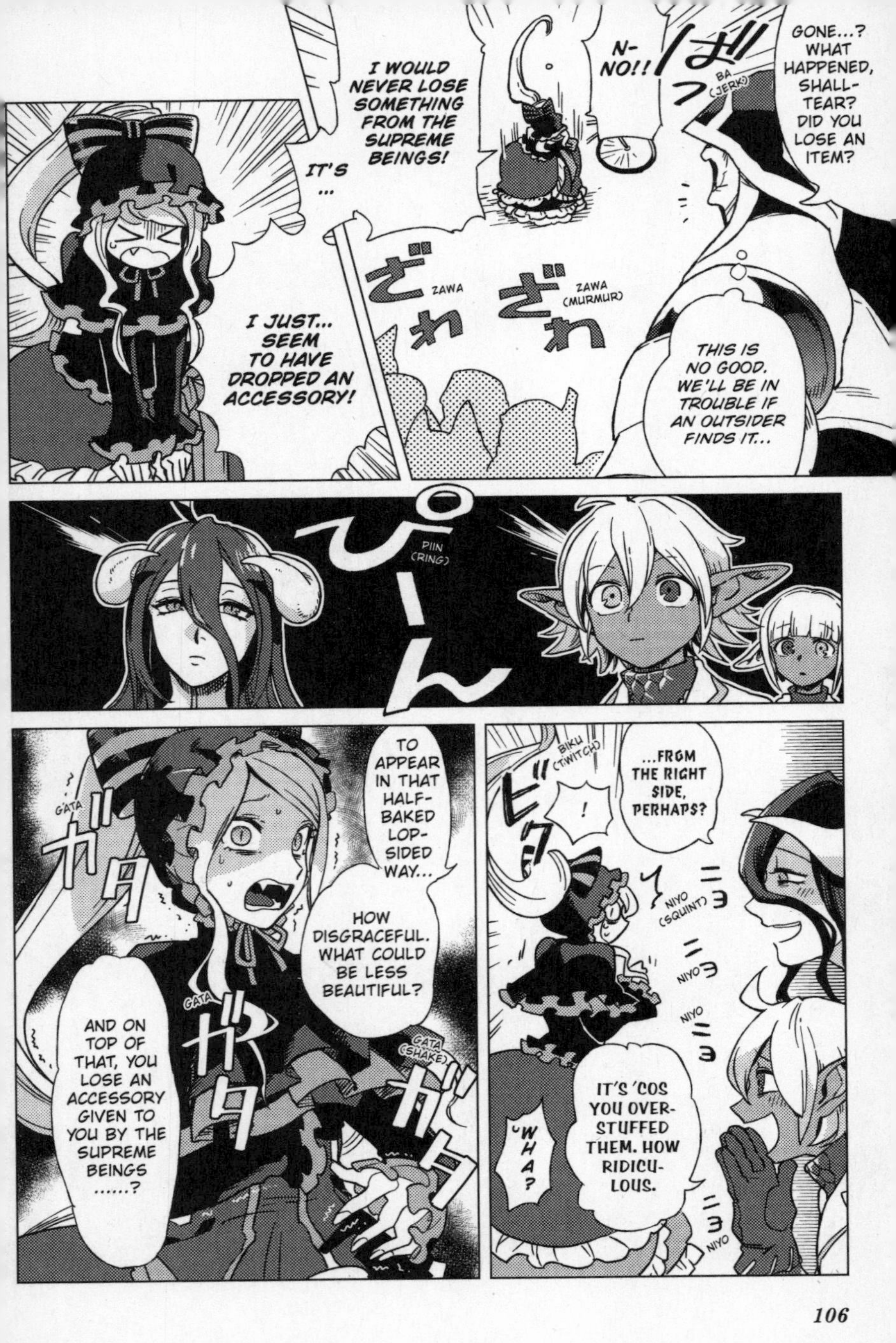
GONE...? WHAT HAPPENED, SHALLTEAR? DID YOU LOSE AN ITEM?
BA (JERK)
N-NO!!
I WOULD NEVER LOSE SOMETHING FROM THE SUPREME BEINGS!
IT'S ...
ZAWA (MURMUR)
ZAWA
THIS IS NO GOOD. WE'LL BE IN TROUBLE IF AN OUTSIDER FINDS IT...
I JUST... SEEM TO HAVE DROPPED AN ACCESSORY!
PIIN (RING)
...FROM THE RIGHT SIDE, PERHAPS?
BIKU (TWITCH)
!
NIYO (SQUINT)
NIYO
NIYO
IT'S 'COS YOU OVERSTUFFED THEM. HOW RIDICULOUS.
WHA?
NIYO
TO APPEAR IN THAT HALF-BAKED LOPSIDED WAY...
HOW DISGRACEFUL. WHAT COULD BE LESS BEAUTIFUL?
GATA
GATA
GATA (SHAKE)
AND ON TOP OF THAT, YOU LOSE AN ACCESSORY GIVEN TO YOU BY THE SUPREME BEINGS ......?

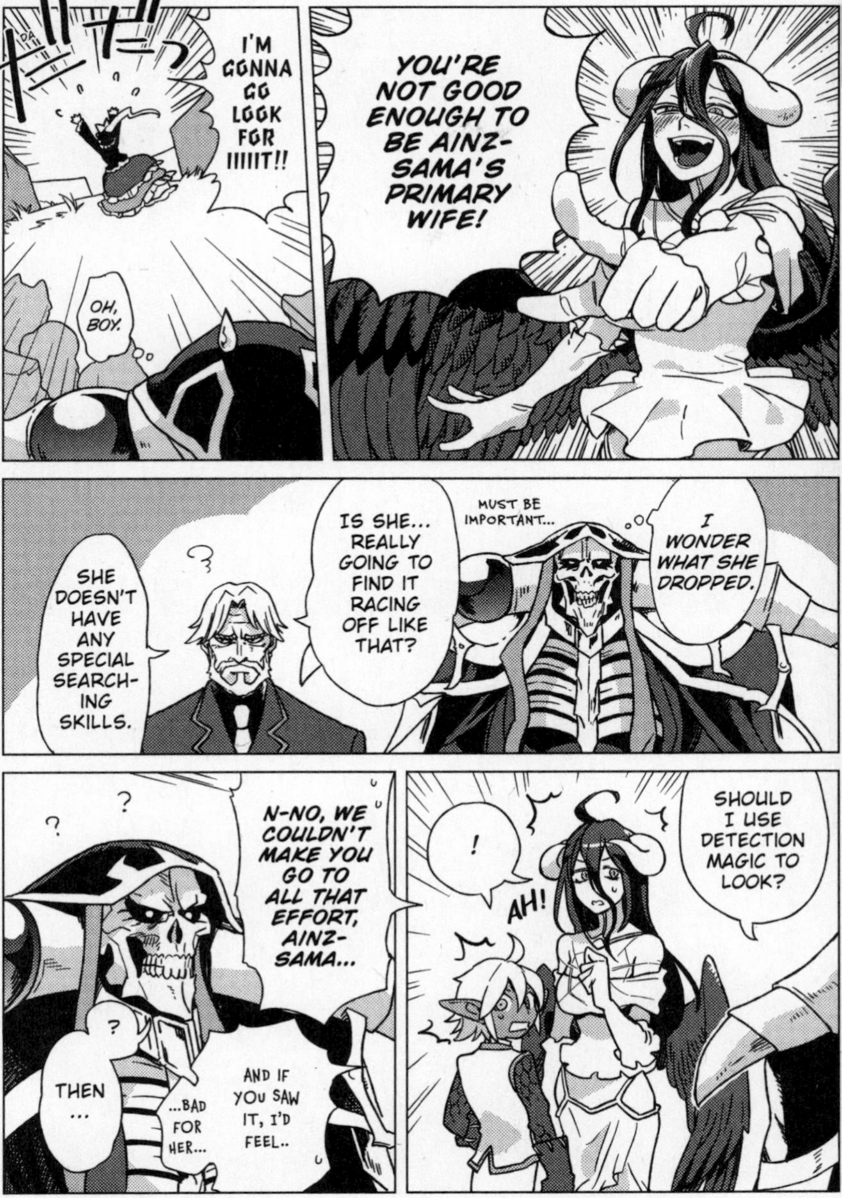
YOU'RE NOT GOOD ENOUGH TO BE AINZ-SAMA'S PRIMARY WIFE!
DA (DASH)
DA
I'M GONNA GO LOOK FOR IIIIIIT!!
OH, BOY.
I WONDER WHAT SHE DROPPED.
MUST BE IMPORTANT...
IS SHE... REALLY GOING TO FIND IT RACING OFF LIKE THAT?
SHE DOESN'T HAVE ANY SPECIAL SEARCHING SKILLS.
SHOULD I USE DETECTION MAGIC TO LOOK?
!
AH!
N-NO, WE COULDN'T MAKE YOU GO TO ALL THAT EFFORT, AINZ-SAMA...
AND IF YOU SAW IT, I'D FEEL..
...BAD FOR HER...
?
THEN ...

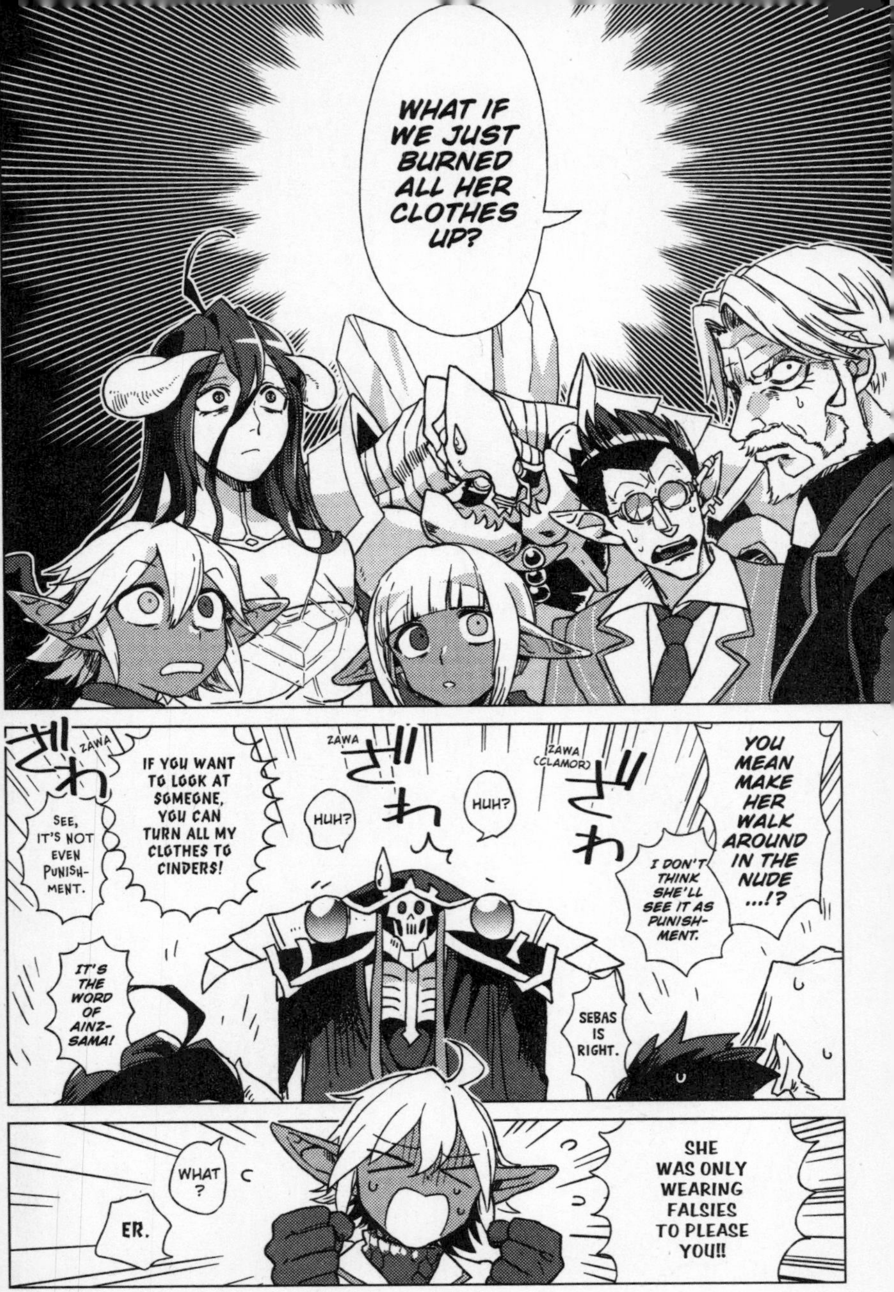
WHAT IF WE JUST BURNED ALL HER CLOTHES UP?
YOU MEAN MAKE HER WALK AROUND IN THE NUDE ...!?
ZAWA (CLAMOR)
I DON'T THINK SHE'LL SEE IT AS PUNISHMENT.
HUH?
ZAWA
HUH?
IF YOU WANT TO LOOK AT SOMEONE, YOU CAN TURN ALL MY CLOTHES TO CINDERS!
ZAWA
SEE, IT'S NOT EVEN PUNISHMENT.
SEBAS IS RIGHT.
IT'S THE WORD OF AINZ-SAMA!
SHE WAS ONLY WEARING FALSIES TO PLEASE YOU!!
WHAT?
ER.

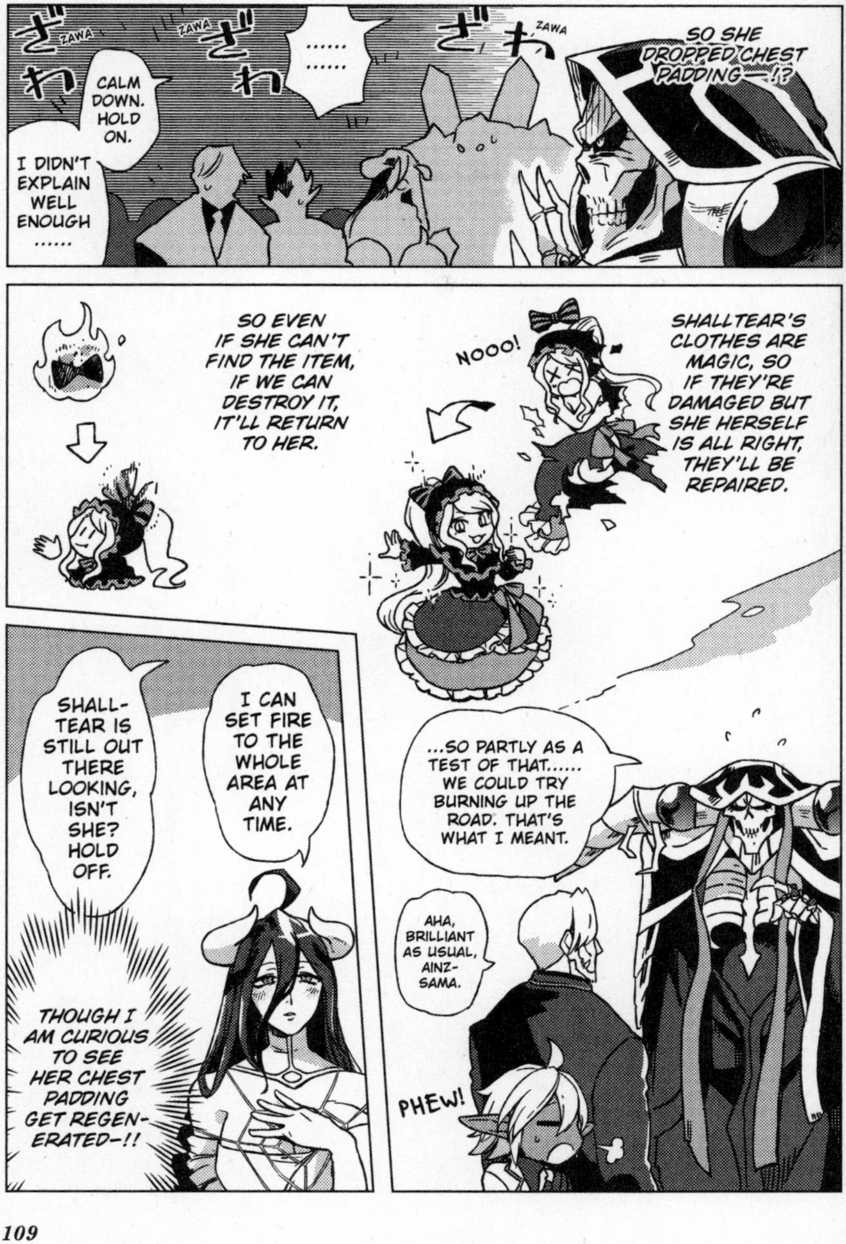
SO SHE DROPPED CHEST PADDING—!?
ZAWA
ざわ
ZAWA
ざわ
......
......
ZAWA
ざわ
CALM DOWN. HOLD ON.
I DIDN'T EXPLAIN WELL ENOUGH......
SHALLTEAR'S CLOTHES ARE MAGIC, SO IF THEY'RE DAMAGED BUT SHE HERSELF IS ALL RIGHT, THEY'LL BE REPAIRED.
NOOO!
SO EVEN IF SHE CAN'T FIND THE ITEM, IF WE CAN DESTROY IT, IT'LL RETURN TO HER.
...SO PARTLY AS A TEST OF THAT...... WE COULD TRY BURNING UP THE ROAD. THAT'S WHAT I MEANT.
AHA, BRILLIANT AS USUAL, AINZ-SAMA.
PHEW!
I CAN SET FIRE TO THE WHOLE AREA AT ANY TIME.
SHALL-TEAR IS STILL OUT THERE LOOKING, ISN'T SHE? HOLD OFF.
THOUGH I AM CURIOUS TO SEE HER CHEST PADDING GET REGENER-ERATED-!!

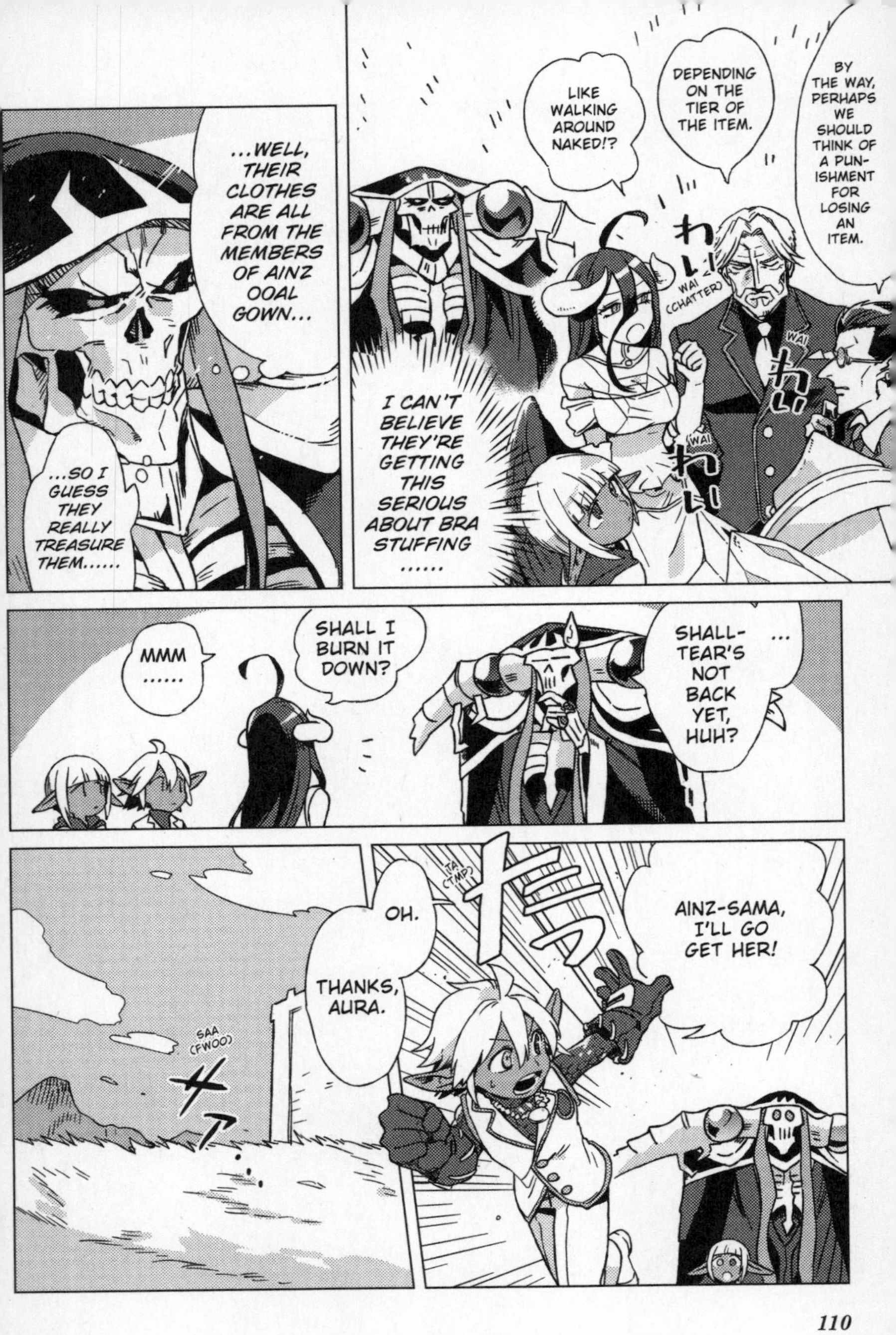

BY THE WAY, PERHAPS WE SHOULD THINK OF A PUNISHMENT FOR LOSING AN ITEM.
DEPENDING ON THE TIER OF THE ITEM.
LIKE WALKING AROUND NAKED!?
WAI (CHATTER)
WAI
WAI
I CAN'T BELIEVE THEY'RE GETTING THIS SERIOUS ABOUT BRA STUFFING ......
...WELL, THEIR CLOTHES ARE ALL FROM THE MEMBERS OF AINZ OOAL GOWN...
...SO I GUESS THEY REALLY TREASURE THEM......
SHALL-TEAR'S NOT BACK YET, HUH? ...
SHALL I BURN IT DOWN?
MMM ......
AINZ-SAMA, I'LL GO GET HER!
TA (TMP)
OH.
THANKS, AURA.
SAA (FWOO)

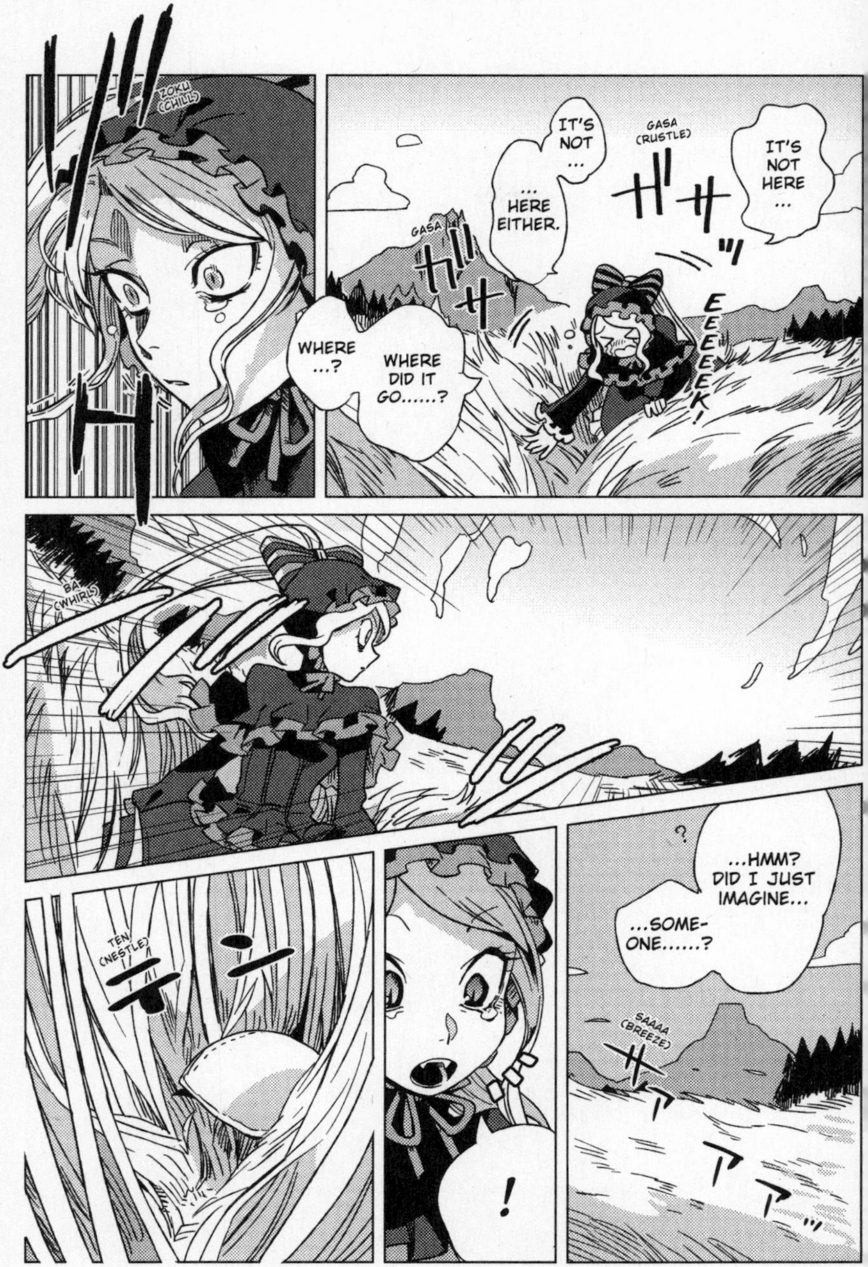
IT'S NOT HERE ...
GASA (RUSTLE)
IT'S NOT ...
... HERE EITHER.
GASA
EEEEEEK!
WHERE ...?
WHERE DID IT GO......?
ZOKU (CHILL)
BA (WHIRL)
...HMM? DID I JUST IMAGINE...
...SOME-ONE......?
SAAAA (BREEZE)
?
!
TEN (NESTLE)

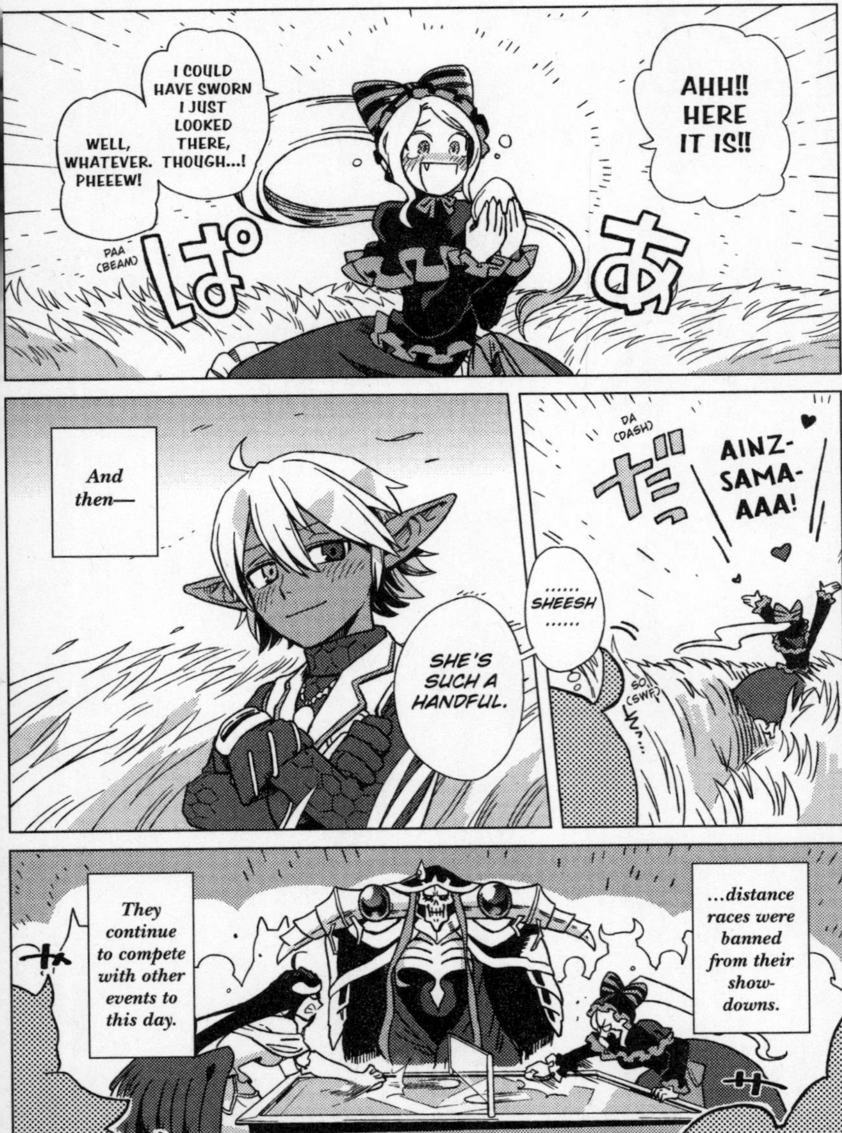
AHH!! HERE IT IS!!
あ
ぱ
PAA (BEAM)
I COULD HAVE SWORN I JUST LOOKED THERE, THOUGH...!
WELL, WHATEVER. PHEEEW!
AINZ-SAMA-AAA!
だっ
DA (DASH)
SO (SWF)
......SHEESH......
And then—
SHE'S SUCH A HANDFUL.
...distance races were banned from their show-downs.
They continue to compete with other events to this day.

OVERLORD
À LA CARTE

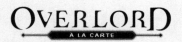

OVERLORD
À LA CARTE

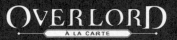

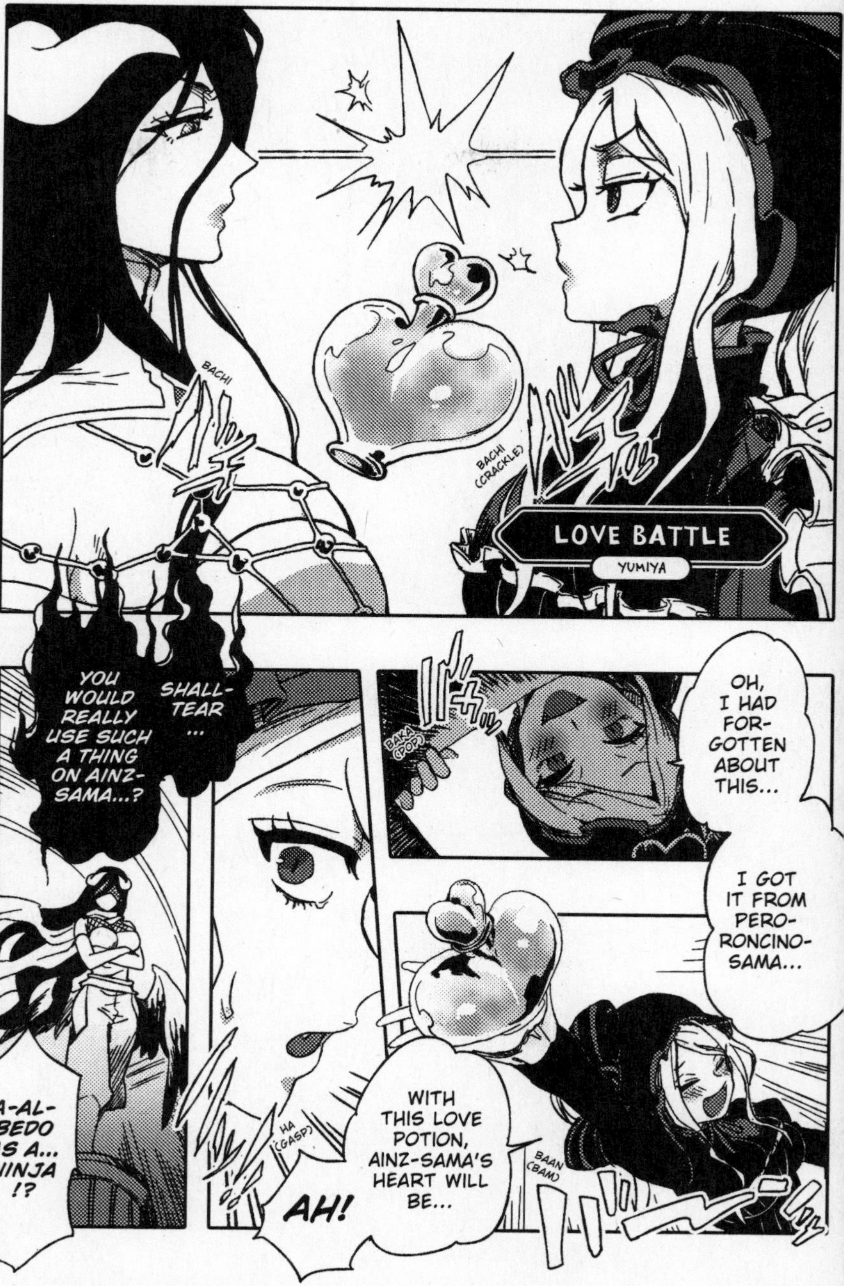
BACHI (CRACKLE)
BACHI
LOVE BATTLE
YUMIYA
BAKA (POP)
OH, I HAD FOR-GOTTEN ABOUT THIS...
I GOT IT FROM PERO-RONCINO-SAMA...
WITH THIS LOVE POTION, AINZ-SAMA'S HEART WILL BE...
BAAN (BAM)
HA (GASP)
AH!
SHALL-TEAR ...
YOU WOULD REALLY USE SUCH A THING ON AINZ-SAMA...?
A-AL-BEDO AS A... NINJA !?

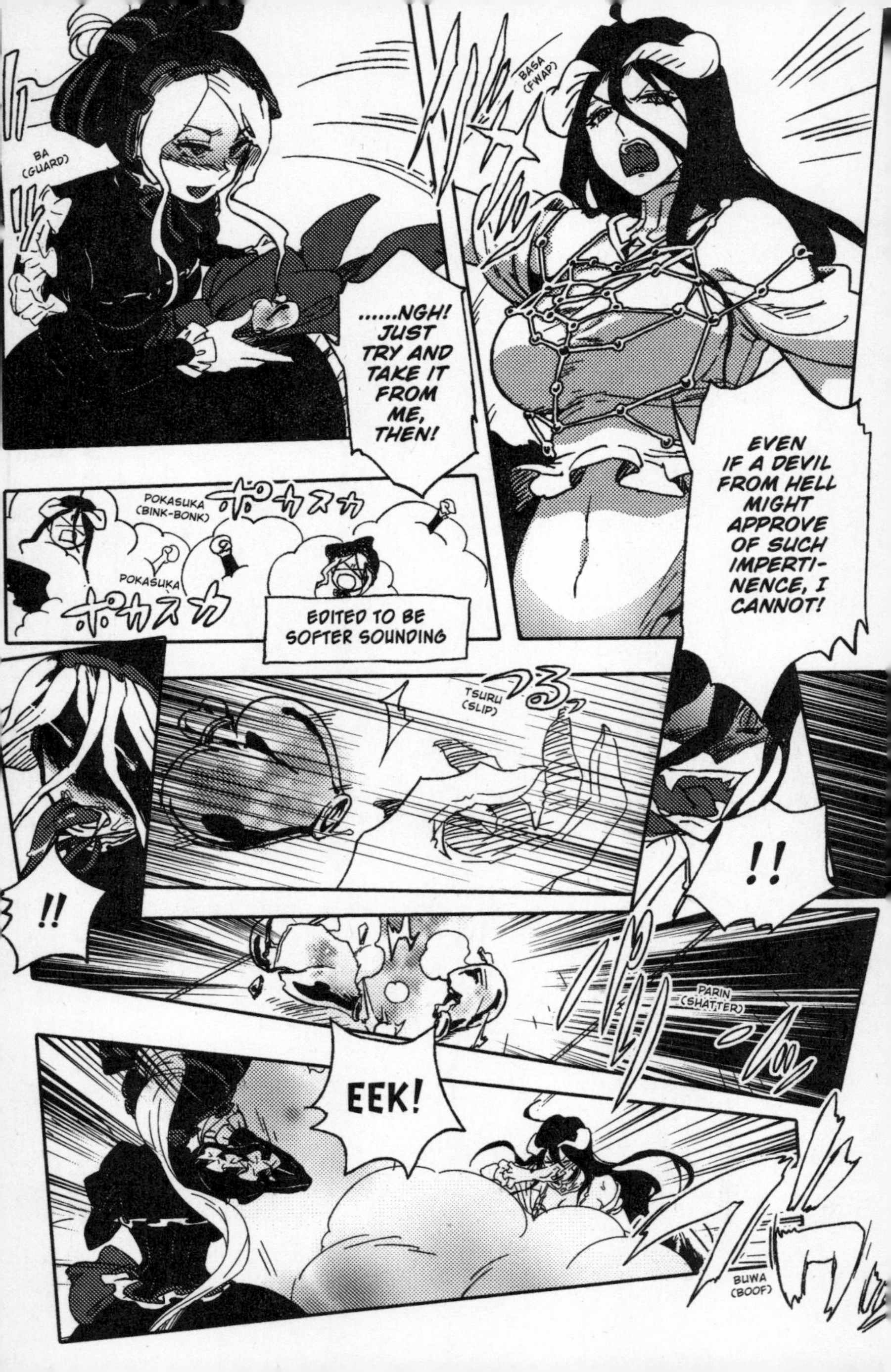
BASA (FWAP)
EVEN IF A DEVIL FROM HELL MIGHT APPROVE OF SUCH IMPERTINENCE, I CANNOT!
BA (GUARD)
......NGH! JUST TRY AND TAKE IT FROM ME, THEN!
POKASUKA (BINK-BONK) ポカスカ
POKASUKA ポカスカ
EDITED TO BE SOFTER SOUNDING
!!
TSURU (SLIP) つるっ
!!
PARIN (SHATTER)
EEK!
BUWA (BOOF)

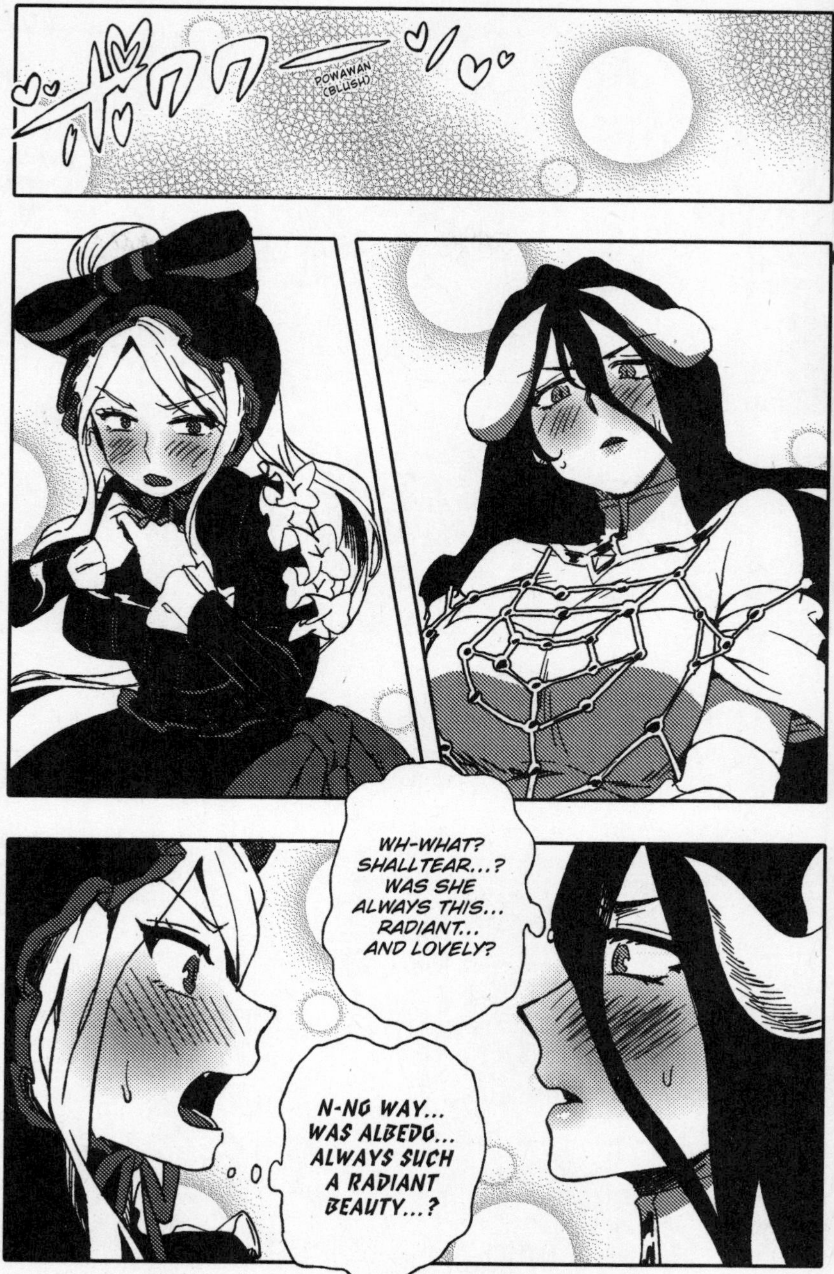
POWAWAN (BLUSH)
WH-WHAT? SHALLTEAR...? WAS SHE ALWAYS THIS... RADIANT... AND LOVELY?
N-NO WAY... WAS ALBEDO... ALWAYS SUCH A RADIANT BEAUTY...?

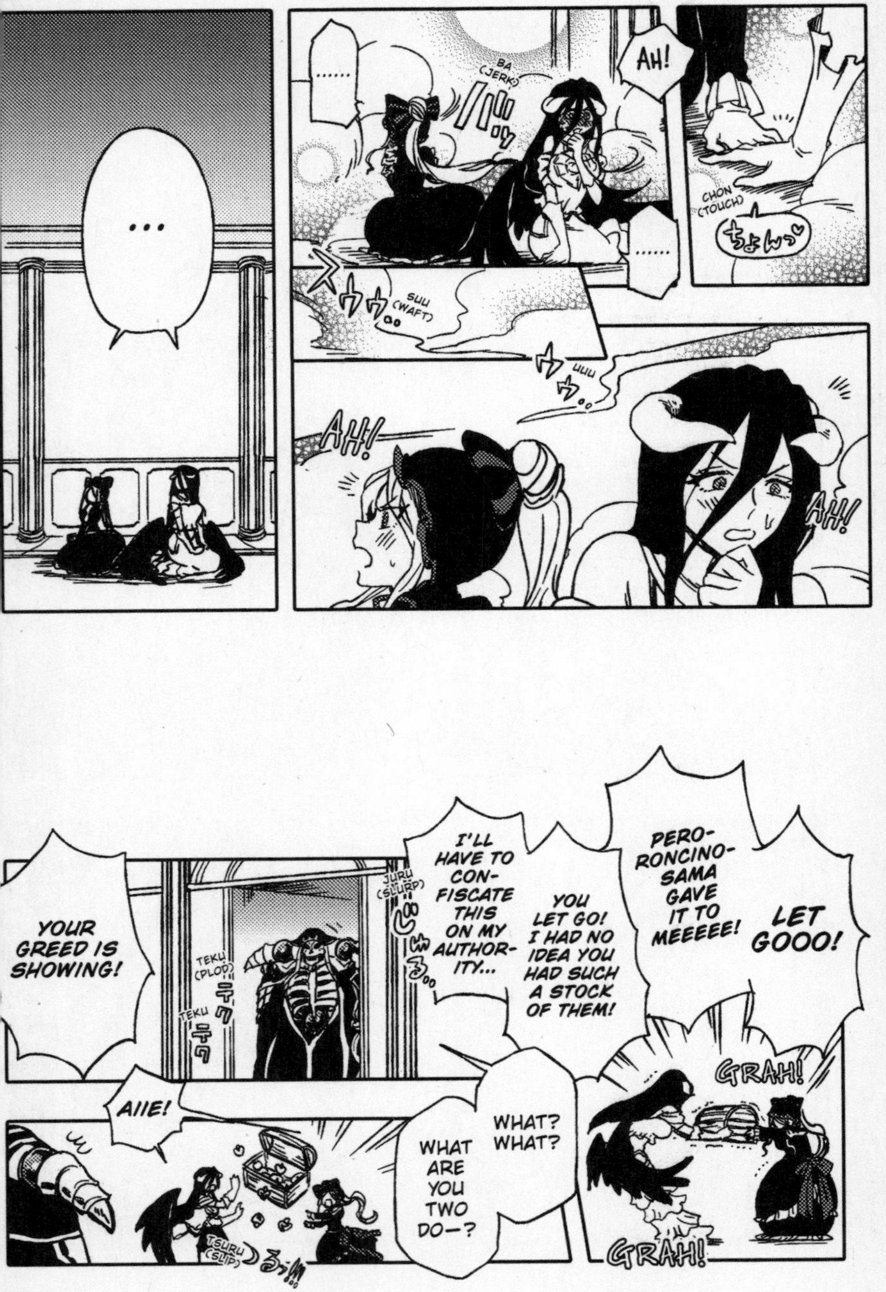
AH!
CHON (TOUCH)
ちょんっ
BA (JERK)
......
......
SUU (WAFT)
UUU
AH!
AH!
...
LET GOOO!
PERO-RONCINO-SAMA GAVE IT TO MEEEEE!
YOU LET GO! I HAD NO IDEA YOU HAD SUCH A STOCK OF THEM!
I'LL HAVE TO CON-FISCATE THIS ON MY AUTHOR-ITY...
GRAH!
GRAH!
JURU (SLURP)
TEKU (PLOD)
TEKU
YOUR GREED IS SHOWING!
WHAT? WHAT?
WHAT ARE YOU TWO DO—?
AIIE!
TSURU (SLIP)

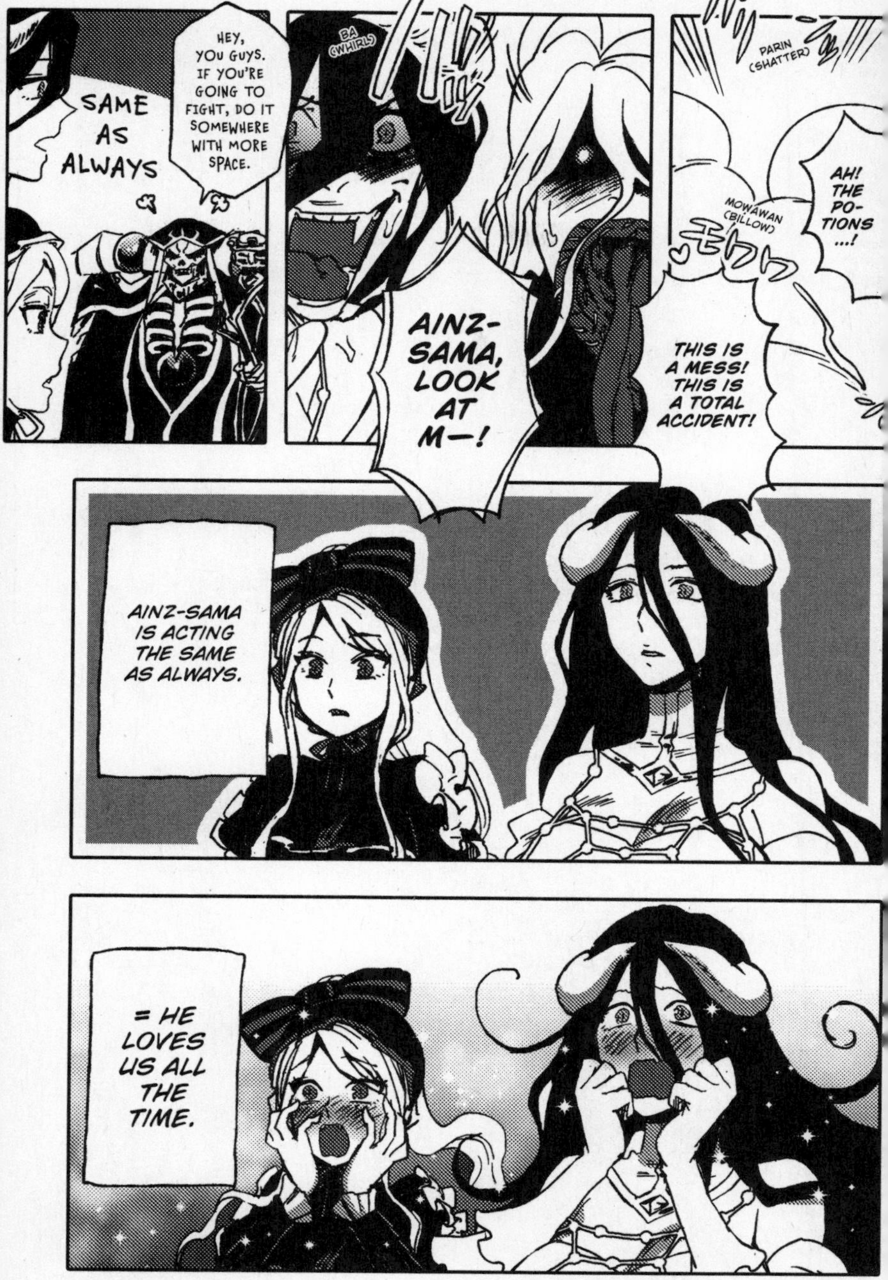
PARIN (SHATTER)
AH! THE POTIONS...!
MOWAWAN (BILLOW)
THIS IS A MESS! THIS IS A TOTAL ACCIDENT!
BA (WHIRL)
AINZ-SAMA, LOOK AT M—!
HEY, YOU GUYS. IF YOU'RE GOING TO FIGHT, DO IT SOMEWHERE WITH MORE SPACE.
SAME AS ALWAYS
AINZ-SAMA IS ACTING THE SAME AS ALWAYS.
= HE LOVES US ALL THE TIME.

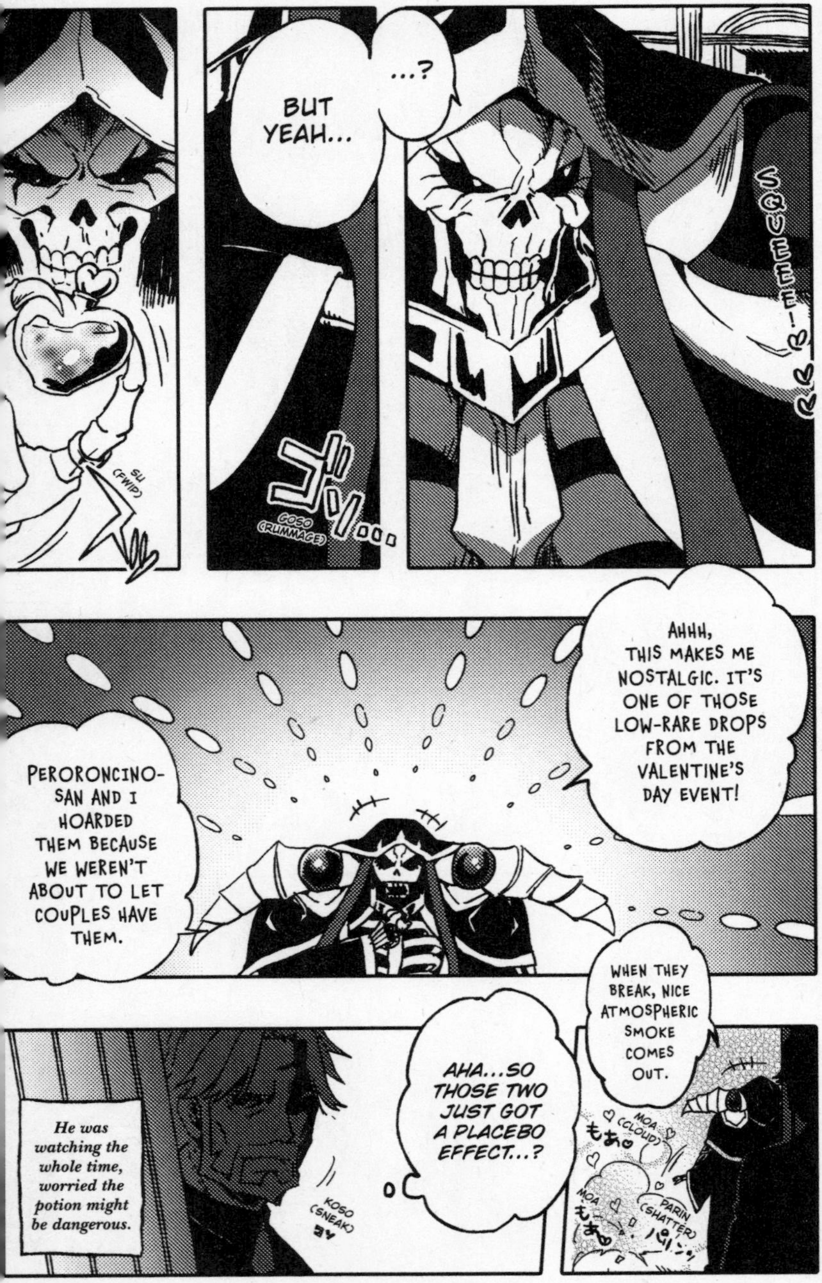
...?
SQUEEE!
BUT YEAH...
GOSO (RUMMAGE)
SU (FWIP)
AHHH, THIS MAKES ME NOSTALGIC. IT'S ONE OF THOSE LOW-RARE DROPS FROM THE VALENTINE'S DAY EVENT!
PERORONCINO-SAN AND I HOARDED THEM BECAUSE WE WEREN'T ABOUT TO LET COUPLES HAVE THEM.
WHEN THEY BREAK, NICE ATMOSPHERIC SMOKE COMES OUT.
MOA (CLOUD)
PARIN (SHATTER)
MOA
AHA...SO THOSE TWO JUST GOT A PLACEBO EFFECT...?
KOSO (SNEAK)
He was watching the whole time, worried the potion might be dangerous.

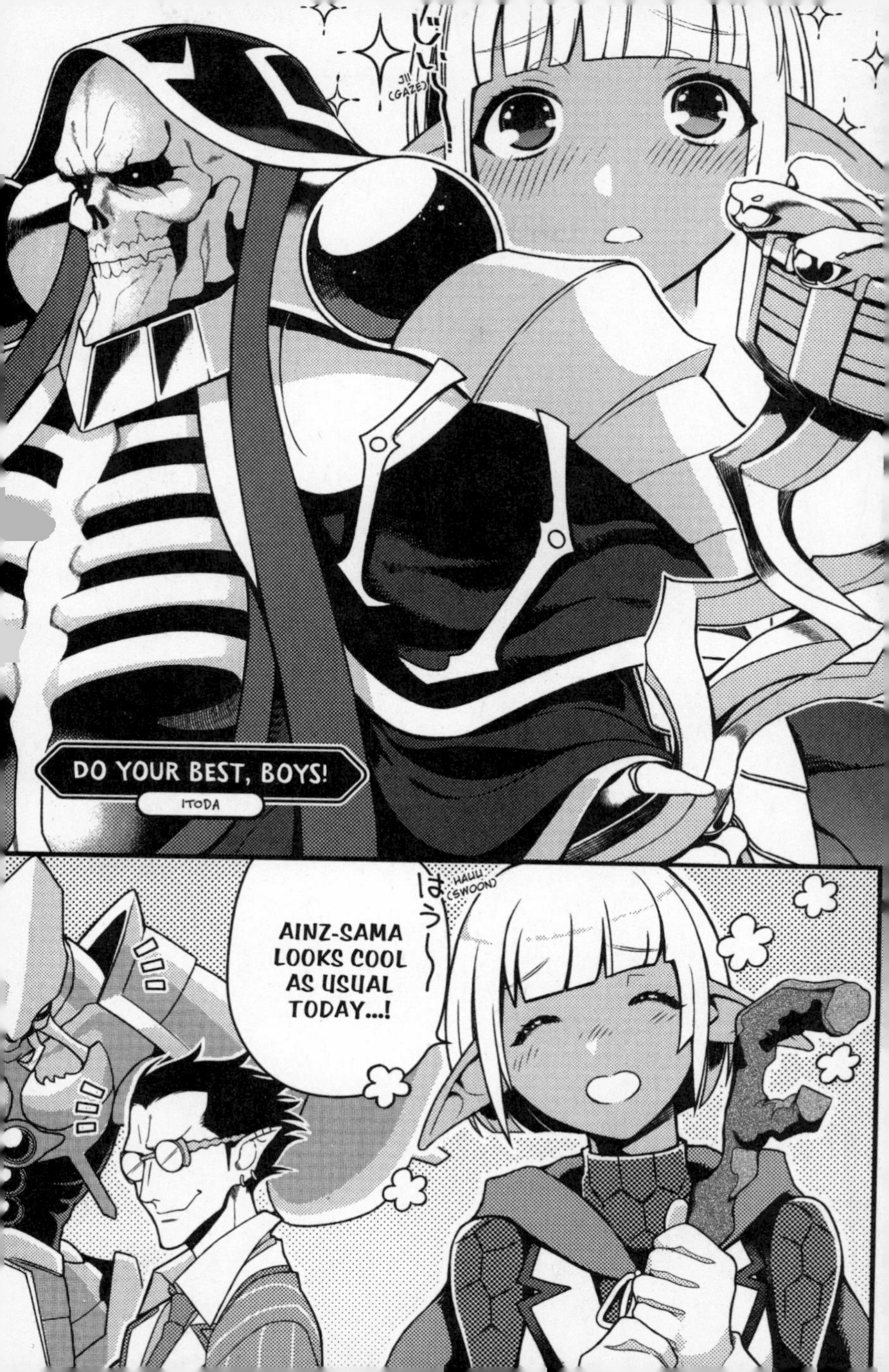

じー
JII (GAZE)
DO YOUR BEST, BOYS!
ITODA
はうー
HAUU (SWOON)
AINZ-SAMA LOOKS COOL AS USUAL TODAY...!

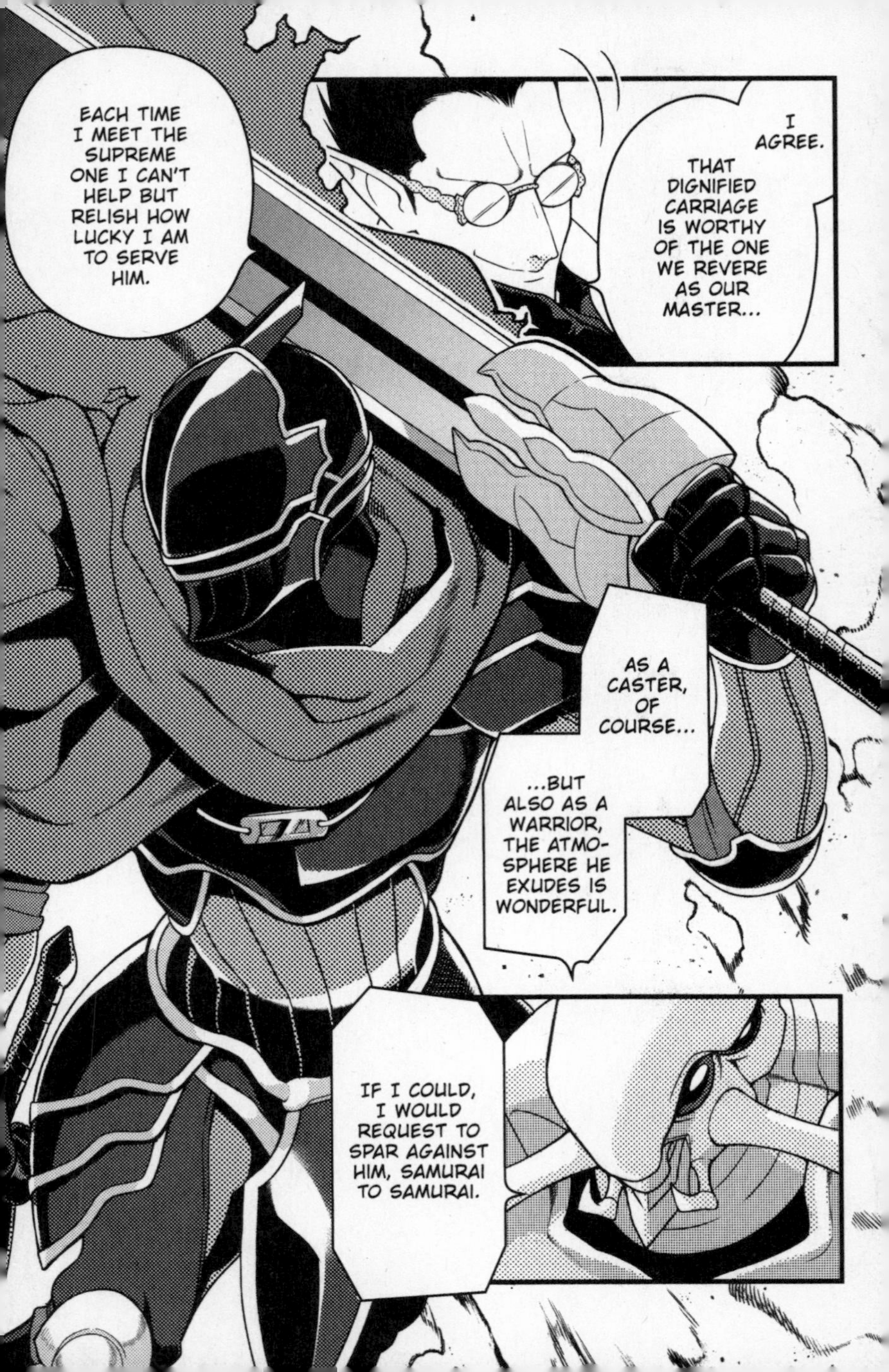

EACH TIME I MEET THE SUPREME ONE I CAN'T HELP BUT RELISH HOW LUCKY I AM TO SERVE HIM.
I AGREE.
THAT DIGNIFIED CARRIAGE IS WORTHY OF THE ONE WE REVERE AS OUR MASTER...
AS A CASTER, OF COURSE...
...BUT ALSO AS A WARRIOR, THE ATMOSPHERE HE EXUDES IS WONDERFUL.
IF I COULD, I WOULD REQUEST TO SPAR AGAINST HIM, SAMURAI TO SAMURAI.

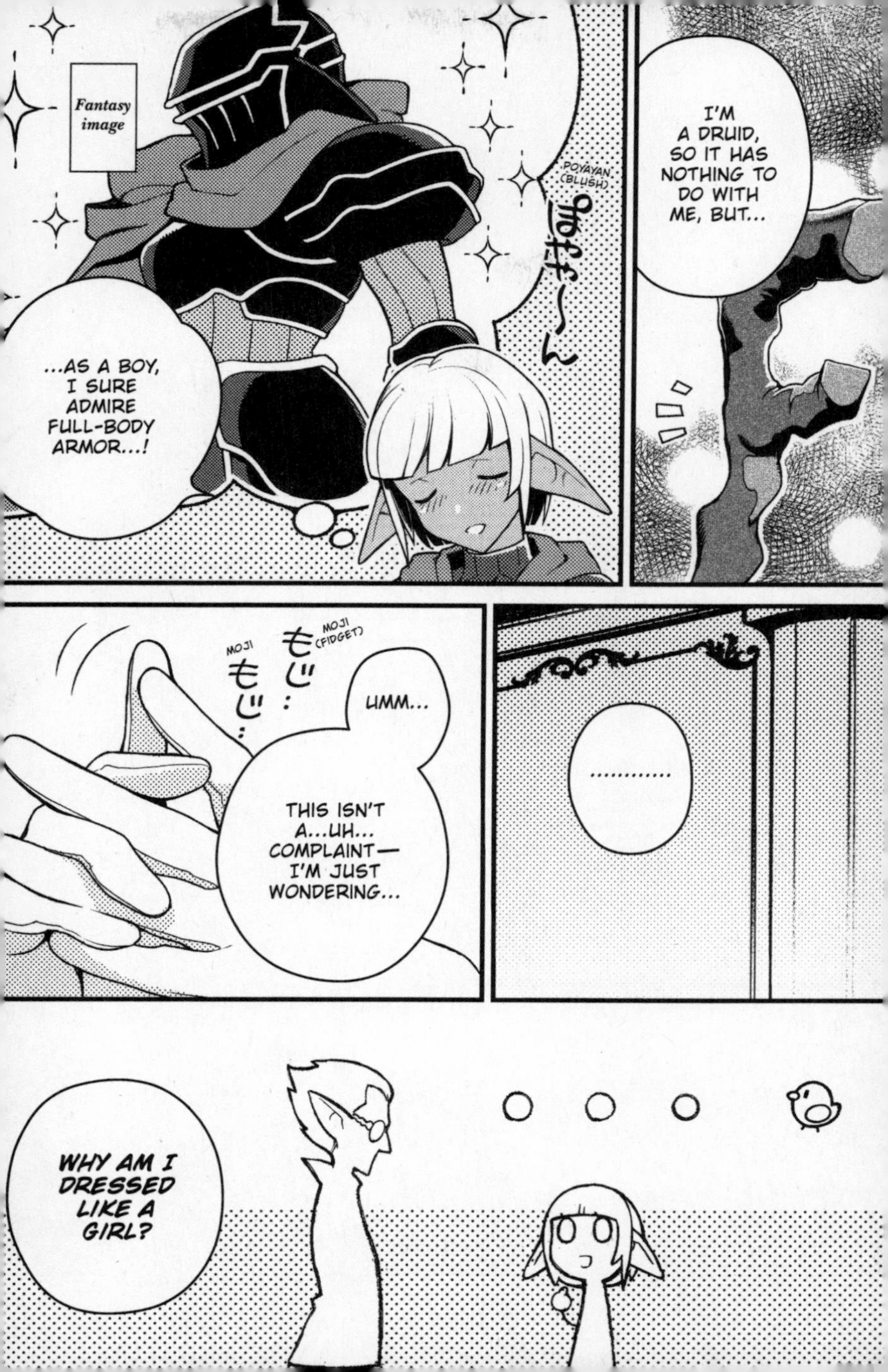
I'M A DRUID, SO IT HAS NOTHING TO DO WITH ME, BUT...
Fantasy image
POYAYAN (BLUSH)
ぽやや～ん
...AS A BOY, I SURE ADMIRE FULL-BODY ARMOR...!
....
MOJI (FIDGET)
もじ…
MOJI
もじ…
UMM...
THIS ISN'T A...UH... COMPLAINT—I'M JUST WONDERING...
WHY AM I DRESSED LIKE A GIRL?

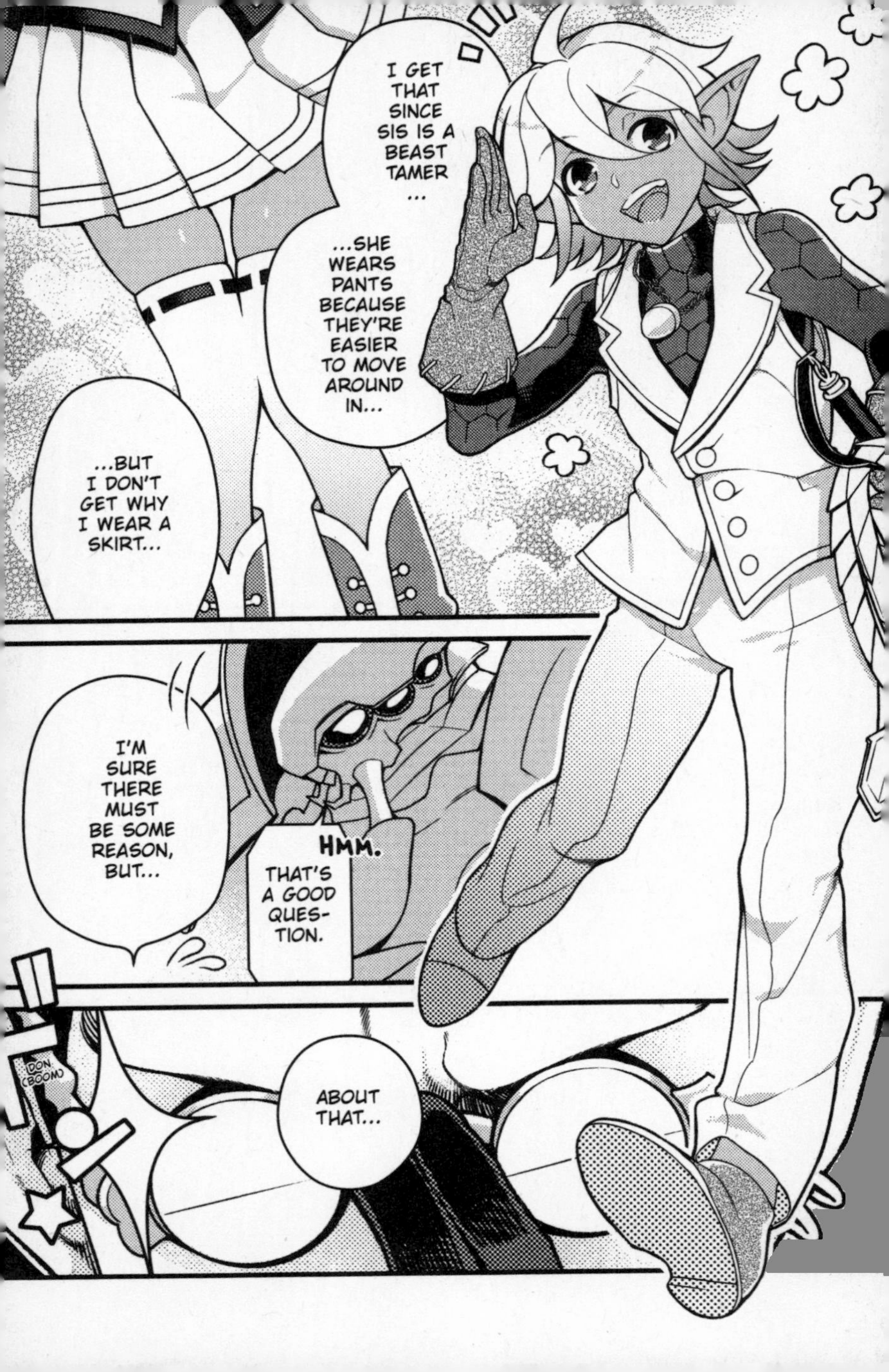
I GET THAT SINCE SIS IS A BEAST TAMER...
...SHE WEARS PANTS BECAUSE THEY'RE EASIER TO MOVE AROUND IN...
...BUT I DON'T GET WHY I WEAR A SKIRT...
HMM.
THAT'S A GOOD QUESTION.
I'M SURE THERE MUST BE SOME REASON, BUT...
ABOUT THAT...
DON (BOOM)

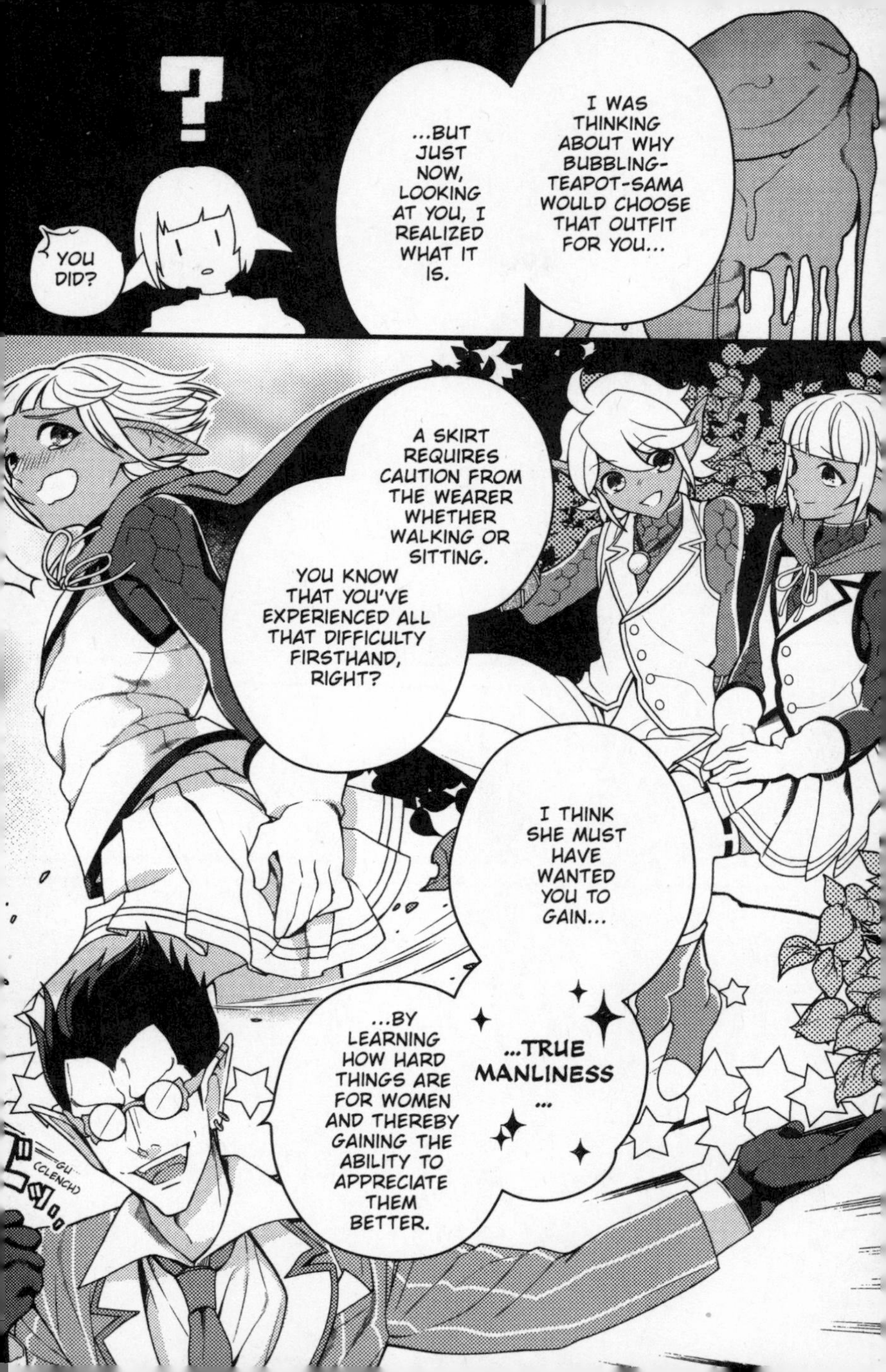
I WAS THINKING ABOUT WHY BUBBLING-TEAPOT-SAMA WOULD CHOOSE THAT OUTFIT FOR YOU...
...BUT JUST NOW, LOOKING AT YOU, I REALIZED WHAT IT IS.
?
YOU DID?
A SKIRT REQUIRES CAUTION FROM THE WEARER WHETHER WALKING OR SITTING.
YOU KNOW THAT YOU'VE EXPERIENCED ALL THAT DIFFICULTY FIRSTHAND, RIGHT?
I THINK SHE MUST HAVE WANTED YOU TO GAIN...
...TRUE MANLINESS...
...BY LEARNING HOW HARD THINGS ARE FOR WOMEN AND THEREBY GAINING THE ABILITY TO APPRECIATE THEM BETTER.
GU (CLENCH)

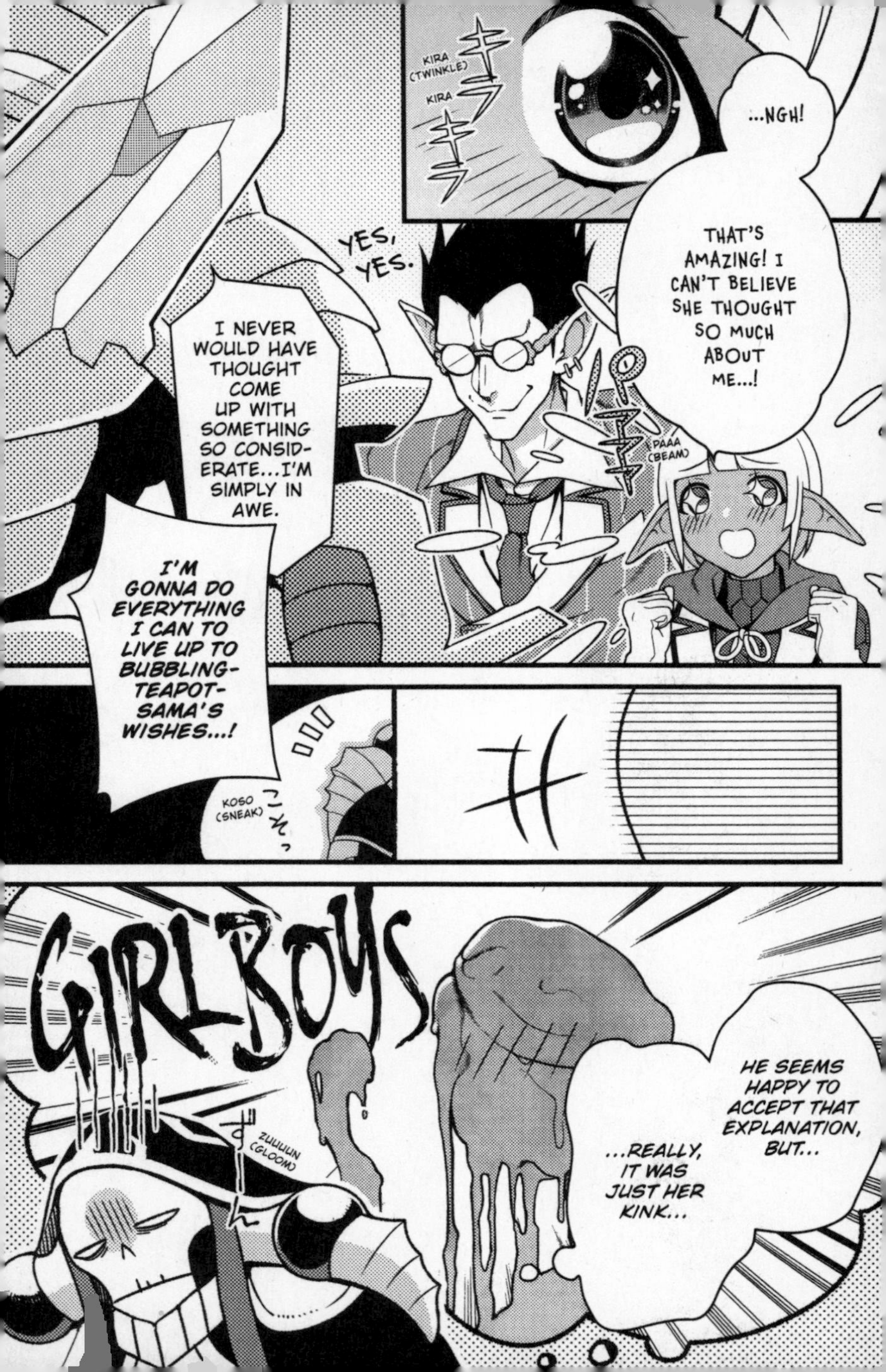
KIRA (TWINKLE)
KIRA
...NGH!
THAT'S AMAZING! I CAN'T BELIEVE SHE THOUGHT SO MUCH ABOUT ME...!
PAAA (BEAM)
YES, YES.
I NEVER WOULD HAVE THOUGHT COME UP WITH SOMETHING SO CONSIDERATE...I'M SIMPLY IN AWE.
I'M GONNA DO EVERYTHING I CAN TO LIVE UP TO BUBBLING-TEAPOT-SAMA'S WISHES...!
!!!
KOSO (SNEAK)
HE SEEMS HAPPY TO ACCEPT THAT EXPLANATION, BUT...
...REALLY, IT WAS JUST HER KINK...
GIRL BOYS
ZUUUUN (GLOOM)

Overlord in 4-Panel Comics

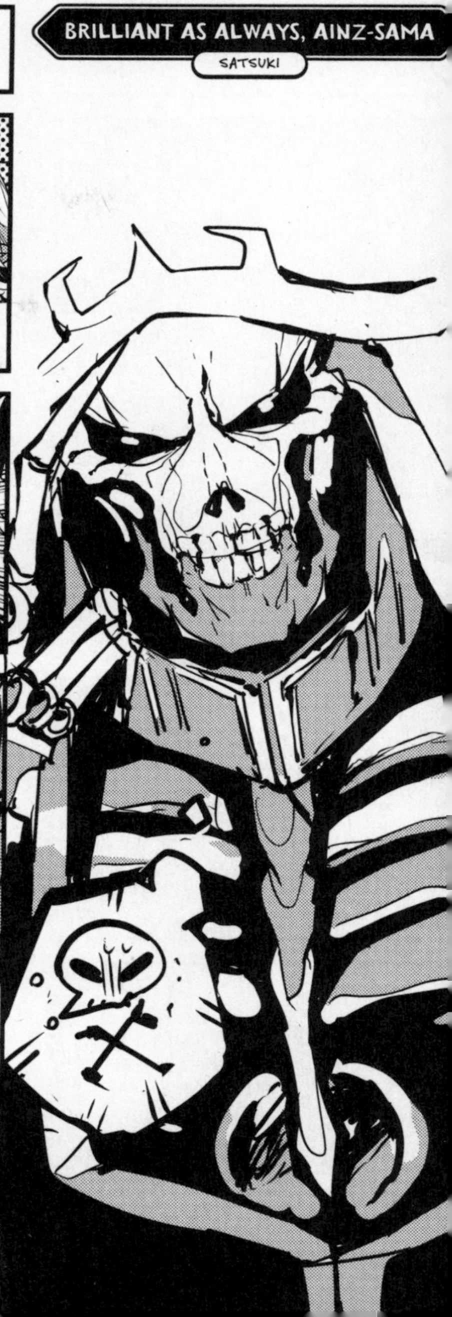
BRILLIANT AS ALWAYS, AINZ-SAMA
SATSUKI

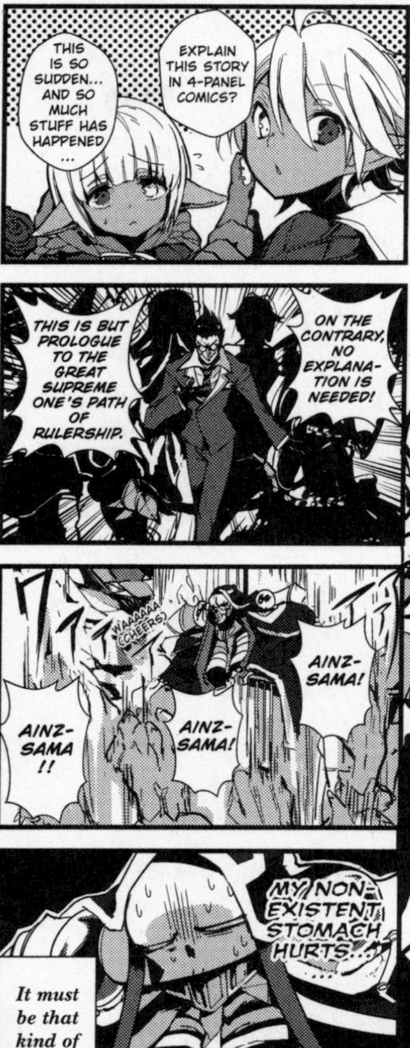
EXPLAIN THIS STORY IN 4-PANEL COMICS?
THIS IS SO SUDDEN... AND SO MUCH STUFF HAS HAPPENED...
ON THE CONTRARY, NO EXPLANATION IS NEEDED!
THIS IS BUT PROLOGUE TO THE GREAT SUPREME ONE'S PATH OF RULERSHIP.
AINZ-SAMA!
WAAAAAA (CHEERS)
AINZ-SAMA!
AINZ-SAMA !!
MY NON-EXISTENT STOMACH HURTS...
It must be that kind of story.

If Brain Were a Little Stronger

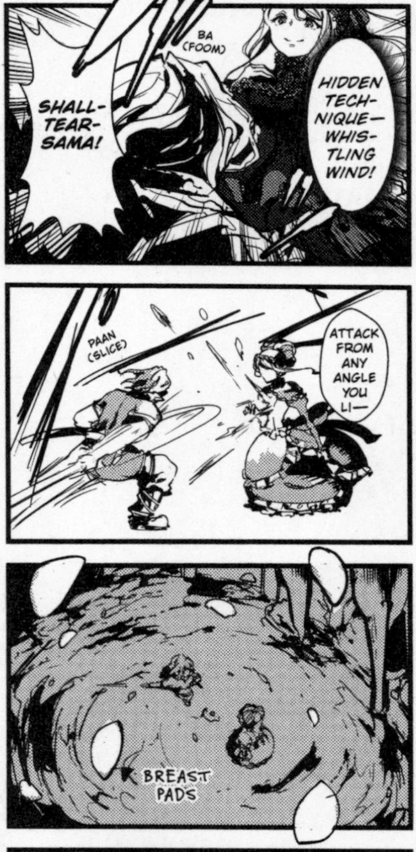
HIDDEN TECHNIQUE—WHISTLING WIND!
BA (FOOM)
SHALLTEAR-SAMA!
ATTACK FROM ANY ANGLE YOU LI—
PAAN (SLICE)
BREAST PADS
AHA. WHAT THICK ARMOR YOU HAVE...!
BAAN (BOOM)
He gets beaten to a pulp after this.

Brilliant, Ainz-sama

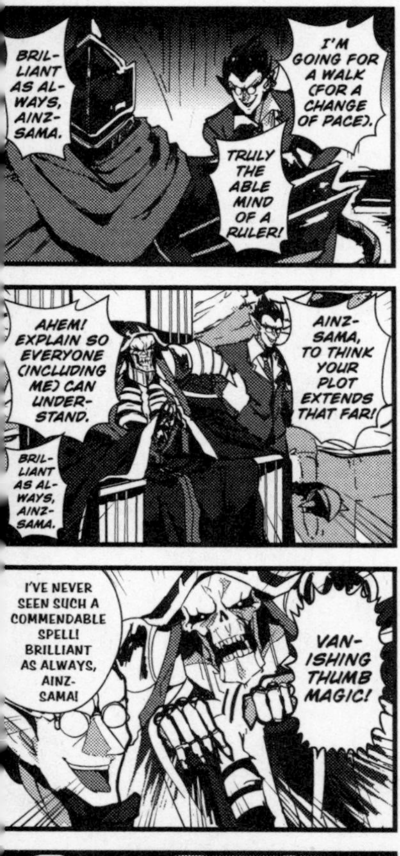
I'M GOING FOR A WALK (FOR A CHANGE OF PACE).
TRULY THE ABLE MIND OF A RULER!
BRILLIANT AS ALWAYS, AINZ-SAMA.
AINZ-SAMA, TO THINK YOUR PLOT EXTENDS THAT FAR!
AHEM! EXPLAIN SO EVERYONE (INCLUDING ME) CAN UNDERSTAND.
BRILLIANT AS ALWAYS, AINZ-SAMA.
VANISHING THUMB MAGIC!
I'VE NEVER SEEN SUCH A COMMENDABLE SPELL! BRILLIANT AS ALWAYS, AINZ-SAMA!
DOES IT EVEN MATTER WHAT I DO?
WELL, I THINK THAT LAST ONE WAS A STRETCH.

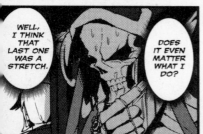

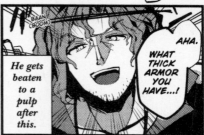

The Dream

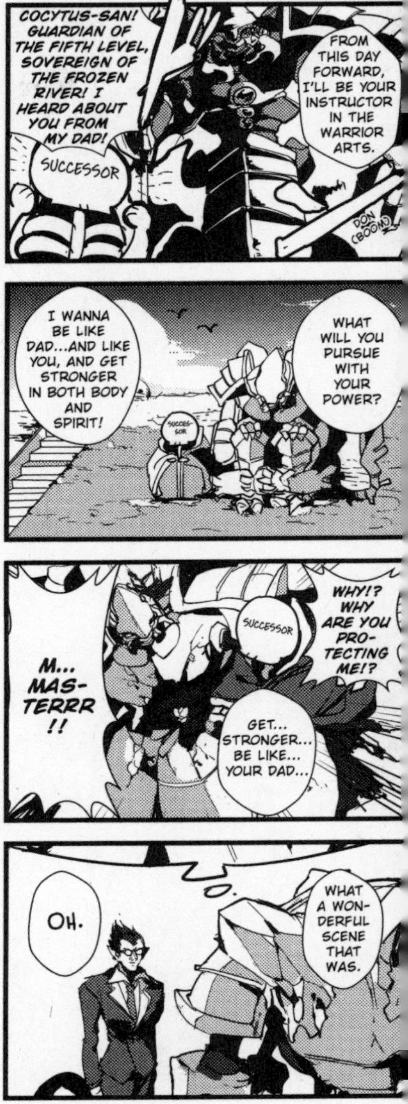
FROM THIS DAY FORWARD, I'LL BE YOUR INSTRUCTOR IN THE WARRIOR ARTS.
COCYTUS-SAN! GUARDIAN OF THE FIFTH LEVEL, SOVEREIGN OF THE FROZEN RIVER! I HEARD ABOUT YOU FROM MY DAD!
SUCCESSOR
DON (BOOM)
WHAT WILL YOU PURSUE WITH YOUR POWER?
I WANNA BE LIKE DAD...AND LIKE YOU, AND GET STRONGER IN BOTH BODY AND SPIRIT!
SUCCES-SOR
WHY!? WHY ARE YOU PRO-TECTING ME!?
SUCCESSOR
GET... STRONGER... BE LIKE... YOUR DAD...
M... MAS-TERRR !!
WHAT A WON-DERFUL SCENE THAT WAS.
OH.

Looks Ten, Actually Seventy-Six

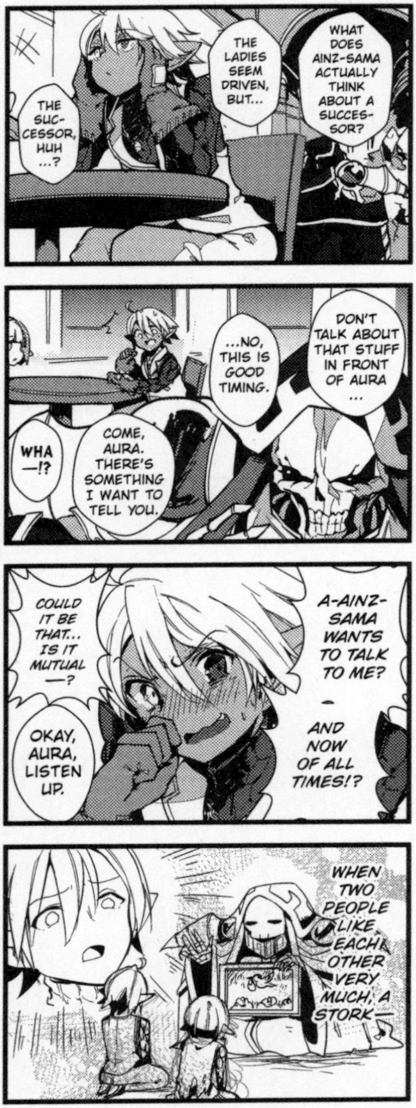
WHAT DOES AINZ-SAMA ACTUALLY THINK ABOUT A SUCCES-SOR?
THE LADIES SEEM DRIVEN, BUT...
THE SUC-CESSOR, HUH ...?
DON'T TALK ABOUT THAT STUFF IN FRONT OF AURA ...
...NO, THIS IS GOOD TIMING.
COME, AURA. THERE'S SOMETHING I WANT TO TELL YOU.
WHA —!?
A-AINZ-SAMA WANTS TO TALK TO ME?
AND NOW OF ALL TIMES!?
COULD IT BE THAT... IS IT MUTUAL —?
OKAY, AURA, LISTEN UP.
WHEN TWO PEOPLE LIKE EACH OTHER VERY MUCH, A STORK—

The Wheel

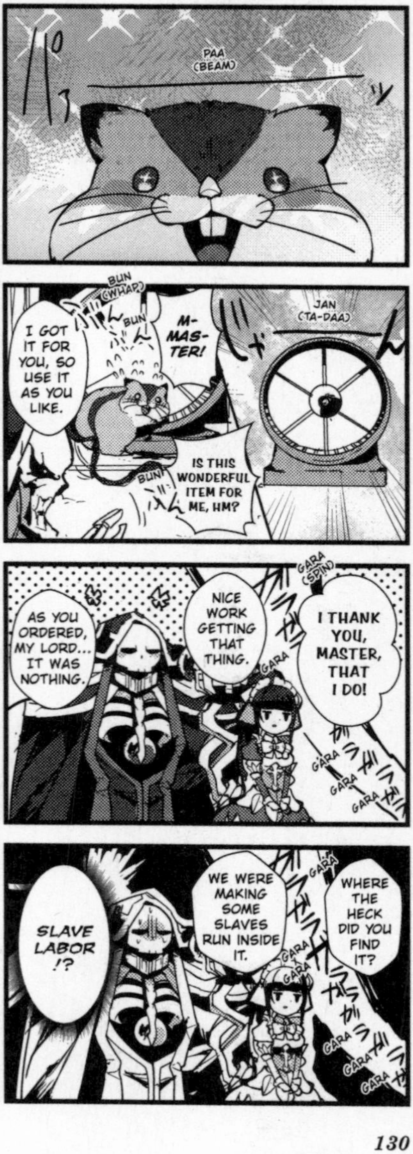
PAA (BEAM)
JAN (TA-DAA)
M-MASTER!
BUN (WHAP)
BUN
I GOT IT FOR YOU, SO USE IT AS YOU LIKE.
IS THIS WONDERFUL ITEM FOR ME, HM?
BUN
GARA (SPIN)
I THANK YOU, MASTER, THAT I DO!
NICE WORK GETTING THAT THING.
AS YOU ORDERED, MY LORD... IT WAS NOTHING.
GARA
GARA
GARA
GARA
GARA
WHERE THE HECK DID YOU FIND IT?
WE WERE MAKING SOME SLAVES RUN INSIDE IT.
SLAVE LABOR!?
GARA
GARA
GARA
GARA
GARA

The Wheel Spins On

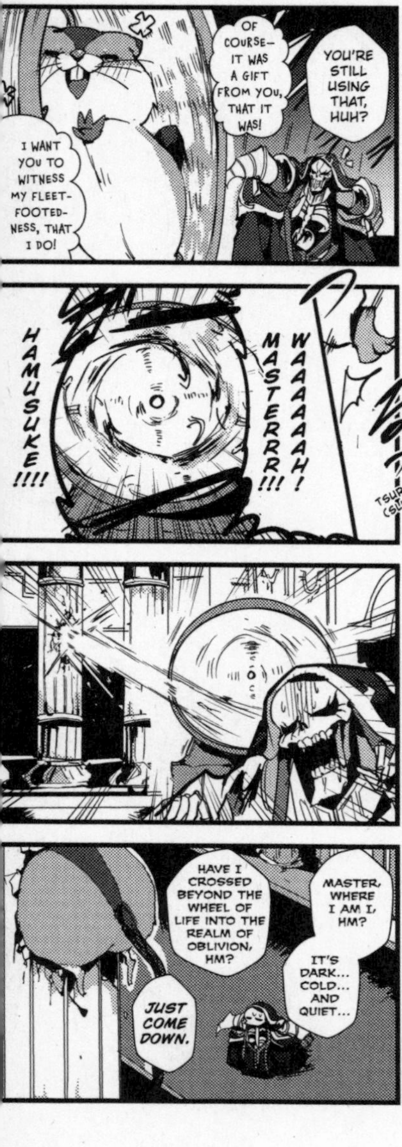
YOU'RE STILL USING THAT, HUH?
OF COURSE— IT WAS A GIFT FROM YOU, THAT IT WAS!
I WANT YOU TO WITNESS MY FLEET-FOOTEDNESS, THAT I DO!
WAAAAAAAH! MASTERRR!!!
HAMUSUKE!!!!
TSURU (SLIP)
MASTER, WHERE AM I, HM?
HAVE I CROSSED BEYOND THE WHEEL OF LIFE INTO THE REALM OF OBLIVION, HM?
IT'S DARK... COLD... AND QUIET...
JUST COME DOWN.

Nabe and the Swords of Darkness

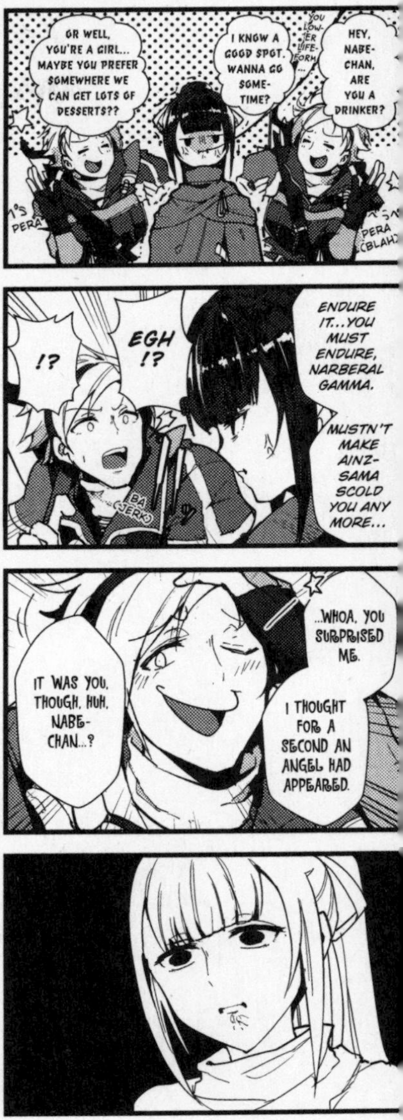
HEY, NABE-CHAN, ARE YOU A DRINKER?
YOU LOWER LIFE-FORM...
I KNOW A GOOD SPOT. WANNA GO SOME-TIME?
OR WELL, YOU'RE A GIRL... MAYBE YOU PREFER SOMEWHERE WE CAN GET LOTS OF DESSERTS??
PERA (BLAH)
PERA
ENDURE IT...YOU MUST ENDURE, NARBERAL GAMMA.
MUSTN'T MAKE AINZ-SAMA SCOLD YOU ANY MORE...
EGH!?
!?
BA (JERK)
...WHOA, YOU SURPRISED ME.
I THOUGHT FOR A SECOND AN ANGEL HAD APPEARED.
IT WAS YOU, THOUGH, HUH, NABE-CHAN...?

Nabe and the Swords of Darkness 2

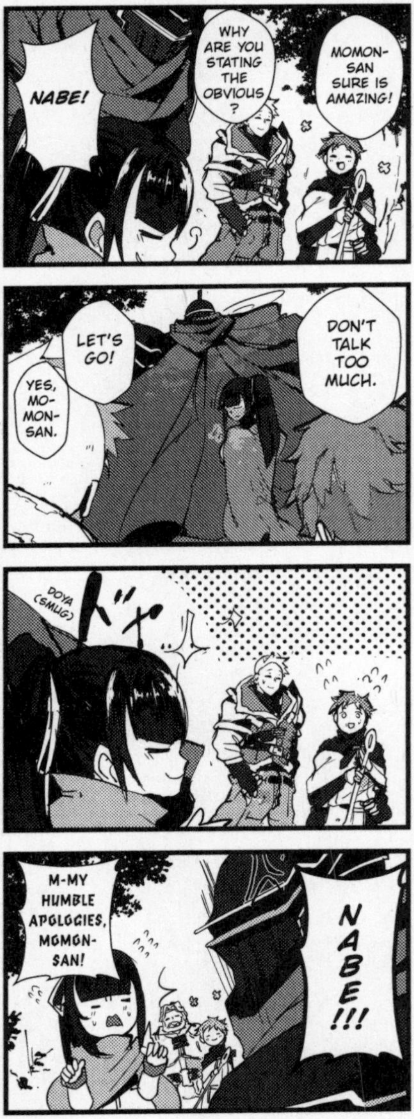
MOMON-SAN SURE IS AMAZING!
WHY ARE YOU STATING THE OBVIOUS?
NABE!
DON'T TALK TOO MUCH.
LET'S GO!
YES, MOMON-SAN.
DOYA (SMUG)
NABE!!!
M-MY HUMBLE APOLOGIES, MOMON-SAN!

The Quiz Show

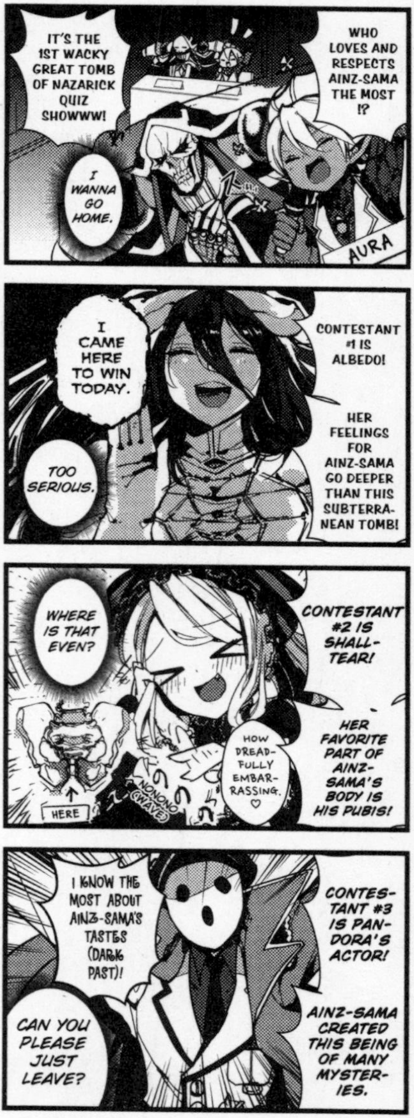
WHO LOVES AND RESPECTS AINZ-SAMA THE MOST !?
IT'S THE 1ST WACKY GREAT TOMB OF NAZARICK QUIZ SHOWWW!
I WANNA GO HOME.
AURA
CONTESTANT #1 IS ALBEDO!
HER FEELINGS FOR AINZ-SAMA GO DEEPER THAN THIS SUBTERRANEAN TOMB!
I CAME HERE TO WIN TODAY.
TOO SERIOUS.
CONTESTANT #2 IS SHALLTEAR!
HER FAVORITE PART OF AINZ-SAMA'S BODY IS HIS PUBIS!
WHERE IS THAT EVEN?
HOW DREADFULLY EMBARRASSING. ♡
NONONO (WAVE)
HERE
CONTESTANT #3 IS PANDORA'S ACTOR!
AINZ-SAMA CREATED THIS BEING OF MANY MYSTERIES.
I KNOW THE MOST ABOUT AINZ-SAMA'S TASTES (DARK PAST)!
CAN YOU PLEASE JUST LEAVE?

The Quiz Show Continues

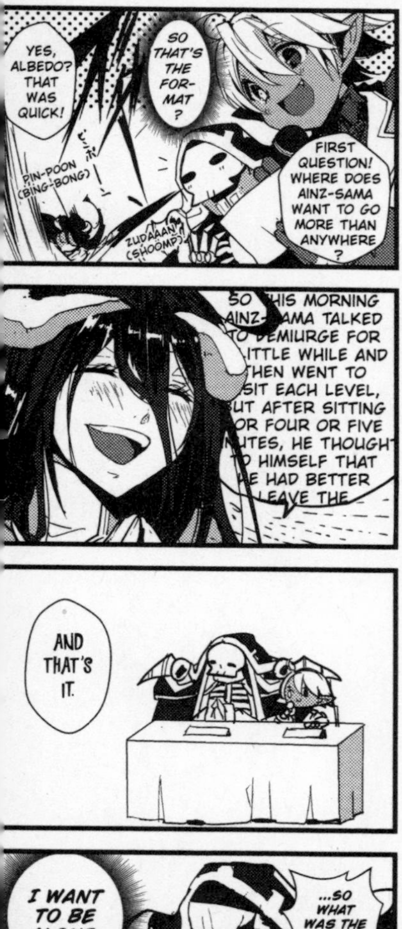
SO THAT'S THE FORMAT?
FIRST QUESTION! WHERE DOES AINZ-SAMA WANT TO GO MORE THAN ANYWHERE?
YES, ALBEDO? THAT WAS QUICK!
PIN-POON (BING-BONG)
ZUDAAAN (SHOOMP)
SO THIS MORNING AINZ-SAMA TALKED TO DEMIURGE FOR A LITTLE WHILE AND THEN WENT TO VISIT EACH LEVEL, BUT AFTER SITTING FOR FOUR OR FIVE MINUTES, HE THOUGHT TO HIMSELF THAT HE HAD BETTER LEAVE THE
AND THAT'S IT.
...SO WHAT WAS THE ANSWER, AINZ-SAMA?
I WANT TO BE ALONE.
There was never a second show.

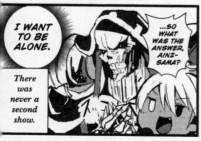

OVERLORD

À LA CARTE

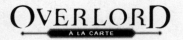

OVERLORD
À LA CARTE

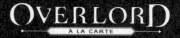

THE GREAT TOMB SWITCH

RYOSAN

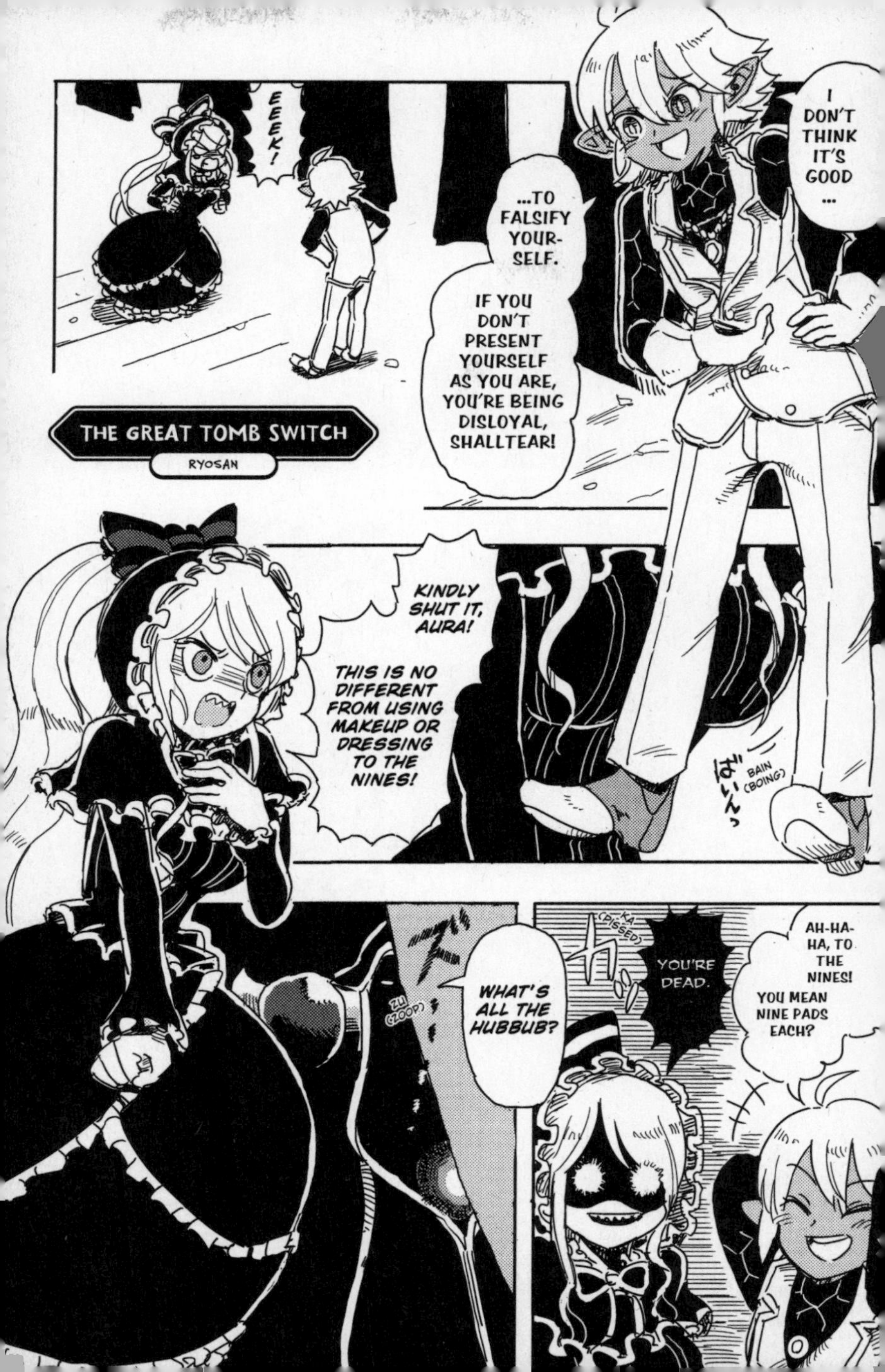
I DON'T THINK IT'S GOOD...
...TO FALSIFY YOURSELF.
IF YOU DON'T PRESENT YOURSELF AS YOU ARE, YOU'RE BEING DISLOYAL, SHALLTEAR!
EEEK!
BAIN (BOING)
KINDLY SHUT IT, AURA!
THIS IS NO DIFFERENT FROM USING MAKEUP OR DRESSING TO THE NINES!
AH-HA-HA, TO THE NINES!
YOU MEAN NINE PADS EACH?
KA (PISSED)
YOU'RE DEAD.
ZU (ZOOP)
WHAT'S ALL THE HUBBUB?

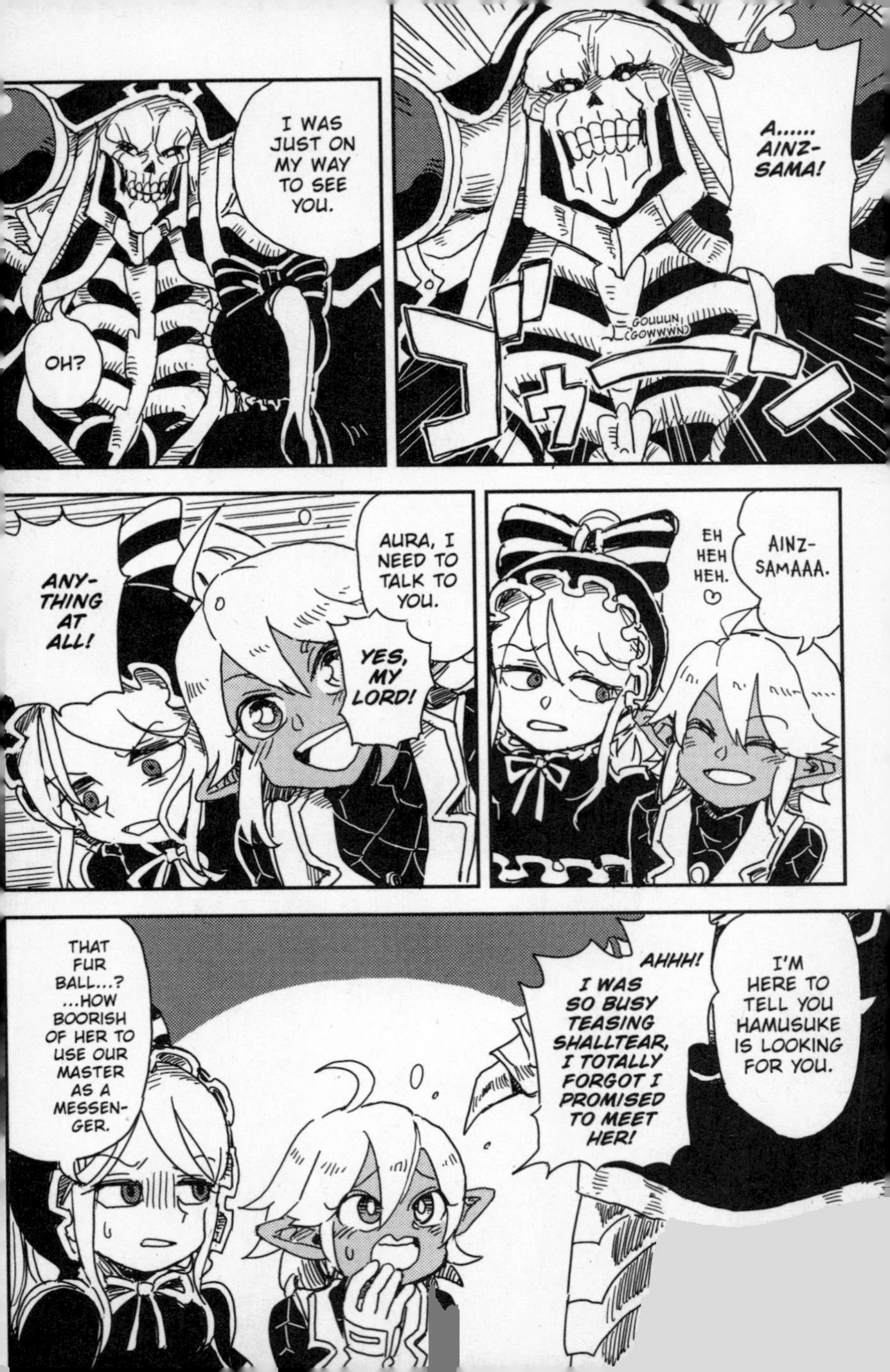
A...... AINZ-SAMA!
GOUUUN (GOWWWN)
I WAS JUST ON MY WAY TO SEE YOU.
OH?
AINZ-SAMAAA.
EH HEH HEH. ♡
AURA, I NEED TO TALK TO YOU.
YES, MY LORD!
ANYTHING AT ALL!
I'M HERE TO TELL YOU HAMUSUKE IS LOOKING FOR YOU.
AHHH! I WAS SO BUSY TEASING SHALLTEAR, I TOTALLY FORGOT I PROMISED TO MEET HER!
THAT FUR BALL...? ...HOW BOORISH OF HER TO USE OUR MASTER AS A MESSENGER.

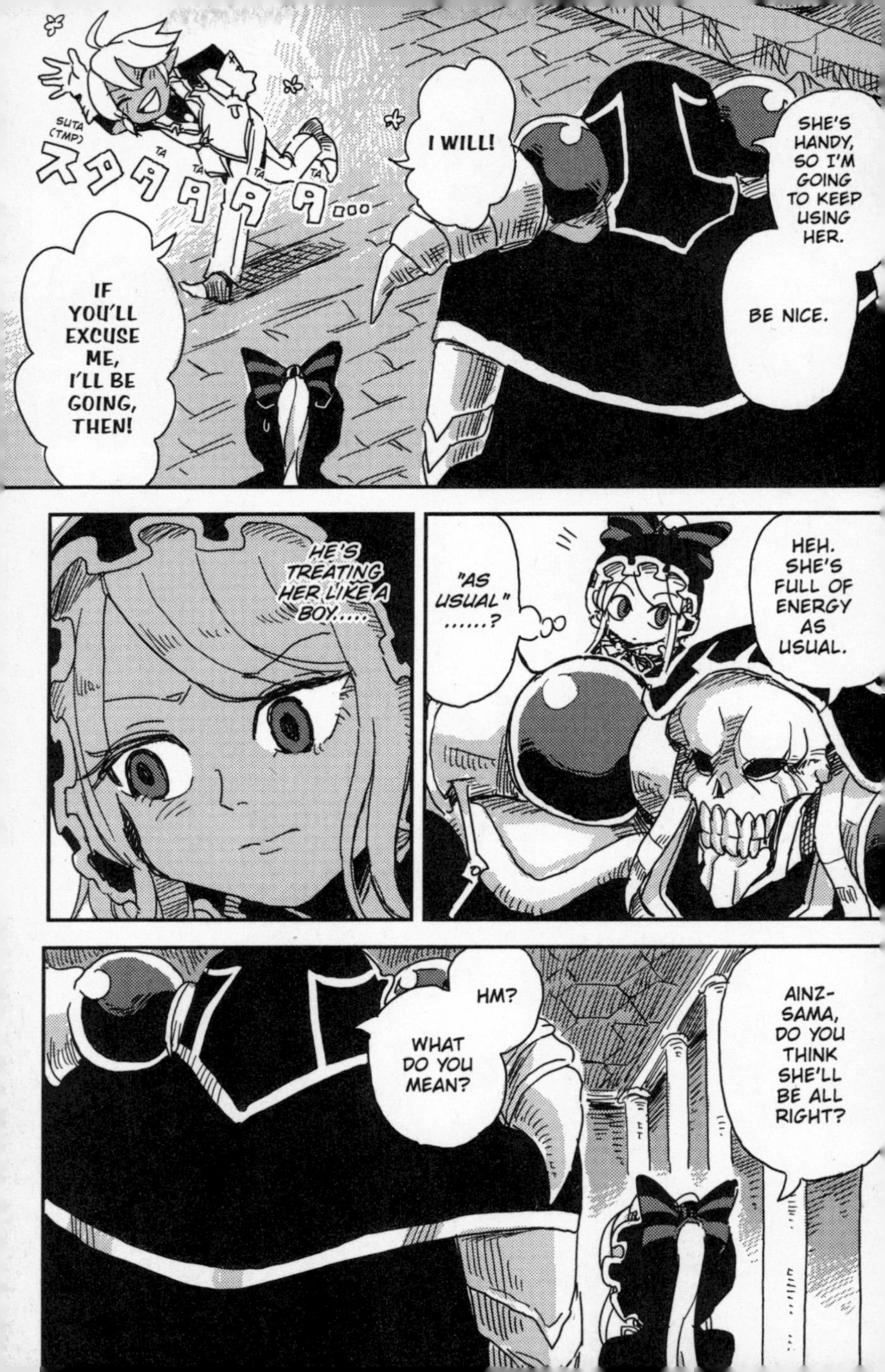
SHE'S HANDY, SO I'M GOING TO KEEP USING HER.
BE NICE.
I WILL!
SUTA (TMP)
スタタタタ...
TA TA TA TA
IF YOU'LL EXCUSE ME, I'LL BE GOING, THEN!
HEH. SHE'S FULL OF ENERGY AS USUAL.
"AS USUAL"......?
HE'S TREATING HER LIKE A BOY.....
AINZ-SAMA, DO YOU THINK SHE'LL BE ALL RIGHT?
HM?
WHAT DO YOU MEAN?

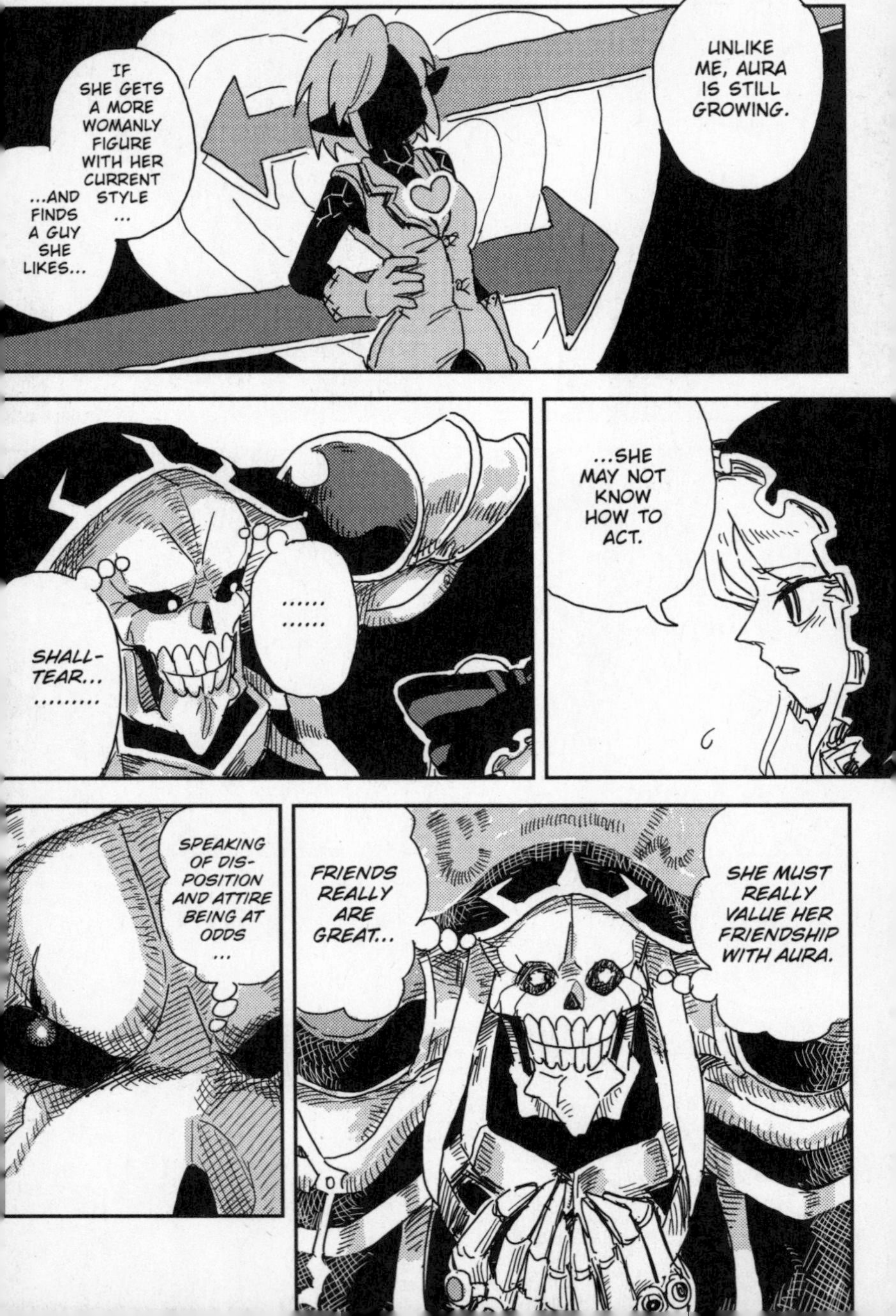
UNLIKE ME, AURA IS STILL GROWING.
IF SHE GETS A MORE WOMANLY FIGURE WITH HER CURRENT STYLE ...
...AND FINDS A GUY SHE LIKES...
...SHE MAY NOT KNOW HOW TO ACT.
....
SHALL-TEAR... ....
SHE MUST REALLY VALUE HER FRIENDSHIP WITH AURA.
FRIENDS REALLY ARE GREAT...
SPEAKING OF DIS-POSITION AND ATTIRE BEING AT ODDS ...

BAK!
(SNAP)

YOU'RE RIGHT ABOUT AURA.

THE SAME GOES FOR MARE TOO. I'D BE A LITTLE WORRIED IF HE GOT ALL MANLY THE WAY HE IS...

THAT WOULD BE INTENSE.

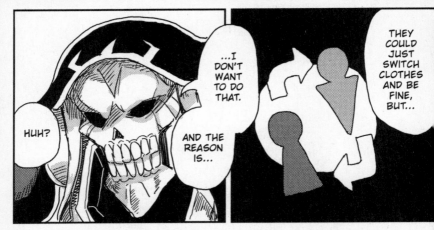

THEY COULD JUST SWITCH CLOTHES AND BE FINE, BUT...

...I DON'T WANT TO DO THAT.

AND THE REASON IS...

HUH?

SHALL-TEAR ......?

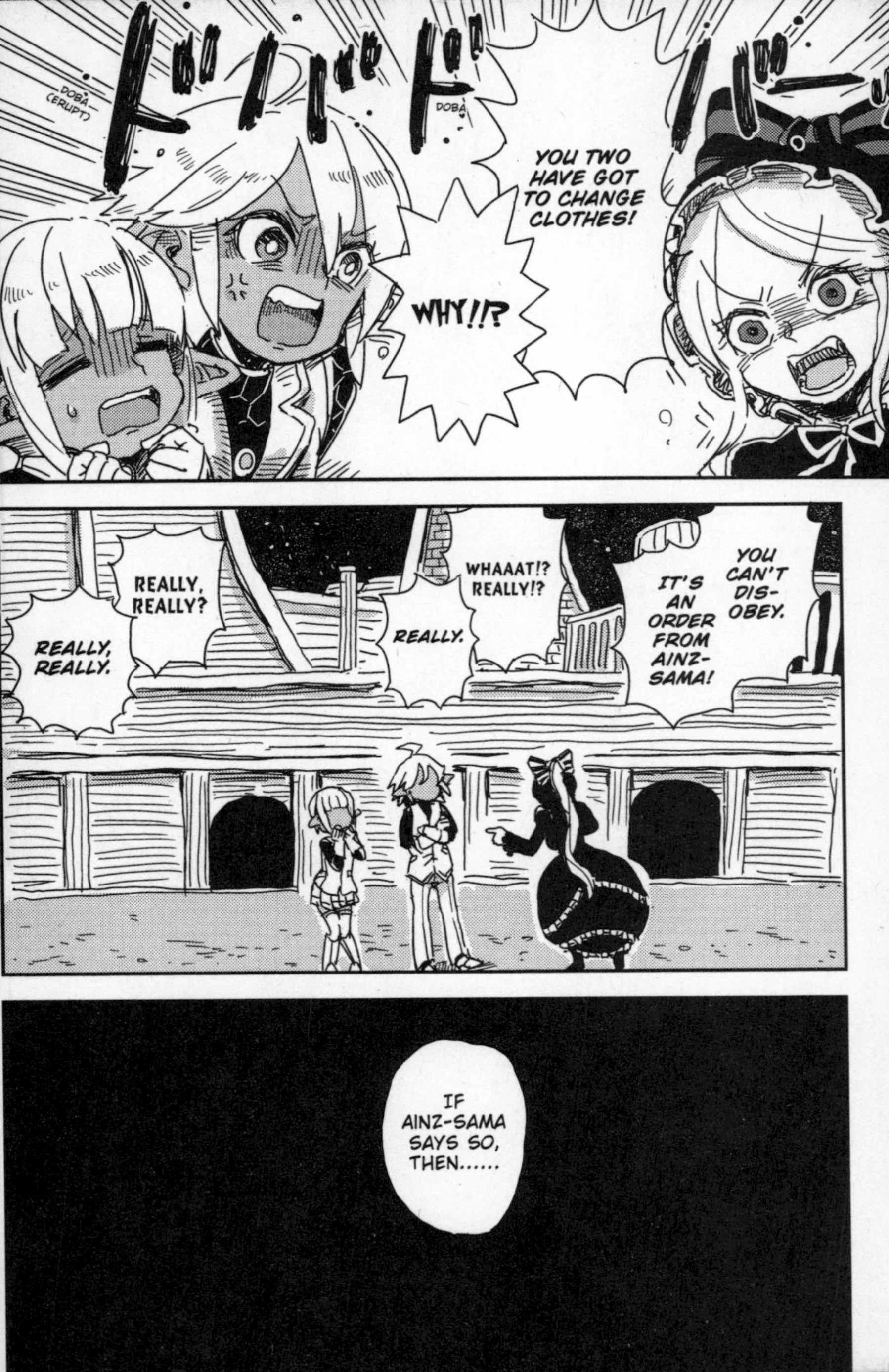
YOU TWO HAVE GOT TO CHANGE CLOTHES!
WHY!!?
DOBA
DOBA (ERUPT)
YOU CAN'T DIS-OBEY.
IT'S AN ORDER FROM AINZ-SAMA!
WHAAAT!? REALLY!?
REALLY.
REALLY, REALLY?
REALLY, REALLY.
IF AINZ-SAMA SAYS SO, THEN......

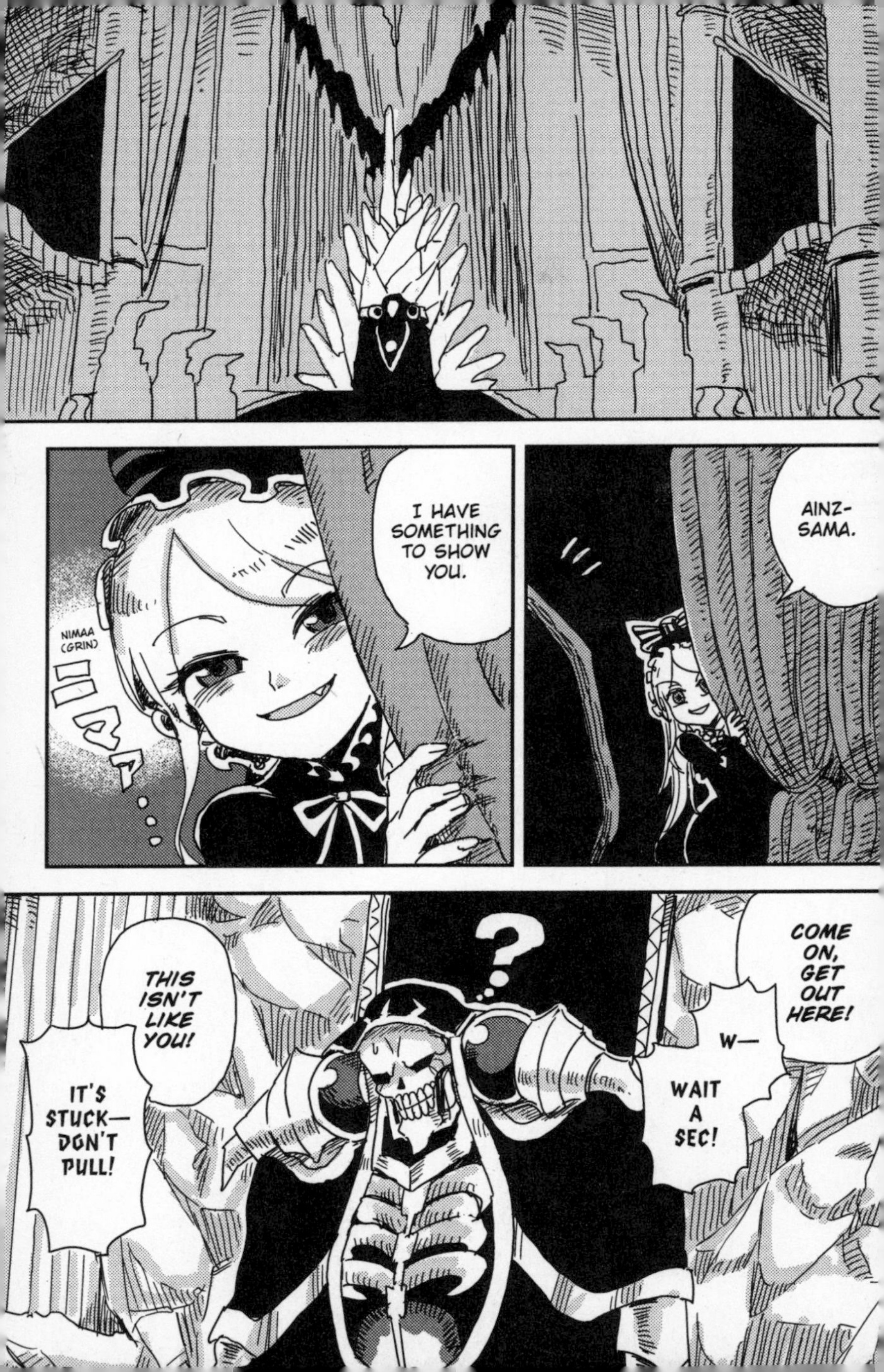
AINZ-SAMA.
I HAVE SOMETHING TO SHOW YOU.
NIMAA (GRIN)
COME ON, GET OUT HERE!
W—
WAIT A SEC!
THIS ISN'T LIKE YOU!
IT'S STUCK— DON'T PULL!

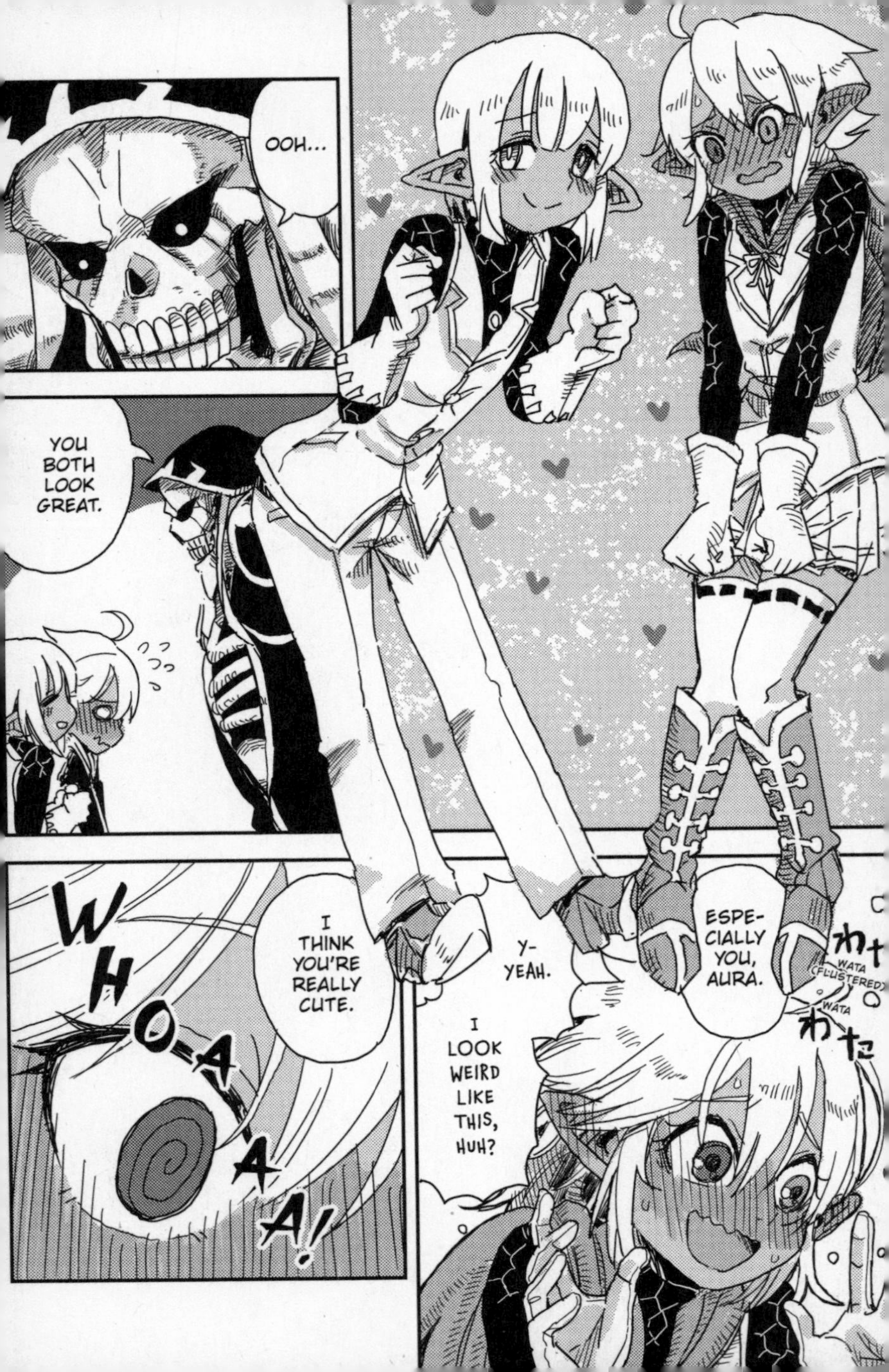
OOH...
YOU BOTH LOOK GREAT.
ESPE-CIALLY YOU, AURA.
わた WATA (FLUSTERED)
わた WATA
Y-YEAH.
I LOOK WEIRD LIKE THIS, HUH?
I THINK YOU'RE REALLY CUTE.
WHOA-A-A-A!

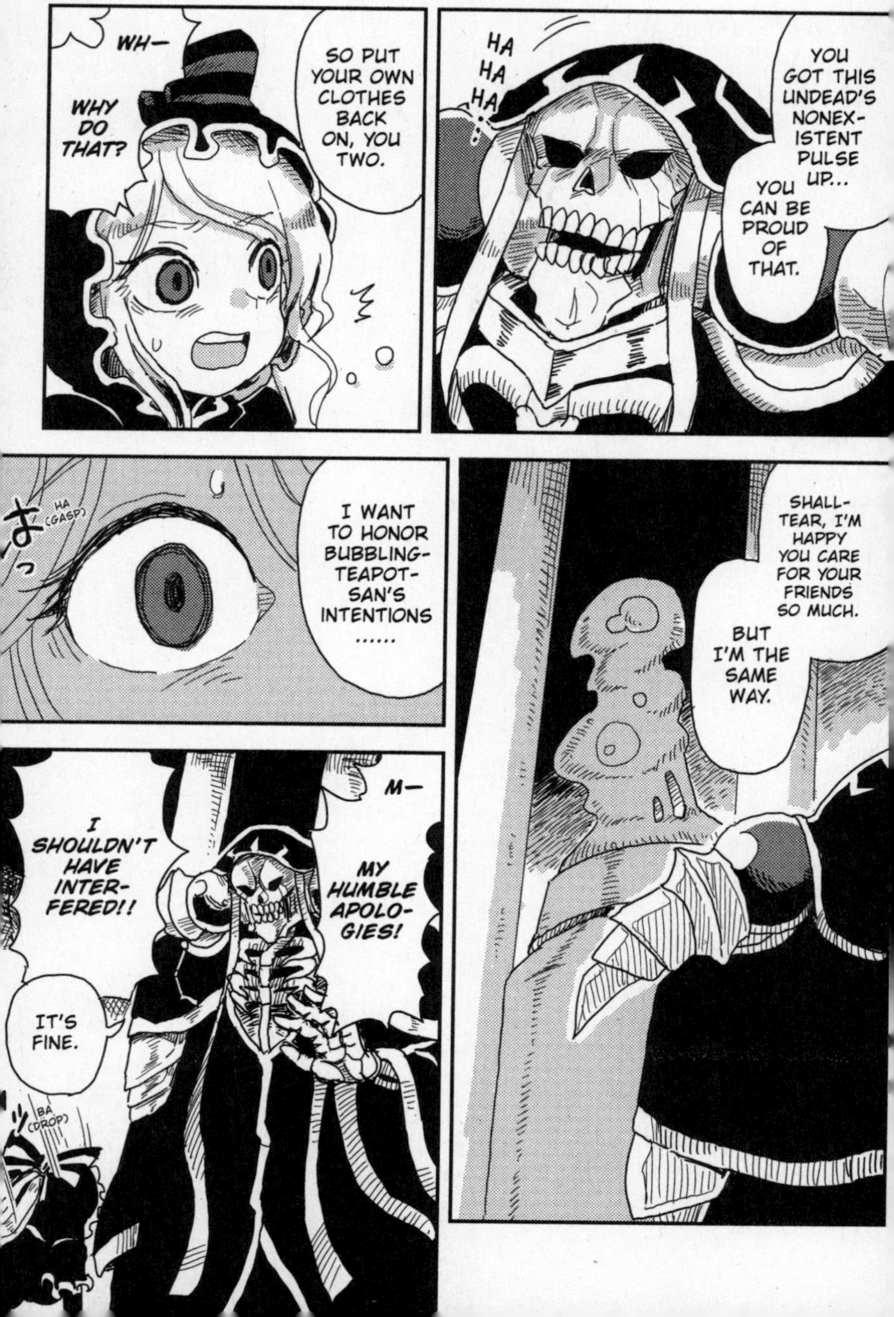
HA HA HA
YOU GOT THIS UNDEAD'S NONEXISTENT PULSE UP...
YOU CAN BE PROUD OF THAT.
SO PUT YOUR OWN CLOTHES BACK ON, YOU TWO.
WH—
WHY DO THAT?
SHALLTEAR, I'M HAPPY YOU CARE FOR YOUR FRIENDS SO MUCH.
BUT I'M THE SAME WAY.
I WANT TO HONOR BUBBLING-TEAPOT-SAN'S INTENTIONS ......
HA (GASP)
M—
MY HUMBLE APOLOGIES!
I SHOULDN'T HAVE INTERFERED!!
IT'S FINE.
BA (DROP)

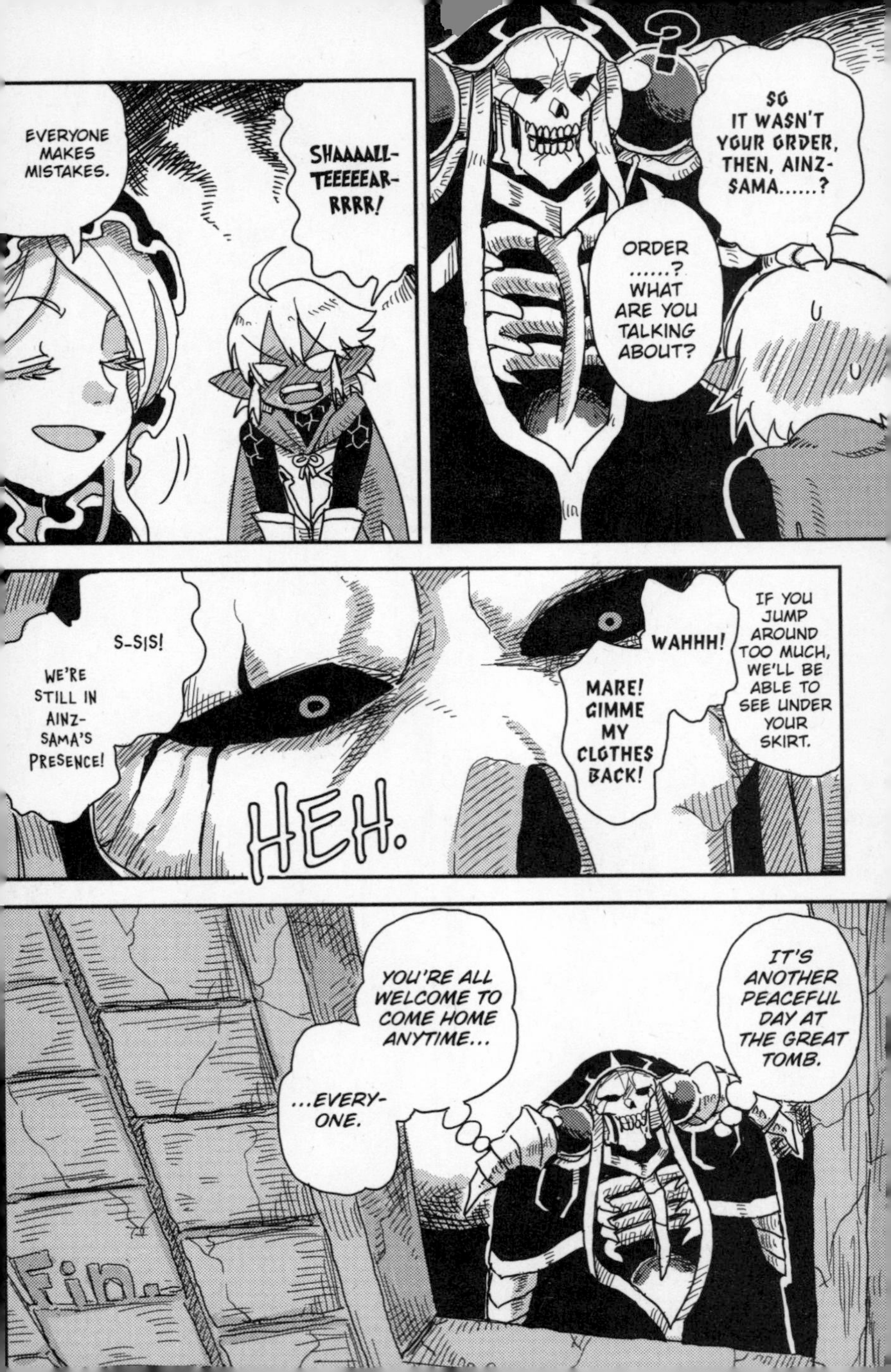
SO IT WASN'T YOUR ORDER, THEN, AINZ-SAMA......?
ORDER ......? WHAT ARE YOU TALKING ABOUT?
SHAAAALL-TEEEEEAR-RRRR!
EVERYONE MAKES MISTAKES.
IF YOU JUMP AROUND TOO MUCH, WE'LL BE ABLE TO SEE UNDER YOUR SKIRT.
WAHHH!
MARE! GIMME MY CLOTHES BACK!
S-SIS!
WE'RE STILL IN AINZ-SAMA'S PRESENCE!
HEH.
IT'S ANOTHER PEACEFUL DAY AT THE GREAT TOMB.
YOU'RE ALL WELCOME TO COME HOME ANYTIME...
...EVERY-ONE.
Fin.

OVERLORD

À LA CARTE

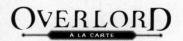

COMMENTS

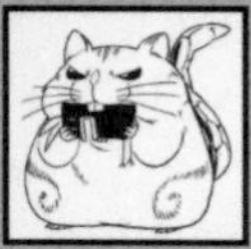

NAME: **Hugin Miyama** || **Cover/Color Illustration**

I got to draw everyone from Nazarick having a fun time together on the front cover!
Hamusuke's fluffy body soothes me.

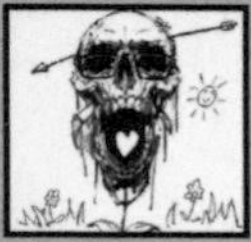

NAME: **so-bin** || **Color Illustration**

I didn't do anything! Thanks to all the people who participated!
It was more than I expected. I hope we can do more volumes.

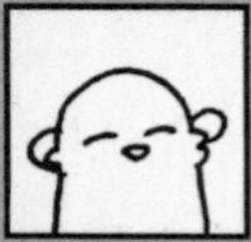

NAME: **Kanao Araki** || TITLE: **Operation Boobs**

Thank you for inviting me to participate!!!
Looking forward to season two!!!!!

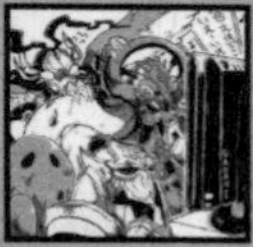

NAME: **Akudo GAZARI** || TITLE: **The Pandora Revolution**

Congratulations on season two of the anime being green-lit.
I'm just so thankful we get to see the brave figure of Ainz-sama and his actions, as well as the flourishing of Nazarick on TV again. Glory to Ainz Ooal Gown going forward as well!

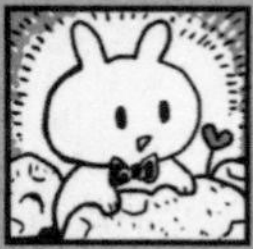

NAME: **Jirou Oimoto** || TITLE: **Seasons of Nazarick!**

Once I started thinking, there were so many jokes I could have done, forcing me to narrow down the list of characters and events, but it was really fun to draw a bunch of characters and Ainz's mental reactions to them! I hope people enjoy the heartwarming ones as well as the dangerous ones.

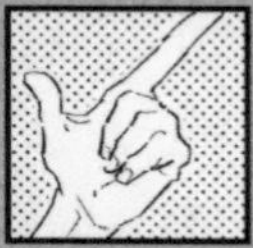

NAME: **Sunako** || TITLE: **Nazarick Chitchat Diary**

Congratulations on the anthology's release!
I like the relationship between Aura and Shalltear.

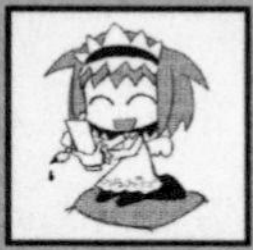

NAME: **Kou1** || TITLE: **The Supreme Magical Beast Namer**

I went into a kind of trance drawing Ainz's teeth...

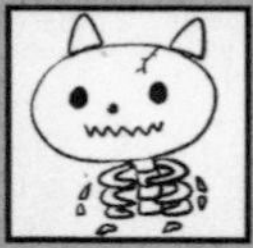

NAME: **Anri Sakano** || TITLE: **Hamusuke ★ Dresses Up**

Congratulations on season two of the anime!
I've never done something with so much beast and calcium flavor, so it was fun!
I wanna try riding Hamusuke sometime.

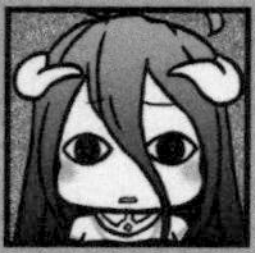

NAME: Maya Mizuki || **TITLE:** Mr. Ovalo

I love *Overlord*, so I'm so happy I got to draw some manga for it!
I love Ainz-sama and all the floor guardians, so I wanted to include as many characters as possible! Thank you so much!!

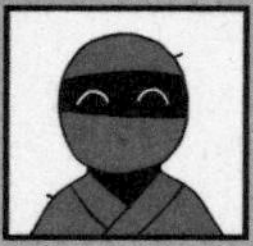

NAME: match || **TITLE:** Two Hundred(ish) Supreme Bones

When I first saw the visuals for Albedo, I thought she was gorgeous, but she's sure a surprise once you get to know her! She's total horndo—ly wonderful character, even better than I anticipated. I like how she's even more fun when Shalltear is around.

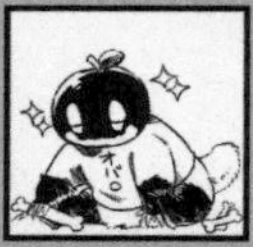

NAME: U Seta || **TITLE:** A Special Meeting Regarding Ages Six and Up

Congratulations on the anthology! I'm honored to have been invited to participate.
I love seeing the busy days of the members of Nazarick as they chat and do other mundane stuff like eating and fighting—it's too adorable. Thank you!

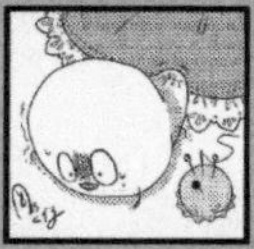

NAME: Kuko Okano || **TITLE:** Master's First Time

Hello, my name is Kuko Okano.
Thank you very much for inviting me to participate in the anthology.
All the girls are so adorable, I can't help myself.

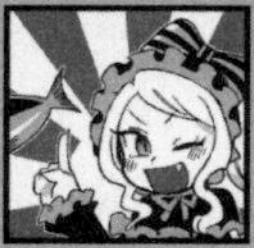

NAME: Michiru Burio || **TITLE:** Shalltear's Lost Item

I'm honored to participate in such a great series' anthology. Thank you!
I'm praying for eternal glory to the guild and ever more cuteness for Shalltear-chan!

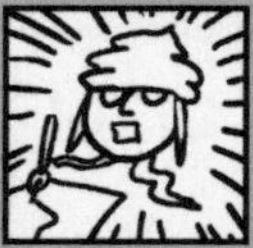

NAME: Yumiya || **TITLE:** Love Battle

Thank you for inviting me to participate! I had fun drawing this.
I love Ainz-sama...

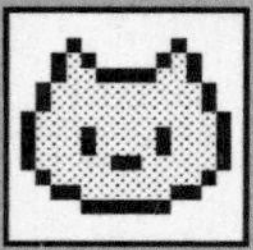

NAME: Itoda || **TITLE:** Do Your Best, Boys!

Thank you for inviting me to participate!
I hope everyone was able to enjoy my story at least a little.

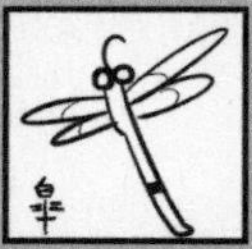

NAME: Satsuki || **TITLE:** Brilliant as Always, Ainz-sama

I'm so happy I could draw some manga for this series I love so much.
I hope we can continue enjoying this series, not only as novels but as anime, movies, manga, and so on, forever.

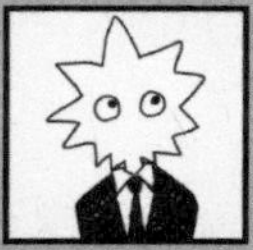

NAME: Ryosan || **TITLE:** The Great Tomb Switch

Ever since I was a kid, I've had this preconception that the earlier the girl appears, the more likely she is to be the main love interest. And Aura is the most like a heroine, I think. Please take the Aura route.

OVERLORD à la Carte ❶

Various Artists
Original Story: Kugane Maruyama
Character Design: so-bin

Translation: Emily Balistrieri • **Lettering: Rochelle Gancio**

OVERLORD KOUSHIKI COMIC À LA CARTE Volume 1
©2012 Kugane Maruyama
First published in Japan in 2018 by KADOKAWA CORPORATION, Tokyo.
English Translation rights arranged with KADOKAWA CORPORATION, Tokyo
through TUTTLE-MORI AGENCY, INC., Tokyo.

English translation © 2019 by Yen Press, LLC

Yen Press
150 West 30th Street, 19th Floor
New York, NY 10001

Visit us at yenpress.com
facebook.com/yenpress
twitter.com/yenpress
yenpress.tumblr.com
instagram.com/yenpress

First Yen Press Edition: August 2019

Yen Press is an imprint of Yen Press, LLC.
The Yen Press name and logo are trademarks of Yen Press, LLC.

Library of Congress Control Number: 2019942576

ISBNs: 978-1-9753-8490-6 (paperback)
       978-1-9753-5892-1 (ebook)

10 9 8 7 6 5 4 3 2 1

WOR

Printed in the United States of America